THE EXILE

MARK OLDFIELD was born in
Sheffield, and now lives in Kent.
He holds a PhD in criminology.

By the same author

THE SENTINEL

THE EXILE

MARK OLDFIELD

HEAD
of ZEUS

Paperback ISBN: 9781781851531
Ebook ISBN: 9781781851548

Typeset by Adrian McLaughlin
Printed in the UK by Clays Ltd, St Ive's Plc

Head of Zeus Ltd
Clerkenwell House
45–47 Clerkenwell Green
London EC1R 0HT
WWW.HEADOFZEUS.COM

For Viv

Seeking to forget makes exile all the longer;
the secret of redemption lies in remembrance.
Richard von Weizsäcker

We do not believe in government through the voting booth.
General Francisco Franco Bahamonde

The whole country shakes with indignation faced with these
heartless men who, with fire and terror, want to plunge popular
and democratic Spain into an inferno of terror.
But they shall not pass.
Isidora Dolores Ibárruri Gómez,
'La Pasionaria'

The squad moved slowly on the mountain path, hemmed in by ranks of dark pines. If they spoke, they spoke in whispers. This deep in enemy territory, there was always the possibility of ambush.

The men were anarchists, more accustomed to theoretical debate than war. Only a month ago, they had left training camp eager for combat with raised fists and cries of Viva La Republica! *Now, their numbers depleted by the harsh calculus of war, they resembled the refugees they passed on the way to the front. Most expected life would be hard in the militia. None expected it would be as hard as this.*

The commander saw the sullen looks as he gave orders, the muted threats of desertion. He reminded them the mission was vital for the Republic. He was a gifted speaker, and the men were placated by his words. Some had read his poems before the war though it was the Poet's martial skills they valued now. As they sheltered under the dripping trees, the Poet revealed their objective. They were to meet one of their observers and escort her back to their lines. The men exchanged uneasy glances. Risking their lives for a spy – and a woman at that – was not an appealing prospect.

It was late afternoon when they saw the small woodcutter's hut on the flank of the mountain, dwarfed by pine woods on the slopes above. Tired by the long march, the men threw down their packs and rifles. In the distance, they heard the dull rumble of artillery fire. The sound distracted them, though they were more distracted by the bundle in the woman's arms as she came out of the hut. No one was expecting the spy to have a newborn child. It was a surprise, the Poet told the men, not at all what he was expecting.

Nor was he expecting the dark-clad troops as they emerged from the trees to encircle the squad. A harsh voice offered a simple choice: surrender or die.

It was not much of a choice.

CHAPTER I

SAN SEBASTIÁN, THURSDAY, 30 SEPTEMBER 1954

A pale sun was setting behind dark-smudged clouds and the biting wind from the sea signalled a coming storm. Fernando Etxarte tightened his overcoat collar as he crossed the Zurriola Bridge. Two hundred metres away, the heavy sea surged into the narrow river mouth, smashing against the rocks in great bursts of spray that sparkled in the insipid light of the street lamps along the riverbank. The wind was raw and Etxarte was glad of the meagre protection of his Basque beret.

The honeyed glow of lights in the shops and bars at the far side of the bridge held the promise of shelter from the imminent storm. But Etxarte had an appointment to keep. Ignoring the rain, he hurried on, passing static lines of trucks and slow, grumbling cars rattling out greasy exhaust fumes into the fierce wind. Now and again, horse-drawn carts laden with goods slowed the traffic, provoking frequent blasts from exasperated drivers' horns.

Etxarte crossed the road at the end of the bridge, heading into the dense warren of buildings clustered between the river and the harbour. The dark mass of Monte Urgull loomed over him, its steep sides towering over the port, the old fortress on top of the hill now skeletal in whirling showers of rain blown in from the sea. He continued through the narrow streets to the darkened Plaza 18 de Julio, his footsteps echoing under the covered walkway around the sides of the square. Long ago they held bullfights here: mounted nobles dramatically ending the raging attacks of *toros bravos* with the thrust of a spear. Once, there were bright numbers above the first-floor balconies where families had rented seats for the fights.

Now, the faded figures looked down on a poorly illuminated row of shops and bars, while above them were shabby apartments, their shutters rattling in the wind, the bird cages on the balconies empty and abandoned until the spring.

At the far end of the square Etxarte came to a small, dingy bar, with a long, zinc-topped counter and a handful of tables along the walls. He paused in the doorway, brushing rainwater from his overcoat, grateful for the warmth inside. Hesitant electric light peered through irregular clouds of black tobacco smoke. A dozen conversations echoed round the bar, some animated and strident, others conducted warily, in low, measured voices. It was a cheerful place despite its spartan interior, a place to drink and smoke and, for those who had money, to sample from the selection of badly prepared tapas on offer.

Etxarte saw the salesman at once. Tall and bulky, a dark coat and hat. He looked successful, judging by the smart cut of his clothes. In fact, he must be very successful, Etxarte thought. You needed to earn good money to eat enough to maintain a bulk like that. Etxarte leaned against the bar and waved to the barman, ordering *patxaran* before he turned to the man in the dark coat.

'Señor Ramirez?'

'You must be Señor Etxarte.'

'That's me. Another drink?'

'Not when I'm working,' Ramirez said. 'Well, perhaps just a brandy. A large one.'

The barman brought the drinks. They drank in silence.

Ramirez leaned over Etxarte's glass and inhaled suspiciously. 'What is that?'

'*Patxaran*. A Basque speciality. Made with local berries and anís.'

'*Joder*. It smells like something you'd buy at a pharmacy.'

'It's an acquired taste,' Etxarte said, defensively.

'So is buggery. And it's no reason to try that either.'

Etxarte frowned. He was here to do business, yet the salesman seemed to have taken an immediate dislike to him. Etxarte had

4

expected a little more seriousness and less aggression, given the nature of their business. After all, he was the customer.

'Did you bring the goods, Señor Ramirez?'

The big man looked at him fiercely. 'Not here. Too many flapping ears. Pay the bill and we'll talk outside.'

Etxarte did so, wincing at the tab the salesman had run up. Still, he reasoned, it was for the Cause. Everything he did these days was. The salesman was waiting outside. Grey sheets of rain swept the desolate square and water fell noisily from the awnings of bars and shops, forming pools of water the colour of dull steel on the cobbles.

'Dismal night,' Ramirez said. 'You have fucking awful weather here.'

'But convenient for us, *verdad*?' Etxarte smiled. 'It's an ill wind...'

'Discretion. That's what these transactions require,' Ramirez said, pulling on leather gloves. 'Where do we meet your friends?'

'I'd rather not say.'

'Of course. Security should always be a prime consideration. So I deal with you?'

'I'm not actually responsible for buying equipment, Señor Ramirez. We have a quartermaster to do that. We don't meet with him; in fact, we don't even know who he is, it's safer that way. But the cell is a collective, so all our decisions are made as a group. One voice, one people – and all for Euskadi, *Señor* Ramirez.'

'*Bueno*. I'll deal with all of you together. That's been my intention all along.' Ramirez lit a cigarette and breathed blue smoke into the wavering curtain of rain. 'What's really important to me is being paid, as I'm sure you understand.'

'*De acuerdo*. You'll appreciate I can't tell you where we're meeting the others. The fascists are constantly trying to infiltrate our movement, so we have to be careful. I'll give you directions as we drive. In the dark you won't remember the route we take. And of course, I'll accompany you back here again, after the transaction.'

'Fine. My car's parked in the boulevard near the town hall.'

5

As they made their way towards the boulevard, the rain grew heavier. Etxarte saw rivulets of water falling from the rim of the salesman's black homburg as he hurried to a line of parked cars.

'Here's my car.'

'A Buick? *Hombre*, that must have cost you plenty.'

'The rewards in this business are considerable,' Ramirez said. 'But then, so are the risks.' He opened the door and climbed into the driver's seat. Etxarte scurried to the other side and scrambled in, glad to be out of the freezing rain.

'So,' Ramirez said, 'which way do I go?'

As Etxarte gave him sparse directions, the Buick's big engine growled into life and the car slid forward, arcs of rain flickering in the pale headlights. Within a few minutes they left the lights of the city behind and the darkness closed in. Etxarte directed Ramirez in monosyllables as they followed the contours of the foothills. Ramirez made little conversation. Etxarte took that for professional discretion: no questions asked, no superfluous information to compromise either party. Very professional. No wonder Señor Ramirez came so highly recommended.

'So your leader won't be here tonight?' Ramirez asked, staring ahead into the darkness beyond the headlights.

'It isn't necessary,' Etxarte said. 'We make tactical decisions within the group. But the quartermaster sources our equipment and arms and passes on communications between us and other cells in the region. He keeps his identity secret from the cell and keeps in touch using coded messages. That way, if anyone's captured and tortured, they can't betray the entire movement.'

'Very effective.' Ramirez nodded. 'You're clearly very well organised.'

Etxarte smiled. It was a long time since anyone had praised his efforts.

The road began to rise into a black mass of hills. Etxarte leaned forward and pointed to a gate by a steeply sloping field.

'It's just through that gate. You'll see lights on your right and a track up to the house.'

'Thank God for that,' Ramirez grunted. 'I thought we going to end up in France. And you know what they say about the French.'

The car slowed as Ramirez turned the Buick onto the rough track leading up to the house. A couple of hundred metres away, the headlights illuminated the outline of a whitewashed farmhouse. Faint lights flickered through cracks in the shutters.

'What do they say about the French?' Etxarte asked.

Ramirez brought the car to halt. The farmhouse was in the typical Basque style: a whitewashed, half-timbered exterior, a red-tiled roof, shutters on the windows.

'They say they're all fucking bastards who have their road signs painted with a German translation on the back. That way, when there's a war, they surrender and then turn the signs round.' Ramirez opened the car door, laughing heartily at his own joke.

The front door of the farmhouse opened, spilling weak light over the car. A young man with a mop of unkempt hair peered out at them through thick, round-rimmed glasses.

'*Kaixo. Ongi etorri.*'

Etxarte returned his greeting. '*Kaixo*, Patxi. Are we all here?'

'We're two short tonight, comrade.'

The young man saw Ramirez who was busy dragging long canvas bags from the car. '*Kaixo.*'

Ramirez looked at him blankly. 'I don't understand a word of Basque.'

The young man grinned sheepishly. 'Sorry. We prefer not to speak the language of the oppressor when we're together. I'm Patxi Zubiondo. And your name, Señor…?'

'This is Señor Ramirez,' Etxarte said, struggling with one of the canvas bags. '*Venga*, Patxi, we need a hand here. These guns won't carry themselves.'

The young man hurried forwards. 'Sorry, Señor Ramirez. Sometimes I forget myself, I get so animated by the Cause.'

'The Cause?' Ramirez asked, handing the young man a couple of canvas bags.

7

The bags were heavy, Patxi noticed, feeling the hard, sharp outlines of their contents. He felt growing excitement. The revolution was beginning at last.

'Our cause. Freedom for the Basque homeland, you'd say in Spanish. In Basque it's *Euskadi ta askatasuna*. That's what we're thinking of calling our resistance movement.'

'Quite a mouthful.' Ramirez nodded. 'You could always shorten it to ETA. People would remember it more easily. You could put it on your notepaper.' Patxi smiled, unsure if Ramirez was joking.

The men carried the canvas bags into the house, stamping mud from their shoes on the reed mat. Patxi dried his spectacles with a handkerchief as he led Ramirez across the hall and through a thick wooden door into a large room with a raised platform at one end. Rows of benches faced the platform.

'This used to be the local school,' Etxarte explained, 'before the fascists closed it and made speaking Basque illegal.'

Six more young people were waiting in the schoolhouse: four men, one with the worst attempt at a beard Ramirez had ever seen, and two young women. One was ugly, which Ramirez had rather expected, and one was not, which rather surprised him since revolutionaries were, in his experience, uniformly ugly. Still, business was business. It always ended the same way, no matter who he dealt with.

The group came over to Etxarte, one at a time, whispering something in a low voice. Etxarte slapped each one on the shoulder as they went over to the benches to take a seat.

'What was that all about?' Ramirez asked.

'A password. It's how we identify members of the group. I shouldn't really tell you.'

'Don't then,' Ramirez said.

The young people were whispering, impatient for proceedings to begin.

'It can't hurt.' Etxarte lowered his voice. 'It's quite moving actually. "*In the mountains, the snows are burning.*"'

'Very nice,' Ramirez muttered, without interest. He climbed onto the dais and placed the canvas bags on the table.

Etxarte and Patxi passed the rest of the bags to him. The salesman was strong, Patxi noticed, seeing how easily Ramirez carried the heavy canvas bags, one in each hand. The others waited on the two rows of benches, eyes bright and excited. Ramirez noticed that when Patxi jumped down from the dais, he went to sit with the good-looking woman.

Politely, Etxarte motioned Ramirez to a chair. Ramirez was very relaxed, a real professional, no doubt about it, Etxarte thought. And, since it had been his decision to approach Ramirez, it also reflected well on him.

'Comrades,' Etxarte said, 'please welcome Señor Ramirez, who, as you know, is here to do some important business with us.'

A hesitant ripple of self-conscious applause.

'Before we begin our negotiations, perhaps you'd like to say a few words, Señor Ramirez?' Etxarte took a step back.

Ramirez got to his feet. 'Is this place secure?' he asked, looking round the schoolroom. There was only one window to his right, and that was shuttered and barred. The only other exit was the door to the corridor. He jumped down from the platform, walked over to the door and turned the key. He returned, putting the key in his pocket, and leaped onto the dais with an athleticism surprising for such a big man. 'You can't be too careful,' he said. Etxarte nodded vigorously. This all seemed highly professional.

Ramirez looked down at his audience. 'Tell me, have any of you handled a gun before?' The good-looking woman raised her hand.

'You, señorita? What kind of gun was it?'

'My grandfather's shotgun. We shot rabbits for the pot.'

'You've shot rabbits?' Ramirez stifled a laugh. 'Well, that's a start. None of you will starve, at any rate.'

'If I can shoot rabbits, I can shoot the murderers of the *guardia civil*.' She glared defiantly at Ramirez and sat down to applause from her comrades.

'Good point, señorita, there are a number of *guardia civiles* I'd gladly shoot myself.' Ramirez chuckled, drawing complicit laughter. 'Perhaps you'd all like to see the weapons now?' Their faces told him they would.

Ramirez slowly unzipped the canvas bags, taking out the rifles carefully and passing them down into impatient hands. 'Six American M1 rifles, gas-operated, clip-fed with eight rounds to a clip. Accurate to around four hundred metres.' He paused, watching the group handle the weapons with affected familiarity.

'Are these loaded?' It was the ugly woman.

'Of course not. I don't want you blowing your heads off before you pay me.'

'Actually, we need to discuss that,' Etxarte said. 'We're a little short of money.'

Ramirez turned to stare at him. The atmosphere in the room changed.

'That's a handicap in any business,' said Ramirez. 'We agreed on payment upfront. Like the signs in the bars tell you, don't ask for credit.'

'There are greater issues at stake here,' the more attractive of the two women said, getting to her feet. 'We're fighting for a cause, señor. We're willing to die for our country and we need arms, yet you talk only of money. Don't you have any principles?'

'Several,' Ramirez said, 'and the most important is never sell things to someone who can't pay.' He paused to light a cigarette and exhaled a stream of smoke. 'I've got six very efficient rifles here,' he continued, 'possession of which, incidentally, will bring an automatic death sentence if you're caught. However, you don't have anything to fire from them.'

'We can buy bullets from someone else,' one of the young men muttered.

'You think it's that easy?' Ramirez snorted. 'How will you know it's not Franco's secret police you're dealing with? That happens all the time to people like you.'

'Comrades, please,' Etxarte said. 'Perhaps we can explain our plans in more detail to Señor Ramirez. Show him we're sincere. Maybe we could have the rifles on a lease. When the struggle is over, he could be paid then.' He took a bulky brown paper envelope from his inside pocket. 'Would this serve as a deposit at least, Señor Ramirez? Five hundred *Yanqui* dollars – it's all we could raise.' He placed the envelope on the table.

'What's this "Señor" business?' the man with the appalling beard said. 'We reject bourgeois formality. What's your first name, Compañero Ramirez?'

Ramirez sighed and glanced at his watch. It was time to put an end to this. 'There are three points I need to make, *comrade*.' He emphasised the word with sudden malice. 'The first is that what you are doing is highly dangerous – as I said, the possession of weapons is treachery and the penalty for treachery is death. Second, that's the worst fucking beard I've ever seen and you should be ashamed of it.' He stopped and finished his cigarette. He threw it down and ground it out with his heel. 'You can't be too careful in a wooden building,' he said, smiling.

'So what's the third?' the young man shouted, incensed by the insult to his beard.

'The third?' Ramirez stared at him. 'My name is Comandante Guzmán of the *Brigada Especial. Buenas noches.*'

The others in the audience shuffled, suddenly uncomfortable and confused. The bearded young man leaped up, brandishing the rifle like a club. 'I don't believe you. If you were a policeman you'd have arrested us by now.'

Guzmán nodded. 'If I were a normal policeman, I would. But I'm not. Those weapons are only here to make things look right for the coroner.'

'You're trapped,' the young man said. 'We'll beat you to death with your own rifles.'

Guzmán reached into his jacket and drew the Browning semi-automatic in a smooth motion that ended with the muzzle of the gun pointing at the bearded man's face. One of the women gasped. The rest were shocked into silence, eyes fixed on the pistol in his hand.

Guzmán shot the bearded man in the forehead. Blood and brain tissue spattered those behind him and the ugly woman gasped as the bullet exited the back of the man's skull, hitting her in the chest. The bearded man had fallen onto two of his startled comrades and before they could push his body away, Guzmán shot them. The other woman made a break for it, leaping from her seat and running towards the door. The door Guzmán had locked.

Guzmán shot her between the shoulder blades. The impact threw her forwards into the door and she clutched at the handle with rapidly ebbing strength, fighting to stay on her feet. Guzmán fired again. This time, the bullet struck a few inches above the base of her spine, opening another red flower on her pale cotton dress. She slid down the door to the ground, leaving irregular crimson trails as she went. The other students remained in their seats, frozen with fear and shock. They died without resistance.

The ensuing silence was immense – at least for Etxarte, sitting on the dais, white-faced, his ears ringing from the gunfire, staring dully at the carnage a couple of metres away. The familiar meeting place was suddenly unreal, haunted by strange smells. Acrid gun smoke drifted over the corpses, mingling with the smell of burned clothing and a charnel odour he recognised from market day. The smell of fresh blood. The evening had turned to nightmare and that nightmare was now striding towards Etxarte, dark eyes glinting as he slammed another magazine of ammunition into the Browning as he stepped up onto the dais.

'I told you I'd deal with you all together.' He took out a packet of Bisontes, lifted it to his mouth and took a cigarette between his lips. He glanced round, suddenly remembering something, and went over to the table, took the envelope of money and shoved it into his pocket, keeping the pistol pointed at Etxarte.

'*Quieres*?' Guzmán held out the packet with his left hand.

Etxarte stared at the muzzle of the pistol. He shook his head. 'I don't smoke.'

The shot hit him in the middle of his chest, smashing him backwards, still seated. The muzzle flash ignited the material of his shirt around the entry wound. Small flames licked up around the growing dark stain.

'You do now,' Guzmán said.

Guzmán left the mechanical clatter of the hotel lift and strode across the lobby to the reception desk. He was not in a good mood. It was two in the morning and he had got lost several times driving back from the job at the schoolhouse. Maps were like people: little use in daylight and by night completely hopeless. With certain exceptions, obviously.

The night porter gave him a sheet of hotel notepaper with a name scrawled on it in childish handwriting. 'This gentleman called several times, Señor Ramirez.'

Guzmán looked at the paper. The name was a code. The caller was Coronel Gutierrez.

'Is there a telephone in my room?'

'No, señor,' the porter muttered. He worked nights precisely to avoid human contact and had already exceeded the limits of his usual conversations with guests.

'So where the fuck can I find one?'

The man pointed to the telephone at the end of the desk. 'There's one there, señor.'

'But then you'd be able to listen to my conversation,' Guzmán said. 'Where's the manager's office?'

'Only the manager is allowed to use that room I'm afraid, señor.' Guzmán realised the porter was keeping his voice down so as not to disturb sleeping residents. That was gross provocation. Physical violence would draw too much attention at this time of night. Merely arguing with the simpleton was clearly worthless. That left the option of out-and-out terror. Guzmán pulled the Browning from its holster and reached across the counter to press the muzzle against the night porter's forehead.

13

'And only I am allowed to use this, you fucking *badulaque*,' Guzmán said, thumbing back the hammer. 'If I pull the trigger, most of what passes for your brain will be splashed over that wall behind you. So, let me ask you again. And, since I'm talking rationally, using the language of good Christians and being exceptionally' – he pushed the muzzle of the pistol harder against the man's sweat-sheened forehead – 'exceptionally polite in the face of your rudeness, tell me where the fucking manager's office is. Or you'll die. And no one, *absolutamente nadie, coño*, will care, I promise you.' He paused, pacified for a moment by the exercise of his frenetic vocabulary of violence. 'Is that clear?'

The night porter tried to nod, which was foolish since Guzmán's pistol was still pressed against his forehead. 'It's the door behind the gentleman.'

Guzmán turned to look without taking the gun from the man's head. 'Good. I'll use the phone in there. I want some supper as well. Get me a bottle of brandy and a large sandwich and do it quickly. But knock first or I'll shoot you in the doorway, *entendido*?'

The porter was shaking violently and the chance to make up for whatever he had done to bring Guzmán's anger down on him was highly appealing. 'Understood, señor. Although I don't know where I can get a bottle of brandy at this time of night. The bar's locked.'

Guzmán walked over to the door of the manager's office and opened it, feeling for the light switch. The room was suddenly bathed in a sickly glow like an undertaker's candle. He turned. 'For all I care, *hombre*, you can prise it out of the hand of a dying nun in the gutter. Just fuck off and do it.' He slammed the door in the porter's face.

Guzmán sat at the manager's desk. Out of professional habit, he tried the drawers. They were locked. That suggested the possibility of discovering something incriminating. It would be worth searching the room before he left. If nothing else, perhaps he would find something that would enable him to coerce the manager into not charging him for his room.

He dialled a Madrid number and listened to the phone ringing at the other end. *National Security*, he thought angrily, *and they're all fucking asleep.*

A knock at the door as the night porter came in bearing a tray with a length of hurriedly sliced loaf stuffed with chorizo, and a bottle of Carlos Tercero. The porter placed the plate on the desk, and next to it, the bottle of brandy with an insultingly small glass.

Guzmán noticed an envelope on the tray. 'What's this?'

'Your mail, sir.'

Guzmán gestured for him to leave and listened to the phone ringing, using his free hand to open the bottle. As he raised the bottle to his mouth, someone answered.

'Is that you, Guzmán?' Gutierrez didn't sound happy. But then, he rarely did.

'*Buenas noches, mi Coronel.* Times must be hard if you've got to answer the phone at this time of night.'

'This is my personal number now, Guzmán, so do try to address me correctly, will you? I've been a *general de brigada* since last week.'

Guzmán shook a fist at the wall of the office. *Mierda. Every fucker gets promotion but me. I've done everything they asked and more and the cabrónes piss on me. Puta madre.*

'No need to congratulate me, Guzmán. How are things in the Basque Country?'

'Fine. I met with the clients earlier this evening.'

'And how did the negotiations go?'

Guzmán swallowed a mouthful of brandy. 'Abandoned due to sudden bereavement.'

'Really? I didn't expect you'd do it so quickly. How many?'

'Eight.' Guzmán felt a spasm of anger at the sudden silence. 'What?'

'There were supposed to be ten.'

'Eight showed up. The organiser, Etxarte, said two couldn't make it. There's also a quartermaster, but he keeps his distance so he can't betray them if he's captured.' He swallowed more brandy. 'You didn't mention a quartermaster in your briefing.'

'That's because I didn't know, Guzmán. So don't fucking gloat.'

'I can only work with the information I'm given,' Guzmán said, gloating. 'There's a password. Actually more than a word, because Basques can't say anything in less than half a page. "*In the mountains, the snows are burning*" – that's how they recognise one another.'

'Very poetic,' Gutiérrez sneered. 'Now you're up there, *Comandante*, there's some more business to attend to and it's a little more important than learning a few Basque phrases. You've heard about El Lobo since you arrived, I imagine?'

'Of course. He hides up in the hills among the wolves and goats. Shoots at the local *policía* and *guardia civil* from time to time. He's just a bandit – not a problem for the security services.' A long silence. It was the silence that always preceded some ludicrously demeaning order from Gutierrez. Guzmán clenched his fist.

'A bandit?' Gutierrez snorted. 'You haven't noticed that the underground press refer to El Lobo as a guerrilla hero who's returned to continue the Civil War? How there are groups of young Basques wanting to join him in his struggle against the State?'

'So what? Look how I dealt with those traitors this evening. One clip of ammunition – well, two – and they're gone. Send the *guardia* after this Lobo.'

Silence. Guzmán realised where this was leading. 'I'm not doing it. You told me—'

'Things have changed,' Gutierrez cut in. 'El Lobo robbed an army payroll truck earlier today, not ten miles from Bilbao. He left four *guardia civiles* dead and got away with a great deal of money. Real money as well: dollars, not pesetas. There's uproar here. The Basque region is supposed to be calm. When I said you were in the area, Franco told me to give you the job.'

Guzmán took another swig of brandy. *So, Franco remembers I'm useful?* 'All right, I'll go after El Lobo.'

'Excellent. We want him dead as soon as possible. And not a hero's death either: we don't want him to become a martyr. Is that clear?'

'Absolutely. Where do I start?'

'There's a village up in the hills called Oroitz. El Lobo's been very active round there. I understand there's a *guardia* barracks there so you can use the squad as you see fit.'

'*Bueno.* I'll go up there and take a look,' Guzmán said, 'but I'll need some of my boys from the *Brigada Especial* to get a job like this done quickly.'

'I've already arranged for someone to join you up there, *Comandante*. He was about to be posted to Calle Robles, I think he'll be of use to you.'

'One man?'

'I believe you know him,' Gutiérrez said. 'Corporal Ochoa.'

'Ochoa?' Guzmán grumbled. 'I remember him. But he's a photographer, for fuck's sake. And he's miserable.'

'He's a good man, and in any case, he's all I can spare. He'll arrive the day after tomorrow. We've also got a number of informants in the area, so naturally I'll pass on any information from them as soon as it's available.'

'Who's going to handle communications between us?'

'Capitán Viana is coming up there to deal with that side of things. He's just transferred to us from naval intelligence. I haven't met him in person yet, but I've heard good things about him. He'll be in touch in the next day or so.'

Guzmán looked at his sandwich, wishing Gutiérrez would fuck off. 'Is that all?'

'Not yet,' Gutiérrez sighed. 'There are certain complications.'

Guzmán realised he was not going to like this. 'What might they be?'

'Firstly, General Mellado, the Military Governor, is causing problems. He's asked Franco for permission to implement martial law over the entire region.'

'Mellado's a character,' Guzmán said. 'We used to call him Madman in the war. He's always been overenthusiastic.'

'Far too enthusiastic for my liking, Guzmán. Frankly, if I had my way we'd get rid of him. He's a part of the past now, it's time he retired. But Franco's not keen on removing him. He hates change.'

'No change there, then,' Guzmán muttered. 'Why do you want rid of him so much?'

'Don't get me started. Mainly because he doesn't realise we need to be aware of our image abroad these days. We need foreign trade and the economy is still a shambles.'

'Last year, you said the American trade deal would solve all our problems.'

'And so it will, when they finally part with the money,' Gutierrez said. 'But the *Yanquis* have a peculiar aversion to the ways we deal with issues of public order. If General Mellado sends in his troops, it would cause massive unrest and if the bodies start piling up, the Americans will turn pale and pull the plug on the deal. We'll remain a nation of paupers.'

'Has anyone told Mellado that?'

'You worked with him, didn't you? He's not a great listener.'

'I could have a word,' Guzmán suggested. 'I'm sure he'll see sense.'

'Do that. Remind him that Franco himself has forbidden him to take action.'

'I will. Is that all for tonight?'

'I hope I'm not keeping you from your bed, Guzmán? Because there are other factors you need to know about. Things that make the situation even more sensitive.'

Here we go. Guzmán waited in silence for the bad news.

'The US Ambassador is holidaying in France,' Gutierrez said, 'Biarritz, to be exact.' He's taking the US Special Envoy with him, the man who's going to hand over the money for the trade deal next week.'

Guzmán exhaled loudly. 'So what?'

'My point is, the two Americans we'd least like to be near the Basque country right now are practically camped out on the border. We don't want their holiday spoiled by reports about Spain's internal problems.'

'I'll be discreet.' Guzmán took another pull of brandy.

'Good, and it goes without saying that you're explicitly forbidden to cross the border into France, *Comandante*. An international incident would be disastrous.'

Guzmán picked up a pencil lying by the blotter on the desk. 'I've got the message.'

'I hope so, because otherwise Madrid will be a distant memory for you.'

'I'm looking at a map of the area as we speak,' Guzmán said, doodling on the blotter. 'I've already identified the key issue.'

'I imagine that involves working out your chances of survival?' Gutiérrez's voice was faint and distorted. 'I'd forgotten your close attention to detail. Just don't expect to be paid for working through the night.'

Before Guzmán could tell him to fuck himself, Gutierrez hung up.

Guzmán swallowed another mouthful of brandy and looked down at his doodle; his chances of survival did not depend upon the calculation of unfeasible odds or the likelihood of failure. They hinged on a simple axis between the two outcomes now scrawled on the blotter, competing with the mosaic pattern of innumerable coffee cups. *Him or me.*

That was enough strategic planning for one night and he reached for the sandwich. Strangely, the night porter had made it just the way he liked: roughly cut bread with the chorizo hacked into thick greasy chunks. Things were looking up. Once this job was completed, he could be back in Madrid within days.

The envelope was still lying on the tray. Guzmán picked it up, seeing the crest of the Military Governor's office. He tore it open and slid out the embossed card:

THE MILITARY GOVERNOR GENERAL JOSÉ MELLADO
REQUESTS THE PRESENCE OF DON LEOPOLDO GUZMÁN

AT A CHARITY DINNER IN SUPPORT OF THE
SECCIÓN FEMENINA OF THE FALANGE.

FRIDAY, 1 OCTOBER 1954. 8.00 P.M. PROMPT.
BLACK TIE.

Guzmán groaned. An evening with the parasites and sycophants of the party was a dismal proposition, even if it did involve a free meal, particularly since the members of the *Sección Femenina* resembled a troupe of third-rate Italian opera singers, although marginally larger, perhaps.

It was time to get some rest but, tired as he was, Guzmán found it hard to break the habit of a lifetime. He took out his key ring and used one of the locksmith's picks attached to it to open the manager's drawers. Despite a thorough search, he found nothing incriminating and went to his room, taking the half-empty bottle with him for a nightcap.

Weak light from a single bulb threw angular shadows over the cheap furniture as he lay on the bed in his squalid room, unable to sleep. The mattress was hard and the pillow smelled of ancient sweat and tobacco. As he rolled onto his back, he saw a large carved effigy of the crucified Christ on the wall above. If that fell, it would kill him. The thought amused him.

Outside, the rain had stopped and a languid breeze stirred the faded curtains. Through the window, he heard the slow rhythm of breaking waves. Irritated, Guzmán stormed across the room and slammed the shutters. Freed from the disturbing cadences of the sea, he sank into his habitual dreams of gunfire, explosions and screaming.

Most of the prisoners were killed at once, avoiding the inconvenience of guarding them.

Those chosen were forced to their knees as the legionnaires took up position behind them, waiting as their officer lit his cigarette before he gave the order to fire. Moments later, four were left alive. The Poet, the woman and two others. They would be questioned later.

The woman was allowed to carry her baby. If she tried to flee she would not get far.

Two hours later, the enemy camp emerged from the mist, a sprawl of dark vehicles, long rows of tents and sandbagged gun emplacements a hundred metres from a ruined village. As they walked, some of the Moors baited the woman with dark threats of what awaited her. Unimpressed, she cursed their mothers, colourfully and without repetition. She was still cursing as the prisoners were bundled down a flight of steps into the cellar of a ruined building.

The men were bound to chairs retrieved from the rubble. Unsure what to do with the woman and her baby, the Moors pushed her onto a chair and left her cradling the infant, staring at her captors with icy hatred. She had no illusions about her fate. It was usual to let the Moors have captured militia women. Few survived that and those who did were killed anyway.

The Moors snapped to attention as their officer came stamping down into the cellar. A tall, sullen-faced teniente. He took the woman by the arm and led her up the stairs. The Moors laughed, guessing the officer's intention. Rank always had its privileges.

Outside, the teniente directed the woman along the side of the house until they were out of sight of the camp. She sat on a low wall, amusing the baby with her rag doll. Once he was certain they could not be overhead, the teniente finally spoke.

'What the fuck are you doing here?'

She tilted her head to one side. A familiar gesture. 'I was going to ask you the same thing, chico.'

CHAPTER 2

MADRID, JULY 2010, CALLE MONTERA

To the women on the street she was Gabriela. To the men who came to buy, she was nothing. As she looked away from the road she caught her reflection in the grimy window of a tattoo parlour, a vague image sketched in dark lines and muted tones. A short, clinging dress, high heels, her pale face indistinct in the smeared glass. Out of the corner of her eye she noticed the man across the street waving impatiently towards the intersection with the main road. She knew what that meant. It was time to sell herself.

Gabriela teetered towards the kerb, unsteady on the cheap high heels. From here, it was a five-minute walk into the heart of Madrid for tourists. But the sightseers on this street weren't interested in shopping or culture. They came to buy women.

This was a feeling she would never get used to, waiting by the kerb as the cars rolled by, drivers inspecting her with the same attention they gave to buying a shirt. Probably less.

A green SEAT Ibiza pulled up. The driver kept the engine running, beckoning her with his finger. Gabriela started walking towards the car.

'*Oyes, niña.*' It was the black girl a few metres up the street. She lowered her voice. 'I know that one. Be careful, he's weird.'

Gabriela smiled. They were all fucking weird as far as she was concerned.

The man leaned through the window to look her over. 'Got a name, *princesa*?'

She stayed half a metre from the car. 'Gabriela.'

'How much?' He lifted his right hand, letting her see the thick wad of euros. She wasn't impressed. He had no intention of paying her that.

'For what?' She put her hand on her hip and stared at him, pale but defiant.

'Anal.' Like he was ordering pizza.

'Thirty.'

He grinned. 'Fifty and forget the condom.'

'OK.' Across the street, a fair-haired woman stepped off the pavement as Gabriela opened the car door and bent to climb inside. A sudden surprised gasp as the man leaned forward and grabbed her wrist, pulling her off balance. A sharp pain shot through her side as he dragged her into the car, trying to push her down between the passenger seat and the dash, out of sight. 'Keep quiet, *puta*,' he muttered, 'or I'll cut you.'

She stopped struggling and let herself fall against him, the sudden impact making him loosen his grip. She pressed her foot against the dashboard, keeping her weight pressed against him, as she fumbled in her belt.

'Keep still, you little whore,' he muttered, trying to get a grip on her arm.

Gabriela twisted round, pushing the muzzle of the pistol into his face. 'Move and I'll blow your fucking head off.'

He looked at her, eyes wide, his mouth sagging open.

She heard footsteps and then the driver's door was wrenched open and the fair-haired woman leaned in, pressing her service pistol against the back of the man's head.

'Take the money.' His voice was trembling.

'We're not robbing you, *cabrón*,' the woman said. '*Guardia civil*: you're under arrest.' He didn't resist as she dragged him from the car and cuffed his hands behind his back. Gabriela got out, noticing the women lining the street a few moments ago had slipped away.

The blonde woman was frisking the driver. 'Well, well.' She turned to Gabriela. 'Look what your friend's carrying.' She threw a large paper bag down onto the pavement.

Gabriela picked it up and examined the wraps of kitchen foil. 'Looks like coke to me.'

'I think you're right.' Eva nodded. 'There's a lot of it.'

'It's only for personal use,' the man protested.

Gabriela shrugged. 'There's enough here to charge you with dealing.' She gave him a contemptuous look as she took an evidence bag from her pocket and bagged up the wraps. 'Not your lucky day, *amigo*.'

A green and white patrol car stopped at the kerb. Gabriela watched the driver as she got out. A tall black woman wearing sergeant's stripes.

'Hey, Mendez,' Eva called. 'Still living the life of luxury up in HQ? When are you going to get a proper job?'

'Fuck you too.' Mendez grinned. She looked at Gabriela. 'Had a makeover, Ana María?' She raised her hand to her mouth. 'Or should I call you Gabriela?'

'Very funny,' Galíndez said. 'Did you drive here just to admire my clothes?'

'Hardly.' Mendez noticed the prisoner. 'Who's your friend?'

'He tried to buy her sexual services.' Eva nodded towards Galíndez.

'*Jesús*, was that ever a mistake,' Mendez laughed. Another patrol car drew up behind her vehicle. Two uniformed officers came over and took the prisoner to the car.

'You're wanted at HQ, Ana,' Mendez said, as they watched the patrol car drive off.

'Who wants me?' Galíndez asked.

'Apparently the disciplinary board have reached a decision about you'

'Shit.' Galíndez was suddenly attentive. 'Do you know what it is?'

Mendez shrugged. 'Hop in the car and let's find out.'

'Is that OK, Eva?' Galíndez asked. 'I've still got twenty minutes of my shift left.'

'Go ahead, Ana. You've done a good job here. I know this wasn't your first choice.'

Galíndez shrugged. 'It was my only choice.'

'Good luck with the board,' Eva said. 'I sent them a glowing report on your work.'

'Thanks.' As Galíndez followed Mendez to the car, some of the girls across the road shouted abuse, thinking Galíndez was being arrested.

She fastened her seat belt. 'So you've no idea what their decision is?'

Mendez pulled away and drove past the women now taking up their places again at the side of the road. 'It's one of two things, Ana. You're fired or you're not. You could flip a coin.'

Galíndez thought about it. 'I'd rather not.'

MADRID 2010, CUARTEL GENERAL DE LA GUARDIA CIVIL

Galíndez came out of the locker room and went back across the corridor into the forensics office. Mendez was waiting by her desk.

Mendez wolf-whistled. 'Look at you. When was the last time you wore uniform, Ana?'

Galíndez frowned, self-conscious. 'A while.' She smoothed her shirt. 'Do I look OK?'

'Christ,' Mendez said, 'it's only *Capitán* Fuentes. You're not scared of him, are you?'

'I'm worried about what he's going to tell me.'

'Better get it over with then.' Mendez pointed to the *capitán*'s glass-walled office at the far end of the main room. 'Don't keep him waiting.'

Galíndez paused outside the office and took a deep breath. She knocked on the door and went in.

'Ana.' Fuentes came out from behind his desk to shake hands. 'You're looking well.'

'Thanks, I'm pretty much back to normal.' That wasn't entirely true, though it was better not to say so.

Fuentes beckoned her to the visitor's chair and went back behind his desk. She saw the brown envelope on his desk and swallowed.

'Don't look like that.' Fuentes smiled as he slipped a sheet of paper from the envelope. 'I don't bite.'

'Sorry, *jefe*, I'm just tense. This thing's been hanging over me for months.'

'I hear you did a good job in Vice,' Fuentes said. 'That was a good move to offer to help them out while they're short-staffed. The disciplinary board were impressed.'

'I hope they were impressed with other aspects of my career as well?'

'They cleared you of breaking the *guardia* code of conduct, if that's what you were wondering about?' Fuentes grinned. 'You're reinstated, Ana. Welcome back.'

Galíndez lifted a hand to her face and wiped the corner of her eye. 'Just like that?'

'Your uncle Ramiro explained to the board how you were sent to the *comisaría* to investigate certain things relating to extremist terrorism. He may even have used the words Al Qaeda, I'm not entirely sure.'

'And the unauthorised firearm charge?'

'It was authorised,' Fuentes said, expressionless. 'I only found the paperwork recently, it had fallen down behind my desk.'

Galíndez's eyes widened. She knew there'd been no paperwork. 'You're saying that you both covered for me?'

Fuentes looked down for a moment. 'No, Ana, I'm not saying that and neither is General Ortiz. What's happened is that we clarified the circumstances around the explosion in Guzmán's *comisaría*. And because everything has been clarified, you keep your job. Understood?'

There was only one possible answer and she gave it. 'I understand perfectly, *jefe*.'

'Naturally, because of the security aspect, all of this will be kept secret.' He toyed with the papers on his desk, distracted. 'Your father and I were friends, Ana. He'd have done the same if the situation was reversed, as would Ramiro.'

Galíndez sat back in her chair, suddenly relaxed. 'I bet you, Dad and Ramiro were like the three musketeers back in the day, boss.'

Fuentes' eyes twinkled. 'Something like that, Ana. We all joined up around the same time, Ramiro in seventy-eight and your dad and me in seventy-nine.'

'So you were friends with Ramiro when his children died?'

'That's right.' Fuentes nodded. 'That was awful. Everyone wanted to help but you know what he's like, he does things his way. Does he ever talk about it?'

Galíndez shook her head. 'No, never.' She bit her lip. 'We're not on very good terms at the moment, after what happened last year. And there was the incident when I left hospital.'

'You mean when he punched that reporter?' Fuentes laughed. 'It served him right for shoving his mic in your face.'

'Ramiro punched him on national TV, boss. He lost the NATO job because of it.' She sighed. 'He must have thought he was back in the eighties with you and my dad.'

'It was another world back then.' Fuentes sat back, remembering. 'Madrid was like the wild west. Franco had only been dead three years. No one knew if the army would stage a coup and the politicians weren't sure what to do next.'

'It must have been weird,' Galíndez agreed, 'given that Franco had used the *guardia* to keep him in power for so long.'

Fuentes nodded. 'True. In fact, some of the jobs we got were still connected to the old regime. Have you heard of the pensioners' deliveries?'

She shook her head.

'Unofficial payments to retired *guardia* officers,' Fuentes said, a little uncomfortable. 'For services rendered to the regime. Dirty tricks, rough stuff, maybe even murder, for all I know. The payments were always in cash and they assigned the monthly deliveries to new recruits like your dad and me. Miguel had quite a few on his list. He used to have this joke, he called them *La*

Docena Sucia – like that American film, *The Dirty Dozen*. Because I was a rookie, I only got one.'

'Did you know what your guy did to deserve the extra money?'

'No idea. He was an old Dutchman, Herr Linderman. He was a nasty piece of work. I dropped off his money every month for nearly three years and he never once said thanks. One day, I arrived to make the delivery and found him dead in his chair.' He smiled. 'Sorry, Ana. Here I am going on about the past and I've not even asked how you are.'

'I'm feeling great,' Galíndez said, 'especially now I know I'm not going to be fired.'

'I think you can go far in the *guardia*, Ana. You've got your dad's energy,' Fuentes said, suddenly serious. 'But there's a condition attached to you coming back and it's from the top so please don't argue.' He gave her a long look. 'It's the Guzmán investigation.'

'What about it?' She jerked forward, suddenly tense.

'It's over. The *guardia* directorate don't think it's worth the trouble of pursuing a long-dead secret policeman.'

'But the public want to know what happened to him.'

'Actually, *you* want to know what happened to him, Ana María. I don't think most of the public care one way or the other.' He saw her expression. 'Christ, you've kept your job. Be thankful. The Guzmán investigation wasn't going anywhere in any case.' He looked down at the paper on his desk. 'The directorate also took an interest in this right-wing group you thought were watching you, the *Centinelas*?'

She stared, suddenly anxious, trying to keep her voice natural. 'What about them?'

'We made extensive inquiries. They don't exist.'

'But Judge Delgado was investigating them.' Galíndez frowned. 'I gave him some evidence about them.'

'Don't you read the news? Judge Delgado was impeached for improper use of public funds six weeks ago. I think you'll find he's going to be occupied for quite some time as he tries to clear his name. Those cases go on for ever.'

'But we also had Guzmán's diary,' Galíndez persisted. 'It was written in code.'

'No, it wasn't.' Fuentes opened a drawer and took out a slim package wrapped in brown paper. 'Here, you can keep it. You were right, it seemed to be in code but cryptographics finally concluded that it's just a diary.' He slide the package towards her. 'The message from the top is no more Guzmán.' He met her gaze and held it. 'Got that?'

Galíndez chewed her knuckle, wondering whether to argue. 'I've got it, *jefe*.'

'That's the spirit,' Fuentes said, more cheerful. 'On a different note, I wondered if you'd like to come over to our place for a meal? Mercedes thought after all that's happened, you might like some home cooking. Would Sunday suit you?'

'That would be great, *jefe*. I haven't seen your girls since you brought them in last year.'

'They've grown.' Fuentes smiled, 'and they're twice as much trouble. Inés still wants to be a forensic scientist.'

'She's a bright girl.' Galíndez nodded. 'Should I go and start work, then?'

'Not yet. You've some leave left over from last year. I think you ought to take it.'

'But I've only just come back.'

'I think you're going to want to take a couple of days off.' Fuentes waved to someone standing outside the office. The door opened and Mendez came in.

'Has she recovered from the shock?' Mendez asked.

Fuentes nodded. 'I think so, *Sargento*. Probably time to give her another, I think.'

Mendez held out a file. 'Present for you, Ana.'

Galíndez opened the file. 'What's this, a welcome-back card?'

'We got a message from a *guardia* post in the Basque country,' Mendez said. 'The boss thought you might be interested.'

'And what was this message from Euskadi?' The change in Galíndez's voice as she pronounced the Basque word wasn't lost on the other two. They knew how she felt about Basques. After what had happened to her father, no one blamed her.

'Just this and that.' Mendez smiled, noncommittal.

'I'm not going to beg.'

'*Jesús*, just tell her, will you?' Fuentes grumbled.

'OK,' Mendez said. 'I got a call from a Sargento Atienza. He's based near a place called Legutio. It's near Vitoria. There's a reservoir with water sports, fishing and stuff.'

Galíndez raised an eyebrow. 'You booked me a holiday?'

'Legutio used to be called Villarreal back in the Civil War,' Mendez said, ignoring her. 'It's where they started the final invasion of the Basque country in 1937.'

'Water sports and history. My lucky day.'

'Atienza says there was a village nearby that was shelled heavily during the fighting.'

'This is like those programmes on hotel TV,' Galíndez cut in. 'But less interesting.'

'They're knocking down what's left of the old village to build a sports complex,' Mendez continued, 'but when they came to demolish one of the houses, they found it was built on top of an older building with a big cellar. There was some stuff in it.'

Galíndez noticed the change in her voice. 'What kind of stuff?'

'He said it looked like an execution. There are bodies. Skeletons, I should say.'

'A war grave?' Galíndez asked, disappointed. 'So why did he contact you?'

'He didn't, he contacted you. I've been checking your email while you've been off.'

'OK, but why me? Don't they have their own forensic unit?'

'He remembered your requests last year for information about Guzmán.'

Galíndez felt gooseflesh on her arms. 'And?'

'It was Guzmán,' Mendez said. 'There's something that identifies him as the killer.'

31

Galíndez let it sink in for a moment. '*Jefe*, you know what you just said?'

'I said the official investigation is over. What you do in your own time is up to you.'

Galíndez looked at him, deep in thought.

'It's a four-hour drive,' Fuentes said. 'Just promise me you'll keep out of trouble.'

'Of course.' Galíndez looked at her watch. 'It's only two o'clock now. I can drive up this afternoon. I'll phone to let them know I'm coming.'

'Wait.' Fuentes looked at Mendez. 'You know what happened at Legutio, don't you?'

'I was about to mention it.'

Galíndez glanced from one to the other. Neither looked happy. 'What?'

'Two years ago, ETA parked a car full of explosives near the *cuartel* one night,' Fuentes said. 'It destroyed the building. It was a wonder there was only one person killed.'

Galíndez remembered 2008 well, though for other reasons. Sitting at Aunt Carmen's side in a hospital room, watching chemicals flow through plastic tubes into her veins. Preparing for her new job in the *guardia* as she dealt with the funeral arrangements.

'Go as Señorita Galíndez,' Fuentes said, interrupting her thoughts. 'Don't carry anything that identifies you as *guardia*. And you'll need a weapon.'

'I've still got the pistol they issued me in Vice.'

'Good. Don't let anyone see you're armed. Word gets around fast up there.'

'I'll be careful.'

'Be really careful, Ana.' Mendez put a hand on her arm. 'ETA don't play games.'

Galíndez shrugged her hand away. 'I saw them murder my father, remember?'

'I'm just saying,' Mendez protested. 'There's a phone number for the *sargento* in these papers. I've printed out the route for you as well.'

'Thanks.' Galíndez took the papers from her. She got up. 'I mean it, thank you both.'

'But when you get back, you draw a line under Guzmán and move on,' Fuentes said as she went to the door. Galíndez raised a hand in acknowledgement.

'I hope she doesn't use the satnav,' Fuentes said, once Galíndez had gone. 'She always breaks them. She doesn't look clumsy, but very often, they come back in pieces.'

'Strange,' Mendez agreed.

'I just hope whatever's up there is worth the drive.'

'It will be to her,' Mendez said. 'She's obsessed with Guzmán.'

Fuentes put his papers back into the envelope. 'She seemed angry, don't you think?'

'Ana's got quite a temper when she gets going, boss,' Mendez said. 'Takes after her father, I heard.'

Fuentes finished his coffee. '*Jesús Cristo*, I hope not.'

MADRID 2010, GLORIETA DE PIRÁMIDES

The lights changed and an impatient line of traffic surged down into the underground section of the M-30. Galíndez followed the tunnel, emerging back into daylight on the Avenida de la Paz, hemmed in on both sides by tiers of apartment buildings, tall high-rises of burnished glass and steel glinting in the bright sun. Half an hour later, she joined the A-1 and headed north. She reached forward and switched off the satnav. There were two hundred kilometres of motorway to go before she needed to think about directions again.

A car roared past, horn blaring as she pulled into the inside lane out of his way. She saw the driver's raised finger and angrily returned his gesture. *Jesús*, she was tense enough without morons like him winding her up. She drove on, her actions becoming automatic as she brooded about Guzmán. It was one thing for Fuentes to tell her to drop her investigation, it was another to

33

accept it. Most of Guzmán's crimes still remained hidden, waiting to be discovered. That was a challenge she wanted to take on.

Lost in thought, Galíndez didn't notice as she left the last isolated suburbs of Madrid behind. She was still dwelling on Guzmán, the way he got away with his crimes just as her father's murderer had. Before she'd been hospitalised, if the topic arose, she'd always said she wanted *Papá*'s killer behind bars. There were times now when she harboured darker, more violent ambitions.

The pain began somewhere near Burgos. At first, Galíndez ignored it, staring at the endless line of the motorway in front of her. When it got worse, she slowed, crossing lanes to pull in at a service station. In the car park, screened from the road by a ragged line of trees, she tried to relax the way they'd shown her in the pain management sessions in the hospital. It hadn't worked then and it didn't now.

She watched the constant motion of traffic through the trees. Words hammered around her head, words she would never utter to anyone. *I'm a mess. A fucking mess.* She put her hand over her mouth, struggling for control. She hadn't given in to her emotions all the time she'd been in hospital and she wasn't going to start now, in a dusty service station on the outskirts of an industrial park. She just needed time. The memory of what had happened to her would fade, she was sure, but there were other, more permanent signs of her encounter with Guzmán's malevolent legacy that time couldn't erase.

She slipped a hand inside her shirt, tracing the line of scar tissue running down her ribs. She was lucky to be alive, the doctors said. Lucky because the shrapnel had only slashed her side, rather than embedding itself in her body. Recalling the pain of that still made her break out in a sweat. Lucky? The only piece of luck had been when she'd lost consciousness.

She left the car and wandered into the anonymous labyrinth of the service station. In the women's toilets, she splashed her face with water, seeing her reflection in the mirror above the sink. A pale face, dark weary eyes. She glanced round, checking if any of the cubicles were occupied. Satisfied she was alone, she took a plastic container from her pocket, twisted off the cap and shook two tablets into her palm. She swallowed them quickly and ran the tap, cupping her hands to catch enough brackish water to wash them down.

By the time she joined the queue at the coffee shop, the painkillers had started to take effect. The assistant behind the counter made a joke as she put her order on a tray and Galíndez laughed out loud, her eyes twinkling as she shared the joke. Returning to her car she sat in the back seat, alternating sips of coffee with mouthfuls of sweet roll. When she'd finished, she took out the plastic container and counted the tablets. Ten left. No more pills once those were gone, she promised. Not unless the pain got too bad. She got behind the wheel and started the engine.

She passed the industrial sprawl on the outskirts of Burgos in a haze, her eyes dry and heavy. The last thing she needed was to doze off and wake up in a ditch so she turned on the radio, selecting a chat show to keep her awake. She caught the words 'Franco's crimes' and turned up the volume, suddenly interested as she heard a woman's voice, strangely familiar, her words fast and breathless, excited by her own erudition.

'Perhaps the worst of the crimes committed during the dictatorship was the wholesale theft and sale of newborn babies carried out with the knowledge and often the assistance of the regime's police and security services. Although many believe the practice ended when Franco died, the lucrative trade continued for years after his death.'

The voice continued but Galíndez was no longer listening. No wonder the speaker sounded familiar, it was Luisa Ordoñez. On the radio, Luisa's voice was calm and authoritative, far from the wheedling tone she deployed when she and Galíndez were lovers.

Another woman was speaking now: 'If you've just joined us, my name's Isabel Morente and you're listening to *Tardes con Isabel*. My guest today is Profesora Luisa Ordoñez, head of the School of Historical Discourse Analysis at Madrid's Complutense University.

We're talking about issues relating to the *niños robados*, the thousands of children taken from their parents at birth by doctors and medical staff who took advantage of their positions to then sell them. If these issues have affected you, call our helpline on—'

Galíndez turned off the radio.

Passing signs for Vitoria airport, Galíndez saw the white control tower in the distance, wavering in the heat. That might be about to change, she noticed. To the north, the horizon was lined with black clouds. She left the motorway at exit 355, passing through Gamarra Menor, a village of white-walled Basque *caserios*, chalet-style timbered houses with red tiled roofs and timbered portals. Her stomach tightened. *You're in the Basque Country now, Ana.* A couple of kilometres later, she pulled over to call Sargento Atienza.

'*Hola*, Sarge, it's Ana Galíndez. I'm ten kilometres from Legutio. Can I visit the site?'

'Sorry, I'm tied up for the rest of this afternoon, Ana. Can we meet up in the morning?'

'I wanted to get a look at it today. I don't mind going alone.'

'Thing is, we've had some trouble with the local workers on the site,' Atienza said. 'It'll be better if I come with you and bring a couple of my guys.'

She frowned. 'That sounds serious, what's the problem?'

'Nothing we can't handle,' Atienza said, 'but it pays to be careful.'

She sighed. 'OK, I'll take your advice. But I need somewhere to stay – any ideas?'

'No problem. When you arrive, drive into the centre of the village, park near the tourist office and then walk down the street towards the main square. There's a *pensión* called the Aralar. It's a bit old-fashioned but it's cheap and comfortable. I'll drive over and collect you in the morning.' He paused. 'You didn't come in uniform, did you?'

'I'm a forensic scientist,' Galíndez said. 'Plain clothes.'

'Good, because you need to be careful. It's best if no one knows you're GC. If anyone asks, say you're a hiker.' He took a breath. 'Have you got Madrid licence plates?'

'You know, you're starting to make me feel paranoid, *Sargento*.'

'There's no need,' Atienza said. 'But a lot of people from Madrid have had their cars vandalised by the local youth. They call it *Kale Borroka*, it's supposed to be a form of low-level urban resistance. They cut their teeth on that and then move up to the big league once they've toughened up.'

'The big league being ETA?'

'Like I said, just be careful.'

'I will.' Galíndez ended the call. Atienza's warning was a stark reminder she wasn't on holiday here. She'd inspect the site tomorrow and be away before dark.

Back in the car, she reached under her seat, feeling for the Glock in its polymer holster. That was a comfort. As she started the engine, she felt the plastic container of tablets in her back pocket. That was a comfort too.

Something glimmered in the distance: the fleeting glint of light on water. Seconds later, a deep roll of thunder.

A hundred metres ahead, the shrubs and trees lining the roadside ended abruptly in a long patch of scarred concrete, separated from the road by a wire fence. Puzzled, she slowed and pulled up by the fence to check where she was. Legutio was just up the road, she realised, poring over the map. This strange concrete scar was all that remained of the *guardia cuartel* destroyed by ETA's bomb two years ago. She started the engine and drove on, following the Urrunaga Dam, the dark waters flickering beneath elongated stammers of lightning.

The village was small and it took only a few minutes to find the Pensión Aralar. Just as the *sargento* said, the place was a little dilapidated but had a homely feel, with an ancient dining room on the ground floor. Her room was comfortable and from the window she had a spectacular view of the dam as the storm rolled in. Within a few minutes, sudden whip-cracks of thunder exploded overhead as gusting rain drummed relentlessly against the windows.

That evening, Galíndez ate alone in the big stone-floored dining room. She had no appetite and asked the *dueña* for something light. Señora Olibari returned with a bottle of red wine and a large plate of *txipirones*, baby squid served in their ink. Galíndez savoured the tender squid, mopping up the ink with bread. The fresh taste of the sea made her hungry and she was considering ordering something else when the *dueña* returned with the dish of the day, *trucha a la Navarra*, a fat lake trout, wrapped in slices of Serrano ham and baked until crisp, the trout soaking up the salty juices of the meat. Galíndez ate the trout with relish, washing it down with more wine. The food made her cheerful and the old lady commented on her flushed cheeks as she brought Galíndez a thick slice of Basque gateau and a glass of purple liquid with two dark berries lurking beneath the surface.

'Home-made *patxaran*, señorita. It's good for you.' Señora Olibari spread several coloured brochures on the table. 'If you're sightseeing, you might be interested in some of these.' As Galíndez took the brochures, the old lady looked at the dark rings around her eyes. 'It's a man, isn't it, *querida*?' she said sadly. 'That's why you're not sleeping.'

Galíndez looked up, her cheeks full of gateau, and nodded. Satisfied with her hearty appetite, if not her sleeping habits, Señora Olibari returned to the kitchen. Galíndez tried a sip of *patxaran*. It was certainly an acquired taste, she decided, though she drank it for its alleged medicinal value as she flicked through the tourist leaflets.

A visit to the Lauburu Agro Farm didn't excite her and she pushed the leaflet aside. Another brochure advertised a guided walk up the Pico de Mari, a tall peak said to be used as a perch by a Basque goddess, while yet another colourful flyer extolled La Cueva, a large cave once used by local bootleggers. The photographs of several wax dummies of absinthe makers in nineteenth-century costume failed to excite her. She had her own itinerary for this trip.

After dinner, the storm passed over and she went to her room to sit by the window, enjoying the cool evening air as she watched the vast expanse of water darken until it merged into the night. Somewhere out on the lake a bird screeched, shrill and unearthly, the echo rippling around the shore. And then an immense silence, broken only by the faint lapping of water and an occasional dull roll of thunder from the departing storm. The silence was disturbing and Galíndez lay awake staring at the bottle of tablets on her bedside table, wondering whether to take a couple. She was still wondering as she fell asleep.

'You're a spy.' Surprise and accusation in his voice.

'Who'd suspect a pregnant woman?' She smiled. 'They were late coming to get me – your invasion slowed them down. In the end I had a goatherd's daughter for a midwife.'

He looked away, angry. 'You know we shoot enemy spies?'

She took a long pull on her cigarette. 'That's rich, chico. Last time I saw you, we were on the same side. You had the uniform and everything. Anyway, you're full of yourself for someone who's – what do you call it? – oh yes, a traitor.'

He glanced round, suddenly wary. 'Don't say that again. And stop calling me chico.'

'You used to like it.'

He snorted. 'You were a whore then. It cost ten pesetas to fuck you.'

'When you paid. I've got an IOU that says you owe me sixty pesetas.' She put a hand on his arm, soft and tentative. 'So what do I call you now?'

He told her his name. That was his only name now, he said, his voice heavy with threat. 'Why did you volunteer to be a spy?'

'To fight the fascists, like you were supposed to. That's why they sent you to Badajoz.'

He tossed the cigarette away, a chain of red sparks in the dusk. 'Things changed.' He peered at the infant nestling in her arms. 'Who's the father?'

She raised an eyebrow. 'You're the smart one, chico. Work it out.'

'How? You must have fucked half the regiment.'

'Until I gave it up and signed up for active service.' A faint smile on her lips. 'I only had one man after that – and that wasn't for very long – remember?'

He glared at her. 'Joder, what am I going to do with you?'

'I don't know,' her eyes widened with feigned innocence, 'but I'd say you've got some thinking to do.'

CHAPTER 3

SAN SEBASTIÁN, OCTOBER 1954,
RESIDENCIA DEL GOBERNADOR MILITAR

Guzmán sank back into the soft leather seat of one of General Mellado's limousines, struggling to breathe. For the hundredth time, he ran a finger under the tight winged collar, trying to loosen the deadly grip of his bow tie. Formal dinners were best avoided as far as he was concerned but there was no avoiding this one. General Mellado not only demanded he attend, he'd sent a car for him.

'If you want a drink, *jefe*, there's booze in that cabinet in front of you,' the driver said, as courteously as could be expected of a man with so many scars across his face.

Guzmán opened the door of the cocktail cabinet and glanced at its contents. A large range of spirits and mixers, a shaker, jars of olives and cocktail cherries. Everything a man might need, he thought, noticing the Walter PPK in a leather holder on one side of the cabinet

'The general said you were with the Moors in the war, *jefe*?'

A moment's surprise. Of all the things Guzmán expected from a thug like him, conversation wasn't one of them. 'I commanded a squad of Moors for a while,' he said. 'Anti-insurgency work in the mountains.'

'You kill any of them, sir?'

'Of course not,' Guzmán said. 'They were on our side.'

'I would have killed them,' the *legionario* muttered. 'I'd have got a machine gun and shot the fucking lot.' He banged the steering wheel with his fist.

'They were good soldiers,' Guzmán said. 'And they never complained either.'

'I fucking hate them,' the legionnaire said, glancing at Guzmán in his mirror. 'When I was with the general in Morocco, we killed plenty of them.'

'That was different.' Guzmán shrugged. 'We were at war with them then.'

The driver drew his index finger across his throat. 'In the desert, the general used to pay one *real* for every Moor's head we cut. We made good money.'

'The general certainly knows how to get the best out of his men,' Guzmán sneered, knowing most legionnaires wouldn't have joined up without the opportunity to indulge their murderous inclinations on a regular basis.

The legionnaire nodded. 'We come across one of their schools one day. They were teaching kids to read and write in heathen. By the time we'd done, there were heads everywhere. Can't remember how much I made, but it was a lot.'

The limousine crunched to a halt on the gravel drive in front of the mansion.

'It must have been tough, fighting children,' Guzmán said. 'Did you get a medal?'

'We did what we were told. That was what we were there for.'

Guzmán opened the door. 'Those days are over,' he said and got out.

'Hang on, I'm supposed to get a tip. The going rate's a hundred pesetas. The general himself set that.'

'Then go and ask him for a hundred fucking pesetas.' Guzmán slammed the door and walked off towards the mansion.

The white marble façade of the building was illuminated by the dazzling beams of two very large searchlights on the lawn. Guzmán went up the steps to the entrance, shielding his eyes from the blinding light. Several military policemen with sub-machine guns were standing inside the doorway. One stepped forward to confirm Guzmán's identity.

'*Buenas, Comandante*. Sorry about the lights, they're brighter than the general expected. But as he says, they'll come in handy if there's an air raid.'

'I'm sure,' Guzmán agreed. 'Do you want me to leave my pistol?'

'No, sir. The general said it would be an insult to a war hero like you.' He pointed to a long hallway. 'Go down that hall and follow the path through the cloisters.'

Guzmán set off down the hall. The door at the end opened into a cloistered garden, surrounded by elegant alabaster walkways. As he walked, he noticed the thick iron bars of a heavy door set into an alcove. Cells were always of interest and he looked round casually to make sure he was alone. Cautiously, he put his hands against the door and pushed. It opened into a narrow stone passageway, so low he was almost obliged to stoop. Vague light shone through a narrow slit in the wall at the end of the passage. Ahead on the right were three dark metal doors, reinforced with steel bands.

Quietly, he opened the flap of the spyhole on the nearest door and peered in. A woman was sitting on the bed in the cell, her right hand cuffed to the metal frame. Aware of his presence, she glanced up and looked away quickly. He heard her rapid breathing, saw the bruises round her eyes. She was terrified. He opened the spy flaps on the other two doors and saw a woman in each cell. He went back along the passageway.

'Excuse me, señor?' Guzmán looked down, seeing the bars of a cell set below ground level. A pale face looked up at him, a young woman, about sixteen or seventeen, he guessed.

'I've been arrested,' she whispered. 'They won't let me tell my parents. *Mamá* will be worried sick.' She pushed a sheet of notepaper through the bars, 'Please let her know I'm here.'

'I don't know what you've done. Just tell the truth when they question you.'

'Please, for the sake of the Blessed Virgin, señor?'

Guzmán took the paper from her and put it in his jacket pocket. 'What's your name?'

'María Vidal,' she whispered. 'God bless you.'

Guzmán went back into the garden. Across the path, something rustled in the shrubs. He drew the Browning and thumbed back the hammer. 'Come out with your hands up.'

A man came out of the bushes. Young, sallow-faced, his hair a gleaming helmet of brilliantined curls. An expensive dinner jacket that must have cost a fortune on the black market.

'Who the fuck are you?' Guzmán grunted. 'I could have blown your head off.'

'Rafael Faisán, assistant to General Mellado. May I ask who the gentleman is?'

'Guzmán, *Brigada Especial*.'

'I'm afraid those cells are private, *Comandante*.'

'I got lost,' Guzmán growled. 'Who are those women you've got locked up?'

'The mothers of girls we arrested for attending resistance meetings. The general has been questioning them.'

'I bet he has,' Guzmán said. 'In the war, he used to keep captured Republican women in his HQ for his personal use. He called them his harem.'

'The general does as he sees fit,' Faisán said, primly. 'It's not for me to comment.'

'So where are the daughters?' Guzmán asked. 'Maybe one of them will know something about the resistance cell I wiped out last night.'

'Sorry, *Comandante*. They're all in solitary until the autumn ball. General's orders.'

'What, Mellado arrests them and then invites their daughters to a dance?'

'Exactly so. It helps them reflect on their foolishness. Like nuns.'

'I doubt that's true. The general was an old goat in the war – I'm sure he still is.'

'That was the war, sir. Now it's a matter of public order. Will there be anything else?'

'Yes.' Guzmán nodded. 'Use that tone of voice again, and I'll beat you senseless.'

'My apologies,' Faisán muttered hastily. 'If you'd come this way?'

Guzmán followed him into the courtyard. The young man knocked at an imposing door emblazoned with gilt letters:

GENERAL JOSÉ MELLADO, MILITARY GOVERNOR

Someone bellowed from inside, though it was hard to know what was said since the phrase consisted entirely of obscenities. Faisán opened the door and ushered him in.

General Mellado was sitting in an ornate chair, wreathed in a thick cloud of cigar smoke. He wore full dress uniform, the buttons straining with the effort of containing his corpulent bulk, his brilliantly polished riding boots resting on an antique table stolen from one or other of the wealthy left-wingers he executed the moment the city surrendered.

'Can't you knock, boy?' Mellado roared. 'I might have had my prick in my hand.'

Faisán blinked unhappily, unsettled by the thought.

The general hadn't changed much, thought Guzmán. There was still the black patch over his right eye, the scar running down his cheek and the missing ring finger on his left hand, all the work of Moroccan tribesmen who had taken advantage of his reckless courage in battle to use him for target practice.

'You took your time.' Mellado chuckled. 'Out whoring, were you?'

'Bit early for that, *mi General*.'

'It's never too early, *amigo*. Christ, I've already had two of the prisoners this morning, one of them over that desk.' He turned to Faisán. 'Isn't that right?'

'It is indeed, General,' Faisán muttered.

Guzmán couldn't help noticing the general was more than a little drunk.

'Brandy, Leo?' Without waiting for a reply, Mellado poured two large glasses.

'Very kind.' Guzmán took the glass and inhaled the fragrant aroma. 'To what do I owe the pleasure of this invitation?'

'Gutierrez called earlier. He said you're here to get this bastard El Lobo.'

'I am,' Guzmán agreed. 'Can you tell me anything about him?'

'I'll tell you one thing,' Mellado said. 'The fucker's a crack shot. In several of the robberies, he shot out the tyres and then killed both guards as they tried to flee.'

'He's not the only one who can shoot straight,' Guzmán said. 'In the meantime, I'm looking forward to a few drinks at your dinner before I go off into the hills.'

'Good lad.' Mellado grinned. 'I thought an evening with the old crones of the Falange would be just the thing before you got started.'

'I hope the food's better than the company.'

'Don't worry, lad, you'll eat well. This operation's secret, is it?'

'Very secret,' Guzmán agreed. 'Franco's ordered Gutierrez to keep it under wraps.'

'I can't stand Gutierrez.' Mellado scowled. 'What do you make of him?'

Guzmán said nothing and the general's deep laugh echoed round the room. 'You think he's a prick too?'

'I didn't say that. He's my boss.'

'I like that. It's diplomatic. You want to know how I'd handle El Lobo if I was you?'

'Of course,' Guzmán said. 'How many books have you written on military strategy?'

Mellado beamed. 'Seven, if you count the one on the use of cavalry.'

'So what do you advise?' Guzmán asked, getting as near to flattery as he ever would.

Mellado's puce face set with concentration. 'It's a typical anti-insurgency situation. You've got limited resources so you go up into the hills after him, destroy his supply lines and stop him being resupplied. Once you do that, he'll have to look round for more supplies or try to get away. That's when you take him.'

Mellado was describing Guzmán's intended plan of action though he refrained from telling him so. 'Thanks for your help, General.'

The general shrugged modestly. 'Killing a bandit's worthless if you ignore the wider context, Leo. Know what I think we should really do?'

'I understand you're in favour of military action?'

'Of course.' Mellado snorted. 'You need fear to keep order. These Basques need to see bodies in the streets to remind them this is Spain and not Euskadi or whatever they call it.'

'We also need investment from abroad,' said Guzmán. 'The *Yanquis* don't understand how we do things in Spain. We need to keep them sweet until we get their money.'

'*Joder*, they'll ruin the country with that approach,' Mellado grunted. 'The fucking foreigners are taking over. You know what we had here this summer?'

Guzmán shook his head. From Mellado's tone of voice, he imagined it must have been an outbreak of plague.

'A fucking international film festival.' Mellado snorted. 'With actors and actresses. There was even a prize for the best one.'

'Who won?' Guzmán asked. Not that he cared.

Mellado shook his head despondently. 'Some nonsense called *Sierra Maldita* about a village where half the people were sterile and the other half fertile. He gave a deep sigh. 'At least it was Spanish nonsense. Next year, they're going to invite foreigners to come and show their films. Just imagine how that will corrupt young people.'

Guzmán gave a vague shrug. He liked foreign films.

Anyway, I'd better get off,' Mellado said. 'I need to get spruced up so I can face a room filled with sanctimonious old hags.' He turned to Faisán. 'Did you get a couple of whores to sit with the *comandante*?'

Faisán looked at the general open-mouthed. 'I thought the general was joking.' His horrified expression lasted only a moment as Mellado punched him in the face, sending him stumbling backwards into the coat rack by the door.

'No whores?' Mellado hissed. 'You were given explicit instructions and you failed to obey.' He took a kick at Faisán. 'Try harder next time, *chico*.' He smirked at Guzmán as he went to the door. 'He's still learning. I've put him in charge of executing an anarchist. Let's see what he makes of that.' He slammed the door behind him as he went out into the courtyard.

'I'm sorry, *Comandante*,' Faisán said. 'I'll just get a cloth from the general's inner sanctum to stop the bleeding.' He hurried away to a door at the end of the office.

Since Faisán had left the door open, Guzmán leaned in, curious. In the far corner of the room, Faisán was dabbing blood from his lip with a field dressing. But what interested Guzmán was the machine in the centre of the room, an angular contraption of metal and wood with leather straps hanging from it. 'Is that what I think it is?'

'A portable garrotte.' Faisán nodded proudly. 'The latest model.'

Guzmán ran a hand over the garrotte, admiring its sinister elegance. The device consisted of a heavy iron base holding a wooden column about four feet high fitted with a small seat for the victim. A pair of leather restraints were fitted to the base for the victim's ankles with another pair behind the seat to secure the wrists.

Guzmán saw a label on the packing case. 'Mind if I take this? I'd like to get one of these for my *comisaría* in Madrid. I'll order it from them if they're any good.'

'Be my guest, sir.' Faisán nodded. 'It's a French company, we find them most reliable.'

'Typical,' Guzmán grunted. 'We don't make things any more in this country.' He pulled the label from the case and glanced at it before putting it in his wallet.

ÇUBIRY PÈRE ET FILS, AGENTS D'EXPORTATION

26 RUE DE VICTOR HUGO, ST JEAN PIED DE PORT, FRANCE

I'll leave you to it,' he went on. 'I'm going to go and find my table.'

Faisán came after him. 'Could I ask you about this thing with the anarchist, sir?'

'What about it?'

'I don't really know how these things should be done. What would you advise?'

'Don't mess about with the garrotte,' Guzmán said. 'Shoot him. Tell him he's about to die and put a round in the back of his head while he's praying.'

'He's an anarchist, *Comandante*,' Faisán protested. 'He won't want to pray.'

'They all want to pray when the time comes, believe me.' Guzmán laughed.

Guzmán's feet echoed on the marble steps leading to the banqueting hall. From inside, he heard the clatter of cutlery and crockery. As he reached the entrance, a woman stepped out from behind one of the Doric columns flanking the ornate doors. It was not a pleasant surprise. Her unkempt dark hair and thick calves together with her hopeless Spanish accent led Guzmán to think she was French.

'*Comandante* Guzmán?' A tobacco-stained smile. 'Jeanette Duclos, I am *journaliste*. Can I ask you about the bandit?'

Guzmán stared at her. 'What did you say?'

'I hear something about a bandit, El Lobo, he has robbed many banks, I hear?'

'I hope whoever you heard that from has left the country.'

'So, will you tell me about him?'

He shook his head. 'Perhaps in France you can ask the police questions without getting a slap but this is Spain. You won't write anything without official approval.'

'*Excusez-moi*, I will write what I wish. It is a free country.'

'Of course it's not, *mademoiselle*, don't be ridiculous,' Guzmán said. 'Spain is a dictatorship. Write anything without prior approval and you'll go to jail.'

Exasperated, he pushed her aside and went into the hall, hearing a stream of curses, though, since they were in French, they were wasted on him.

Guzmán found his table and made himself comfortable. He saw the place setting next to him. *Señorita Magdalena Torres.* Some rotund harpy, he imagined, probably the elderly daughter of a long-deceased colonel. He took a look at the setting opposite and groaned. A bishop. That meant the conversation would be about money, football or women, possibly even God if the bishop wasn't Spanish. His only hope was that the food would be good, though that would be scant consolation for tolerating such tedious company.

A waiter went by and Guzmán deftly reached up to pluck a glass from the tray. He lit a cigarette and sat back, sipping the expensive champagne as the social élite of the town filed in, preening and self-important as they hurried to their places. He smiled at their disappointment as they found themselves seated at the back of the room, an indication of the contempt the general held for them.

As he watched, a portly matron bustled into the crowded dining room. On her ample bosom he saw the yolk and arrows insignia of the Falange. Perhaps this was Señorita Torres. Then he breathed a sigh of relief as the woman joined several other ladies ensconced at a table near the general's dais. Bottles of water only, he noted. It was an image of hell.

A sudden movement at the door caught his eye as a late arrival hurried in. He took a long look and then, feeling the need for another drink, called the waiter, though he kept his eyes fixed on the blonde woman now standing in the doorway.

As he watched, the woman pushed a stray lock of hair into place and then strolled into the banqueting hall as if she owned it. She wore an expensive powder-blue silk dress that accentuated her figure as she picked her way around the tables, examining the place settings. Casually, Guzmán tried to loosen the collar of his bow tie again.

'Ah, here I am.' The woman smiled, seeing her name on the place card at Guzmán's side. He leaped up to hold her chair and she slid into the seat with supple grace. She turned to thank him. Blue piercing eyes. Scarlet lips that matched her expensively manicured nails. She gave a vague wave and a waiter came scuttling over. Guzmán didn't blame him.

'Brandy,' she told the waiter. 'A double.'

'Do you always drink brandy this early in the evening, señorita?' Guzmán asked.

'I really don't think you need worry about that, señor. I drink what I like, when I like.' She called the waiter back. 'The gentleman will have a brandy as well.'

Guzmán offered his hand. 'Leo Guzmán. You're Señorita Torres, I believe?'

'Heavens, you must be a detective, Señor Guzmán.' She offered him a cigarette from a monogrammed silver case. Blond tobacco, he noticed, probably American. He took the cigarette anyway, though he would find it weak and uninteresting. Unlike Señorita Torres.

'You're right, I am a policeman,' he said as he lit her cigarette. 'I saw your name on the place setting and thought you'd probably be an old dear who knits socks for the party. I'm very glad you're not.'

Magdalena gave him a faint smile. 'I find it quite a relief myself.'

Distracted, he ran a finger inside his collar. 'Do you think it's warm in here?'

'Not really, I found the sea breeze a little cool if anything.' She glanced round as the hall hummed with the noise of hundreds of conversations. 'I often wonder what people at these functions find to talk about, don't you?'

'They talk about themselves,' Guzmán said, trying not to stare at her breasts.

'I expect you're right.' She cast her eye over a table of high-ranking officers. 'That would explain why they all look so bored.'

They were interrupted as the waiter brought their brandies. Magdalena took a sip, looking at Guzmán over the rim of the heavy glass. As she put the glass down, he saw a faint trace of lipstick on the rim. His eyes moved lower, dwelling on the pearls round her neck. Tasteful and expensive, like her clothes. Like her.

'I'm not surprised to meet a policeman here,' she said, observing their fellow guests. 'This place is crawling with black marketeers and criminals.'

'Does that include you?'

She arched an eyebrow. 'Are all policeman so suspicious or is it just you?'

'It's just me. Since I'm not on duty, call me Leo, will you? What shall I call you?'

'Señorita Torres usually works rather well.' Her voice was clipped and precise. 'I mention the criminal element because my father runs a small import business. He trades with all manner of people and a lot of the more disreputable ones are here tonight, unfortunately.'

'Imports? You need to come from an influential family to get on in that business.'

'You know about these things?' Magdalena rested her elbow on the table, letting the smoke from her cigarette spiral upwards. 'Do tell.'

'It's simple enough,' Guzmán said. 'Even a woman can understand it.'

Magdalena pressed a hand to her chest. 'Oh, thank goodness.'

'First, you need a father in the military,' Guzmán continued, 'preferably a confidant of Franco. Failing that, you'd have to bribe someone extremely important – General Mellado would be an excellent choice because he's never offended by people offering him money. In fact, a large number of Republicans paid him vast sums not to execute them during the war.'

'What a softie.' Her smile was contagious, though he was not sure what amused her.

'Not really. He took their cash and then shot them anyway.' He noticed her expression. 'Did I shock you? Military matters can be too strong for a lady. I apologise.'

53

'Christ, you don't have a very good opinion of women, do you?' Magdalena said. 'I thought you were intelligent but I must say, you're doing rather a good job of keeping it hidden.'

Before Guzmán could say any more, the guests rose as the general came down the wide marble stairs, flanked by four grim-faced trumpeters. At the bottom of the stairs, Mellado paused to catch his breath, his face florid. Behind him, his bodyguards stared at the guests with malevolent suspicion. Guzmán noticed the scar-faced driver among them.

As Mellado and his retinue slowly proceeded past the bishop, the old man put down his pipe and reached into an inside pocket, presumably for his tobacco pouch.

A sudden shout from one of the bodyguards. 'He's got a gun.' And then a sudden blur of movement as two of the *legionarios* knocked the bishop from his chair and pinned him to the floor. The remaining bodyguards hurriedly took up position in front of Mellado, pistols aimed at the cowering diners, keeping them covered until the bishop was bundled out of the building, still protesting his innocence.

Magdalena's blue eyes twinkled. 'Am I mistaken or did that gentleman with the scars on his face just refer to the Bishop of Pamplona as a son of a whore?'

'He did,' Guzmán agreed. 'Just before he punched him in the face for a second time.'

With the excitement over, Mellado went to his table on the dais from where he looked down at the other diners, causing the conversations on the nearest tables to fade into nervous silence as he glared at them. Finally, with Faisán's help, the general took his seat alongside the various local dignitaries invited to dine with him. They would be paying for that privilege through the nose, Guzmán was certain.

Mellado was even more drunk than usual, Guzmán noticed, though that was no surprise. There was only one real surprise this evening and that was the woman sitting next to him. She was stunning.

'I knew a Torres,' he whispered. 'He was a general. I hated the sour-faced bastard.'

'Really?' Magdalena put a cigarette in her lips and leaned forward for a light. She sat back and exhaled a ball of smoke. 'Not *the* General Torres, the Butcher of Bilbao?'

'That's him. In my opinion, the man was a complete shit.'

'Actually, he still is.' Magdalena smiled demurely. 'He's my father. He owns the biggest importation company in the north of Spain. I'm the general manager, by the way.'

Guzmán reached for his brandy, trying to think of something to say. He was still trying when Mellado tapped his glass with a knife, calling for order. He looked out over the assembled diners, causing fidgeting among some of the guests. Mellado's kitchen might boast a famous French chef, but his reputation for violence had an unsettling effect. No one liked a homicidal host.

'Señores,' Mellado said, bringing his eye to bear on the nervous audience. 'Welcome to my annual fund-raising dinner in support of the *Sección Femenina* of the Falange.' His words were greeted with a ripple of polite applause. Several rotund women sitting nearby blushed gratefully. 'We know the good work these ladies do,' he continued, 'and the work they've done in the past, corralling and imprisoning those verminous whores who contravened the laws of God and Spain by taking part in the conflict against us, betraying both their country and their own natural femininity.'

By now, a number of ruddy matrons were waving their fans with increased vigour. Such eloquent flattery was most unexpected from the Military Governor.

'I'll tell you now,' Mellado said, raising his voice, 'you may think these vinegar-faced dowagers knit things for the party to pass the time while their husbands are out having fun, but they're doing God's work, setting an example to the rabble who still lie in waiting, hoping one day to rise in rebellion. Let me tell you, if that day comes, their blood will run in the streets.'

Faisán leaned forward and muttered something in Mellado's ear. The general held up a hand. 'Naturally, I don't mean the blood of these good ladies. I mean the Reds, the homosexuals and the verminous poor.'

Faisán signalled for the guests to applaud.

'You know the general always insists on a song at these events?' Magdalena whispered.

'I do, unfortunately,' Guzmán agreed. 'Worse, I know all the words.'

Mellado called for quiet. 'Before we eat, I ask you to rise and sing the anthem of our beloved Foreign Legion – not the cowardly French version, crammed with syphilitic criminals, but our very own Spanish foreigners.' He raised his mutilated hand into the air like a baton, pointing his pistol towards the back of the hall with the other. 'Sing, you bastards.' As the guests began the dirge-like anthem, he beat time with his gun as he bawled the words.

'None of the regiment knew who that Legionnaire was
So bold and brash he joined the Legion.'

'Only another ten verses,' Guzmán whispered.

The singing went on for twenty minutes. It seemed so much longer. Overexcited now, the general demanded a second rendition and, as the last line ground to an end, he could contain himself no longer and fired a shot into the ornate ceiling, bringing down a large section of plasterwork onto an unsuspecting dowager. As the staff hurried to her aid, the rest of the guests took their seats, relieved Mellado had done so little damage.

Cheered by both the singing and the opportunity to use live ammunition in a public place, Mellado launched into a speech about the occult underpinnings of democracy for a few minutes until, exhausted, he terminated his rambling discourse and made his way out of the hall, assisted by his bodyguards. His absence lowered the tension in the hall and conversation resumed once more.

Just as Guzmán was enjoying monopolising Señorita Torres's company, a waiter brought him a note inviting him to the general's table.

'Would you excuse me? I'll only be a minute,' he muttered, looking round belligerently at several dapper young officers scattered about the nearby tables.

'Of course. I'll chat to the bishop,' Magdalena said, noticing the bishop tottering back to his seat just in time to prevent the waiter making off with his lobster. The waiter backed away cursing, his hopes of selling the platter on the black market suddenly dashed.

Before Magdalena could speak to him, she sensed someone standing behind her and turned, her eyes narrowing as she saw the short plump man leaning on his walking stick.

'Señor Bárcenas.' Her tone suggested she'd discovered something vile on her shoe.

'Since you're alone, perhaps I should join you?' His voice dripped with bogus charm.

'You most certainly may not. I've already made it quite clear I don't want you as a business partner and I certainly don't want to sit at the same table as you.'

'You'd be wise to accept my offer,' Bárcenas said, spraying spittle.

Magdalena glared at him. 'Was that a threat?'

'It's simple business sense. Your father's incapable of running things and you…' He paused to mop his thick lips.

'What about me?'

'You're a whore.'

Magdalena took a sip of wine. 'Go away, you odious little man.'

'A business like yours needs a man at the helm.' His eyes flicked over her neckline.

'Since I doubled our profits over the last two years, I scarcely think we need the dubious benefit of your presence in the company, Señor Bárcenas.'

'You're alone and women on their own are always vulnerable.'

'I expressed my sentiments a moment ago,' Magdalena said angrily. 'I could rephrase them in the language of the gutter, but it wouldn't be polite to tell you to fuck off. Though, frankly, that's my answer.' Behind Bárcenas, she saw Guzmán returning from the

57

general's table. 'Do go away before you're sorry, Señor Bárcenas.'

'I'll ruin you. It's about time people knew what a slut you are.' Bárcenas frowned.

'Take your offer and shove it up your arse,' Magdalena snapped. She glanced across the table. 'Sorry, Bishop.'

The bishop kept his head down, shovelling lobster into his mouth while keeping a wary eye on the waiter. 'I've heard worse this evening, my child, believe me.'

Bárcenas lifted the cane in his right hand. 'No one talks to me like that.'

'I think the lady made herself clear,' Guzmán said, behind him.

Bárcenas turned, angrily. 'Who do you think you're—'

He didn't finish the sentence. Guzmán snatched the cane from his hand, snapped it and threw the pieces to the floor. 'Get out, before I do the same to you.'

'You wouldn't hit a cripple?' Bárcenas spluttered.

Guzmán shrugged. 'I've had plenty of practice.'

As Bárcenas hobbled away, Magdalena signalled the waiter to bring more wine.

'Who was that?' Guzmán asked.

'Alfredo Bárcenas. He's chairman of the local branch of the party and a black market racketeer.' She unfolded her napkin as the waiter brought her lobster. 'We don't get on.'

Guzmán paused. 'If you like, I'll go after him and beat him senseless, it's no trouble.'

'Don't waste your time.' She ground out her cigarette in the ashtray. 'I thought you'd abandoned me for the general.'

'Do I look stupid?' Guzmán asked. He saw her expression. 'What are you laughing at?'

Magdalena put her hand on his. 'I'm not laughing at you, *Comandante*. I'm enjoying myself.'

Guzmán looked at her for a moment. 'So am I.'

Three hours later, Guzmán and Magdalena were still at their table amid a circle of empty glasses, talking. The staff watched them, wishing they would leave.

'Do you have plans for tomorrow, *Comandante*?'

He nodded. 'I'm going up to the *guardia civil* barracks in Oroitz. My corporal and I have some work to do up there before I can go back to Madrid. How about you?'

'I'm taking my father up to our hunting lodge tomorrow morning. It's not far from Oroitz, perhaps you'd like to call in? You can say hello to him.'

'I'm sure he'd like that. Last time I saw him, I almost ordered my men to shoot him.'

'Really?' She gave him an amused smile. 'Why is he still alive then?'

'It's simple. My men disobeyed me.'

She breathed out smoke. 'You'd have done the world a favour, believe me.' She gave him a long look. 'I really would be grateful if you'd drop by, I could use some support.'

'In that case, I will,' Guzmán said. 'As long as he behaves himself.' As they went out into the courtyard, the scar-faced legionnaire and the rest of Mellado's bodyguards emerged from the shadows.

Scar-face broke the silence. 'Can I have a word, sir?'

'Go ahead,' Magdalena said to Guzmán. 'I've got my car parked out front.'

He raised an eyebrow. 'A woman with a car?'

'I know.' Magdalena laughed. 'Whatever next? I'll wait for you on the drive.' The sound of her heels faded away down the path.

'What can I do for you, soldier?' Guzmán asked.

Scar-face tossed his cigarette to the ground. 'Over here.' He went to the darkened alcove at the end of the cloister. 'I seen you this evening.' The legionnaire's stale breath soured the air. 'Chatting to that *puta* while the general was speaking. Both of you laughing at him.'

Guzmán felt a familiar sensation. A flame held to a fuse. 'What did you just say?'

Scar-face grinned, his broken teeth glinting in the faint light of the courtyard. 'You heard. The general thinks you're his friend. We think different.'

'"We"?' Guzmán repeated. He heard a soft noise behind him and turned. 'You brought your pals,' he said, giving the big shadowy figures a look of contempt.

'We look after the general,' Scar-face said. 'And if you don't behave properly with him, we'll break every fucking bone in your body.'

Guzmán gritted his teeth. 'You're out of line, Private.'

'Don't try and pull rank,' Scar-face muttered. 'Just watch it in future, or we'll come calling.' He spat onto the cobbles. 'But first, we'll call on that blonde you were with.'

Guzmán walked away through the cloisters, hearing their laughter behind him. Four veteran legionnaires would be difficult to take on, even for him, he reflected, standing at the entrance to the mansion. A vein in his temple throbbed.

Magdalena was leaning on one of the Grecian pillars by the entrance, a fox fur stole draped round her shoulders. She exhaled a pale cloud of smoke. 'I'll give you a lift to your hotel if you're ready.'

A red blur swept across his vision. The fuse sparking into flame.

'I think I left something in the general's office. Could you give me five minutes?'

'Of course. I'll wait in the car.'

There were no echoes now as Guzmán retraced his path along the corridor. He walked silently, the way the Moors taught him in the war. At the door to the cloisters he stopped and slipped the trench knife from the scabbard on his calf. The blade glimmered in the darkness. Keeping the knife flat against his leg, he went in search of Scar-face.

It did not take long. Guzmán heard the legionnaire's voice echoing from the alcove where the women's cells were located. One of the prisoners was weeping as the man enunciated the catalogue of torments he was going to subject her to. These men were scum at the best of times, Guzmán knew. With no war to occupy them, Mellado had allowed them to grow presumptuous. Presumption was one thing. Tolerating it was something else. It was weakness.

As Guzmán entered the alcove, Scar-face was standing outside the cell at the far end.

The fuse burned shorter now.

Guzmán walked towards him silently, gauging the distance between them as he raised the knife. He was almost upon him by the time the legionnaire sensed his presence.

'What do you want?' The man's scars had a luminous quality in the dark.

Guzmán adopted a conciliatory tone. 'I came to apologise. I don't want any trouble.'

The man sniggered. Stale wine on his breath. 'You'd better say sorry then.'

'I already left you an apology,' Guzmán said. The knife felt like an extension of his arm.

'Yeah?' Contemptuous. 'Where?'

A sudden tense silence. Guzmán shifted his weight on the balls of his feet, his grip on the knife balanced and comfortable. 'In your mother's cunt.'

He swung the knife, putting his massive strength behind the heavy blade as it sliced open the legionnaire's throat, sending him reeling against the wall, already drowning in his own blood as he fell. Guzmán stepped back to avoid the last spurts of blood, watching the man's final spasms with professional satisfaction.

'Did you find what you were looking for?' Magdalena asked as he got into the car.

Guzmán reached for his cigarettes. 'It turned out I hadn't lost it at all.'

'That must be a relief.' She started the engine and the car moved down the drive. The sentries saluted as they opened the gates. They drove along the sea road, following the curve of the beach. The bay was black, speckled with light from the shore.

'Beautiful, don't you think?' she asked, looking at the bay.

'Very beautiful,' Guzmán said, looking at her.

The car turned into the boulevard and slowed to a halt outside his hotel.

SAN SEBASTIÁN 1954, HOTEL ALMEJA

'Can I offer you a nightcap?'

'I won't, *gracias*,' Magdalena said. 'I never go back to a gentleman's hotel room on the first night. I find my restraint helps develop a certain demeanour in him later on.'

'What kind of demeanour?'

'Why, gratitude, of course.' She brushed his cheek with her lips and got back into the car. Guzmán watched as she gunned the engine and sped away down the boulevard, turning with a squeal of tyres into Calle San Juan. As the roar of the engine died away, he went to the hotel door and hammered on it to wake the night porter.

The bleary-eyed porter opened the door and Guzmán waited at the desk, impatient for his room key. It had been a good night, he reflected, a very good night indeed, and nothing, not even this wooden-headed *badulaque*, could ruin it.

As he handed Guzmán his key, the porter remembered the letter that had arrived earlier in the evening and hurried to retrieve it from the ancient wooden mail rack behind the desk.

Guzmán tore open the envelope and read the short message inside. He had been wrong.

His evening was ruined.

The teniente *did not visit her the next morning. Instead, she was taken upstairs by a myopic corporal in thick spectacles. He led her to one of the ruined houses and waited outside while she washed in a bucket of cold water. Afterwards, they sat on a stone wall and Ochoa held the baby for a while, waving the doll at her until she beamed.*

He took out a battered packet of Superiores. She took the cigarette he offered and leaned forward to let him light it. 'Can I ask your name, Corporal?'

'Segismundo Ochoa, señorita. At your service.'

'Do you have children?'

'Not yet,' Ochoa said. 'I will one day, I hope.'

He was about to escort her back to the cellar when the teniente *returned. After Ochoa had gone, she laughed, seeing the* teniente's *face blackened with soot. 'You look like the devil,' she told him. 'Want me to tell your fortune like I used to?'*

He took her by the arm and started leading her back to the ruined building. 'Stop acting like you know me,' he growled.

'Then help us get away, chico. *If you don't, I'll lay a curse on you.'*

His face darkened. 'Don't joke about things like that.'

'Then help us. Just let me and the little one go on our way, for old times' sake?'

'It might be easier just to kill you.'

'Don't even think about trying that, chico. *I know who you are, remember? In any case, if anything happens to me, the curse stays put for ever.'*

He escorted her back to the cellar in silence. The guards led her back down into the shadows and he walked away, lost in dark thoughts.

She was becoming a problem.

CHAPTER 4

S argento Atienza found Galíndez in the dining room, finishing
off a plate of *jamón, huevos y tomates*. They shook hands and
Atienza asked for coffee when Señora Olibari came to say
good morning. She guessed Atienza was in his fifties from his
greying hair and beard.

He watched her push her plate away. 'You're not leaving that
ham, are you?'

'Go ahead, I'm stuffed.'

'*Gracias.*' Atienza picked up a piece of bread and made a
sandwich with the ham. He glanced at the wood-panelled dining
room. 'I bet this place looked the same fifty years ago.'

'Can we get started?' she asked, impatient. 'I have to be back in
Madrid this evening.'

'Sure, let's go.' Atienza finished his improvised breakfast and
went out into the street. Galíndez picked up her bag of equipment
and followed him. A four-by-four was parked outside. As she
stowed her bag on the back seat, she noticed Atienza lying on the
kerb, checking underneath the vehicle with a small mirror. A
careful, systematic search, something her father should have done
the morning he was killed. Another reminder of where she was.

Atienza finished his inspection and sensed her watching.
'Routine precaution,' he grunted casually as he got behind the
wheel. He'd unfastened the retention strap on his holster, she
noticed. Not so casual after all.

Atienza followed the narrow cobbled street down to the main
road and turned north across a long bridge over a lagoon, heading

towards a series of hills several kilometres away. The clouds had rolled away now and the water glittered. She saw rowing boats and sailboards, people fishing.

'Did you see the remains of the *cuartel* when you arrived?' Atienza asked.

She nodded. 'There wasn't much left. Will they build another?'

'Supposedly, but the local councillors are holding things up. They think if they do that long enough the *guardia* won't come back.' He shrugged. 'Leave them to it, I say.'

They left the road and turned onto a rough dirt track running up the side of a hill overlooking the dam. After a few hundred metres, the track grew too steep to continue.

'Sorry, Ana.' Atienza held up his hands in apology. 'We'll have to walk from here.'

Galíndez looked at the gradient of the steep track, imagining the pain in her ribs as she climbed with the heavy bag of equipment. She shrugged. 'No problem.'

'Can I carry your bag for you?'

She shook her head. 'I don't need any help.'

Further along the hillside, slow lines of construction vehicles were struggling up a makeshift service road leading to the flat ground on top of the hill where the skeletal outline of a crane towered over the half-completed sports complex.

Atienza was talkative and filled her in on most of his life story in the first ten minutes of the walk. It was pretty standard stuff: a daughter who left home at sixteen, unable to tolerate the disruption of his various postings, and then an acrimonious divorce. And now, with retirement looming, he hadn't a clue what he would do in civilian life.

The hilltop was littered with ruined houses. Atienza pointed to some ragged brick walls, none of them more than half a metre high. 'That's the house. Or it was.'

The ruin was surrounded by green and white chequered tape: *Guardia Civil No Pasar*. Two uniformed troopers with submachine guns were standing by the ruins of the house. Both men acknowledged Atienza with a friendly wave. Neither spoke to Galíndez, though she noticed their brusque appraisal.

'This is Juan Carlos,' Atienza said, introducing Galíndez, 'and this is Pepe.'

They grunted, turning their attention to a group of men standing a few metres away.

'Those are the construction workers,' Atienza explained. 'They're waiting for us to sort out what's in this cellar so they can get back to work. They'll lose money if we hold them up much longer.'

Galíndez stopped. One of the men was staring at her. A tall heavy-set guy with a thick beard covering his pointed chin. The 'hare face' they called it up here. A Basque face.

She walked toward him, returning his stare. 'Got a problem?'

He glowered at her. 'Fuck off back to Madrid.'

She felt the vibrations start somewhere deep in her chest, spreading down her arms, her fists clenching. 'What did you call me, you prick?'

A hand gripped her arm. 'Leave the peasants alone,' Atienza said quietly. 'The farmers need lads like him to keep their sheep pregnant.'

Galíndez tensed against his hold on her arm. She heard the metallic rattle of the two troopers readying their weapons.

'Come on,' Atienza muttered. 'We don't want anyone getting hurt. It's bad publicity.'

Galíndez turned reluctantly and started back towards the house. A mocking voice followed her. 'There she goes, down into that cellar to take it up the arse, like all the other whores from Madrid.'

'*Puta madre.*' She spun round, incensed.

Atienza pulled her back. '*Tranquila*, Ana, there'll be trouble if this kicks off.'

'Yeah, Ana, don't start any trouble.' The construction worker grinned. 'Just drop your *bragas* and bend over, that's what you're here for.'

Galíndez glared at him, rigid with anger. She was memorising his face.

The bearded man cackled. 'Look at her shaking. They're all scared when they come here. Make sure to look under your car when you go home, *puta*.' He made a gesture, throwing his hands up in the air. 'Boom.'

'Leave it now, Aïtor,' one of the others muttered.

'Ana, do you want to see what we found or not?' Atienza asked, trying to distract her.

Galíndez threw a last dark look at Aïtor and turned to inspect the ruins.

It had been a large building once. She saw a ragged opening and a flight of steep stone steps descending into dark shadow. 'They're down there?' she asked, putting down her bag.

'That's right.' Atienza pointed to a heap of broken concrete. 'The cellar entrance was sealed up. The concrete cracked when a heavy vehicle got too near. The house was built on the site of an older one, but no one knew about the cellar.'

'Did you touch anything when you went down?'

'When I saw the bones, I guessed what it was,' Atienza said. 'I knew you wouldn't want my DNA all over the place.'

'I wish more of our agents were like you.' Galíndez tied back her hair and took a pair of latex gloves from her bag. She smiled. 'I hate a contaminated crime scene.'

The builder saw her pull the gloves on. 'You've done that before, *muñeca*.'

Galíndez froze. 'If he calls me "babe" again…'

'You know, that's quite a temper you've got,' Atienza said.

'Tell me about it.' Galíndez pushed a strand of hair behind her ear.

'Just be cool, he'll lose interest in a minute.'

'I know what he ought to lose,' she muttered, taking her flashlight from the bag. 'So, what made you contact me about this site, Sargento?'

'Why don't you see for yourself?' He gave her a faint smile. 'I thought I'd save the best till last, like I used to with my daughter's Christmas gifts.'

She felt a sudden warmth towards him for his attempt at being kind. 'I bet your daughter liked that, didn't she?'

He shook his head. 'She can't stand me. When she left home, she got into drugs big time. Three times I tracked her down and brought her home. She just ran off again.' He sighed. 'You know, there's no helping some people and she's one of them.'

Galíndez wished she'd kept her mouth shut.

Fluffy clumps of cobweb clung to her sleeve as she negotiated the shattered stairs, running the flashlight over the debris littering the cellar floor. Shining clouds of dust rose in the white beam. In the rubble, she saw a large angular shape wreathed in cobwebs. Kneeling, she pulled away some of the thick web, revealing an ancient metal chair, lying on its back. She moved the beam to her right, her interest growing as the light picked out a jumble of bones around another chair.

'There are bones everywhere,' Atienza said. 'Were they in an explosion?'

'No, over time, the skeleton falls apart,' Galíndez said, shining the light further into the gloom, seeing the same pattern repeated: another battered metal chair, bones strewn around. Looking closer, she saw the damaged spine, severed between the first and second cervical vertebrae. She took her phone from her pocket and took a picture.

Atienza moved closer and saw the look on her face. 'What have you found?'

'Someone cut off the head. Whoever did it had already hit the victim several times, see?' She pointed to the mark of the impacts on some of the bones. 'He would have been bleeding badly before the fatal blow.' She knelt, examining the floor behind the chair.

'So what are you looking for?' Atienza asked.

'The head, of course.' The beam of her flashlight fell on a pale ball of dusty gossamer. 'There we go.' A skull, the dark hollows of the orbital cavities discernible through the dusty shroud of accumulated cobwebs. A head didn't detach itself and travel two metres without assistance. Something bad had happened here.

'Hello, what's this?' Atienza turned and saw Galíndez kneeling, head down, meticulously examining something. She got up, carefully brushing cobwebs from it. Her eyes suddenly widened. She turned the object towards him. He saw a chipped nose, a small mouth, two faded glassy eyes.

'What's that?' He frowned.

'You've a daughter,' Galíndez said, 'can't you see? It's a doll's head, porcelain, I think.' She shone her torch down at the spot where she'd found it. 'I expect the body was made from cloth or wool. It must have rotted away long since.' She bagged up the head and put it to one side. Her face set with concentration. 'You didn't find any trace of a child's body, did you?'

Atienza shook his head. 'No, I took a good look round and these were the only remains I found.'

Galíndez moved the torchlight over the rubble again. 'Can't see anything. I'll keep an eye out in case. Let's see what else we've got, shall we?'

Atienza pointed his torch into the darkness, a circle of white light flecked by dust. 'There's the other body.'

This one was different. Some of the body was still in the chair, half buried in a sloping pile of rubble that reached up to a ragged fissure near the top of the wall, crudely repaired with concrete, suggesting the damage had been caused by an explosion outside. There was no head here either, though the ribs and spine were kept in place by the debris that engulfed the body. She saw a humerus amid the rubble behind the chair.

Atienza kept his distance, giving her room to work. 'What happened?'

'Part of the wall collapsed,' Galíndez said. 'Probably the result of shell fire. See that?' She played her torch over the sloping mound of rubble, her latex glove eerily white in the beam of the flashlight as she pointed to an irregular patch of concrete where the damage had been repaired. 'It blasted a hole in the wall, and rubble poured down onto the body, that's what's kept it in place all these years.'

She moved closer, bending to examine the scattered bones. '*Mierda*, look at this.' She lifted the skull in both hands, turning it to show the full extent of the damage. 'Someone cut through his skull as if they were taking the top off an egg.'

Atienza looked round. 'What do you make of all this?'

'What it looks like,' Galíndez said, mulling it over, 'is that someone hacked these people to death. I mean he really hacked them, there'd be body parts all over the place.' She glanced at Atienza. 'Are you OK with me talking like this? Some people get a bit squeamish.'

Atienza nodded. 'I've seen worse.'

'Lucky you.' Galíndez played the light over the cellar. 'Is this everything?'

'You sound disappointed.'

She shrugged. 'If this is all we've got, I'm going to try spraying with Luminol.'

'That's the stuff that finds traces of blood, isn't it?'

'With these injuries, there would have been plenty of blood. Using Luminol might just help give me a better idea of how the killings happened.'

'Can I help?' Atienza asked.

She looked at him in surprise, unused to anyone offering to help her in these situations. 'It would be great if you'd operate the camera. You'll need to sit on the stairs about halfway down and hold it steady because we need a prolonged exposure.'

'I think I can do that.'

On the stairs, she found an angle that would take in most of the cellar while keeping the skeletons in view. 'This will do nicely.' She handed him the camera.

Atienza watched as she prepared the mixture, mixing luminol with a catalyst and then pouring it into her spray gun. 'You think there'll be any blood after all these years?'

'*Absolutamente*. Luminol will show blood over a hundred years old. And old blood glows brighter than new. Let's see, shall we?'

She pulled up her face mask and began spraying, careful not to trample any potential evidence. As she reached the far end of the cellar she called to Atienza. 'Press the button, Sarge.'

Atienza obeyed and Galíndez switched off her torch, plunging the cellar into darkness. It was not dark for long. The Luminol began to glow in iridescent blue patterns, covering the cellar floor with intricate geometries of glinting blue light. 'Press it again, Sarge,' she said. The camera shutter snapped, brittle and loud. 'Now move down three or four steps and let's do another.'

He took another photo. 'What do you think, Ana?'

'I think it was a messy killing; there's blood everywhere.'

'So what do you want to do with these skeletons?'

'I doubt we can identify them,' she said, gauging the work involved. 'Maybe you should bury them once your forensics unit has carried out its investigation?'

'There's no local forensics unit,' Atienza said. 'And the construction company has political connections, so my boss doesn't want things held up any longer. If you don't take these bones with you, the guys up top will fill the cellar with concrete and build over it.'

'I'll take them,' she said quickly. 'You said something about saving the best till last?'

'Over here.' Atienza led her to the side of the stairs. 'I left it just where I found it.' He pointed the flashlight at the ground. In the white circle of light she saw a glint of metal.

'Is that a machete?' Growing curiosity in her voice.

'See for yourself.'

'*Mierda*.' Galíndez picked up the weapon with both hands. A scimitar, the curved blade mottled with rust. She brushed away encrusted dirt with her finger. '*Hombre*, there's something written on it.'

Atienza raised his flashlight, illuminating the inscription.

Galíndez looked at it, wide-eyed. '*Puta madre*.'

Two rows of writing. The first consisted of elegant, precisely etched symbols, Arabic by the look of them, worked into the metal with great skill.

The second line ran parallel to the first. Bigger letters, crudely stamped onto the sword:

Capitán Leopoldo Guzmán 16.4.1937

'Is that your man?' Atienza asked.
Galíndez nodded, her eyes still fixed on the blade.

LEGUTIO 2010, PENSIÓN ARALAR

Atienza stood by the entrance to the *pensión*, watching as Galíndez finished putting her forensic kit into the car. She slammed the door. 'Thanks for everything, Sargento.'

'*De nada*. Listen, this is a one-way street, so the best thing is to go straight down and turn in the square at the end, see where those trees are?'

'Got it. Thanks again for helping with the skeletons.'

'You're welcome. I hope those *cabrónes* didn't upset you?'

Galíndez looked away. 'They wound me up, that's all.'

He smiled. 'In this part of the world, that's not the worst thing that can happen. I'll see you around. Maybe I'll look you up if I come to Madrid?'

'Do that.' Galíndez climbed into the car and adjusted her mirror. She leaned out of the window. '*Hasta pronto.*' Atienza shook her hand and walked to his car.

Galíndez eased the car forward. Down a side street she caught a glimpse of the dam, its dark water burnished by the setting sun. Ahead, she saw the square and slowed, ready to turn.

Ten metres away, a figure stepped off the pavement. It was the construction worker, Aïtor, heading for a bar on the other side of the square. Galíndez stopped the engine and gripped the wheel, her knuckles white. When she took her hands away, they were shaking.

The barman looked up. '*Kaixo*, Aïtor. What will you have?'

'Beer.' Aïtor leaned against the bar. 'Nothing like a day's work to build up a thirst.'

The barman held a glass under the tap. The nozzle hissed, spluttering froth.

'Out of beer? I can always go somewhere else.'

'I'll get a new barrel,' the barman said. 'It'll only take a minute.'

'Fine, I'm off for a piss.' Aïtor walked to the rear of the building, through a large tiled area in semi-darkness, wooden tables and benches where the restaurant had once been. At the far end, a murky passageway led to the toilets.

Mikel disconnected the empty barrel and rolled it towards the storeroom. Behind him, he heard a rustle at the door and turned, hoping it was another customer. No such luck: the bar was empty. He shrugged and went to get the new barrel.

In the men's *komun*, Aïtor washed his hands in cold water. The hot tap hadn't worked in years and Mikel still hadn't fixed it. At least there were paper towels today. He dried his hands and tossed the screwed-up towel on the floor with the others, wondering why he still came to this dump. Once, the place had been a popular restaurant. Now, it was just a seedy bar with a dwindling clientele as competition grew from the places springing up round the dam. When they finished the new complex, most customers would take their business there. Certainly he planned to. No more hundred-metre walks to take a piss or hot water taps that never worked.

He stepped out into darkness. Someone had turned out the light in the old restaurant, reducing the passageway to a dark tunnel. At the far end, he saw a figure, framed against the dim light, coming towards him. A pale face emerged from the shadows.

'What did you call me?' Galíndez said.

With just a kilometre to go before she reached the A-1, Galíndez started looking for the slip road. After that, she could look forward to the monotonous three-hour drive back to Madrid. Behind her, she saw the flashing light of a patrol car in her mirror, travelling fast, probably on its way to an accident. As the patrol car passed, it veered in front of her and slowed, forcing her to brake. A hand emerged from the driver's window, pointing to the verge. She pulled over.

The patrol car stopped a few metres ahead. Galíndez killed the engine and waited, rehearsing her story: *No, really, was I going that fast?* An attitude of quiet surprise. *Here's my ID. That's right, I'm guardia – just like my father, actually.* Mendez said stuff like that worked every time and she ought to know, she drove like a lunatic.

Galíndez opened the window as a figure in a hi-vis vest came toward her. Atienza leaned in through the window. 'You want the good news or the bad news?'

'Surprise me.'

'He's not going to press charges. I don't think he could face his pals if they heard you'd beaten the crap out of him.'

Galíndez frowned. 'So what's the bad news?'

'You've got a problem.'

He's guessed about the tablets. Dilated pupils maybe. 'What sort of problem?'

'I think they call it anger management.'

She relaxed. *He doesn't know about the medication.* 'I'm fine,' she said. 'I saw that builder in the square and had a quick word with him.'

'It was a hell of a word: he's got a broken collarbone and two black eyes. Why didn't you tell me if he upset you that much?'

Galíndez stared into the dark, gripping the wheel. 'I'm my father's daughter.'

'What does that mean?'

She turned and met his gaze. 'It means I don't ask anyone to fight my battles for me.'

'Wait here.' Atienza went back to his car and returned with a plastic box under his arm.

'What's that?' Galíndez asked.

'Two chorizo sandwiches, an apple and a flask of strong coffee. You're in a hurry so you might be tempted not to stop and eat. I'm donating my supper to you.'

'*Gracias*,' she said, touched. 'Dinner's on me if you come to Madrid.'

Atienza gave her a wave of acknowledgement and went back to his patrol car.

Galíndez waited for him to drive away before she started her engine. It was dark now, nothing to see but the endless stream of headlights in the opposite lane. She had just taken a bite of chorizo sandwich when her phone buzzed. She took the call, glad for the distraction.

'Ana? It's Mendez. I've got a problem.'

'Only one?'

'Well, two when you get here. I've got a body in the chiller, some hooker who got carved up. I need someone from forensics to sign it off and you're the only one who isn't sick or having a baby – at least as far as I know, anyway. Can you do the DNA stuff for me?'

'I'm near Vitoria right now. Can I do it tomorrow?'

'Sure. Seven thirty,' Mendez said. She hung up.

The road to Madrid became a blur as Galíndez turned her thoughts back to the rusty sword on the back seat. A sword that had killed the three people whose skeletons were bagged up in her boot. Three more killings to be added to the list of Guzmán's bloody deeds. It was unlikely she'd ever know why those people were killed but at least there could be no doubt as to the killer's identity. His name was inscribed on the blade, for God's sake.

Next morning, Ochoa was ordered to photograph the prisoners. The three men ignored him. The woman was nursing the baby and she lowered her head to shield the child from the camera with a curtain of black hair.

Later, as Ochoa passed General Torres's tent, he heard Torres and the teniente *talking. Curious, Ochoa paused and lit a cigarette, glancing round as he blew a long breath of smoke into the damp air. There were no guards nearby and he sidled closer to listen to their discussion.*

The general was giving orders for the execution of the prisoners.

Foreign journalists had arrived, the general said. Reporters from the Catholic Herald: *their accounts of the war were key to winning the support of the US government. Because of that, it was best they were not aware of the executions. Which meant, said the general, the* teniente *should kill them tomorrow evening, while the reporters were being entertained in the mess. There would be ample time to kill the Reds without alerting the* Yanquis.

Once the executions were completed, the general went on, it would be a kindness if the baby were to be adopted. He had a couple in mind, good Catholics, members of the party, too. A childless couple like them deserved a child far more than the Red whore down in the cellar.

Adoption would be for the best, the teniente *agreed.*

A nurse from the Sección Femenina *would care for the infant until the new parents could be contacted, General Torres continued. They were a wealthy couple and they would pay handsomely for the child. Naturally, the* teniente *would be rewarded for his assistance in the matter. And, of course, for his silence.*

Naturally, the teniente *agreed.*

Outside the tent, Ochoa heard footsteps approaching and saw one of the regular soldiers, a big surly private. The man warned him not to get so close to the general's tent. If he didn't want a bullet in the back, he should fuck off out of it.

Ochoa took his advice.

CHAPTER 5

SAN SEBASTIÁN, OCTOBER 1954, HOTEL ALMEJA

Guzmán stood at the window of his hotel room looking at the sea through his reflection in the smeared glass. He snatched up the handwritten note and read it again.

You Killed her.

He'd been wrong to think no one knew him here. Someone knew him very well indeed. Deep in thought, he left his room and went out to get a breath of sea air.

They were pulling a drowned man from the harbour as Guzmán walked along the seafront. A crowd had gathered to watch several men in a rowing boat as they struggled to retrieve the corpse from the dirty water. Finally, the men got a grip on the body and manhandled it aboard. It lay on its back, causing gasps of horror among the spectators as they saw the distorted face, the sodden mop of pale blond hair above wide, staring blue eyes. Some know-it-all in the crowd claimed the man was a sailor, lost from a foreign vessel in the Bahia de Vizcaya. It was a reasonable hypothesis that Guzmán had no reason to doubt, far less to care about, and he left the jabbering crowd by the quay.

As he walked to the Buick, he sensed movement around him. Slow, subtle actions, men holding newspapers but not reading them, others taking an age to light a cigarette, their eyes following him. He slowed, suddenly aware of more men stepping out from behind parked cars and shop doorways, taking up position. He didn't have to turn to know there were others behind him.

A sharp-faced man was walking towards him. The double-breasted leather coat might as well have had *Policía* painted on the back, Guzmán thought.

'Inspector Rivas. Head of General Mellado's Security Police.'

'Guzmán, head of the *Brigada Especial*,' Guzmán said, staring him down. 'Although I'm sure you know that, just as you know that I outrank you. What do you want?'

'I'm investigating the killing of a *legionario* at General Mellado's mansion last night.'

'Legionnaires like killing one another,' Guzmán said. 'What's new?'

'I understand you were talking to the general's bodyguards before you left the mansion. What was your conversation about?'

'One man was my driver earlier in the evening. A big guy with scars on his face. I tipped him a hundred pesetas.' Guzmán met Rivas's eye. 'Why not ask him?'

'He was the man who was killed. There was no money on him.'

'Then it's clear theft was the motive, wouldn't you say, Inspector?' Guzmán smiled. 'Anything else, or shall I call Franco's HQ and let them explain why obstructing me in the course of my duty has cost you your job?'

'You were with Señorita Torres at the dinner, I believe?' Rivas said, ignoring his threat.

Guzmán gritted his teeth. 'You'd do well not to bother her, bearing in mind who her father is.'

Rivas shrugged. 'General Torres doesn't have the clout he used to.'

'No? He's a personal friend of Franco. And since I report to the *caudillo*'s HQ, I'll be very happy to let him know you're bothering one of his old friends.' Guzmán stared into Rivas's eyes until he looked away. 'Understood?'

The inspector's face twitched. 'I'm not suggesting Señorita Torres is implicated in the killing, *Comandante*, but you must appreciate I have to carry out a thorough investigation.'

'Then I suggest you get on with it. And forget about Señorita Torres.'

'This isn't Madrid, *Comandante*,' Rivas muttered. He gestured to the men around him and they melted back into the doors and alleyways.

'Thanks for the geography lesson.' Guzmán turned and walked across the road, straight towards the surly plain-clothes men on the far pavement. Grudgingly, the men moved aside. Ten paces further on, Guzmán stopped and looked back. Across the road, Inspector Rivas was standing stock-still, watching him. Guzmán shrugged and walked unhurriedly into the narrow streets of the old town, feeling Rivas's eyes burning into his back as he went.

SAN SEBASTIÁN 1954, CAFÉ SOL, PLAZA 18 DE JULIO

There was still an hour before Ochoa's train got in and Guzmán took a seat at a café in the plaza. He inspected the walkway on the far side of the square with a practised eye, noticing brief, hurried movement as someone slipped out of sight behind a kiosk.

He ordered coffee and a brandy to accompany it. The brandy was cheap and rough though far less offensive than the coffee, which tasted as if it was made from powdered acorn flour. If the price didn't reflect that, there would be trouble.

He looked up, hearing the tapping of heels on the cobbles. A gypsy was coming across the square, making straight for him.

'*Buenos días*,' the gypsy said deferentially. Guzmán liked that.

'I apologise for bothering you,' she added, thinking he was ignoring her.

Since Guzmán was ignoring her, he liked her persistence less. He gave her a critical glance. Tall, curiously masculine, troublingly big hands. A gaunt, cadaverous face with high cheekbones, skin coarsened by the sun or, more likely, drink. Her attempt at a smile revealed a missing front tooth. No, he was mistaken: teeth. Since she wasn't selling faded flowers stolen from the cemetery, that could only mean one thing. He stayed silent, waiting for her to reveal it.

'This will come as a surprise, señor...' she began.

'You're a whore.' Guzmán shrugged. 'I'm not surprised at all.'

'Is the gentleman clairvoyant?'

'No, I'm a policeman.' He saw her expression change. 'Don't worry, gypsy whores are very low on my list.'

'There's a list?' she asked, worried now.

'There's always a list.' He stared at her hands again. 'Are you sure you're not a man?'

The gypsy shrugged. 'Who can ever be sure of anything in this life?'

It was a good answer, managing to avoid his question entirely. That gave him confidence in her. 'Do you tell fortunes?'

She took a pack of cards from her tattered bag and set them on the table. The cards were greasy and much handled, rather like their owner, he imagined.

'If you'd be kind enough to select four cards, señor?'

He chose the cards, and watched the gypsy arrange them on the table.

'The cards suggest it's time to let go of the past. Is there a lady you want to forget?'

Guzmán leaned forward, startling her. 'Which card is that?'

'The card of Death, señor, though it doesn't always indicate someone dying.'

'But it can,' he said, thinking of El Lobo. 'Dying with a bullet in them, perhaps?'

The gypsy swallowed, drawing attention to her Adam's apple. 'It's possible.'

Guzmán reached for his wallet and counted out several bills. 'Here's forty pesetas.'

'You could have fucked me for half that,' she muttered ungratefully.

'No doubt,' Guzmán said. 'Though the cost of the penicillin after would have been prohibitive. I don't know why you're complaining: forty pesetas will buy you something to eat.'

'Yes,' the gypsy agreed, 'two bags of roast chestnuts.'

'And I very much hope you enjoy them, señora,' Guzmán said, dismissing her. She began to gather up her cards. 'Have that brandy if you like,' he added. 'It's foul.'

The gypsy downed the brandy in one gulp and turned to go.

'Wait,' Guzmán said. 'Can you lift a curse?'

'It depends, señor. Is the person who cursed you still alive?'

He shook his head and the gypsy sighed as her hopes of extracting more money from him were dashed. 'Unfortunately not. The curse stays in place until your death in such cases.'

Guzmán put his wallet away. 'Then I'll bid you good day, señora. Or señor.'

Across the square, a man was watching him from a seat outside one of the dingy bars under the covered walkway. The same man who had been hiding behind the tobacconist's kiosk twenty minutes earlier. Aware of Guzmán's gaze, he looked down at his newspaper.

As the gypsy went across the square towards the harbour, the man got up and came over. He was tall and rangy with an expression that looked like he'd been drinking vinegar. It was possible he was one of Inspector Rivas's goons, though Guzmán doubted it. His clothes were too expensive for a local policeman. That was confirmed when the man took a seat at the next table and sat looking out at the square.

'You'll be Capitán Viana, I take it?' Guzmán said.

The man glanced around the square suspiciously. Since the square was deserted, the gesture annoyed Guzmán intensely. 'You can never be sure who's listening,' he muttered.

'Never mind your paranoia,' Guzmán said. 'Just tell me how you're going to handle the communications for this operation, and look at me while you're talking, not that paper.'

Reluctantly, Viana looked up. 'I'm working undercover at the local police station. Gutierrez will send telegrams to me, I'll decode them and then deliver them to your hotel.'

'And when I'm in the mountains?'

'We can radio you at the *guardia cuartel*, or I can send communications by courier.'

Guzmán got to his feet. 'I expect Gutierrez told you I have my own ways of working?'

'He said you're insubordinate and unorthodox,' Viana said. 'Among other things.'

'You should know better than to gossip about your colleagues,' Guzmán growled. 'Just be sure you do a good job on this operation. If you don't, I'll come looking for you.'

Viana looked up, his eyes glinting. 'I can handle myself, *Comandante*.'

'I'm sure you do every night,' Guzmán said. 'But answer me like that again and I'll put you in a wheelchair.' He saw the waiter coming towards them. 'There are two things I expect on an operation like this, Viana.'

'Which are?'

'The first is don't talk to me with a face like a choirboy going into confession with a bent priest.' Guzmán took his bill from the waiter and slapped it down onto the table in front of Viana. 'The second is you pick up the tab. Remember to keep in touch, won't you?'

Gutierrez was right about Guzmán, Viana thought, watching him go. No wonder the *general de brigada* had promised him special instructions on how to handle the *comandante*.

SAN SEBASTIÁN 1954, ESTACIÓN DEL NORTE, PASEO DE FRANCIA

Guzmán drove across town to the Santa Catalina Bridge. The town was livening up. Every street corner was lined with boys hawking newspapers, and here and there gypsies were shining shoes, using neat alcohol that removed all stains but would split the leather within a few hours. Further along, lines of women queued outside every food shop, all hoping the produce would not sell out before their turn came.

On the far side of the bridge, he turned into the Paseo de Francia and pulled over by a patch of waste land across the road from the smoke-stained North Station. Along the front of the station, a line of stony-faced passengers queued patiently at a ticket window. Guzmán observed them without interest as he finished his cigarette, watching the smoke from a departing train stretch and fade on the sea breeze.

A few passengers came out of the station entrance, among them a pasty-faced man struggling with several large camera cases. He peered uncertainly across the road through his thick glasses and finally recognised Guzmán. He staggered across the road with his luggage.

'Good trip?' Guzmán asked as he put Ochoa's bags in the boot.

'Not bad, sir,' said Ochoa. 'Although it wasn't all that good either.'

'Fuck me, Corporal,' Guzmán snapped, 'it's been seventeen years and you've still got that same miserable disposition you had in the war.'

'The station's packed with young women,' Ochoa said, in an attempt at conversation.

'You always were hopeless with small talk,' Guzmán grunted. 'Just get in.' He looked down and saw a small leather case. 'Is this yours as well?'

Ochoa snatched up the case. 'I carry this camera with me all the time. Just in case.' He paused. 'Who's that watching us across the street?'

At the front of the station, Inspector Rivas was standing near the queue for the ticket office. Two of his men waited by the entrance, thinking Guzmán wouldn't notice them.

'Local police. Someone was killed last night, I think he suspects me.'

Ochoa gave Guzmán a strange look. Guzmán ignored it.

'Nice car, sir,' Ochoa said instead, admiring the Buick. 'Must have cost a fortune.'

'Not really. I confiscated it from an enemy of the state.'

He pulled out of the car park, still glowering at Rivas in the rear-view mirror. 'So what's this job, *jefe*?' Ochoa asked.

'We're tracking down a bandit.'

'Just us?'

'The American ambassador is on holiday just across the border. Franco doesn't want his vacation disturbed by talk of bandits.' Guzmán turned to stare at Ochoa. 'And by talk, Corporal, I mean killing the bastard.'

'I gathered that, sir.' Ochoa nodded. 'So what's our plan?'

'Remember the counter-insurgency work I did up here in the war?'

Ochoa nodded. 'It'd be hard to forget that, wouldn't it?'

Guzmán leaned forward. 'I'm not talking about *that*. Christ, remember what was said when the war ended? There are things we don't talk about. Everyone in the *Brigada Especial* agreed to that, you included.' He changed gear noisily and headed out of town.

'You were in the press corps when we were at Villarreal,' he continued, annoyed by the silence. 'Did you do that for the rest of the war?'

Ochoa nodded. 'After you were posted south, I took pictures of Red atrocities.'

'How? You weren't behind their lines.'

'I used any bodies I could find. First, I'd mess their faces up with a bayonet or a brick and then take a picture. Our newspapers published them, saying they were the work of the Reds.'

'Christ, it's always the quiet ones,' Guzmán said. 'You must have seen a fair few corpses then, even if the only shooting you did was with a camera?'

'I certainly did, *jefe*. I was there when we captured Toledo.'

Guzmán exhaled a cloud of smoke. 'I bet you didn't take pictures of that.'

'I went to watch them take over the hospital,' Ochoa said. 'There were two hundred patients, most too badly injured to get out of bed. After they killed the doctors, the *legionarios* raped the nurses and then killed them. Then they went through the hospital, slaughtering the patients as they went. It's not the sort of thing you forget.'

'Of course you can.' Guzmán took a drag on his cigarette. 'Just get on with your life.'

'Is that what you did?' Ochoa said. 'After Villarreal?'

'For fuck's sake,' Guzmán snapped. 'What did I just say about things we don't talk about? Villarreal's in the past and that's where it's staying.'

'See, I haven't forgotten it,' Ochoa said. 'I have these nightmares…'

'Stop that now, Corporal, or you'll end up in the madhouse,' Guzmán said, angrily. 'And when you come out in thirty years' time and you're begging outside Atocha station like a flea-ridden dog, don't shake your tin cup at me because you'll get fuck all.' He glared at him. 'Got it? Change the fucking subject.'

'Yes, sir.' Ochoa nodded. He looked out of the window at the sheer slopes towering over them on either side of the road. 'Where are we?'

OROITZ 1954

The wind came from the mountains in cold violent flurries. Guzmán stood by the side of the Buick, surrounded by the shredded remains of his map. That map had failed him for the last time, he thought, watching the scattered pieces dancing away on the breeze.

Ochoa came back from examining an old wooden sign a few metres down the road. 'It isn't a road sign,' he shouted, trying to make himself heard above the wind.

'What does it say?'

Ochoa shrugged. 'Beware of cattle.'

'The sooner I get back to Madrid, the better.' Guzmán stared belligerently at a vast landscape devoid of cows. He cocked his head. 'What's that noise?'

Someone was coming down the road. Guzmán reached into his jacket for the Browning, noticing Ochoa draw his pistol as he moved away, making them a harder target.

The noise grew louder as a figure appeared from behind a bank of gorse and rough shrubs. An ancient shepherd, wearing what appeared to be a filthy carpet. The strange noise Guzmán heard was his singing. The wind picked up again, changing direction. Suddenly, Guzmán became aware that the man was, in fact, wrapped in a sheepskin, a very old one, judging from the smell. He holstered his pistol and concentrated on getting upwind.

The old man's smile was a row of evil-looking stumps. 'Are the gentleman lost?'

Guzmán thought that was perfectly clear, even to a reeking peasant like him. Since they needed his help, he refrained from saying so.

'I'm looking for Oroitz, *Abuelo.*' He spoke slowly, presuming the man was an idiot. Most country people were in his experience.

The old man pointed to a faint cluster of houses clinging haphazardly to the lower slopes of a mountain several kilometres across the valley. 'Oroitz.' He pointed again, in case Guzmán hadn't understood. '*Bai.*'

'Watch it, *Abuelo*, it's illegal to speak Basque,' Guzmán warned. 'Tell me, if we walk up that track over there, can we get to the village?'

The old man nodded. 'That track takes you there eventually, señor, though it's very wet, so you'll probably get those nice shoes muddy. And then you have to climb up through the rocks and that'll be quite a struggle because the ground gets really steep there.'

Guzmán's scowl was growing deeper by the minute. He began taking his bags out of the boot. 'Will the car be safe if I leave it here?'

'Leave it?' the old man asked, surprised. 'Why would the gentleman do that?'

Country folk: every last one wooden-headed. No wonder Franco shot so many. 'Because I'm not going to carry it, am I?'

88

'I thought perhaps the señor might take the road since he has an automobile.'

'Road?' Guzmán's eyes narrowed. 'What road?'

The old man pointed to a faint grey ribbon in the distance. 'That road. You follow it over the hill and it branches off up the side of the mountain to Oroitz. An easy drive, señor.'

Guzmán threw the bags back in the car. 'You thought I'd prefer going up a muddy track rather than drive?'

'The gentleman is from Madrid. Things are done differently there.'

Guzmán stared at him, suspiciously. 'How do you know I'm from Madrid?'

The shepherd shrugged. 'From the gentleman's licence plates, of course.'

Guzmán got behind the wheel. The old man watched him without blinking.

'Do you want a lift, *Abuelo*?'

The old man exposed the shattered remnants of his teeth as he smiled. '*Eskerrik asko.*'

Guzmán pulled the choke angrily. '*Por Dios*, speak like a Christian, will you? Spanish. Not Basque. *Entiendes*?'

'I understand, señor.'

Ochoa opened the rear door and the shepherd scrambled onto the back seat. Ochoa slammed the door and climbed into the passenger seat alongside Guzmán. They looked at one another for a moment.

'I'll open a window,' Ochoa said.

'Open it wide.' Guzmán started the engine and the tyres grated on the track as he headed towards the distant road.

Ochoa turned to offer the old man a cigarette. 'Got a name, *Abuelo*?'

'Mikel Aingeru, *para servirle*,' the old man said politely, dipping into the pack of cigarettes. He took three, Ochoa noticed.

'Do you know where General Torres's hunting lodge is?' Guzmán asked.

'Of course.' The old man leaned forward between the two front seats, giving them a waft of his vile breath. 'See where the road turns left up the mountain? That's where we're going. If you carry straight on, you come to the general's lodge after a few kilometres.'

The shepherd was correct: the road did climb up the side of the mountain, so steeply that Guzmán was forced to slow to a crawl. The effect on the old man was immediate. No longer disturbed by the movement of the car, he began snoring loudly, his face resting against the window, steaming the glass with his fetid breath.

After a few hundred metres the road opened out onto a piece of flat ground near the village. Guzmán pulled over and killed the engine.

'That's quite a view,' Ochoa said, accepting Guzmán's offer of a Bisonte. An ancient hand emerged from between the seats and plucked a cigarette from the pack.

'You're awake, then?' Guzmán said, half turning. 'We've arrived.'

'So I see.' Mikel leaned forward to let Ochoa give him a light.

'Let's take a look round,' Guzmán said to Ochoa.

'I'll stay and watch your bags.' The old man yawned, giving them an unwanted view of his gums. 'This car is so comfortable, I could sleep in it all night.'

'You could if I let you,' Guzmán muttered. He climbed out of the car and looked round at the spectacular view. Above them, shards of cloud clung to the slopes of the mountain, hiding the peak. Behind him, he heard the sound of Ochoa's camera as he began taking photographs.

The village consisted of a short steep track with buildings on either side. The appearance of the houses told of centuries under rain-filled skies, scoured by the eternal mountain winds. The idea of living here horrified him. No bars or whores and no gambling. Just ancient houses being worn away by time and rain, much like their occupants, he supposed.

The clouds around the mountain were starting to break up, and he watched as the world below slowly emerged from the mist. Within twenty minutes he found himself looking out over a great landscape, rugged and beautiful in equal measure. Not that he cared. It wasn't Madrid and for that reason alone, he hated it.

Guzmán returned to the car and tapped on the window to wake the old man, recoiling from the smell as he opened the door. As he rummaged among the bags in the boot for his hat, he sensed the shepherd peering over his shoulder.

'Hold this for a second.' Guzmán handed the old man a long leather case.

'The señor has a rifle?' Mikel looked at Guzmán in surprise. '*Cuídese*, señor. The *guardia* shoot people for carrying weapons.' He inclined his head towards the barracks a hundred metres down the hillside, joined to the village by a steep narrow path. A frayed plume of smoke rose from a chimney, and over the entrance to the *comisaría* the yellow and red flag stuttered in the breeze.

'Not that we need the *guardia* to kill us here,' Mikel said. 'We fight among ourselves. *Hombre*, two nights ago, they found eight bodies in the school at Ihintza. Students, all shot dead. Seems they'd got hold of some weapons and fallen out. What a thing to happen, eh?'

Guzmán looked at him without blinking. 'It's a tragedy.'

'Who knows what goes on in these young ones' minds? I blame the parents, señor.'

'*Absolutamente*,' Guzmán agreed, knowing that what had happened to the students in the schoolhouse had been planned weeks earlier by Gutierrez and his staff in Madrid.

'It was nice to meet you,' he added, pointedly.

'The pleasure was mine, señor. *Agur*.' The old man set off up towards the village.

'You've forgotten something.'

The shepherd grinned. '*Lo siento.* I nearly walked off with the gentleman's rifle.'

'Nearly.' Guzmán retrieved the heavy leather case from Mikel Aingeru and watched the old man wander away, leaving an odour of ancient sheepskin behind. He stowed the weapon safely in the car and called Ochoa to join him as he went down the track leading to the *cuartel*.

'It's not Madrid, is it, sir?'

Guzmán glowered at him. 'Strangely enough, Corporal, I'd noted that.'

OROITZ 1954, CUARTEL DE LA GUARDIA CIVIL

The building was typical *guardia* architecture, an ugly, cheaply constructed blockhouse made of defective concrete bought from dishonest contactors and built by incompetent builders. Most of the builders' efforts seemed to have gone into carving the traditional *Todo por la Patria* over the entrance, and even the lettering of that was skewed. Guzmán could picture the layout inside: a few offices, an armoury and a squad room that stank of sweat, farts and cabbage. By the door, a civil guard was polishing his boots. He looked up as they approached. 'Want something?'

Good, Guzmán thought, *it would never do to arrive somewhere and be dealt with courteously. That would just make things boring.* 'We're staying in the village,' he said. 'We're here to present our documents.'

'Quite right too.' The trooper held out his hand with blatant disinterest.

Guzmán handed over his papers and watched the man's face change as he read the pass issued by Franco's HQ.

'*Perdón, mi Comandante.* We had no idea you were coming. *A sus ordenes.*'

Somewhere inside the *cuartel*, a woman screamed. '*Qué pasa?*' Guzmán asked, walking briskly towards the entrance.

'Sargento León is questioning someone, sir. I wouldn't interrupt if I was you.'

Ignoring him, Guzmán went into the building and marched down the dingy corridor, the monotony of its mildewed walls punctuated by khaki doors with peeling paint. The woman cried out again, from a room to their right. Ochoa stood back as Guzmán opened the door.

There were two men inside. One had his back to them, the other was a burly *sargento*, holding a young woman against the far wall, his big hand round her throat. The girl's face was flushed and her blouse was torn at the neck. The men were arguing.

'Mind your own fucking business, Corporal,' the *sargento* growled. 'She's a suspect. I'll do what I like with her.'

'She can't be a suspect,' the corporal protested. 'She hasn't done anything wrong.'

'You think so? She'll confess to anything in an hour or two. You know what they say: old enough to bleed, old enough to butcher. Time she found out what women are for.'

Guzmán stepped into the room. '*Buenos días.*'

'Who the fuck are you?' the big *sargento* growled. 'Throw him out, *Cabo.*'

The corporal looked at Guzmán and saw trouble. 'Who are you, señor?'

'Read this.' Guzmán handed the corporal his papers. 'Out loud.'

'Stuff it up your arse, I'm busy,' the *sargento* said. Noticing his momentary distraction, the young woman took the opportunity to bite his hand. He cursed, pushing her against the wall, trying without success to pin her arms to her sides. She lashed out with her foot and caught him in the shin. He glared at her. 'I'll teach you to bite me, *puta.*'

He was a big bastard, Guzmán noticed. Still, so was he.

'You'd better hear this,' the corporal said.

'I told you to throw them out.' The *sargento* let go of the girl and she slumped against the wall, her eyes bright, though not with tears. She seemed to be looking for something sharp.

'I'm questioning this prisoner,' the *sargento* said. 'And I don't like being interrupted, so piss off, unless you want the same treatment.'

'What? You're going to feel my tits as well?' Guzmán sneered.

'Listen to this, Sarge.' The corporal's voice rose in disbelief. '"His Excellency, Head of State, *Caudillo* by the Grace of God, *Generalísimo* Don Francisco Franco requests that the holder of this document, *Comandante* Leopoldo Guzmán, of the Special Brigade, be afforded any assistance said officer may request of any public servant whether civil or military. Any order or instruction from said officer may not be countermanded by a commissioned officer below the rank of *coronel* and even then said officer must first communicate with General HQ to obtain approval. Further, be aware that the above mentioned Don Leopoldo Guzmán is authorised to bear firearms at all times.'" The corporal stared at the sergeant. 'It's signed by Franco himself.'

'Which means,' Guzmán growled, 'you two ladies start behaving in a proper manner or I'll take appropriate measures.' He reached into his jacket for a cigarette. 'But suit yourselves, I've always enjoyed firing squads.'

'*A sus ordenes, mi Comandante.*' The corporal snapped to attention.

The *sargento* was less impressed. 'You might be something in Madrid but this is my territory and things are done my way here.'

'This land doesn't belong to you Spaniards,' the young woman cut in. 'It's Basque and always has been.'

'Quiet, bitch.' León drew back his fist.

Guzmán sprang forward, seizing the *sargento*'s wrist and twisting his arm to pull him away from the girl. León tried to break free but he was too slow and Guzmán slammed him back against the wall before driving a couple of hard punches into his belly. Gasping for breath, the *sargento* looked up just as Guzmán's head-butt hit him in the face, sending him backwards, scattering piles of papers from the desk as he fell. He lay on the floor, clutching his nose, trying to staunch the flow of blood. 'Shoot the fucker, Corporal.'

Caught between fear of Guzmán and fear of his *sargento*, the corporal made a half-hearted attempt to draw his pistol. Something clicked behind him and his hand froze before the gun left the holster.

'I wouldn't do that,' Ochoa said, his pistol aimed at the corporal's head.

The corporal raised his hands. He gave the *sargento* an embarrassed shrug.

'Useless fuck,' León spluttered.

Guzmán frowned as he looked down at the sergeant. 'I know you, don't I?'

'In the war.' León's teeth were red with blood. 'You were commanding those Moors.'

'And you were wiping General Torres's arse, I recall,' Guzmán said, 'with your tongue.'

'At least I didn't spend my days with a bunch of heathens,' León sneered.

Guzmán stamped on León's crotch. The *sargento* howled and rolled onto his side, clutching his groin. 'You're finished here,' Guzmán said. 'Pack your bags.'

León struggled to his knees and spat blood onto the floor. 'You can't do that.'

'I just did,' Guzmán said. 'And start referring to me by rank, *cabrón*.'

The *sargento*'s pig-like eyes narrowed. '*Sí, mi Comandante.*'

Guzmán noticed the young woman standing by the door, watching events with interest. 'You'd better come with me, señorita.' She didn't blink. *I'm losing my touch.*

As he went into the corridor, Guzmán called to Ochoa. 'Go to the radio room and arrange the *sargento*'s immediate transfer.'

Guzmán took the young woman outside. They stood looking at the spectacular view of the valley and the mountains, listening to the noise of the flag rippling in the breeze.

'Don't you think it's beautiful here, señor?' she asked.

Guzmán paused for a moment before answering. 'No.'

Inside the *cuartel*, León was throwing his things into a kitbag. Some of the men gathered round, watching him pack. 'It's too bad, Sarge,' one said. 'You had a good thing going here.'

León turned on him, his face red with anger as he slung his

kitbag over his shoulder. 'That bastard won't be here long. They can't hack it, those Madrid types.'

'Why is he here?'

León tapped the side of his swollen nose with a finger. 'That's for you to find out, Chavez. And if he gets any messages, I'd like to know about them too.'

'There'd be something in it for me, would there, *Sargento*?'

León hoisted his bag onto his shoulder. 'Isn't there always?' He walked to the door rubbing his injured crotch. 'He'll be sorry he messed with me.'

Guzmán took out his cigarette case and offered the young woman a cigarette. When she refused, he lit one, observing her through a wreath of smoke. She was about eighteen or nineteen, pretty, too, her oval face framed by sleek black hair. But it was her eyes he noticed most. They were like the sea before a storm.

'Why are you looking at me like that, señor?'

'You seem familiar – I wondered if we'd met before?'

She smiled. 'We Basques all look alike. The hare face, we call it.'

'That must be it. Do you live in the village, señorita?'

'I live there.' She pointed down the valley to a distant farmhouse.

'You live with your parents, I suppose?'

'With my aunt. My parents are dead.' She looked at him through strands of wind-blown hair. 'You Spaniards killed them in your war.'

In Madrid, he would have slapped her for that. 'We're all Spanish,' he said. 'One Spain, united and free. Haven't you heard the party members chanting that at their meetings?'

She looked at him, amused. 'Monkeys will do anything for a banana.'

'I think you should go home to your aunt, *niña*. And try thinking before you speak in future, otherwise you'll get yourself into some real trouble.'

'Don't call me *niña*,' she said indignantly. 'I'm a woman, not a little girl.'

'I think the expression you're looking for is "*muchísimas gracias*", Guzmán said. 'I just got you out of a nasty situation.'

'*Eskerrik asko.*' She ignored his frown at the Basque words. 'Why did you help me?'

He shrugged. 'I can't stand bullies. How come the *sargento* detained you?'

'I said something in Euskara about him being a pig.'

'That was foolish, don't you know it's illegal to speak Basque?'

'Many things are illegal that shouldn't be. And there was the *brujería* as well.'

'What witchcraft?'

'We study the old ways. Some Spaniards think it's anti-Catholic.'

'You should be careful. Not everyone understands such things.' He looked up at the mountain and peered at a row of dark holes in the steep hillside overlooking the road. 'What are those?' he asked, pointing. 'Caves?'

'It's the Fortaleza de Zumalacárregui. It was built in the eighteen thirties during the First Carlist War. They built it to stop the enemy from using the road.'

'Did it?'

'Not really.' Nieves smiled. 'They built a new road.' Her face brightened. 'Why don't you visit us one morning, Señor Guzmán? My aunt's a marvellous cook.'

'I'll try and drop by,' Guzmán said, liking the sound of home cooking. 'But what's your name? I can't call without knowing who I'm visiting.'

'Nieves Arestigui. *Para servirle.*' She held out her hand, suddenly formal.

'And I'm at your service.' He took her hand. 'In return for me pulling that *sargento* off you, would you do me a small favour?'

'Don't worry.' Nieves inclined her head to one side. 'I won't tell anyone about the man from Madrid who's a friend of Franco.' A cheeky grin. 'Most will know soon anyway. People round here are terrible gossips and Sargento León isn't renowned for his discretion.'

'Sargento León is packing his bags.'

'Don't you know what the shepherds say? Squash a tick and another takes its place. *Agur*, Señor Guzmán.' She walked away down the rocky track to the valley, her black hair fluttering round her shoulders like a raven.

Guzmán stared after her. A sudden faint memory, the sound of boots on stone.

Corporal Ochoa was waiting by the entrance to the *cuartel* and Guzmán went to join him, pulling his jacket tight against the breeze.

'Have they got clean bedding in there?' Guzmán asked.

'They've got bedding, though it's none too clean.' Ochoa fidgeted for a moment. 'That young lady, sir. Don't you think—'

'They all look the same round here,' Guzmán snapped. 'And I told you before, we don't talk about those things.' He pushed his face towards Ochoa. 'I don't usually have to repeat my instructions to fucking corporals.'

They walked up the track in silence. Guzmán saw the sunset staining the sky over the mountain and lifted his binoculars. 'There's something up there,' he muttered, peering at the darkening slopes. He tensed, quickly focusing on the ridge. 'What the fuck?'

High above them, a line of strangely dressed horsemen were moving along the ridge. Guzmán stared at the profusion of improbable headgear: plumed hats, spiked Prussian helmets and military kepis, great knee-boots and frock coats, swords hanging from their belts. Bright ribbons plaited into the manes and tails of their horses. And then, as the sun slid below the horizon, the detail of the ridge and the horsemen merged into the night, leaving only the obscure bulk of the mountain outlined for a moment against the dying light.

She cradled the baby as she talked to the Poet. Being a poet, he was naturally romantic and it had taken very little time for him to fall for her. That was not unusual, given her beauty, rare in an army whore. Most men were glad to have her for the short time their money bought them in her bed, but not the Poet. He was more enamoured by her allegiance to the Cause: it had been his idea for her to give up whoring and join the militia. After the war, they would forget what she had done, he said. Things would be different then, they would shed the old identities forced on them by the class struggle and adopt new ones more suited to the brave new world that would be built upon the ashes of fascism.

At first, she had been enchanted by his idealism and his exotic English accent, though his bourgeois prudishness irritated her. Where others had clamoured for her favours, the Poet kept his distance. Love was an arbitrary and self-indulgent distraction, he argued, a waste of vital energies better spent on preparing for the revolution.

Though she indulged him, she found his opinions tenuous and inconsistent, built as they were on theories and dogma, though she did not say so. That was not the only thing she kept from him. There was another, younger man in her heart. The young soldier who queued patiently for his turn with her in the year before the war. Sometimes she let him stay longer, and they would talk in low voices about a future neither of them could envisage.

She abandoned whoring as war became inevitable, choosing to join a militia to play her part in the defeat of fascism. A while later, the young man and his regiment were despatched to Badajoz. When the city fell, she assumed he was dead or a prisoner.

It was then she volunteered for the undercover mission, posing as a peasant in a woodsman's hut in the mountains, observing the movements of the fascists and relaying them to the Republican command. It was a quiet isolated existence, though it was only when she found she was pregnant that she realised just how isolated she was. In the end, she and the baby survived. And she intended to survive now, as long as the teniente *did the right thing and helped them. Not as if he had any choice in the matter.*

It was dark when a nurse came down into the musty shadows of the cellar. She held whispered conversation with the Moors, mentioning the general's name several times.

The woman looked up from the baby, her face pale as the nurse held out her arms for the child. A routine medical check, the nurse said, the baby would be back in an hour.

She fought hard to keep the child, though it was always a losing battle. Her male comrades shouted support, straining against their bonds impotently as the nurse bustled away up the stairs holding the child. After a moment, one of the Moors ambled after her.

The woman tried to follow the nurse but the Moorish soldiers held her back and bound her to the chair. Her comrades heard her cries but stayed quiet, shamed by their helplessness. Even the Poet had no words for an event like this.

At the top of the stairs, the light faded into night. Far off, they heard the sound of singing and revelry. A party of some sort. And then shouting, growing nearer, the sound of boots as someone came down the stone steps. A dark bulky figure, a curved sword glinting in the darkness. For a moment the dank air was tense and silent.

It was not silent for long.

CHAPTER 6

Mendez pulled the sheet from the dead girl's body. An emaciated figure, a gaunt face framed by greasy blonde hair. Savage knife wounds to her chest and abdomen.

'*Joder*, look at that.' Mendez shook her head slowly. 'The bastard nearly gutted her.'

Galíndez finished putting on her gloves. 'Who did it, her pimp?'

'No surprise there.' Mendez put a wad of forms on a desk by the wall. 'When you've done the samples can you fill these in? You'll have to leave most of the details blank because all we know so far is that she was called Zora Ivanova. How old would you say she is?'

'Fifteen, sixteen, maybe? She's very skinny.' Galíndez leaned forward to examine the body. 'And she was using. See? Track marks on both arms. Same old pattern, probably got her hooked and then forced her to go on the game to pay for her next hit. And his, most likely.'

'You could write the script,' Mendez agreed. 'Hey, thanks for coming in like this at such short notice. What time did you get back?'

'Late,' Galíndez said, inspecting needle marks between the girl's toes. 'As in so late I'm pissed off I had to come in here first thing.'

'What if I buy you a coffee? Will that get you off my case?'

'You don't get off that easily.' Galíndez smiled. 'It's got to be a big one.'

'Whatever you like, *doctora*. How do you want it?'

'Strong and black, please.'

'Hey, that's me you're talking about, Ana.'

Galíndez looked up from the corpse. '*Sí*, and too hot to handle.'

'So my husband says. I'll get the coffee, you two talk amongst yourselves.'

As Mendez went to the vending machine, Galíndez began collecting samples for the DNA test, thinking how strange it was that the presence of a dead body created a sudden need for humour. It might seem odd to an outsider, but it was their way of dealing with the fact that someone had got this frail young woman hooked on heroin before forcing her to work the streets. And then, for some reason, he'd butchered her. If you didn't laugh you'd have to cry. That was what they said in the locker room. And in the *guardia*, no one wanted to be seen crying. That was fine by her.

By the time Mendez got back with the coffee, Galíndez had the tissue samples labelled and ready for the lab. She'd even begun the paperwork, Mendez noticed.

'Leave the forms,' Mendez said. 'Just sign them and I'll do the rest. It's only fair.' She paused. 'Hey, the boss said something about you being on TV this Friday?'

'I've got to do a five-minute interview with RTVE. I have to say I'm looking forward to going back to work, that sort of thing.'

Mendez noticed a box in the corner of the lab. 'Is that's why you've been shopping?'

Galíndez nodded. 'I thought I should look smart for the interview.' She opened the box to show Mendez the boots nestling in a bed of tissue paper.

Mendez whistled, seeing the name on the box. '*Hostia*, how much were these?'

'Far too much.'

'Let's have a look.' Mendez watched as she pulled the boots on. 'They look great, Ana.'

'They do, but I don't think I can walk in them.' Galíndez took a few careful steps, noticing the staccato tap of the heels. '*Dios mio*, they're really noisy, aren't they?'

'Really, really noisy,' Mendez agreed. 'You'd think for all that money they could quieten them down or something.' She pointed to the plastic bag lying on the floor alongside the shoebox. 'What else did you get?'

'This?' Galíndez lifted the bag and took out the sword. 'It was at the site of the killing up in the Basque country.'

'You look like Sinbad the Sailor,' Mendez said. 'It's a scimitar, isn't it?'

'I think so.' Galíndez held out the sword so Mendez could see the inscription. 'See?'

Mendez saw the name stamped on the blade. 'It's Guzmán's?'

'Seems so. And there were the skeletons of three people he'd killed with this. In fact, I've got them in my car boot. I don't suppose…?'

'Not again,' Mendez groaned. 'We've got problems accommodating the recently deceased without you bringing in the remains of people who died seventy-odd years ago.'

Galíndez narrowed her eyes. 'I just thought, seeing as how you owe me…'

Mendez threw up her hands. 'Not the evil eye, Ana, I give in. There's a bit of room left in the basement. I'll sort it out for you later. And then we're quits, right?'

'Absolutely, Sarge. Hey, I don't suppose you know what language this is?'

'Not really, we speak Spanish in the Dominican Republic. Is it Arabic?'

'I wondered about that.' Galíndez nodded.

'I know someone who'll know.' Mendez went over to the phone and dialled an internal number. 'Can I speak to Teniente Bouchareb, please?' She waited as someone fetched him to the phone. '*Hola*, Sami, it's me. Can you pop up to Lab Five for a minute? We need a little of your linguistic expertise. OK, thanks.' She put the phone down. 'Sami does a lot of translating for ethnic minority prisoners,' she said, seeing Galíndez's inquiring look.

A knock at the door as Lieutenant Bouchareb came in. He

pointed to the body on the trolley. 'I can't interpret for dead people, Sarge.'

'You're slipping then,' Mendez said. 'Do you know Ana María Galíndez?'

Bouchareb smiled. 'You were on one of my diversity induction courses, weren't you?'

'That's right,' Galíndez said, 'and I really enjoyed it.' She held out the sword. 'Any chance you can tell me what this Arabic writing says?'

Bouchareb peered at the sword. 'It's not Arabic,' he said, 'it's Persian.'

'Persian?' Galíndez echoed. 'Can you read it?'

'I certainly can, I even know where this comes from. It's a verse by Omar Khayyám.' He took the sword from her and read:

'"Drink wine. This is life eternal. This is all that youth will give you. It is the season for wine, roses and drunken friends. Be happy for this moment. This moment is your life."'

Galíndez looked at him, disappointed. 'I thought Guzmán might have got this from some Moroccan troops in the Civil War. The Persians didn't fight for Franco, did they?'

'Not as far as I know.'

'Thanks anyway.'

'No problem.' Bouchareb bustled out through the swing doors.

Galíndez stared hard at the inscription. 'Persian.'

'So now you know,' Mendez said. 'It's a nice verse, don't you think?'

'I think it's a bit sickly.' Galíndez was distracted, wondering what Luisa would make of this. She'd probably write a book on how Guzmán was really a romantic poet.

She glanced at her watch. 'Shit. I'm going to be late for my last appointment with the shrink so he can certify I'm officially fit for work. Another hour of my life wasted.'

'I don't know why you say that,' Mendez said. 'An hour with a man who actually listens when you're talking? Heaven.'

Galíndez snatched up her bag. 'Can I leave the sword here?'

'Sure,' Mendez said. 'Maybe you've got some laundry you'd like me to do as well?'

'Next time.' Galíndez hurried to the door. 'Got to run.'

'I wouldn't,' Mendez called after her. 'Not in those heels.'

MADRID 2010, HOSPITAL CLÍNICO SAN CARLOS

'Make yourself comfortable, Ana María.' Dr Fernandez waved her to an expensive leather chair as he looked over his notes. Galíndez sank into the chair and listened as Fernandez summarised the course of therapy she'd undertaken with him, noting her cooperation and her refreshing willingness to be open. She was tempted to explain how she'd prepared for each session by reading psychology journals from the university library's online collection. No wonder her responses made her seem such a well-balanced individual: they were based on extensive research. Shrinks needed a bit of directing before they reached the right conclusion.

Not that Fernandez was unpleasant. Certainly he was much nicer than the ones she'd seen as a girl, following her parents' deaths. Dour-faced men bullying and hectoring her.

Pleasant though he was, the course of treatment with Dr Fernandez stuck to the usual pattern. Each session consisted of him trying to isolate some aspect of her life within one psychological category or another, focusing endlessly on irrelevant detail until she wanted to scream with boredom. But attending these sessions was non-negotiable. The *guardia* required confirmation she was psychologically fit to return to work.

'So what have you been doing this week, Ana?' Fernandez asked.

'I finished my stint with the Vice Squad and now I'm about to start work back at HQ.' She decided to omit her trip to the Basque country. She wanted to avoid talking about Guzmán.

Fernandez pointed to her skinned knuckles. 'Did you hurt your hand?'

'I did it at the gym. Working out helps me cope with stress.'

'Any more blackouts?'

'None since the ones last year during the Guzmán investigation.'

'Do you still think about Guzmán much? Your commanding officer said you were utterly determined to track him down, almost to the point of obsession.'

'Of course I think about him,' she said. 'I was carrying out an investigation into his activities. But obsessed with him? Definitely not.'

Fernandez seemed satisfied with her answer. 'I agree, Ana María.'

Galíndez smiled. She'd worked hard to create that impression.

'Well, we've reached the end of our sessions,' Fernandez said. 'As far as I'm concerned, you're fit to go back to work and that's what I'm putting in my report.'

Galíndez could have kissed him. Almost.

'I'm a little concerned about your amnesia,' he said, consulting his notes. 'There was so much happened to you as a child, your father's murder and then your mother's suicide. It's no wonder you blanked out your early experiences.'

'Naturally, it was upsetting, but I got over it.'

'There's something I'd like to suggest that might help. Nothing radical, just something to try and prompt some recall. Do you still have any of your parents' possessions?'

'A few.'

'And how long is it since you looked at any of those things?'

She shrugged. 'A couple of years, maybe.'

'Perhaps it would be an idea to take another look and see if they evoke any memories?' Fernandez said. 'Unless you'd find it too upsetting?'

'No, I'll try it,' Galíndez said, anxious to get away.

'We're done. Thanks for being so cooperative.' Fernandez closed his notebook.

Galíndez smiled as she shook his hand. 'Thank you, doctor. It's been very helpful.'

*

Once she was out of the office, Galíndez breathed a sigh of relief. Fernandez's suggestion to take a look at *Mamá* and *Papá*'s stuff made sense. She had nothing to fear from the past. She headed home.

The door of her building slammed behind her, reverberating around the stone walls of the entrance hall. She checked her mailbox before going upstairs to her flat, unlocking the three reinforced locks with practised ease. Inside, she opened the window and an aromatic mist of garlic and hot oil drifted up from the bar below. A sudden chorus of laughter. That was what she loved about living in the centre of the city: she was never completely alone.

She went into the bedroom and took a large cardboard box from the wardrobe. She saw the stamp of the *guardia civil* as she opened the lid. A musty smell. Perhaps it was the smell of home, though if it was she didn't remember. All her memories of the Galíndez house were of a place of mourning. Aunts and uncles dressed in black. Men in *guardia* dress uniforms, muttering in low voices. Her mother wearing too much lipstick, propped up in a corner with a drink in her hand, whispering to people, her shrill laugh false and foolish. A house of whispers, adult faces looking down at her, giving instructions that usually began with *don't...*

Settling in her armchair, she put the box on her lap and opened the lid, inhaling the sudden dark odour of leather and tobacco. She hadn't been truthful with Dr Fernandez about the last time she'd inspected the contents of this box. She'd never looked at them.

As she dipped into the box, the musky odour grew stronger. Her fingers brushed over something smooth. A leather belt, and not just any belt, she realised as she lifted it from the box. *Papá*'s gun belt with the holster still attached. She opened the catch on the holster, and saw the Star 400 semi-automatic. She smiled. Uncle Ramiro had packed this. Only he could think a young woman would want to remember her dead father by having his service pistol. She slid the weapon from its holster, her eyes widening as she realised it was still loaded. She removed the magazine and put the pistol to one side.

Slowly, she inspected the other contents. Here was a gaudy Madonna, bundled together with a few items that called her mother's aesthetic taste sharply into question. Cheap domestic relics made all the more poignant knowing they belonged to a life cut short seventeen years ago. She picked up *Mamá*'s purse and stroked the scuffed leather, raising it to her nose. A musty odour of violets, suddenly growing stronger. The purse went onto the floor with the other discarded things, though the sickly sweet scent remained, thick and cloying.

She reached into the box and lifted out a black and white photograph. A young woman in a sundress, her long black hair tied back. *Mamá*, the garden behind her a little out of focus, though the blurred foliage suggested summer. An awkward, shy smile. Around her neck, the engagement present *Papá* gave her, a delicate silver chain with her initials at the centre, *AMG*. *Amaranta María Galíndez*. Probably taken around the time her parents married in 1978, she guessed. She put the picture to one side, wondering what had happened to the silver chain. Since they both had the same initials, it would be nice to wear it.

Disappointingly, the chain wasn't in the box. That was unfortunate, since the rest of these things meant nothing to her. *Papá*'s tobacco pouch, a few flakes of pungent black tobacco still clinging to the leather. Six rather cheap-looking dessert spoons in a presentation box. An unwanted wedding present, perhaps. It was clear *Mamá* had never used them. In fact, Galíndez realised, she couldn't care less about any of this stuff.

She trailed her fingers idly over the jumbled items, deep in thought. That was it then, her legacy, a box full of dusty items even a junk shop wouldn't want. Her thoughts were interrupted as she felt something pressed flat against the bottom of the box. Another framed photograph, *Mamá* and *Papá* standing together in a garden. He was in uniform, his patent-leather tricorne under one arm, the other draped around *Mamá*'s shoulders. She was clearly annoyed, resisting his attempt to pull her close for the photo. Behind them, scattered on the grass, she saw a young child's toys, a battered teddy bear and a doll. *My toys.* A sudden chill as she remembered them.

A flash of light pulsed across her vision. She looked up, wondering if the overhead light was faulty. Of course not, it was afternoon, the light wasn't on. Far off, she heard faint white noise, growing louder. Her hands felt strangely cold and clumsy, her fingers no longer obeyed her. *Oh God, not again.* The photograph slipped from her fingers. A muffled crack of breaking glass. She tried to get up but her legs folded under her and she fell, feeling the floor suddenly pressing hard against her face. And then the noise began to subside as grey mist obscured the daylight and she slipped into a darkness tinged with the faint smell of violets.

A dull pulse of painful light, red and luminous against her eyelids as the late afternoon sun jolted her into consciousness. Galíndez was lying across the cardboard box, the hard edges pressed painfully against her body. *It's happened again.* She struggled to get up, her legs uncertain and weak as she hauled herself into the armchair. A strange metallic taste in her mouth. The photo of *Mamá* and *Papá* was lying in the fireplace and she leaned forward to retrieve it. The glass was cracked and the top of the frame had come away, attached now only by a thread of glue. A small wedge of white paper protruded from the gap between the photo and the thin card behind. She felt a pang of disappointment. *Mierda. I only have to touch something and it breaks.* She poked the broken frame. The top piece wouldn't fit back in place because the wedge of paper was in the way. Maybe if she pulled it out, the broken piece would slot back.

She eased the folded paper from the frame. It was longer than she'd expected, yellowing, folded repeatedly to reduce its size. Unfolding the paper, she saw ruled lines covered in faded writing. It was a list, written in *Papá*'s angular script. Two columns, each with a heading: *Nombre, Comisaría*. Some names were annotated, scored through with a pencil and a date added to the right of the entry. Twelve entries in all, only two that weren't crossed out. *José Luis Colina* and the other, a few lines below: *Segismundo Ochoa*.

Even in her dulled state of consciousness, Galíndez realised what this was. Twelve names. What was it Fuentes said *Papá* called them? His Dirty Dozen. *Papá*'s pensioners, the retired *guardia* officers paid for their silence. The dates on the paper ranged from March 1981 through to September 1991, the year before *Papá* was murdered. A sudden insight: the entry headed *Comisaría* indicated the barracks where these men were based before their retirement. Jose Luis Colina at Carabanchel and Segismundo Ochoa at Calle Robles. That was interesting, given that Calle Robles was Guzmán's old HQ. If Ochoa worked with Guzmán, he must have witnessed some of the *comandante*'s dirty deeds. Christ, he might be the only living witness. Maybe he'd welcome a chance to talk about the old days, though it seemed unlikely, since he'd been taking *guardia* hush money for years. Perhaps she could do it another way? Get him talking and secretly record it. If he was alive, that was, given that the last entry on this list was made twenty years ago. *Nothing ventured…* She reached for the phone directory.

There were fifteen 'S. Ochoas' in the directory. One was a young greengrocer, South American from his accent. A second call got the answering machine of a Madrid language school. Several Ochoas didn't answer, one was abusive, refusing to believe she wasn't selling something, and another made a very improper suggestion. She slammed the phone down on the overexcited Ochoa and dialled the next name in the book. The call was answered almost at once. An elderly man's voice.

'Señor Ochoa? *Buenas tardes*. This is Teniente Galíndez of the *guardia civil*.'

'*Muy buenas, Teniente*.' A slight pause. 'I don't think we've met, have we?'

He sounded pleasant enough. For a moment, she was tempted to come clean and tell him why she was calling. She didn't. 'No, I'm new to the area.'

'Galíndez?' She heard his rasping breath down the line. 'Your father wasn't in the *guardia*, was he?'

It's him. She tried to control the excitement in her voice. 'No, he wasn't.'

'Are you calling about my money?' Ochoa asked. 'I don't know why there's suddenly a problem after all these years. It was always so straightforward before.'

'Sorry to hear that,' she said, improvising. 'So you haven't received your payment?'

'Not for three months, *Teniente*. I'm a veteran, you know, guarantees were made. I've always honoured my side of the bargain. I keep all that stuff we don't talk about to myself.'

What don't we talk about? 'Now I've taken over your case, we'll soon get things sorted. The paperwork isn't in order, that's the problem.'

'Typical,' he snorted. 'The woman who used to bring it was hopeless.'

'Tell me about it. Look, we owe you three months' money. What if I bring it round myself and we put in an extra month's payment as compensation? How does that sound?'

'It sounds very fair,' Ochoa muttered. 'I'm not trying to be awkward.'

'Of course not. Let's see, I've got your phone number here but the address is a bit blurred, my colleague didn't keep very good records.'

'*Piso* 3, fourth floor, thirty-two Calle de Mira el Río Baja,' Ochoa said quickly.

'*Momentito*.' Galíndez checked her phone diary. 'Would next Tuesday be convenient, say ten o'clock?'

'That's fine,' Ochoa agreed. 'So what happened to the other lady?'

More improvisation. 'She left. I'm afraid she wasn't cut out for the *guardia*.'

'Doesn't surprise me. She said she'd come at nine and rolled up at two. Always offhand as well, no respect. I don't know why they let them in the country, let alone the *guardia civil*.'

'Ten o'clock Tuesday then, Señor Ochoa. I won't be late.'

'I hope you're better-looking than the last one,' Ochoa grumbled as he hung up.

Galíndez punched the air. Finally, someone who had worked with Guzmán. He must have a few tales to tell. An idea struck her. *He hopes I'm better-looking than the last one? I'd better make an effort then.* In the corner of the room she noticed the box containing her expensive new boots. Maybe Señor Ochoa would appreciate a woman in heels like those.

Ochoa sat in his tent, talking in pidgin Spanish to two of the Moors. The teniente *was to be posted south very soon, they said. He was a good leader and a fierce warrior so they had got him a gift. Did the corporal think he would accept it? Ochoa examined the curved blade of the sword and saw the* teniente's *name stamped on it. It would be very acceptable. Was the writing in their language? It was not, the Moors said. They had looted the sword from the museum at Badajoz. One of their number was a blacksmith and he had stamped the* teniente's *name on the blade. Ochoa assured them the* teniente *would be delighted with their gift and ushered them out into the night.*

There were other issues on the corporal's mind that weighed much more heavily than the Moors' sword. Of all the things that he might do during this war, Ochoa never thought treason would be one of them. Nor that he would so readily choose such a course of action. Nonetheless, his mind was made up. He had seen things no man should see during this war but he was damned if he would stand by while the woman was killed along with the others and her baby sold to some rich party member. Even so, the corporal was not a brave man and he was reminded of that a few moments later when the first shells of another Republican counter-attack burst across the edge of the camp.

Ochoa pulled on his oilskin coat and went outside, deciding to take advantage of the confusion to slip into the cellar and try to free the woman. Once that was done, his plan was hazy. In fact, it was non-existent. He would have to take his chances.

As he ran through the slanting rain, he saw a plume of smoke rising above the house where the prisoners were held. A shell had blown a hole in the wall of the building at ground level and men

113

were bustling about in confusion, shouting that someone had escaped. Ochoa listened avidly, thinking perhaps it was the woman who had got free. Someone pushed him aside and he saw the big private who guarded the general's tent bellowing instructions to someone. As Ochoa listened, he realised the man was referring to the prisoners as corpses.

Puzzled, Ochoa looked at his watch. The killings were supposed to take place after eight o'clock and it was only a quarter to. Suddenly chilled, he hurried into the cellar. The air was thick with the acrid smell of fear. And another odour, dark and earthy: the stench of fresh blood. Halfway down the steps he paused and raised the camera quickly, determined to capture the horror of the moment, trying not to see the subjects illuminated in the momentary brilliance of the flash.

At the bottom of the steps he found a lantern and lit it, throwing weak light over the dingy cellar. Something bitter and sharp rose in his throat as he stared at the bodies in front of him. Vast, open wounds, a decapitation. Missing limbs. Everywhere, the glint of blood, thick and black in the lantern light. Ochoa stared, unable to look away from the carnage. Someone had hacked the helpless prisoners to pieces.

And then he saw her, still bound to the overturned chair. Saw the terrible wounds to her neck, the deep vicious gashes slashed across her chest, the arm almost severed at the shoulder. And below the chair, almost lost in the darkness, a pale round oval, resting in a pool of blood. Ochoa looked away quickly, unable to bring himself to look at the child's corpse.

As he struggled for control, the woman's eyes opened, white orbs against the dark mask of blood that was her face. Something grey and pink protruded from a huge cleft in the top of her head. She shuddered with involuntary spasms as she tried to speak. Ochoa leaned closer to hear her words. 'Guzmán did this.'

They were her last words and Ochoa fled.

Outside, the air was fresh and damp. Something glittered in the darkness and Ochoa saw Guzmán a few metres away, the curved sword gripped in his hand, the blade streaked with dark stains. Ochoa took a step forward and stumbled over the body lying in front of him, scrambling away in horror as he saw the nurse's uniform with the yolk and arrows of the Falange, soaked in blood from the savage cut across the woman's throat. And, clutched tight in her dead hand, the baby's stained blanket.

Ochoa got to his feet and stared at Guzmán. Someone was screaming. Ochoa realised it was him. And then, as his words were cut off in a torrent of scalding bile, he turned and ran.

CHAPTER 7

OROITZ, OCTOBER 1954, CUARTEL DE LA GUARDIA CIVIL

t was an hour after dawn as the civil guards stumbled out of their grim concrete *cuartel*, unused to being roused from their beds at such an early hour. Guzmán and Ochoa watched the men line up, their tricornes and oilskin capes dark against the pale sky. A moment later, Guzmán's bellowed instructions echoed over the sloping hillside.

'The corporal and I are pearls before swine,' he shouted. 'In case you have trouble working it out, that means you're the swine.' He strode along the line as if looking for someone to punch. 'I've got news for you: we're going after El Lobo.'

The men shuffled unhappily. The *comandante* was talking about combat. That was not something they were accustomed to.

'We're going to make life difficult for him,' Guzmán continued. 'He must have hiding places for his supplies up there. Well, not for much longer. You're going to find them and destroy them.' He gave the men a piercing glare. 'Any questions?'

A hand went up, somewhat uncertain. 'How will we find these hiding places, sir?'

'With your fucking eyes, *imbécil*, how do think?' Guzmán shouted. 'Old huts, barns, caves, holes in the fucking ground. *Jesús*, do I have to spell it out?'

The man shook his head. 'It wouldn't help, I can't read, sir.'

Guzmán sighed. Nothing about these men suggested a fighting force ready to take on a hardened bandit in his own territory.

Another hand went up. 'What's your name, private?'

'Quintana, sir.' The man shuffled uncomfortably. 'What happens if we run into El Lobo?'

'We kill him,' Guzmán said. He waited in vain for a positive response.

'From now on, everyone pulls their weight,' he continued. 'You got away with that shit when León was here, but you're under military discipline now. Who knows what that means?'

A row of blank faces. The *guardia* provided meals and accommodation and the chance to take a bribe now and again. These men had little knowledge of rules and regulations.

Met by their silence, Guzmán answered the question. 'It means if you disobey an order, or show cowardice in the face of the enemy, you'll be shot. And what's more, it'll be me who shoots you. That clear?'

If it was not, no one said so. Most of the squad were looking at the ground.

'I'll take that emphatic silence as a yes,' Guzmán went on. 'When we run into El Lobo, we engage him, kill him and hand over his body to the top brass. Is that understood or shall I draw you a picture?'

Reluctantly, Quintana raised his hand. 'Thing is, sir, we're not the best of shots. We're only issued five rounds apiece each month.'

'*Madre mía*,' Guzmán muttered. 'Corporal, I want these men issued with the regulation amount of ammunition.'

Quintana's hand went up. 'You again?' Guzmán's voice was getting louder now.

'We've never had any proper training with our rifles, sir. They only send the worst troopers up here as a punishment.'

'Then you're no longer the worst troopers in the *guardia*,' Guzmán said. 'I forbid it. Corporal Ochoa will instruct you in the use of weapons and basic combat procedure for the next couple of days. By then, I expect you to be capable of dealing with a solitary bandit.' His eyes widened as Quintana's hand went up. '*Joder*, what now?'

'It's not just El Lobo up there. There are things in those mountains best left alone.'

'Oh really?' Guzmán snorted, exasperated. 'Like what?'

'Like the Çubiry, sir.'

'Çubiry?' Guzmán frowned. 'I thought they were a shipping company?'

Quintana swallowed, hard. 'They're more than that, *Comandante*. The family's had a reputation for being smugglers and cut-throats for over a hundred years.'

Guzmán frowned. 'Do they wear stupid hats and ride horses?'

'That's them.' Quintana nodded.

'We saw them last night, riding around on that ridge like they owned it. Why haven't you been up there after them if they're smugglers?'

'We don't mess with them,' Quintana said. 'They're a rough lot.'

Guzmán heard the others muttering agreement. 'Shut the fuck up. You carry out this mission or you'll face a court-martial. And you know what? You'd have General Mellado as the judge.' He saw fear on their faces. 'Naturally he'll have you shot within the hour.'

Cowed, the men sensibly refrained from any further questions.

'Now that I've inspired these gentlemen, I'll leave them to you, Corporal,' Guzmán said. 'I'm going to drive down the valley to take a look round. I'll be back this afternoon and I'll expect to see these morons have made some progress.'

Ochoa saluted. '*A sus ordenes.*'

Standing at the back of the squad, Chávez narrowed his eyes as they watched Guzmán going up the steep track to the village. 'El Lobo,' he whispered to the men on either side of him. 'Let's see what Sargento León makes of that.'

The whispering stopped as Ochoa took a rifle from a man at the front and held it up. 'This, gentlemen, is the Mauser 1893 model,' he said, peering at them through his thick lenses. 'The rifle that lost us an empire.' He looked at them disparagingly. 'An appropriate weapon for you lot, I'd say.'

OROITZ 1954, LAUBURU FARM

Guzmán parked by an ancient stone bridge. On the far side, an old

118

wooden sign pointed into the woods on either side of the stream: *Lauburu Farm*. He followed the dirt path through dappled shadows thrown by a line of ancient trees flanking the stream. Sudden shards of light danced off the water, flickering over the mossy rocks on the riverbank.

He emerged from the wood and crossed a dirt track towards a white farmhouse, its walls reinforced with beams of dark timber, topped with a low-angled roof of red clay tiles. Though the garden was empty, he had a feeling of being watched and looked back the way he'd come, seeing no one. When he turned to the house again, Nieves Arestigui was standing in the doorway watching him.

'*Kaixo*, Señor Guzmán.' A shy smile. '*Ongi etorri.*'

Another woman appeared at Nieves' side. In her thirties, she had the same almond face and black hair of her niece, though with a more interesting figure, Guzmán observed.

'*Buenos días.*' She shook his hand with gentle formality. 'I'm Nieves' aunt, Begoña Arestigui. You must be the policeman sent to catch El Lobo?'

'Nieves has a strange way of keeping a secret,' Guzmán said.

'I only told her what happened with Sargento León,' said Nieves. 'In any case, I did tell you nothing stays secret for long in a place like this.'

'Won't you sit down?' Begoña pointed to a wooden table by the front door. 'We'd better make the most of this weather while we can.'

Guzmán looked up at the sky. 'I'm sure it will last a while longer, señora. There's not a cloud in sight.'

'Oh no,' Begoña insisted. 'It's going to rain. I can smell it.'

Guzmán saw only a few faint clouds covering the taller peaks of the distant mountains. Begoña was wrong but he wasn't going to contradict her in her own home.

A tallow-haired lad was walking up the track. He saw them and gave them an awkward wave. '*Kaixo*, Señorita Begoña, *Kaixo*, Señorita Nieves.'

'One of the family?' Guzmán asked, watching the young man disappear into the trees.

'That's Patxi Gabilondo,' Begoña said. 'He does odd jobs for us.' She smiled. 'He's in love with Nieves.'

'Señor Guzmán doesn't want to know that,' Nieves muttered.

'Can I get you something to eat?' Begoña asked. 'A *bocadillo de filete* and a glass of home-made cider?'

'Much appreciated.' Guzmán nodded. 'Walking gives a man an appetite.'

Begoña got up. 'Nieves, talk to the señor while I get him some food.'

Casually, Guzmán watched the movement of Begoña's hips as she went into the house. A fine-looking woman. Strong but not hefty like many farm girls.

'So you think people in the village noticed my visit to the *cuartel*?'

'What do you expect?' Nieves said. 'No one within twenty kilometres has a motor car, let alone one like yours. And you gave Mikel Aingeru a lift. He's not exactly tight-lipped.' She looked at him, curious. 'When you saved me from Sargento León, you had a pass signed by Franco. Does that mean you're important?'

He shrugged. 'I used to think so.'

'So you're not important?' A tinge of disappointment in her voice.

Guzmán scowled. 'It's hard to say at the moment. Does it matter?'

'Life is very dull here, Señor Guzmán,' Nieves said. 'If you were made minister of war or something in a year or two, I'd be able to tell people I knew you when you were just a policeman. People round here like interesting gossip.'

'"Just a policeman"?' Guzmán said. 'I'm a *comandante*. There's no "just" about that.'

Nieves tilted her head to one side and smiled. 'I knew you were important.'

Begoña returned with a bottle of cider and some glasses. Leaving Nieves to pour the drinks, she went back into the kitchen. Guzmán watched again, paying furtive attention to the sway of her hips. A couple of minutes later, he smelled frying steak and the hard tang of garlic. A good-looking woman who could cook. *Hostia.*

'Nieves? It's about to rain,' Begoña called. 'Better bring Señor Guzmán indoors.'

'*Bai berehala.*' Nieves saw his expression. 'I know, *comandante.* Speaking Basque is illegal.' She crossed her wrists and held them out, as if waiting for the handcuffs.

'Don't push your luck,' Guzmán said. As he followed her indoors, he smiled to himself: there was not a rain cloud in sight and the only smell was that of frying steak.

Nieves showed him to a seat in Grandfather Arestigui's study. The appearance of the room, with its antiquated furniture and dark wood cabinets filled with mounted butterflies and pressed flowers, suggested Grandpa was expected back at any minute.

Guzmán saw a row of small rural scenes. 'Did your *abuelo* paint these?'

'The oil paintings are his,' Nieves said. 'Those are mine.'

She pointed to three paintings on the far side of the fireplace. Guzmán expected light, airy depictions of grassy slopes and wild flowers, the distracted whimsy of a young woman's mind. He was wrong. Nieves' paintings were dark statements of brooding threat: angry troubled skies beneath which skeletal figures trudged across a harsh terrain, unaware of the clawed hands reaching towards them from the ground.

'You paint very well, señorita.'

'Grandfather was a real painter,' Nieves said, suddenly shy. 'I just paint what I feel.'

Since the imagination of a young woman was alien territory, he refrained from asking what those feelings might be.

Nieves interrupted his thoughts. 'So you're here to kill El Lobo?'

'Who told you that?' Guzmán asked, suspiciously. 'I never said anything about El Lobo.'

Nieves shrugged. 'There's nothing else to bring an important man like you up here.'

'I may not kill him,' Guzmán lied. 'I might arrest him.'

'But then he'd try to escape and you'd shoot him. The *guardia* do that, I've heard.'

'You're very knowledgeable about police procedures.' He took a sip of cider and smacked his lips. 'That's good stuff.'

'Listen,' Nieves leaned forward conspiratorially, 'you know when you called Begoña "señora"?' Guzmán nodded, taking another large swig of cider.

'Well, she isn't.' Nieves glanced towards the door to make sure she couldn't be overheard. 'She's Señorita Arestigui, so there's no husband to catch you looking at her arse as you did a few minutes ago, though you should be more subtle. She'd be shocked.' A gentle laugh. 'She's not very worldly about men, I'm afraid.'

'And you are?' He laughed. 'Keep that up and it'll be your arse that gets kicked.'

'What are you talking about?' Begoña asked, as she put Guzmán's plate on the table. His mouth watered as he saw the large slice of rare beef smothered in soft red peppers and garlic.

'Señor Guzmán has a steady job in the *policía*,' Nieves said. 'He probably earns at least five hundred pesetas a week and he likes your cooking.'

'Is she trying to marry me off?' Begoña laughed, blushing. 'She interviews any man who comes near this farm to see if he's a potential suitor.'

'If I left it to you, we'd never know how suitable they were,' Nieves said. 'I'll get Señor Guzmán's coffee.'

'She has a very inquisitive nature,' Begoña said after Nieves had gone.

'She'd make a good policeman,' Guzmán said. 'Though it's not a job for women.'

'The very idea.' Begoña smiled. They both laughed at the absurdity of it.

'So her mother died in the war?'

Begoña nodded. 'My sister was the black sheep of the family, I'm afraid. She fought for the Republic and unfortunately she died for it.'

'And you brought her up after Arantxa died?'

Begoña stared at him. 'How do you know my sister's name, *comandante*?'

A sudden, strained silence.

Guzmán shrugged. 'Nieves mentioned it yesterday, when we met.'

'Of course.' Begoña nodded. 'She never knew her, poor thing. She's a good girl. Usually, anyway.'

'Usually?' Guzmán smiled.

'It's nothing really, Señor Guzmán. 'But she has a temper. At school, one of the boys bullied her. She waited for him on the way home from school and broke his nose.'

'Good for her.' Guzmán nodded approvingly. 'How old is she? I find it hard to tell a young woman's age these days.'

'I was born on the twenty-fourth of March 1936,' Nieves said. 'So I'm eighteen. Are you investigating me, Señor Guzmán?'

Guzmán turned, surprised to find her standing behind him with his coffee. He'd never heard a sound as she'd come in. 'Not at all, señorita, unless you're a criminal?'

She stared at him, narrowing black eyes. 'I speak Basque. That's criminal, isn't it?'

Begoña looked at her niece in horror. 'For heaven's sake, Nieves. Be quiet.'

'Just don't speak it in front of me,' Guzmán muttered. He changed the subject. 'Didn't you tell me Sargento León objected to you practising witchcraft?'

'Among other things.' Nieves nodded. 'Does that bother you as well, Señor Guzmán?'

'Not at all, I have an interest in the occult. My *comisaría* was built on the site of an old convent used by the Inquisition.'

'How horrible,' said Begoña.

Nieves leaned forward, suddenly interested. 'Is it haunted?'

He nodded. 'Possibly, I haven't explored all of the vaults yet, but I've heard things.'

'Vaults?' Nieves was wide-eyed. 'Are the instruments of torture still there?'

'They are,' Guzmán said with a certain pride. 'Though it's all sealed up. Only a few people go down there.' *And I'm the only one who comes back up.* 'They burned the nuns at the stake,' he added. 'Apparently they were worshipping God, but it was the wrong god. That was when the Inquisition stepped in.'

'I'll bet the vaults are haunted.'

'What on earth interests you in such things, señor?' Begoña asked.

'I like to think there are things we don't know about, knowledge that's secret and out of the control of ordinary mortals.'

'You mean a higher power?' Begoña asked. 'You should go to church more often.'

'I went through the war hearing people beg God to help them.' Guzmán shrugged. 'Most of them died. They'd have been better asking a witch for a charm. That's what I did.'

'Some people think we're witches.' Nieves was sitting in shadow, her eyes so dark both iris and pupil appeared to merge.

'Really?' Guzmán sipped his coffee. 'And are you?'

'*Hombre*, if we were witches, there'd be no *guardia civil* in that *cuartel*, just a few toads in three-cornered hats,' Begoña scoffed. 'We respect the old ways.'

'And what do the old ways tell you?'

'They tell us about how to live in our land,' Nieves cut in. 'About the gods and creatures that lurk in the valleys. They show us the way time is carved into the landscape.' She stared at him, her dark eyes luminous. 'Do you realise, Señor Guzmán, that we call things by the names they were given when they were first created?'

'And that isn't witchcraft,' Begoña added, 'no matter what the Spanish think.'

'Stop saying "Spanish" like that, as if it's an insult,' Guzmán said. 'Officially, you're Spanish.'

'We know,' Nieves said. 'We've seen the posters on the walls in San Sebastián: "If you're Spanish, speak Spanish."' She grinned. 'So we speak Basque.'

'You can see why I worry about her, can't you?' said Begoña.

'She can't keep her mouth shut. I keep telling her there's no such thing as free speech in Spain.'

'Absolutely,' Guzmán agreed, thinking Begoña seemed a sensible woman.

'Are you a detective, Señor Guzmán?' Nieves asked, suddenly animated. 'I read a book about a detective. *Sherlock Holmes y el Sabueso de los Baskerville*.'

'In a way I am,' Guzmán said. 'I work in the *Brigada Especial*. We find missing people.'

'I'm sure the *comandante* doesn't have much time for reading.' Begoña gave him a sharp look. 'Not with all those people he has to find.'

'Señor Guzmán is a friend of Franco,' Nieves said. 'He has a pass signed by him.'

'Half the country are policemen these days,' Begoña muttered. 'And all of them are friends of Franco. He doesn't stay in power because we love him.'

There was a sudden silence. Guzmán was astonished by her outburst. If she'd said that in his *comisaría* he would have knocked her to the floor. Begoña looked down, her cheeks glowing.

He broke the silence. 'I hear General Torres has a hunting lodge out here?'

'That's right, it's along the old road,' Begoña said. 'We do some work for his company from time to time. Farmers like us don't earn much, so we make a bit extra by making souvenir paperweights. The Torres Company buy them from us and sell them in French seaside towns.'

'Although it's hardly worth the effort,' Nieves added. 'Torres don't pay well.'

'We do all right.' Begoña turned to Guzmán. 'General Torres's daughter collects the figures every month. She has her own car, can you imagine that?'

He had imagined a great deal about Señorita Torres, though he refrained from saying so.

'We leave the figures in a sack by the bridge,' Nieves cut in.

'And she leaves the money there in a tin. That way she doesn't have to talk to us.'

'Why don't you talk to her?'

Begoña laughed, embarrassed. 'She's used to mixing with people in high society. She wouldn't have much to say to the likes of us, we're just peasants to her.'

'And she mixes with the fascists,' Nieves added with an outraged expression. 'I heard that Franco's her godfather.'

'That's just a rumour,' Begoña said. She touched her hair, suddenly self-conscious. 'She's very beautiful, you know, she looks like that American actress.' She looked at Nieves inquiringly. '*Como se llama esa rubia?*'

'Graciela Kelly,' said Nieves. 'We saw her in *Solo ante el Peligro*, remember? Gary Cooper was in it as well.'

'Kelly? So that's how you say it?' Guzmán said. 'You speak English then, señorita?'

'Goodness, no,' Begoña said, flattered. 'Just a few words I heard at the travelling cinema when it came to Oroitz.'

Guzmán remembered his mission. 'I imagine you ladies know this region well?'

'Better than most,' Begoña agreed. Or it might have been Nieves, he wasn't sure.

'I need to take a patrol up onto the ridge. Is there an easy way up?'

Nieves looked at her aunt. Begoña shrugged. 'That might work.'

'What might work?' Guzmán looked at them, puzzled. 'She didn't say anything.'

A faint light shimmered round them. Something to do with the lamp, he imagined.

'La Escalera de Mari.'

He stared, unable to tell who was talking. 'Who is this Mari?'

'The goddess. She rules the storms, the land and what lies beneath.'

'Sometimes she's half woman, half tree.'

'Stop that,' Guzmán said, confused by their merging voices. 'How do I get up there?'

The light around them faded.

'It's a narrow ravine,' Nieves said. 'It's the route the smugglers use. You follow the track from the valley up the slopes, and eventually you reach the cliffs below the ridge. Then, you either climb them or you go through Mari's Stair.'

'Thanks, I'll try that.' Guzmán glanced at his watch. 'I must go. I'll be in Oroitz for a few days so perhaps I'll see you again?'

Begoña smiled. 'I do hope so, Señor Guzmán.'

Outside, he saw a straw doll nestling over the door, a safeguard against the evil eye.

'I told you it would rain,' Begoña said as the first hesitant drops pattered on the leaves. In the distance, a faint rattle of gunfire rolled over the hillside. Nieves and Begoña looked at one another, uneasy. '*Dios mio*,' Begoña whispered, 'it sounds just like the war.'

'My corporal's giving the men some target practice,' he said. 'Nothing to worry about.'

He walked along the path into the trees, then stopped and lit a cigarette, thinking about Nieves, the dark fire of her eyes, the gestures she made with her head.

All that was a long time ago.

He was seeing ghosts.

OROITZ 1954, TORRES PABELLÓN DE CAZA

The Buick turned a wooded bend and Guzmán saw the hunting lodge, a sombre half-timbered building with a red-tiled roof. On the first floor, a couple of windows had been opened and the white curtains rose and fell in the slight breeze. The windows downstairs were still shuttered, though a pile of expensive luggage near the front door suggested Magdalena and her father had arrived.

He parked by the gate and walked down the gravel path. A black Hispano Suiza was parked on the far side of the garden and nearby he saw Magdalena's bright red Pegaso. The latest model, he noticed, and paused to admire the sleek curves of a vehicle made for the racetrack.

As he turned to the front door, a sudden blast of the Pegaso's horn made him look back. Magdalena waved to him from the driver's seat. Her blonde hair was freshly styled, her clothes simple but very expensive; even he could tell that as he went to greet her, admiring the firm line of her calves as she slid from the low-slung roadster. 'Did I surprise you? I was fiddling with the brake, that's why you didn't see me.'

'It's a very pleasant surprise, señorita,' he said. As she came nearer, he noticed her delicate perfume and leaned closer.

'What's the matter, Leo, do I smell?'

'I'm not complaining. Your perfume is delightful, Señorita Torres.'

'I'm so glad, because a bottle of this costs more than you get paid in a month.'

'I'm not surprised.'

'For God's sake, stop beating about the bush, will you?' Magdalena said, suddenly impatient. 'Surely you don't really want to discuss perfume? The answer's yes.'

'Really?' Guzmán moved closer. 'What was the question?'

She sighed. 'You were about to invite me to dinner tomorrow night.'

'Of course I was. Where am I taking you?'

'Casa Juanxto. It's the best restaurant in town. Shall we meet at the Hotel María Cristina at eight thirty?'

'I look forward to it.'

She lowered her voice. 'Father's in the house. Can you bear to say hello? It won't take long, I promise. I have to get back to town for a business meeting soon.'

He paused, on the verge of refusing. 'Would you like me to?'

'Yes, just say hello, will you? The worst he can do is insult you.'

'It wouldn't be the first time,' Guzmán said, distracted by the movement of her skirt as she turned towards the front door.

Torres was old and feeble now, he thought. It was not worth wasting his anger on him, especially over something so long ago. But though the details were vague, the memory of his grievance against the general still burned, bright and insistent. Like a curse.

Magdalena led him down a long hall, decked out with a profusion of weapons, framed certificates and photographs. The typical decor of a military man. A door on the right was open and he followed her into a lounge decorated in various depressing shades of brown. A tan leather empire sofa faced the window.

The general was sitting in a wooden straight-backed chair by one of the shuttered windows and turned, locking his small angry eyes on Guzmán. Torres still had most of his hair, though it was thin and white now. He was fatter than Guzmán remembered.

'Is that you, Guzmán?' Torres asked, peering myopically at him.

Guzmán took a step closer. 'Your eyesight's gone, has it?'

'Don't forget I'm a general.' Torres's voice was like a petulant child.

'You *were* a general,' Guzmán growled. 'Though not a very good one.'

'And you were insubordinate,' Torres snapped. 'You never showed me any respect.'

'That was because I never respected you.'

'Excuse me, *Comandante*.' Magdalena put a restraining hand on his arm. 'I must get Father settled so I can return to San Sebastián.' She leaned closer to whisper, 'Then you can go.'

Guzmán was cheered by that. 'Can I help with those shutters?'

'Esteban's gone to get a screwdriver,' Torres said. 'They've been fastened too tightly.'

'Esteban?'

'Esteban Jiménez, our warehouse manager,' Magdalena said. 'He drove Father here and he's going to stay with him.' She smiled. 'It's most awfully modern, we've had an office made for Esteban with a desk and everything. I'll just go and see where he is.'

'This is what I've become,' Torres muttered, giving a despairing look. 'I can't even run my own company, I have to let a woman do it.' He peered at Guzmán with rheumy eyes. 'I want Magda to stay here until after the harvest ball but she won't listen. Tell her, will you? Make her see sense. She never listens to me.'

Guzmán gave him an evil look. 'I'm not surprised, no one else does.'

Torres peered at the thin strips of light slanting in through the shutters. 'It's too dark in here. Why aren't the shutters open?'

Magdalena returned, accompanied by a thin dark-haired man. His emaciated frame spoke of malnourishment or TB. Guzmán decided it might well be TB and held his breath as they shook hands.

'I'll open this shutter so you can get some sun on you, General,' Jiménez said as he started to unscrew the brackets holding it closed.

'In the absence of any staff, I suppose I'll make the coffee,' Magdalena sighed.

'Shall I help you?' Guzmán was already sick of Torres's miserable company.

'No, but you can help Esteban. I don't think he's accustomed to using tools.'

'I've nearly got this screw out,' Jiménez grunted. From his t one, Guzmán wondered if he was about to complain that he'd broken a nail.

'Why don't you move out of his way, General?' Guzmán suggested. 'He can work faster without you in the way.'

Torres lifted his hands in a helpless gesture. 'I have trouble getting up.'

'I can manage, honestly,' Jiménez said. 'You stay right where you are, General.'

He removed the last screw from the bracket and pulled the shutter open. Torres grunted, turning his face from the bright sunlight.

Behind him, Guzmán heard the rattle of cups and saucers as Magdalena brought their coffee. He looked through the window at the autumn colours on the hillside overlooking the house. A sudden metallic flash among the trees. Branches moving.

'Coffee's ready, gentlemen,' Magdalena said.

Guzmán stared. Someone was up on the hillside. A mounted man, pinpoints of sunlight reflecting from the bridle of his horse.

Jiménez took the bracket and went to a door on the far side of the lounge.

Guzmán stared at the rider, half hidden in the trees, looking down through a telescope.

'Coffee,' Magdalena said, more emphatic this time. 'I'm not the maid.'

It was not a telescope the rider was holding.

'Biscuits if you want them,' Magdalena said, impatiently. 'I won't ask again.'

Guzmán turned, shouting a warning.

A sharp crack at the window. Breaking glass. Tumbling echoes down the valley.

General Torres slumped sideways in his chair. Behind him, Guzmán heard crockery shatter on the floor. He twisted round and saw Magdalena, lying with her back against the sofa, arms limp. Broken cups and saucers were strewn around her, a growing stain extending over the carpet from the coffee pot. It was the blood he noticed most. Spattered over her face and hair, a dark slick extending from her chest to her waist. He started crawling towards her.

Her eyes opened. 'Leo?' A distant voice.

He scrambled to her side. 'Where does it hurt?'

She pointed to the window. Guzmán turned and saw General Torres slumped in the faded armchair. A portion of his head was gone, most of it was splashed over Magdalena.

'Stay here.' He ran down the hall, working the slide on the Browning as he dashed through the front door, squinting in the bright sunlight.

A bullet hissed into the gravel path before he even heard the shot and Guzmán ducked behind a tree, shouting to Magdalena to stay inside. A moment later, a second shot whined off the garden wall in a mist of powdered stone.

And then, at the top of the hillside, the horse and rider appeared. Glancing out from behind the tree, Guzmán aimed the pistol with both hands, though he had no chance of hitting him at this range. The horseman raised the rifle above his head in a triumphal gesture before turning the horse into a grove of trees on the hilltop.

Guzmán went back into the house, raging. 'I'll kill that bastard,' he grunted, shoving the Browning back into its holster.

Magdalena's eyes widened, surprised by his anger. 'At least you're alive, Leo.'

'How the fuck could a bandit know I was here? This mission is secret.'

'I have no idea, but I'd be grateful if you would temper your language, *Comandante*.'

Guzmán nodded. 'Sorry.'

He took out two Bisontes, put them in his lips and lit them. 'Let's go outside,' he said, giving her one of the cigarettes.

She took a long drag and coughed. 'We'd better go out the back. The rear of the house isn't overlooked.'

He followed her through the kitchen into a small herb garden. They sat side by side on a low stone wall in silence. Magdalena reached out and took his hand. Guzmán looked down at the whiteness of her skin and her crimson nails against his big sun-browned fists. An unusual sensation. Had he not been so angry, he could almost have enjoyed it.

Magdalena touched the congealing blood on her blouse. 'Papa's dead,' she whispered as if he might have doubted it.

Accustomed to death, Guzmán was much less used to regretting it. 'I'm sorry.'

'Don't be a hypocrite, you hated him. I heard it in your voice. Mind you, so did I. He tried to do something to me when I was thirteen. I never forgave him for that.'

He decided not to ask. 'He's gone. There's no use wasting energy hating him now.'

'I'll direct my energies in whatever direction I wish,' Magdalena snapped. 'And even though I own my father's company now, I'll never forgive him.'

Guzmán was tempted to say the same thing, though since he would have had to explain his reasons, he did not. 'How long had you been here when I arrived?' he asked, reverting to being a policeman.

A vague shrug. 'Ten minutes, perhaps. Esteban unlocked the door and helped Father into the lounge. He put him in the chair by the window and then went to get a screwdriver so he could open the shutters.'

Guzmán's eyes narrowed. 'Was that your father's favourite chair?'

'No. The room was stuffy since the lodge hadn't been used since July. Esteban said something about Papa getting some fresh air.'

'Did he.' It was not a question. 'Where is Jiménez anyway?'

'I think he's probably cowering in the bushes. He isn't very brave. In fact he's...'

'A coward?'

'One might prefer to say gentle, Leo.'

Guzmán snorted. 'You mean he's a *maricón*?'

'Indeed. Papa was surprisingly tolerant about it.'

Because he was weak, Guzmán thought. *Too weak to maintain a decent prejudice.*

She took a last pull on her cigarette and threw it away. 'Should we call the police?'

'I'd rather not tell anyone yet,' Guzmán said, thinking fast. 'Your father was a national hero: there'll be an outcry when Franco finds out he's been murdered. I was supposed to keep the hunt for El Lobo a secret.'

She took his hand again. 'That's most inconvenient for you. I'm sorry.'

'Inconvenient?' He saw the headlines, the call from Franco's HQ. And then a lifetime of poverty stretching before him. 'It's more than inconvenient, I'll be fucked.'

'Isn't there anything you can do?' Magdalena asked.

'It would all be different if your father died from natural causes.'

'You really are fucked then, if you'll excuse my language.'

'Suppose he died of a heart attack?' he said. 'At least, that's what we say happened.'

'You mean you want me to cover up my father's death?'

'More or less.' Guzmán nodded. 'It's a lot to ask, I know.'

She gave him a long look. 'What do you suggest we do?'

'We follow his last wish to be buried quietly without a funeral, here at the lodge.' Guzmán said, improvising rapidly.

'I really don't care what we do with him,' Magdalena said, 'but I'll need a death certificate so I can inherit the company. And you'll never get a death certificate because no doctor in Spain would mistake a bullet wound for a heart attack.'

'Isn't there a German doctor in San Sebastián?'

'There's Dr Pfeiffer. He's a very proper sort, I doubt he'd help in something like this.'

'What do you mean "proper sort"?'

'Oh, you know, an ex-military man.' She frowned. 'What's so funny?'

'He'll provide us with a death certificate, all right,' Guzmán said. 'I'll bury your father here, at the back of the house. You drive into town for your meeting and I'll come over tomorrow morning to say the words that will make Dr Pfeiffer only too pleased to help.'

'Which are?'

'Nuremburg is one and money is the other.'

'You think he's a war criminal?'

Guzmán smiled. 'Why else would he be living in Spain?'

OROITZ 1954, CUARTEL DE LA GUARDIA CIVIL

It was evening by the time Guzmán finished the grave and manhandled the late General Torres into it. Magdalena drove back to San Sebastián, her composure fully restored, having taken a shower and changed into a silk dress that stopped Guzmán in his tracks as watched her climb into her car. He leaned through the window to say goodbye and received a chaste kiss on the cheek for his trouble.

'*Hasta mañana, Comandante*,' Magdalena whispered.

Guzmán drove back to Oroitz and parked up by the village.

As he walked down the narrow track to the *cuartel*, he realised something else had been going on here beside target practice. Two bodies lay near the door, wrapped in bloodstained sheets. Ochoa appeared in the doorway.

Guzmán nudged one of the corpses with his boot. 'Who are the stiffs, Corporal?'

'Reyes and Nistal,' Ochoa said. 'So the others say. I don't know all their names yet.'

'So what happened?' Guzmán said. 'When I asked you to give them some target practice I didn't mean they should shoot each other.'

'I think it was El Lobo,' Ochoa said. 'I took the squad for a route march up onto the hillside. We were ambushed as we climbed the track. He dropped these two with head shots. I got the others into an extended line and we opened up on him. The lads did their best.'

'Which wasn't much, given that it was one man against sixteen.'

'They tried, *jefe*. I tried to outflank him but he rode off before I could get near.'

'What time was this?'

'About two thirty.'

'But that's when he shot General Torres. The lodge is across the valley from where you were. It would take at least two hours to get from there to the lodge. You know what this means?'

Ochoa shook his head. 'What?'

'There's more than one gunman up there.' Furious, Guzmán threw his cigarette butt to the ground near the corpses. 'And the bastard nearly shot me. I don't know who he's got with him, but I'll tell you this: they're not coming down from those hills alive.'

He stood for a moment, fists clenched as he stared up at the mountains. Far off, a campfire flickered on the ridge, a tiny speck of light in the darkness.

'I've got business in town tomorrow, Corporal,' Guzmán said, calmer now. 'You've got one more day to get the squad into shape. Then we're going into the hills after El Lobo.'

'What if the men aren't ready, *jefe*?'

Guzmán shrugged. 'That's their problem.'

CHAPTER 8

MADRID, JULY 2010, BAR SALTAMONTES, CALLE DEL ALCALDE
SÁINZ DE BARANDA

An expensive cocktail bar, angular black metal fittings, subtle lighting reflected on the long chrome and glass bar. The place was empty but for a woman perched on a stool at the bar, nursing her third drink. The barman darted an admiring glance at her, noting the expensive clothes, the immaculately styled hair framing the delicate beauty of her face. A face that turned heads in the street. But, beautiful as Isabel Morente was, it was her voice that made her famous: her radio show *Tardes con Isabel* attracted huge audiences. Until today.

'Drowning your sorrows after what happened this morning, señorita?'

'You heard the programme?' She looked at her empty glass, wondering about another.

'I always listen to your show, although it isn't usually as exciting as it was today. Did you plan to quit before you went on air?'

Isabel shook her head. 'Not at all. But after the phone-in about the Galíndez Inquiry started, we kept getting call after call saying the *guardia* should fire her because she is gay. After an hour of that, I just lost it.'

'You certainly did. And you told him exactly what you thought, señorita. You also came out in front of half a million listeners.' The barman rubbed a hand across his stubble. 'That took courage. You get my respect.'

'That's not what my bosses said.' Isabel sighed.

'No? What did they say?'

'Oh, this and that. "You're fired" is the bit I remember most.'

'Well, you stuck up for your principles, señorita. Although…'

Isabel frowned. 'Although what?'

The barman shrugged. 'You have to be able to afford principles. Take me. I'd quit this job today because of the lousy pay, the long hours serving journalists who stay until five in the morning, puke on the floor and then leave shitty tips. But I don't quit because I can't afford to. Working on radio is different, I guess. All that money must give you some leeway.'

'*Hombre*, I wish that was true. I'm stuck with a big mortgage on a flat in the city centre that I only bought so I could get to the studio every day at six a.m. and I've been working twelve hours a day so my social life has been non-existent and now I've got no job.'

'All the same, you said your piece and I bet most of Madrid heard it. Good for you.' He wiped the counter with a towel. 'Can I get you anything else?'

'No thanks. *La cuenta por favor.*' Isabel slid her credit card across the counter.

The barman pushed the card into the reader. 'I'll turn the sound up on the TV. Hey, look, it's about the Galíndez case.'

The TV showed a flight of steps, the camera slowly zooming in on two figures standing together at the bottom of the steps. One dressed in a stylish trench coat, holding a microphone, the other in a black suit, her hair tied back.

'*The* guardia civil *have now officially confirmed that Dr Galíndez has been completely exonerated of breaking the* guardia civil *code of conduct and has been reinstated following her suspension. Dr Galíndez is with me now. Buenas días.*'

'Buenas días.'

'See? You were right to have faith in her, Señorita Morente.' The barman looked down at the credit-card reader and frowned.

'Is there something wrong with my card?'

'I'm afraid it's been declined, señorita. You're over your credit limit.'

'*Mierda*. I've got another somewhere in my bag. Hang on.'

The barman slid her card back across the bar. 'Forget it. It's on the house.'

'*Gracias.*' Isabel turned to look at the TV as the camera closed in on the woman being interviewed. Despite her slight build there was a certain quiet confidence in the way Galíndez carried herself. Dark hair tied back tight, a pale face, her eyes ringed with shadow. The thin line of her lips suggested she hadn't smiled in a long time. She stared into the camera as if looking for something. A moment later, as the interview ended, she put on her sunglasses and turned away towards the main road.

'*Hola*? Penny for them, Señorita Morente?'

'What?' Isabel twisted round on the bar stool, startled. 'Sorry, I was miles away.'

'I said since you lost your job sticking up for her, maybe you could ask Dr Galíndez for an interview. You're a reporter, after all. Might be worth a try.'

'That's a brilliant idea,' Isabel said. 'Maybe there's even a book to be written about, God, what's his name, the one she was investigating?'

'Guzmán, wasn't it?'

'That's him. I could take her research findings and make them more accessible to a wider audience. She's had so much publicity recently, it might even be a bestseller.'

'Go for it. And this could be your lucky day, because from what I just saw on TV, she's coming this way. I reckon she'll pass the door any minute.'

Isabel shook her head. 'I can't just jump out at her like that.'

'Why not? You're a journalist, aren't you?'

'I am, but I don't want to intrude.' Isabel thought about it for a moment and then got down from the bar stool, suddenly energised. 'I tell you what, if she agrees, I'm coming back here to pay that bill.'

'Ay, señorita.' The barman smiled. 'That's what they all say.'

Galíndez walked slowly, glad to be away from the TV cameras. As she turned the corner, she reached up and untied her hair, shaking it loose. Perhaps now the media would lose interest in her and she could go back to being that woman from Forensics again.

As she crossed the street, she noticed a cocktail bar, its dark metal and glass interior vague behind the smoked glass window. She thought briefly about going in for a drink, but the only customer was a woman talking to the barman. Both were staring at her. Galíndez decided to give the place a miss and turned away.

'Excuse me?'

A woman was standing in the doorway. High cheekbones, striking green eyes and annoyingly healthy hair. She seemed familiar.

'My name's Isabel Morente. I do a daytime radio show. Or I did.'

'I've heard it a few times,' said Galíndez, recognising her. '*Buenas Días*, isn't it?'

'That's a different station. My show's *Tardes con Isabel*. Well, it was, anyway. I was fired this morning.'

'Sorry to hear it,' said Galíndez. 'Why did they do that?'

Isabel shrugged. 'I swore at some of the people who called in to discuss your case.'

Galíndez raised her eyebrows. 'Thanks for the support, though it's a shame about your job. I wish there was something I could do.'

'Actually, there is,' said Isabel. 'I wondered if you'd collaborate with me on a book about your investigation. "In search of Guzmán", something like that? I'll write it if you provide the material.'

Galíndez didn't need to think it over. 'It's a great idea. I'd like that.'

'So it's a deal?' Isabel gave her a broad smile. 'It will get your Guzmán story to a wider audience and address another issue close to my heart.'

'What's that?'

'It'll keep me from starving. My career will be in meltdown after what happened.'

'We can't have that.' Galíndez smiled. 'Here's my card. Give me a call.'

'Thanks,' Isabel said. 'I look forward to working with you. *Hasta pronto.*'

As Galíndez walked towards the metro, a black four-by-four pulled out of a parking bay a few metres ahead. Two men got out. Big men with expressionless faces, dark shades and shoulder holsters. The taller of the two went to the door of the car and opened it. His menacing stare turned to a slightly less menacing smile. 'Get in please, Dr Galíndez.'

There was no way she could handle both of them. Maybe she should just run.

A gruff voice boomed from inside the vehicle. '*Jesús Cristo*, get in, will you?'

Galíndez peered into the gloomy interior. 'Uncle Ramiro?'

'These men are paid by the hour, so stop keeping them waiting and get in. I haven't got all day,' Ramiro grumbled, impatient as ever.

Galíndez slid into the rear seat. She waited until one of the men slammed the door before turning on Ramiro. 'Do you know your men aren't wearing any ID? The code of conduct strictly says officers must—'

'*Jesús*, Ana María, you sound like a policewoman. Regulations this, regulations that, blah, blah, blah.' Ramiro shrugged. 'They aren't *guardia*, they're Special Forces. They don't have a code of conduct and even if they did, it would be top secret.'

Galíndez glowered at him. 'Why all the secrecy?'

'If you'd shut up for a moment, I could tell you. And don't start lecturing me about secrecy, you never even told me you were gay.'

'It wasn't any of your business. It still isn't, come to that.'

He sighed. 'That's what your *tía* Teresa said, only louder.'

'In any case,' Galíndez continued, 'it's hard to tell you anything. You're not very approachable. You're grumpy and you explode at the slightest—'

'*Puta madre*, not fucking approachable – me?' Ramiro bellowed.

'You should have met my father. They didn't call him Iron Hand for nothing. I'm a pussy cat in comparison.'

'You're second in command of the *guardia*. I have to put in twice as much effort to show I can do the job without your help.' She paused, realising she was shouting.

'I know the feeling, Ana. My father deliberately made life in the *guardia* hard to make me prove myself. At least I don't do that to you.' He narrowed his eyes. 'Yet.'

'I never meant to harm your reputation,' Galíndez said quietly. I'm really sorry you lost the NATO posting because of me.' She frowned. 'Although you did punch that reporter who was bothering me. That might have counted against you.'

'Call me old-fashioned if you like, but I won't have people manhandle you like that,' Ramiro muttered. He fidgeted, uncomfortably. 'Unless you want them to, obviously.'

Galíndez laughed. 'Stop while you're ahead, uncle. I caused trouble for you, and I'm sorry. I know how much you wanted that posting and I know you lost it because of me.'

His eyes twinkled. 'Not at all. Having a gay niece seems to have worked wonders.'

She frowned. 'What are you talking about?'

'I got a call from NATO High Command earlier today. They have lots of gay troops now, Dutch and Germans, I imagine. Having a commander who understands the issues and who's had to publicly defend attacks on his niece because of her sexuality are key skills for a modern NATO commander. At least that's what their press officer said.' He grinned. 'In fact, punching the reporter showed my caring side.'

'So they offered you the job? *Enhorabuena*, Tio Ramiro.'

'And one favour deserves another, no?' Ramiro smiled. 'So my friends here are going to give you a lift.' He tapped on the glass partition and the big bodyguard started the engine.

'Where are you giving me a lift to?'

'I think you'll like it,' Ramiro said. 'Call it an early Christmas present.' Awkwardly, he put his arm round her. 'I know you don't want people to think of you just as my niece. But I do want to help you use your talents, Ana.'

'You didn't answer my question,' Galíndez said.

'Don't worry, I won't come in with you. It's best you talk to her woman to woman.'

'But who am I going to meet, Uncle Ramiro?'

'Someone very important,' Ramiro said as the car moved into traffic on Calle de Goya. 'At least, she thinks so.'

MADRID 2010, MINISTERIO DEL INTERIOR, CALLE AMADOR DE LOS RÍOS

Galíndez looked round the empty meeting room, bored by its faded curtains and dull wallpaper. She went back down the hall to the reception desk. 'Are you sure I'm expected?'

The receptionist gave her a dazzling smile. 'Definitely, Dr Galíndez. Just have a seat in there, someone will be with you soon.' The phone rang and the receptionist took the call.

Galíndez returned to the meeting room and paced around the table, wondering who she was going to meet. Some civil servant, she imagined. Maybe they were doing a press release about her returning to work.

The door opened and a smartly dressed woman entered, accompanied by two men in suits. The men took up position on either side of the doors, watching impassively as the woman came over to shake Galíndez's hand. 'A pleasure to meet you, Ana, I'm Rosario Calderón.'

Galíndez didn't needed an introduction. The Minister of the Interior was one of the most powerful politicians in the government.

'You're probably wondering why I asked you here,' Calderón said, waving Galíndez to a chair. 'I have to confess I've taken an interest in your work.'

'Can I ask why?' Galíndez asked, flustered.

'For one reason, it's very interesting,' Calderón replied. 'And from the mail I get, a great many members of the public are also interested in your work on Comandante Guzmán. In fact, the data from our focus groups shows huge support for exposing his crimes.' She gave Galíndez a long careful look. 'The data also show a high level of public confidence in you.'

'But they don't know anything about me.' Galíndez narrowed her eyes. 'Do they?'

'Oh no.' Calderón smiled. 'But they think they do, which is the important thing.'

'Important for who?'

'The focus-group research identified several characteristics the public associate with you: integrity, perseverance and courage. They also see you as a loner, conducting a difficult investigation without complaint.'

'Really? Some of my colleagues think I never stop complaining.'

'That might be true.' Calderón laughed. 'But the public don't think so. And being young and attractive doesn't hurt either. You particularly appeal to a younger demographic, I'm told.' She gave Galíndez a knowing look. 'Higher approval ratings amongst women as well.'

'So they approve of me even though they know nothing about me?'

'Of course, all they need is an image. After that, they weave their own narrative.'

Galíndez decided not to argue.

'So,' Calderón continued, 'your work not only resonates with the public, they also like you.' She looked at Galíndez and held her gaze. 'That means they'll believe what you tell them.'

'I've always wanted to address public concerns through my work.'

'And naturally, the public's concern is the government's concern. That's why we want you to investigate certain criminal activities that began during the dictatorship.'

Galíndez was taken by surprise. 'What crimes?'

'With the election coming up, the government is keen to show it's addressing public concerns about crimes from the Franco era. We'd like you to focus on the *niños robados*.'

Galíndez frowned. 'The election's not far off. It'll be hard to carry out in-depth research in so short a time.'

'It's true you can't examine every crime,' Calderón said. 'But you could draw some broad-brush conclusions, highlight the involvement of employees of the regime in the theft of children, that sort of thing.'

'It would be too general. People want more detail about what went on, surely?'

'People want a convincing narrative,' Calderón said impatiently. 'I think you can provide that, and in doing so you'll reassure them that the government is doing something.'

'You mean you want me to win votes for you?'

'I wouldn't say no to that.' Calderón gave Galíndez a charming smile. 'But this research will be good for you as well.' She looked at Galíndez intently. 'Don't you want something done about the stolen children?'

'Of course. It's horrendous that it's been ignored for so long.'

'That's precisely why we want you to investigate,' said Calderón. 'There are links between Franco's regime and the theft of maybe three hundred thousand children. Maybe you could show the involvement of the secret police in the sale of infants, for example.'

Galíndez tensed, suddenly sensing the possibilities. 'You mean Guzmán?'

'You're the expert.' Calderón shrugged. 'And you've already collected information on him, so it makes sense to include anything relevant in this piece of work.'

'I have to say, the information I've got isn't very conclusive so far.'

'You don't seem like someone who gives up easily, Ana.'

'I'm not. But the *guardia* have said I can't continue the Guzmán investigation.'

'You won't be working for them,' Calderón said. 'You'll be working independently, on secondment to the university, though the Ministry will be funding you.'

Galíndez looked at her, interested now. 'Have you cleared this with the *guardia*?'

'Remind me, who's in charge of the *guardia civil*?' Calderón said, amused. 'Oh yes, I remember. It's me. In any case, your uncle Ramiro thinks it's an excellent idea.'

'I'm still not convinced there's a reason to think Guzmán was involved in child theft.'

'Oh, he was involved all right,' Calderón said. 'Look.'

She pushed a red manila folder across the table. Galíndez read the label. *The Abduction and Subsequent Forced Adoption of Roberto Enrique Martinez.* Inside she saw a faded adoption certificate for one R. Martinez, age 7. The signature of the adoptive mother, a Señora Peralta, and a name in an angry script in the space for *Authorising Officer:* Comandante L. Guzmán.

'Guzmán authorised it?' Galíndez examined the certificate. 'Did he steal the child?'

Calderón shrugged. 'You tell me. But doesn't it give you something to start with?'

'It does, Minister.'

'Good, it's settled then. As of now, you're officially the *Guardia Civil* Research Fellow at the university. We've arranged an office for you and the budget will be in place in a day or so. Is there anyone you could hire as an assistant?'

Galíndez nodded. 'There's a journalist called Isabel Morente, she's doing a book on Guzmán and I know she's looking for work. I'll give her a call later.'

'I knew I could rely on you, Ana. Report back once you've got some substantial evidence.' She gave Galíndez a long hard look. 'Before the election, naturally.'

'Naturally.'

'A lot of the people involved have been dead for years,' Calderón continued, 'so keep a sense of proportion. The issue of the stolen children is an emotive topic according to our focus groups. We want hard evidence with clear-cut conclusions that apportion blame for the child thefts. It's what people want and it will go a long way toward getting us re-elected.'

'And after that?'

'Five years' full funding for your research centre, based on your estimate of the necessary costs. We won't quibble.'

Galíndez felt uncomfortable. Calderón was rushing things, not giving her time to think.

'I'm not going to haggle,' Calderón said. 'I can always approach Profesora Ordoñez – I believe she's done work in this field?'

'Of course I'll do it,' Galíndez said quickly. 'Thank you, Minister.'

'Do this job well, Ana María, and you'll have good reason to thank me.' Calderón stood up. The two men at the back of the room moved fast, opening the doors and checking the corridor outside as the minister walked to the door. 'I'll be in touch.'

The afternoon sun beat down as Galíndez headed for the Metro in the Plaza de Colón. Her initial shock was giving way to excitement. The more she thought about it, the more she agreed with Rosario Calderón: people should know the truth about the *niños robados*. And the secondment would enable her to continue investigating Guzmán without interference. For the first time in a long time, she almost felt happy.

She walked slowly, lost in thought. Since things were looking up, she decided to cook something to celebrate. If the microwave was working, that was. The rush hour was beginning but, deep in thought, she hardly noticed the fumes of the afternoon traffic or the hordes of wilting tourists slumped on benches, studying maps with worried expressions. Nor did she notice the blue Nissan across the road or the tall man behind it, the sunlight twinkling off his facial piercings as he photographed her as she walked into the Metro station.

CHAPTER 9

Tall and strong in his black SS uniform, Dr Hans Jurgen Pfeiffer was a fine example of the Nazi vision of the master race. But the sepia photograph on the wall was dated 1940 and bore little resemblance to the corpulent figure completing General Torres's bogus death certificate as Guzmán towered over him.

'This is highly irregular,' Pfeiffer muttered, 'in my opinion, at least.'

'Keep writing, I don't want your opinion.' Guzmán rummaged in his pocket for a cigarette. 'There's something satisfying about hitting Germans, so get on with it. *Rapido.*'

'Señorita, I appeal to you to protect me from this gentleman,' Pfeiffer whined.

'Don't appeal to me, doctor.' Magdalena's voice was icy. 'I know what you did in your camps.' She stared straight at him. 'I also know the *comandante* will happily turn you over to the War Crimes Commission if you don't do as he asks.'

Guzmán snorted. 'I'd rather give him to the Israelis.' He slapped Pfeiffer on the back. 'Less red tape than the British. They'd string you up as soon as you arrived.'

Pfeiffer continued writing.

Guzmán glared at him with contempt. 'Now sign it.'

Pfeiffer added his name to the document and dabbed it with a square of blotting paper. He took a large brown envelope from a drawer and slipped the certificate into it. 'Your father's death certificate, Fräulein Torres. My heartfelt commiserations on the loss of your papa. Though I must say this is unconventional.'

'So is experimenting on children.' Guzmán looked at his watch. 'So shut up.'

'Thank you for your cooperation, Dr Pfeiffer.' Magdalena offered her hand and Pfeiffer kissed it lightly, clicking his heels with outdated Prussian formality.

As Magdalena walked to the door, Guzmán noticed the doctor's hungry eyes scrutinising the movement of her body beneath the sheer silk dress. He stabbed an angry finger into Pfeiffer's ribs, cutting short his Aryan fantasies. 'Here.' He took an envelope from his jacket and handed it to Pfeiffer. 'Two hundred US dollars. I know I said five hundred but I've taken my commission from it. And not a word about this to anyone, or I'll come back and beat you to death. *Entendido?*'

'Of course. My professional ethics forbid such a thing, *Herr Comandante.*'

Guzmán tapped the Browning in its sleek leather holster. 'So does this.'

Pfeiffer waited until Guzmán had gone before he began searching his cupboards for something containing alcohol. It was a little early, even for him, but his customers would never notice if he'd had a drink or two. Even if they did, it wouldn't matter.

Guzmán followed Magdalena into the street. A light rain had fallen earlier and the cobbles steamed in the autumn sun. The shops were opening, the metal blinds clattering up as the shopkeepers' wives scrubbed the pavement in front of their windows.

'You handled that most efficiently, *comandante.*' Magdalena smiled.

'When in doubt, threaten a Nazi doctor,' Guzmán said modestly. 'In any case, I should thank you. You've saved my neck by agreeing to this.'

The smile left her face. 'It's no more than my father deserved.' She tossed her head, as if shaking away the thought of him. 'By the way, a man came to see me yesterday evening. An Inspector Rivas.'

Guzmán's fists clenched. 'What did he want?'

'He was asking questions about the man who was killed at the Military Governor's charity dinner. Honestly, it was almost as if he suspected you.'

'What did you tell him?' Guzmán asked, his fists still balled tight.

Magdalena raised her face, her blue eyes wide and innocent. 'The truth, of course. That we were together all evening and you never left my sight.'

Guzmán relaxed. An alibi from the daughter of one of Franco's favourite generals would be more than enough to keep Rivas off his back.

'Apart from when you went back to look for something at the end of the evening,' she added. 'I hope that was all right?'

'Of course,' Guzmán said through gritted teeth. 'I'm sure he'll leave me alone now.'

'I do hope so. He seemed a nasty little man.'

'Are we still going to eat at Casa Juanxto tonight?'

'We are, though I warn you, it's expensive. But it's more than worth it.'

Like you, Guzmán thought. 'Eight thirty in the María Cristina then, señorita?'

'I look forward to it.' She kissed his cheek. 'And do stop calling me señorita.'

He watched her walk away, a shadow figure against the bright dusty light, suddenly lost among the crowds of early morning shoppers.

SAN SEBASTIÁN 1954, HOTEL ALMEJA

The hotel was located on the first floor of the building, and as he went up the stairs Guzmán felt the soles of his shoes stick to the carpet. The Almeja was far from clean and not all that comfortable, but since he was paying for it out of his own pocket, it would have to do. He needed somewhere to spend the night, that was certain.

Women like Magdalena rarely went to bed with men because they liked them – unless they were fools. Or gypsies, of course.

As he entered the grimy reception area, Guzmán heard soft rustling in the darkened corridors where sullen women dressed in black were changing the linen in the rooms. Or more likely they were taking sheets from rooms on one side of the corridor and putting them in rooms on the other, sending only the most repugnantly fouled bedding to the laundry.

'What do you want?'

Guzmán looked round, puzzled, since there was no one at the desk. There was no one in the corridor to his right and when he looked to the left, he saw only the immense rump of a hefty chambermaid, her upper body almost lost inside a large wicker basket as she struggled with a tangled mass of sheets. That was her problem, and he turned back to the desk.

Drawers slammed as a dwarf in a gold braided uniform emerged from behind the desk, angrily adjusting his beard. 'Who let you in? Didn't you see the sign saying "No Beggars"?'

'I need a room for tonight,' Guzmán grunted.

'You've come to the right place then,' the dwarf said pompously. 'I'm Heráclito and it's my dubious pleasure to welcome you to the Almeja.'

'I stayed here a couple of days ago,' Guzmán said. 'I know what it's like.'

'And you're back for more?' A derisive laugh. 'Who says the customer's always right?'

'Do you greet all your guests like this?'

'No, sometimes I'm rude.' Heráclito yawned. 'A room, you said?' With an exaggerated sigh, he hopped up onto the chair, slid the register across the desk and pushed a pencil towards Guzmán. 'You know what to do.'

Guzmán scowled as he signed the register. 'Any chance of some civility?'

'Very little,' Heráclito said, examining his signature. 'Though it depends what sort of customer you are, Señor Ramirez. Spend enough on the services I offer and who knows? Speaking of which, if you want a whore, I can provide one. Ten if you've got the money – though I doubt that. If you want a boy, I can arrange it, though naturally with condemnatory repugnance. If there are other services you require – drink, drugs, the use of a Chinese laundry, the services of a private detective or an undertaker – I'll need an hour's notice.'

'I told you, I'm a police officer.'

Heráclito looked up, amused. 'Then you'll require most of those amenities, I imagine. I'll take the money in advance if you like; shall we say a ten per cent discount for cash?'

'Just give me a clean room with a view of the sea.'

'It's fifteen per cent extra for a sea view,' Heráclito said. 'I can't help with the issue of cleanliness.' He gave Guzmán a slightly affronted look. 'This isn't the Ritz.'

'Do what you can,' Guzmán said, turning to the exit. Outside, he took deep breaths of sea air to lighten his mood. That didn't help, so he lit a cigarette and walked down to the harbour, deep in thought. Aggressive dwarves were a problem he could do without.

SAN SEBASTIÁN 1954, HOTEL INGLÉS

Viana lay on the bed, watching the sun go down through the streaked glass. The phone rang and he answered at once. '*Buenas tardes, mi General*.'

'I've got a problem here,' Gutierrez said, dispensing with formalities. 'I need you to pass on a message to Guzmán, telling him to get a move on with this Lobo business.'

'I'll contact him at once,' Viana said.

'You remember I told you Guzmán sometimes needs a nudge to get him moving? He's one of those people who respond well to pressure.'

'Yes, sir. And you were quite clear about how I should apply that if it became necessary.'

'Then get on with it, Captain,' Gutierrez snapped as he hung up.

From the window, Viana stared out at the city, the buildings vague in the feeble light of the street lamps. Around him, stark outlines of houses and tenements, blinds and shutters closed against the night. Empty balconies with caged birds rustling in the dark. Idly, he watched a car drive along the seafront. The car pulled up near the quay and a man and woman got out, their movements subtle and furtive as they leaned against the car. Money changed hands. Such a decadent city, Viana thought, watching them walk down onto the beach. No wonder General Mellado despised it.

SAN SEBASTIÁN 1954, CALLE DE FERMÍN CALBETÓN

Magdalena Torres stood in front of the full-length mirror in her apartment, surrounded by boxes and coloured tissue paper. She checked her appearance, appraising the combination of her new cashmere cardigan, the raw silk blouse from Paris and the skirt from Milan. She ran a hand over her sheer silk stockings, checking the seams were straight. After a last look in the mirror she decided that was quite enough vanity for one day. She looked good. She rather hoped the *comandante* would think so as well.

She walked to the window and looked out, seeing the evening sun turning the bay to silver with its fading light. Her watch said seven thirty. That gave her an hour before she met Comandante Guzmán in the María Cristina. She doubted he would be late to meet a lady.

Magdalena had drawn the curtains against the sun while she dressed and the humidity in the apartment was overbearing. A breath of air was just what she needed before dinner. Folding a lightweight coat over her arm, in case of rain, she left the apartment and went downstairs.

In the lobby, she noticed the *sereno* hanging around as usual, probably peeking in people's mailboxes. She glowered, thinking how repulsive he was with his furtive glances and lecherous expressions.

'Going out, señorita?' Another of his faults: he couldn't look her in the eye.

'Apparently, Señor Alvarez.' She saw no reason to be polite. As she opened the heavy iron and glass door, the sour odour of the street drifted into the lobby. Feeling the watchman's eyes on her back, she turned and gave him an icy look before letting the door swing to with a crash. Still annoyed, she set off down the street towards the Calle Mayor, her heels tapping out a brisk staccato rhythm on the cobbles.

Inside the building, Alvarez sat in the dank vestibule that served as his office. A tiny room that smelled of sweat and cleaning fluid. He would be there all night, as he always was, in case any of the residents forgot their key. Some didn't even take a key when they went out, knowing he would be here to let them in. He remembered what Señor Bárcenas said when he gave him the job, that beggars couldn't be choosers. At the time, Alvarez hadn't realised he was on a par with a beggar. He knew it now.

This was his reward, he thought bitterly. Sitting in this cramped box next to a toilet night after night. His reward for being part of Alfredo Bárcenas's death squad during the war. It wasn't much of a reward for what he'd done. Bárcenas treated him as a lackey, making it clear it wasn't for the likes of him to question why Bárcenas wanted to be kept informed about Señorita Torres's movements. He wanted it, Alvarez did it. It was that simple.

He picked up the phone and dialled a number.

Bárcenas answered. '*Dígame?*'

'Señor Bárcenas, it's Antonio.'

'Who?'

'Antonio Alvarez. Señorita Torres just left. It looks like she's going to the harbour.'

'Well done, Antonio.'

'Would there be a little reward, Señor Bárcenas?'

'All right.' A wheezing sigh. 'If you hurry, you can watch.'

'*Gracias.* Could I have the money for a drink or two as well?'

Alvarez was talking to himself. Bárcenas had hung up.

Magdalena walked by the harbour, looking at the masts of the fishing boats against the setting sun. She paused to watch the crews preparing to sail on the evening tide. As the boats began to leave the harbour, she continued along the quay and climbed the flight of stone steps up to the Bar Acuario and took a seat overlooking the bay.

Below, set in the cliff, she saw the aquarium and remembered when her father used to bring her here as a child. They were not pleasant memories. It was here her father had struck her for the first time when she pointed out one of the fish was actually a crudely painted piece of wood on a wire. He never cared for the truth. Perhaps that was why he and Franco were friends.

The bar was busy and the terrace echoed with the sound of conversations. The smell of frying squid and prawns from the kitchen made her mouth water.

A waiter came rushing to her table, short and fat, beaming his pleasure at seeing her, the way he had since she was a girl. '*Buenas noches*, Señorita Torres. All alone?'

'I've got a date later, Enrique. I just thought I'd watch the sunset for a while.'

'An excellent idea, señorita. Will the señorita take something?'

'*Sí, gin y tónica*, please.'

'And something to go with it? A few gambas and some calamari?'

'Of course, thank you.' She never turned down his suggestions and he never suggested anything she would want to refuse.

Enrique brought her a gin and tonic so strong the tonic was just a faint echo on her tongue. He arranged a plate of prawns and squid on the table, chiding her to eat. Magdalena needed no prompting and drenched a prawn with lemon juice before biting into the salty batter, idly wondering if the *comandante* would like it here. She imagined he would, since they had much in common. That was most unusual in the men she associated with.

At eight fifteen, Magdalena pushed aside her empty glass and prepared to leave. She waited until Enrique was busy before hurrying away, leaving a tip he would otherwise refuse.

The sun had almost set as she made her way along the quayside. The harbour was empty now, the fishing fleet a series of dim lights rising and falling out at sea. The streets were dark and she walked quickly, though not too fast, since she had decided to be ten minutes late. The *comandante* seemed the sort of man who would want to establish himself before a lady arrived. Probably he'd have a drink and a cigarette to freshen up. Ten minutes was adequate time for him to do that without him wondering if she'd stood him up.

Heading into the *casco viejo*, she made her way through the warren of narrow streets, taking the most direct route to the Hotel María Cristina. She stumbled on the cobbles and slowed, not wanting to break a heel. A few more minutes wouldn't hurt, she was sure. The *comandante* would probably take the opportunity to have another drink. Lost in these thoughts, a few minutes passed before she noticed the sounds in the shadowed street behind her. Heavy footsteps that slowed with hers, picking up pace as she began to hurry. She was being followed.

Most people had made their way home for dinner by now and the streets were empty. She paused to look back, seeing only dark buildings, the windows lit by muted lights. She began walking faster, aware of the men following her, the sound of their shoes sharp on the cobbles.

She made a decision. At this rate, they would soon overtake her. She couldn't walk quickly, let alone run in these heels. But if she couldn't outrun them, she could outwit them. She turned a corner and headed into the tangle of narrow alleyways leading to the Iglesia de Santa María. Somewhere down these cobbled lanes she would lose her pursuers and double back to the María Cristina to meet the *comandante*. She was damned if a few would-be thieves were going to spoil her night out.

The street was swathed in darkness and Magdalena stumbled as she turned into the tight confines of another alley, expecting to see the Gothic outline of the church at the far end. She paused, struggling to understand why the familiar surroundings were so different, her stomach tightening as she realised she'd taken a wrong turn and blundered into a blind alley. Anxiously, she turned to retrace her steps.

Two men stood at the entrance to the alley, staring at her in silence, knowing they were blocking her only escape route. Behind them, she heard the sound of someone approaching slowly, accompanied by a dull rhythmic beat. As he turned into the alley, she saw him: a dark corpulent figure, moving awkwardly, supported by his cane.

'*Buenas noches*, Señorita Torres.' The words were exhaled rather than spoken: pursuing her required an effort unwelcome to such a large man.

'Señor Bárcenas.' Her tone suggested she had just stepped in something unpleasant.

Bárcenas leaned on his cane, breathing heavily. 'I told you pride goes before a fall, señorita.' The effort of speaking made him cough. 'And what a fall it's going to be.'

Magdalena glared at him, furious. 'How dare you follow me like this?'

'I dare to do a lot of things, señorita.' The words bubbled in his throat. 'Women should know their place. If they don't, they have to be punished.'

Her eyes glinted with fury. '*Hijo de puta*, lay a hand on me and you'll suffer.'

'That foul mouth needs cleaning,' Bárcenas hissed.

'Stay away.' She stepped back, noticing the other men edging towards her.

Bárcenas paused for breath, illuminated by pale light from a third floor window. 'I want a share of your business,' he wheezed. 'I saw the announcement of your father's death in this evening's newspaper. You're on your own now.'

'True,' she agreed. 'But even so, I reject your offer.'

'You've no choice,' Bárcenas said. 'You won't be able to do much at all after what's going to happen to you.'

'And what's that?' She took another step away from them, feeling rough bricks press against her back. The wall of the building. She was trapped.

Bárcenas rested his hands on the cane. 'Show her, Carlos.'

Carlos came forward, the sallow light glinting on the glass jar in his hands.

'Are you collecting insects? How appropriate for a lizard like you.'

'Let her see,' Bárcenas said, excited now.

Holding the jar away from him, Carlos tipped a few drops of liquid into a pile of newspapers scattered around the garbage bins. A sudden hiss, smoke rising from the paper.

'Acid,' Bárcenas panted. 'You'll have none of that pride when your face looks like a painting left out in the rain. Luckily for you, you won't be able to see it.'

Magdalena opened her bag. 'I assume this is about money?'

'No money on earth will buy you a new face,' Bárcenas whispered.

'I have seventy thousand pesetas here.'

'I don't care. You're going to suffer, *puta*.'

She pressed herself against the wall, still rummaging in her bag.

'Do it, Carlos,' Bárcenas gasped. 'Make sure it goes in her eyes.'

SAN SEBASTIÁN 1954, HOTEL MARÍA CRISTINA

Guzmán lit another cigarette before looking at his watch again. It was five past nine. He had expected Magdalena to be late – that was what women of her class did, after all – but half an hour was pushing it. He leaned back in the leather armchair and looked around the dimly lit lounge. It was a quiet night, a few couples at the tables, some solitary guests on stools at the bar. And no Magdalena. He looked at his watch again. Maybe he'd been wrong about her.

That was disappointing. Magdalena Torres intrigued him: she was argumentative, stubborn and with a tendency towards aggression. He found that combination attractive. It reminded him of someone, though he couldn't think who.

As he reached for his brandy, his hand brushed the red rose lying on the table, its stem wrapped in tissue paper, an impulsive purchase from a gypsy near the seafront. If Magdalena didn't turn up he could always track down the gypsy and get his money back.

His stomach rumbled. Yet another disappointment: he'd booked a table at one of the town's finest restaurants and the thought of the menu made him salivate. It would be a tragedy to arrive late and find all the specials had gone.

'Señor Guzmán?' An apologetic voice. He looked up.

The waiter gestured towards a phone at the end of the bar. 'A call for you, señor.'

Guzmán got to his feet. No doubt this was Magdalena, wanting to cancel. He went to the bar and picked up the phone, anticipating rejection.

It was Magdalena, calling from a phone booth. Her voice was high and strained. That was full-blown hysteria for a woman as composed as her. He heard her words pouring down the line, '... followed me... acid... my face... blind me... Bárcenas... three of them.'

'Where are you?' His voice was thick, anger turning to rage.

'The Iglesia de Santa María, Calle Treinta y Uno de Agosto. Please hurry.'

He slammed down the phone, threw some change on the bar and rushed down the hotel's awning-covered steps to the taxis waiting by the kerb. He climbed into the cab at the head of the line and gave him the address. '*Policía*,' Guzmán told the driver. 'Go as fast as you can. I'll pay double.'

Threats were good but bribes worked much better and the driver accelerated, tyres squealing as he took a left and hurtled down the Alameda del Boulevard. At this time of night, there was little traffic and the taxi raced along the wide avenue towards the sea before taking a violent right into Calle Mayor, almost overturning the cab in the process.

Grim-faced, Guzmán clung to his seat as the cab bounced along the cobbles for a hundred metres before shuddering to a halt. He sprang from the cab, throwing a hundred peseta note onto the seat as he went. He ran fast, the night-black street alive with echoes as he sprinted towards the dark Gothic outline of the basilica.

The church ahead was silent. Anyone lying in wait would gauge his position easily as his footsteps echoed off the dark walls so he slowed, drawing the Browning to scan the darkened building for signs of ambush. As he moved closer, he heard the faint sound of breathing, shallow and rapid. At the top of steps, by the huge double doors, he saw a huddled shape. Someone sitting in the darkness, head lowered.

'Magdalena?'

'Leo.' Slowly, she got to her feet, putting a hand on the wall to steady herself as she hurried down the steps into his arms.

He held her awkwardly, unsure what to do with the Browning as she clung to him.

'It was Bárcenas and his men,' she said, suddenly angry. 'They were going to throw acid in my face to blind me. He was enjoying it.'

He held her face in his hands, checking for signs of harm. 'Where are they now?'

'I'll show you.' She took his arm and led him into one of the narrow side streets. After a few metres, they turned into a blind alley, strewn with trash from the overflowing bins by the walls. 'This is where they trapped me.' She pointed into the shadows. 'Over there.'

Guzmán peered into the reeking darkness. '*Puta madre.*'

Bárcenas lay on his back, staring up at the night sky, his mouth open in surprise. Surprised no doubt by the bullet hole in his forehead. Another corpse stretched out in front of him. The man had fallen forwards, holding the flask as he hit the cobbles, landing face down in the acid. Small wisps of smoke rose around his head. It was a closed coffin for him.

'Where did you get a gun?' Guzmán asked.

'My father worried about assassination attempts. He always

carried one and insisted I do the same.' She ran a hand over her hair. 'He was right, for once.'

'I've worked with a lot of men who couldn't shoot this well,' Guzmán said with professional admiration. As he moved away from the smoking corpse, his foot caught on something and he took out his lighter and snapped it into flame, seeing another body sprawled in the soggy refuse. 'Who the fuck is this?'

'Alvarez, the watchman at my apartment building. He tipped off Bárcenas when I went out and came here to watch the fun.' She looked down at the body. 'Unfortunately for him, I had the last laugh.' She looked again at the bodies. 'What shall we do with them?'

'We'll leave these two here, the police won't care about them, they're nobodies. But Bárcenas is chairman of the local branch of the Falange, it's best if he disappears. I'll bring my car over from the hotel and stick him in the boot. I'll decide what to do with him tomorrow.'

'You can't just make a man disappear,' Magdalena protested.

'I can.' He put his arm round her shoulders and she leaned against him, exhausted.

'I've ruined your evening,' she said. 'Is there some way I can make it up to you?'

'Yes, but if I told you what it was, you'd slap my face.' It was a bad joke and he was sorry he'd said it.

She stayed silent and Guzmán bit his lip, thinking he'd offended her. Then he saw her expression. 'Wouldn't you?'

'Let's get your car and move that,' she said, nodding at Bárcenas. 'Then we'll go to my apartment. I'll fix us some supper after.'

'After what?'

Magdalena rolled her eyes. 'I don't sleep with stupid men, *Comandante*, do keep up.'

SAN SEBASTIÁN 1954, CALLE DE FERMÍN CALBETÓN

The room was almost silent. Steady muffled breathing. A sudden cry. '*Mierda*.'

It was a nightmare even more horrific than usual and Guzmán jerked upright, bathed in sweat. The closed shutters muted the pallid light from the street, creating pale diagonals across the walls. The air was warm and stuffy, filled with a heady odour of sweat, expensive perfume and sex. Magdalena was still asleep, her hair a blonde halo on the pillow. Careful not to wake her, he looked round for his cigarettes and saw them on the dresser by the window, next to his wallet. Since his side of the bed was against the wall, he would have to climb across her to get a smoke. She was sleeping so soundly he decided to forgo the cigarette rather than disturb her.

He lay back and resisted his craving for tobacco for almost a minute before giving up. As he eased himself over her, he felt the warm contours of her body as his weight pressed her into the mattress. He forgot about the cigarette.

Magdalena stirred, her voice distant and soft with sleep. 'God, not again, Leo, please.'

Guzmán grunted in frustration as he climbed from the bed and pulled on his clothes. Once dressed, he lit a cigarette and went to sit beside her on the bed.

She pulled herself up against the headboard. 'What time is it?'

'Half past six. I've got to see the manager of the bank at seven and then drive up to the *cuartel*. We're heading into the mountains today after El Lobo.'

'That's a shame,' Magdalena said. 'The bed will feel empty without you.'

'Don't remind me,' Guzmán grunted. 'Before I go, can I ask you something?'

She brushed a blonde curl from her face. 'As long as you don't ask if I was a virgin. I can't tell you how many men have asked me that.'

'What did your father mean about keeping you away from Mellado's harvest ball?'

Magdalena arranged herself on the pillows and pulled the sheet over her breasts. 'The autumn ball is one of the general's more depraved traditions. He invites his closest and most repulsive friends and sycophants and provides a large number of women, usually people he's had arrested. They have to take part in tableaux, posing in scenes from history or myth, that sort of thing. All in various states of undress, of course.' She blew a long column of smoke up into the air. 'Naturally, Mellado's guests take advantage of them as they wish.'

'Some of those women have been going to resistance meetings,' Guzmán said. 'If they have to run around at his party in their underwear, they can think themselves lucky. It's better than fifteen years in jail for treason.'

'I suppose so,' Magdalena said, grinding out her cigarette in the ashtray on the nightstand. 'Haven't you seen the queues of girls at the station? Their parents send them to stay with relatives until after the ball, terrified they'll be snatched by Mellado's men otherwise.'

Guzmán went to the door. 'Naturally, they're ashamed, but worse things can happen.'

'They can indeed. Often they do.'

'You mean they get hurt?' Rough stuff, he imagined, boisterous games played by men who didn't know their own strength.

'I mean they get killed,' said Magdalena. 'That's why *Papá* wanted me out of the way.'

Guzmán thought about it for a moment. 'That would be a good idea, I'd say.'

She listened to his footsteps as he went downstairs, hearing the loud impact of the front door as it closed behind him. Then she slipped from the bed, retrieved the small Colt from her handbag and reloaded it. No matter how odious her father was, he had been right.

You could never be too careful.

CHAPTER 10

MADRID 2010, UNIVERSIDAD COMPLUTENSE, CALLE DEL
PROFESOR ARANGUREN

The campus was quiet, the lawns patterned with sharp angled shadows. Galíndez parked in the shade of some low trees near the faculty building and wandered across the grounds in search of her new office. Nothing seemed to have changed as she passed the administrative block, feeling a wave of unwelcome nostalgia, remembering last summer, walking with Tali to the car park in the faded light of a summer storm, on their way to search Guzmán's abandoned HQ. Remembering the encroaching sense of threat as they arrived at that grim building, the feeling of accumulated fear and pain inside.

With only three days left until summer break, there were only a few indolent students slouched on the grass near the fountain, watching the shimmering column of water rise into the warm air like sculpted glass. A new sign labelled *Centre for Historical Discourse Analysis* directed her down the side of the old History building. Clearly they had tucked Luisa's new department away at the back of the faculty. That made Galíndez smile: Luisa wasn't a woman to tolerate anything that threatened her status.

At the rear of the faculty building, Galíndez stopped, staring at what had been the visitors' car park. Luisa hadn't been hidden away at all. The new departmental building was a steel and glass construction, two storeys high with rounded asymmetrical contours, the architectural style more Martian than Madrileño. As she approached, Galíndez saw a large stylish foyer. A young man with an optimistic beard was lurking just inside the door, holding a clipboard. He gave Galíndez a disapproving look.

'I'm looking for the new *Guardia Civil* Research Centre,' Galíndez said.

'It's in the main faculty building,' the young man said, fingering his beard self-consciously. 'I thought you were here for Profesora Ordoñez's lecture.' He checked his watch. 'It'll be over in a couple of minutes anyway.'

'Really?' Galíndez said. 'Can I go in and catch the end of it?'

'Just go up those stairs,' he indicated a short flight of metal stairs leading up to some swing doors, 'the doors lead to the back of the lecture theatre.'

Galíndez ran up the stairs. Inside the darkened lecture theatre, she found herself in an aisle behind the last row of seats, looking down the sloping auditorium towards an intricately lit podium from where Luisa was delivering her inaugural lecture. Behind the *profesora*, a huge screen gave a magnified view of her face. It was an impressive use of the EU funds Luisa had secured for the new department, a monument both to her ambition and her ego. The auditorium was full and Galíndez leaned on the balcony behind the final row of seats to listen as Luisa brought her talk to a close.

'Señores.' Luisa moved her gaze over the audience, as if recognising each person in turn. 'Today, I set out the provisional agenda for my new department, an agenda in which actions speak louder than words and yet words are actions. Our main goal is to create an immense work of linguistic analysis, a discursive labyrinth stretching from the Civil War to the Pact of Forgetting and the subsequent disappearance of the dictatorship and its political lexicon.'

Galíndez sighed. Luisa couldn't say if she wanted cream or milk in her coffee in fewer than five hundred words.

'Memory is at the heart of our work,' Luisa continued. 'After all, memory was a central element in the transition from the dictatorship to democracy. Perhaps more correctly I should say the suppression of memory, since the Pact of Forgetting involved an agreement that the military would not resist democracy as long as their crimes during the years of Franco's rule were forgotten. That required all those who suffered during that time to deny it and set it to one side; *to agree it did not happen*. That denial of memory needs to be addressed and rectified using the analytic practices developed in my own ground-breaking work exploring emotion, experience and recall.'

Galíndez rolled her eyes, certain that if Luisa didn't have both hands on her copious notes, she would pat herself on the back.

Luisa wasn't finished. 'The ultimate objective of an interpretative scholar like me is to examine how people give significance to their lives – not by using official histories, compendiums of statistics or sterile chronologies of events stripped of all relevance to lived experience. Instead, we explore hidden places, the lost worlds of human existence and experience whose perspectives have been obscured by the quantification and calibration of positivist science. Counting, categorising and quantifying merely create colourless realms in which human experience is represented using rigid categories to provide a restricted and joyless understanding of what it is to be human.'

Luisa was talking about scientific method and Galíndez narrowed her eyes, suddenly resentful, knowing the *profesora* never missed an opportunity to attack her working practices.

'We must break away, allow the hidden voice to be revealed by our research, and, in doing so, share and understand the worlds of others.' Luisa sounded ecstatic. 'We must judge actions on their own terms not ours, understand their motivations, recognise their frailties and inadequacies, not stand as judge and jury. As Bataille said: "Experience cannot be communicated without bonds of silence, of hiding, of distance." We need to understand those bonds, understand how people came to do things because of circumstance and social environment. Our work on history is about giving a voice to the silenced, the inarticulate and the dead. Ladies and gentlemen, for me as a historian, this work it is not an exercise in measurement or judgement. It is a privilege.'

Oh fuck off. Galíndez gripped the handrail tightly as the audience burst into loud applause. Luisa glanced around the lecture theatre for a moment and then stepped away from the microphone with a sharp swirl worthy of a bullfighter, marking the end of her first lecture in the new centre. Galíndez leaned on the rail, looking down over the rows of people below as they emerged from the dark, suddenly illuminated by the overhead lights. On the podium, Luisa was surrounded by well-wishers, engaged in a pageant of handshakes, air kisses and extravagant embraces as if receiving an Oscar.

She certainly deserved one, Galíndez thought, turning to go. She paused, realising she was being childish. Luisa was what she was, it was Galíndez who was the interloper here. Since they were going to be working only a few metres away from each other, it was probably best to say hello now and get it over with. If Luisa still held a grudge that was just too bad. As she went down the stairs, the last of the audience were melting away, leaving Luisa alone. As Galíndez stepped onto the podium, Luisa looked up from her papers.

'Ana, *probrecita.*' She rushed forward, wrapping her arms around Galíndez, her hands sliding down to clasp her rear. 'It's so good to see you.'

'You too,' Galíndez said, turning her head to avoid Luisa kissing her on the mouth. *Clearly she doesn't hold a grudge.*

'I'm so sorry about what happened to you, my poor darling. Are you OK?'

'I'm fine, thanks,' Galíndez said, wriggling from her grasp. 'I thought I'd just say hello since we're going to be colleagues again.'

'So I heard. I'm very pleased.' Luisa slipped her arm around Galíndez's waist, resting her hand on her hip. 'I miss the intellectual tension between us.'

'Speaking of which, you won't be surprised to hear I'm going to continue my investigation on Guzmán,' Galíndez said, trying to keep Luisa's hand from progressing any further under her shirt.

'Just as I expected.' Luisa nodded. 'Good for you. Just ask if I can be of any help.' She frowned. 'What's this on your ribs?'

'Scar tissue. I was in an explosion, remember?'

Luisa pulled her hand away. 'I'm so sorry. I didn't realise you'd been disfigured.'

'It's nothing when you think how close I was to being killed.'

'You had such a splendid body.' Luisa took a step away from her.

'Are you OK with me continuing the Guzmán investigation?' Galíndez asked, changing the subject.

'Of course.' Luisa smiled. 'In fact, the work you did last year led me to rewrite parts of my manuscript to accommodate your criticism. As you'll have gathered from my talk, my work focuses on the discursive mechanisms employed by people like him. I'm going to call the book *Textual Oppression in Spanish History 1936–1982.*'

'Very appropriate. I'll be using a scientific approach as always.'

Luisa gave her a patronising smile. 'I'm sure you feel you have to.'

'I've got to dash,' Galíndez said, noticing the time. 'I'm meeting my assistant in the new office. Thanks for the flowers you sent when I was in hospital.'

'*De nada.* Let's do lunch soon?' Luisa briefly embraced her, though this time with markedly less enthusiasm.

Galíndez strolled to the History building. This was familiar territory with its dimly lit interior pervaded by a lingering odour of dust. She made her way along the corridor past Seminar Room B and paused for a moment, remembering how she'd first been introduced to Guzmán's crimes in this room filled with black and white images of war. Her mood began to deteriorate as she followed the corridor down a flight of stairs into the basement. A handwritten sign on the wall pointed the way and Galíndez realised dejectedly that the new research centre was located at the end of this low passage, next door to the boiler room. She opened the door.

'Surprise.' Isabel grinned.

Galíndez stepped into the windowless room, trying to hide her disappointment. The sparse office furniture looked suspiciously like a collection of rejects from another department: a few shelves on the back wall, an electric kettle and some mugs. In one corner was a battered whiteboard, with a few marker pens.

'I've worked in nicer places,' Isabel said, pointing to a patch of damp on the wall.

'It's pretty basic,' Galíndez agreed. 'Still, we've got a budget so we can get computers and whatever else we need in the next couple of days. Maybe you could do that?'

'From radio star to purchasing clerk,' Isabel sighed. 'Just as well I like shopping.'

'How come you're early? You said you'd be here at two.'

'I got this.' Isabel reached under the desk and brought out a large cake.

Galíndez raised an eyebrow. 'Is that chocolate cake?'

'It is and if you don't like it, I'll take it home and eat it while I watch TV.'

'You won't.' Galíndez dipped a finger into the icing. 'I love chocolate cake.'

Isabel started slicing the cake. 'A woman was looking for you earlier.'

'Who was she?'

Isabel shrugged. 'She didn't say but she seemed a bit odd. Maybe she's a crazy fan?'

'You're the media star, I don't have fans.'

Isabel sighed. 'Nor do I, since she didn't recognise me. It's always a problem in radio.' She put a slice of cake onto a plate and gave it to Galíndez. 'Thanks for the job, by the way.'

'You're welcome.' Galíndez took a bite of cake. 'It could last a while too. Señora Calderón promised to fund us for the next five years if her party win the next election.'

'And of course you believe politicians' promises, Ana María?'

'At least you've got this,' Galíndez said, gesturing round the dingy room. 'Interesting work and a pleasant boss.' She dabbed her finger into the cake topping again.

'You want to go for a drink tonight, Ana? Celebrate our first day?'

'I'd love to, but my boss phoned me earlier. He and his wife are going to a show and they need a sitter.'

Isabel rolled her eyes. 'How many kids?'

'Two. Inés is twelve and Clari's three. You wouldn't like to come, would you?'

'Sorry, I'm allergic to children.'

'They're sweet, really.'

'I'm sure, but there are some things I just don't do, and kids are one of them.'

Their conversation was interrupted as a woman came into the room. Probably in her fifties, a little older maybe, a gaunt face and unkempt hair. The expression of someone who knew what it was to be unhappy.

'Doctora Galíndez? I'm sorry to bother you.' She had a wild, haunted look that made Galíndez wonder about mental health issues as she shook the woman's nicotine-stained hand.

'Take a seat, señora,' Galíndez said, looking round for a chair. 'My colleague said you were looking for me earlier?'

'That's right, my name's Adelina Solano.'

Isabel stood up. 'Sit here, señora. I'll go to the cafeteria and get some coffee. How do you like yours, Ana María?'

'Double espresso,' Galíndez said. 'How about you, señora?'

Señora Solana gave her a cold look. 'I can't afford it and I don't accept charity.'

Galíndez shrugged and pointed to the cake. 'This is our first day in this new unit, won't you have a slice of cake and a coffee with us?'

'If you're sure,' Adelina Solano muttered, hesitating. 'A white coffee would be nice.'

'*Café con leche* it is.' Isabel went out into the corridor.

'How did you hear about our investigation?' Galíndez asked. 'This is our first day.'

'I tried to get you at the *guardia* HQ. They said you were on secondment here, investigating the stolen children.'

Galíndez brushed a few crumbs from her shirt. 'So, how can I help?'

Once Adelina Solano started, she couldn't stop. 'I was watching TV the other morning and they were talking about your Guzmán investigation. One of the commentators said you seemed to be on a personal crusade. That struck a chord because so am I.'

'Is this about someone lost in the Civil War?' Galíndez cut in. 'We can't investigate individual cases.'

'It's about my daughter, Leticia,' Adelina Solano said, looking her straight in the eye. There was more pain in those eyes than anyone deserved, Galíndez thought.

'I suppose you know about the *niños robados*, Dr Galíndez?'

'I do. Was your daughter one of them?'

Adelina Solano exhaled slowly, trying to compose herself. 'The hospital told me she died at birth, but that was a lie. I'm certain she was stolen.'

Galíndez looked round in vain for a pen and paper. 'Did you go to the *policía*?'

'Of course. But the clinic said they'd cremated the baby, so the police refused to do anything. That was seventeen years ago. No one's done anything since.'

Galíndez sighed. If she started taking individual cases, she'd be working on them until she retired. 'This isn't my area, señora. My main focus is on investigating Guzmán and his links to the stolen children.'

Adelina pursed her lips. 'You sound like Señora Calderón.'

'Do you know her?' Galíndez asked, surprised.

'I tried to get her to do something about my daughter's case, but she wouldn't.'

'There are support groups, aren't there?'

'I used to be spokeswoman for a *niños robados* parents' group. We met regularly with Señora Calderón – that's how I know her. She's like all the others, she did nothing.'

'Didn't the other people in the support group help?'

'Not really.' Adelina shrugged. 'In fact, they threw me out.'

'Why did they do that?'

'I'm too radical for them because I want action, Dr Galíndez.

This has been going on year after year, and all the time, the officials and politicians just make it harder to find out what happened to our children.'

'Even so...' Galíndez saw the look on Adelina's ravaged face and shut up.

'I should have known,' Adelina said, in a tired voice. 'You're like all the others. You listen, patronise me and then show me the door. And nothing gets done to find my daughter.'

'I have to focus on Guzmán,' Galíndez muttered, suddenly defensive.

'No, you don't.' Adelina Solano leaned forward. 'My daughter has grown up without knowing her mother. If you knew what that was like, you'd help.'

'Actually, I do,' Galíndez said quietly. 'When I was eight, my mother killed herself a few months after my father was murdered.'

'Then you, of all people, should help me,' Adelina said with an air of vindication. 'These are her details.' She took some hand-written sheets from her bag and pushed them across the desk. 'I've put down the dates, the name of the clinic and the doctor.' A tear started to trickle down her lined face. She wiped it away. 'I've lost my daughter, my husband and my home. I can't stop now. I have to find my Leticia.' She stared into Galíndez's eyes. 'Help me, Dr Galíndez. I don't know who else to ask.'

Galíndez sighed. 'Even if I agree, there's no guarantee I'll find her.' She ran a hand over her hair, thinking about it. 'Do you have any information that would help me?'

'Oh yes,' Adelina said. 'That parents' group I told you about, the ones who threw me out? Well, I was the driver of their van. In fact, I've still got it at the moment.'

'We don't need a vehicle, señora. But thanks for the offer.'

Adelina frowned, annoyed at being interrupted. 'I was about to say that earlier this morning I drove round to see a priest in a church on Calle Robles. It's in Vallecas.'

'I know where it is,' Galíndez said. 'I was nearly killed there.'

'Then it's a good job I went and got the boxes. You might not have been up to it.'

'Boxes of what?'

'Letters. They're from people who wrote to the Church authorities to complain about their children being stolen. They sent them to priests, bishops and even the archbishop. They've been stored in the church vaults. I thought maybe they could be put to better use.'

'How many?' Galíndez asked. The least she could do was take them off Adelina's hands as a gesture of support. Going through a few letters wouldn't take long.

'About ten thousand.' Adelina watched Galíndez's expression change.

The door opened as Isabel returned with their coffee. 'What's going on?'

'You're just in time to help unload the van,' Galíndez said.

'Read the label on my T-shirt, Ana María,' Isabel muttered. 'Go on.'

Galíndez lifted Isabel's collar. 'Stella McCartney.'

'That's right. And what's this across my chest?'

'Dust mainly, and grease. Or it might be oil. '

'Exactly.' Isabel took the lid off one of the Styrofoam cups and sipped her coffee. 'So why are we filling our new office with all these filthy boxes?'

'The material in them could be really useful.'

Adelina brought in the last box of letters and put it on a desk, raising a cloud of dust. 'I'll take the van back now.'

'She was a character,' Isabel said, going to the door to make sure Adelina was gone. 'I bet she'd have been awkward if you hadn't agreed to help her.'

'She was pretty assertive.' Galíndez nodded.

'You'd better be like that with your kiddies tonight, or they'll run rings round you.'

'Not at all,' Galíndez said, 'they obey my every command. It's the *guardia* training.'

'Really?'

'No, they'll run me into the ground.' She got to her feet. 'I'd better get going, the traffic's going to be heavy out towards Colmenar Viejo.'

'OK.' Isabel took her laptop from her bag. 'I'll check out that office furniture.'

'*Hasta mañana*.' Isabel heard her footsteps fade as she went up the stairs. She opened her laptop and began searching online for office equipment. A loud knock at the door made her look up. 'Did you forget something, Ana?' she laughed, opening the door.

Two men stood outside. One was big, his muscular arms heavily tattooed. The other was older, a fleshy face, rather like a toad, she thought. Both stared at her.

'Hello,' Isabel said. 'What are you doing?'

The big man pointed to the ceiling and Isabel saw the space where some of the ceiling tiles had been removed. 'Electrics, señorita. A few dodgy wires need fixing, don't they, Agustin?' The other man nodded in agreement.

'Don't let me stop you,' Isabel said, suddenly uncomfortable. 'And be careful,' she told the big man as he started up the stepladder, holding a piece of electrical equipment. 'With all those piercings in your face you might get a shock.'

'Takes a lot to shock me,' he laughed, pushing the device into the ceiling cavity.

'I'm sure,' Isabel said as she closed the door.

CHAPTER 11

SAN SEBASTIÁN, OCTOBER 1954, BANCO DE BILBAO

/ T his way, *Comandante.*' The bank manager ushered Guzmán
into a cluttered office ripe with the smell of sweat and black
tobacco. Señor Cifuentes was nervous. That was frequently
the case when Guzmán called on people unannounced.

'How can I be of help to the *Brigada Especial*, Señor Guzmán?'
Cifuentes asked.

'You're aware of the robberies and killings carried out by the
bandit known as El Lobo?' said Guzmán. 'You may not be aware
that he seems to have been remarkably well informed about
movements of money by your bank.'

'The local police questioned the staff a number of times,'
Cifuentes said. A sheen of sweat glistened on his upper lip. 'The
policía didn't suspect anyone here.'

'I do,' Guzmán said. 'Over the next few days, I'm going after El
Lobo with my squad. Life in the mountains will become very
unpleasant for him. When he hears you're transporting a large
sum of money, he'll jump at the chance of such a soft target.'

'But we have no plans to transport any large sums of money in
the near future.'

'That's where you're wrong,' Guzmán said with uncharacteristic
patience. 'I want you to transport a very large amount of money
– five million pesetas will do – and I want you to make sure all
your staff know about it as soon as possible.' He leaned forward.
'Someone here has been giving information to El Lobo. I think
they'll leak this as well.'

Cifuentes stared at him, open-mouthed. 'You can't be serious,
comandante.'

'I'm very serious. This plan has been authorised by the General Directorate of Security, which means it has the *caudillo*'s blessing. What greater reassurance could you want than General Franco's approval?'

'It seems risky to send out a truck carrying so much money after the other robberies. What if something goes wrong?'

Guzmán gave him a suspicious look. 'We'd have lost the war with that kind of thinking.' He narrowed his eyes. 'That's assuming you were on our side?'

Cifuentes fidgeted, uncomfortably. 'There's no question of my loyalty, *Comandante*.'

'Then make sure all your staff think this is just a normal shipment. And remember, if you tell anyone this is a set-up, you'll be in a prison cell before you can blink.'

'I won't say a word.'

'You've three days to arrange it. After the truck leaves the bank, we'll stop it away from prying eyes and fill it with a squad of *guardia civiles*. When El Lobo attacks, he'll be outgunned. Then you'll get your money back and probably a medal for your cooperation.'

'I'll make the arrangements at once,' Cifuentes said.

'Excellent.' Guzmán put on his hat and went to the door. He paused and took a guide book from a rack by the door. 'We're counting on you, Señor Cifuentes.' After giving the manager an intimidatingly painful handshake, he left, leaving Cifuentes mopping his face with a handkerchief. The meeting had gone well, Guzmán thought. Cifuentes had swallowed the lie about having Franco's approval without a moment's hesitation.

Guzmán walked along the seafront watching the pleasure boats in the bay decanting holidaymakers onto the wooden jetty at Santa Clara island and picking up others returning to shore. At the far end of the bay, near Ondarreta Beach, he came to the car park, a patch of rough ground below the casino. The Buick was parked in the shade of a clump of trees. Once inside, he opened the guidebook

176

he'd taken from the bank and turned to the page describing the *Salto de los Enamorados* at Iturralde. The Lovers' Leap was an isolated spot of outstanding natural beauty, the guidebook said, long favoured by suicidal sweethearts, since the deep rapids invariably proved fatal for those desperate enough to hurl themselves into the churning waters. Sadly, the narrowness and depth of the river meant that few bodies were seen again. It was the perfect spot to say goodbye to Señor Bárcenas.

Guzmán eased the Buick out of the car park and drove back along the seafront. Ahead, the traffic was starting to slow, probably held up by a horse and cart, he imagined. As the line of cars came to a standstill, he noticed the uniformed men on the pavements, the lines of canvas-topped trucks parked on the side streets. He leaned out of the window to take a look and swore as he saw what was causing the hold-up. A wooden barricade was pulled across the road, flanked by military vehicles and dozens of grey-uniformed police. A roadblock.

The pavements on either side of the road were swarming with troops and plain-clothes police. Escape was impossible. There was no way he could turn and go back the way he'd come. Any hint that he was trying to avoid the roadblock would result in them stopping and searching the car immediately. His only option was to sit tight and hope the officers wouldn't have the patience to search every vehicle.

He glared through the windscreen at the immobile line of traffic, hands tense on the wheel as he watched the blinking tail lights ahead of him. The vehicles edged forward at snail's pace each time a car was searched and allowed to proceed. One more vehicle and then it was his turn. He gripped the wheel, angry at himself for not throwing Bárcenas into the harbour during the night. Attention to detail was supposed to be his speciality.

A uniformed policeman came forward, holding up his hand. Guzmán stopped and applied the handbrake. He waited, drumming his fingers on the wheel, watching a man in a black leather coat examining the vehicle in front. Finally, with a wave to the men on the roadblock, the officer signalled for them to open the barrier. He turned to Guzmán's car and waved him forward. Guzmán breathed out a string of obscenities as he eased the car alongside Inspector Rivas.

As he pulled up, Rivas saw him and leaned into the window.

'*Buenos días, Comandante*. We won't keep you more than a few minutes.'

'What's happening?' Guzmán asked.

'A senior member of the Falange is missing,' Rivas said. 'Alfredo Bárcenas.'

A bead of sweat ran down the back of Guzmán's neck. 'This is a lot of manpower to look for someone like him.'

'He has political connections in Madrid, *Comandante*. If anything's happened to him, somebody's head will roll, you know what it's like.'

Guzmán did know, though it was the last thing he wanted to hear. 'Men like him often make off with the funds. Have you checked his bank accounts?'

'No, but we will.' Rivas nodded. 'That would be a better result.' He leaned further into the window, suddenly conspiratorial. 'We don't want this to be linked to the shooting.'

Guzmán's frowned. 'What shooting?'

'Officially, there wasn't one. Unofficially, it was a man on the seafront, the evening before last. Someone picked him off from a rooftop. An excellent shot, I must say.'

'I assume it's being covered up?'

'The victim was on a part of the beach where prostitutes hang out after dark,' Rivas said. 'His family were only too pleased for us not to give the matter any publicity.'

'And what time was this?'

'About eight thirty.'

Guzmán thought about it. El Lobo attacked the Torres lodge at two thirty. Six hours was more than enough time to get to San Sebastián, have a meal and then blow someone's head off. He tried to calm himself. *It's like a fucking conspiracy.*

'*Comandante*?' Rivas was staring at him, waiting for an answer.

'Sorry.' Guzmán ran a hand over his face. 'What did you say?'

'I said Señorita Torres confirmed your account of the charity dinner.'

'So I'm off your list of suspects now?' Guzmán feigned a smile.

Rivas was gazing down the road. He spoke without looking at Guzmán. 'Señorita Torres says you left her on two occasions, so I can't rule you out completely. Professional habit, you know how it is.'

Guzmán rubbed the back of his neck. His collar was damp.

Rivas looked at the line of traffic stretching along the seafront. 'Market day, busiest day of the week, and this happens.' He called to two uniformed men standing by the wooden barrier. 'Check the boot you two, *rapido*. Let's get this gentleman on his way.'

Guzmán drummed his fingers on the steering wheel again, wondering how he was going to explain the body. Even if they only arrested him, rather than having the legionnaires beat the fuck out of him at their barracks, the operation to get El Lobo would be ruined. As would his career. He was willing to bet Magdalena wouldn't be intimate with a pauper.

Rivas heard the sudden exclamations from his men as they opened the boot. 'Won't be a minute, *Comandante*.' He turned and walked to the back of the car.

Guzmán took a long breath and tried to think of a credible explanation. It wasn't easy.

A sharp tap on the rear window. Guzmán turned and saw Rivas beckoning him.

'Could you get out of the vehicle, please, *Comandante*?'

Guzmán climbed out, seeing armed men in every direction as he followed Rivas to the rear of the car. The two uniformed officers were leaning into the boot, engaged in a heated discussion about something inside.

He tried to peer into the boot, ready to express his surprise at the find, but Rivas blocked his view as he turned to face him. An apologetic expression.

'Sorry to tell you this, *Comandante*, but someone's broken into your car.'

Guzmán leaned forward, seeing the scratches, the twisted metal of the lid where a crowbar had been used to force the lock.

'Was there anything valuable in there?' Rivas asked.

Guzmán shook his head. 'The only thing in there was worthless. They're welcome to it.'

OROITZ 1954, CUARTEL DE LA GUARDIA CIVIL

The wind from the mountain was sharp, more winter than autumn. Guzmán took the rifle from his car, admiring the tooled leather of the case. A Mauser Karabiner 98k, fitted with a telescopic sight. A fine weapon for killing a bandit.

As he came down the track, he heard the flag stuttering in the cold air. Below it, a line of horses was tied to the rail near the barracks. The lance corporal was standing in the doorway.

'What's up with you?' Guzmán said. 'You look as guilty as a gypsy in handcuffs.'

'The squad's almost ready, sir.'

'Almost?' Guzmán snapped. 'Tell them they've got five minutes.'

Ochoa came out of the *cuartel*. 'Chosen a horse yet, sir?'

'It's so long since I rode I've forgotten what a horse looks like,' Guzmán said. 'Unless it's on a plate, cooked with onions.'

He walked over to the horses, deciding on a big bay mare. 'What's this one called?'

Ochoa grinned. 'Republic.'

'I'm going to ride it, not fuck it,' Guzmán muttered as hauled himself into the saddle. 'While you get the men organised, I'll take this nag for a gallop and remind my arse what it's like to sit on a horse. I'll wait for you by that wood at the bottom of the hillside.' He turned the bay, gave it a flick of his heels and set off down the valley at a canter.

Up on the mountainside, a light flashed, sudden and bright.

Ochoa peered up at the distant rocks. When there was no repetition of the light, he went back into the *cuartel*, shouting to the squad to fall in.

Guzmán urged the horse into a gallop, rediscovering the feeling of being on horseback as he headed towards the small wood. The air was invigorating, clearing his head, though one thought still nagged him: who the fuck had taken Bárcenas's body? He reached the edge of the glade and rode slowly into the trees. Ahead, he heard the sound of running water. The horse slowed as the wood opened out onto a large pool below the sheer hillside.

A stream plunged down the cliff face, smashing in foaming rivulets over the mossy rocks below, patterning the dark pool with endless ripples. He peered into the glassy water, its surface nuanced by sunlight and flecks of foam from the waterfall. Something moved below the surface and he stared, intrigued by a pale shape, wondering about the possibility of some ancient species dwelling in the shadowed pool.

He was mistaken, he realised as the creature burst from the water, gasping at the cold, her long dark hair fanning out, spraying a curtain of glittering beads across the surface. It was Begoña Arestigui. And, Guzmán observed carefully, she was naked. Moments later, a second head burst from the water as Nieves surfaced. Hidden from view, he listened to their chatter, the Basque words rattling like the sound of falling stones.

The opportunity to look at one, let alone two, naked women was rare and he was tempted to linger a while. But he felt strangely uncomfortable amid these pine-scented shadows, the slanting autumn light bright and shimmering with dust. These women had invited him into their house and made him welcome. Now he was spying on them. Worse, he sensed they were aware of his presence.

Reluctantly, he went back into the wood, letting the horse pick its way around the great weathered stones, half-buried in the soft pine mulch. Behind him, the endless cadences of the waterfall reverberated against the hillside. He reined in the horse and sat for a moment, deep in thought. His was a life where survival depended upon action and reaction. Instinct and reflex were preferable to brooding and meditation but he could no longer avoid thinking about this.

He knew exactly where he had seen Nieves Arestigui before. In a moment of caustic recollection, he saw eyes glinting in the light of a lantern. The sound of a man crying. And a woman's voice echoing in the darkness.

Guzmán emerged from the glade as Ochoa and the squad came across the grass towards him in a drumbeat rhythm of muffled hoofs and clanking equipment. He looked along the line of sullen-faced *guardia*, in their tricornes and dark oilskin capes, the long Mausers slung over their backs. 'These boys almost look like the real thing,' he said. 'Almost.'

'Anything in that wood, sir?' Ochoa asked as they started up the track.

'Nothing you need worry about,' Guzmán said. 'Did you check the map?'

Ochoa pointed up at the escarpment. 'It's a straightforward climb until we reach the high pastures. Then we go up through Mari's Stair onto the ridge.'

'You make it sound easy.' Guzmán urged his horse to the track.

Two hours later, the ground became increasingly steep, forcing them to dismount and lead the horses towards the cliffs bordering the ridge.

'That's Mari's Stair,' Ochoa said.

Guzmán took the field glasses and studied the dark gash in the cliff. He was not happy with what he saw. A man with a rifle on the ridge could easily pick off the squad as they struggled along that narrow path. 'There's no other way of getting onto that ridge then?'

Ochoa shook his head.

Guzmán looked up again at the long cliff face.

'Something wrong, *Comandante*?' Ochoa asked, noticing his concentration.

'I saw a flash of light.' Guzmán scanned the cliff with the binoculars again. 'Maybe he's waiting until we go into the ravine. If he does, it's a death trap.'

'So what do we do, *jefe*?'

Guzmán shrugged. 'We need a volunteer.'

'You think it's as bad as that?'

Guzmán took out his cigarettes. 'Have a word with them, Corporal, someone will volunteer. There's always a hero in every squad.'

Ochoa went to talk to the men.

'Though not for long,' Guzmán added, looking at the entrance to the ravine again.

Ten minutes later, the volunteer stood with Guzmán near the mouth of Mari's Stair. It was worse than he'd thought. The track was littered with shattered boulders and heaps of crushed rock while the narrow walls on either side were at least fifteen metres high. Once inside, the men would be almost defenceless.

Guzmán turned to the volunteer. 'What was your name again, trooper?'

The man snapped to attention. 'Machado, *mi Comandante. A sus ordenes.*'

'Did Corporal Ochoa explain what you have to do?'

'Yes, sir,' Machado said, eagerly. 'Scout the trail ahead.'

'But in sections,' Guzmán said. 'I want you to stop every hundred paces. Then we'll send another trooper in and, once he reaches you, you go forward another hundred paces, then he follows and you move on. We do that until everyone's through the ravine. When you're not moving, keep your rifle aimed upwards. If anyone appears up top, shoot them.'

'*A sus ordenes.*' Machado gave Guzmán an annoying salute.

'One thing,' Guzmán said as Machado picked up his rifle.

'*Sí, mi Comandante?*'

'How come you volunteered?'

'My father fought at Anwal. He got a medal. I'd like to show I'm as brave as him.'

Guzmán nodded slowly. 'Off you go then, trooper.' He gestured to Ochoa to join him. 'Did you pick some men to hold the horses?'

'Three.' Ochoa nodded. 'They're staying put on that slope over there until we're through the ravine. That leaves nine men for combat. Eight if we assume Machado might not be with us for very much longer.'

'Look on the bright side, Corporal,' Guzmán said. 'He might look up, see El Lobo and shoot the bastard dead.' He spat onto the rocky ground.

'Or Lobo might not be up there at all, sir.'

Guzmán frowned. 'If I was him, that's where I'd be.'

Machado saw Guzmán's signal and moved into the ravine, weaving around the rocks, glancing up the sheer walls for signs of a sniper. Guzmán stayed by the entrance, watching. Machado was doing all right. Or maybe he was just lucky.

An hour later, Guzmán and Ochoa slipped into the ravine and made their way along the stony track to where the other men were now crouching behind whatever cover they could find, looking along the last stretch of track leading up to the ridge. A hundred metres uphill, with the possibility of attack from any direction.

'You've done well so far, Machado,' Guzmán said, lying alongside him in the cover of a large boulder. 'Now you just have to complete the job. Go up and take a look round. If everything's clear, we'll follow. *Entiendes*?'

Machado grinned. 'Of course, *Comandante. Gracias.*'

'Off you go,' Guzmán said. 'Just take it slow.'

Ochoa joined him as Machado started crawling up the track.

'He wants to be a hero like his papa,' Guzmán said, resting his rifle on the boulder. 'Says his father fought at Anwal.'

Machado was inching over the rough shale, careful not to make any noise.

'Anwal, that's right, sir.'

'That's in Marruecos, isn't it?'

'It is. Nineteen twenty-one, I think.'

'Big battle, was it?' Guzmán watched Machado roll onto his back, checking no one was watching on the cliff walls above.

'Very big,' Ochoa said. 'You know, sir, if Lobo's up there, Machado hasn't a chance.'

Machado was now working his way up towards the thick grass on the ridge.

'I didn't hear you offer to take his place, Corporal,' Guzmán said. 'So what happened in that battle?'

'Anwal?' Ochoa brushed a fly from his face.

Machado reached the top of the gulley, cautious as he moved into the grass.

'Of course fucking Anwal. What have we been talking about for the last five minutes?'

Machado got to his feet, giving them an enthusiastic thumbs up.

'The Moors wiped out the entire army.'

'All of them?' Guzmán worked the bolt on his rifle and put a round into the breech.

'Thirteen thousand,' Ochoa said. 'It was a massacre.'

Machado took off his black leather tricorne and waved for them to join him.

Ochoa started to get up but Guzmán pulled him back. 'Wait.'

'*A por ellos compañeros. Viva España!*' As Machado's war cry echoed down the ravine, the squad rose from hiding and moved forward, bayonets fixed.

The sudden crack of a rifle. A bloom of red mist as the back of Machado's head disintegrated. The sound of the shot rolling over the ridge in laminated echoes. The troopers threw themselves down, hugging the ground.

A bullet whined off the rocks behind them. 'Fuck.' Guzmán dived to the ground as another bullet exploded into the narrow defile, scouring his face with fragments of stone. The troopers cowered, crawling behind anything that looked like it might stop a bullet.

'Useless bastards.' Guzmán ran past them, the rifle at his shoulder as he threw himself into the thick grass, scanning the slopes ahead through the rifle sight. He saw movement in a patch of bushes two hundred metres away. Leaves and branches parting, the subtle actions of someone in hiding. And then, to his left, the percussive rattle of the troopers returning fire. As Guzmán squinted through the rifle sight, a shape appeared in the bushes, a man in a black slouch hat and dark coat, looking through his rifle sight at Guzmán. Aiming.

Guzmán rolled to one side as the bullet whined into the ground where he had been lying a moment earlier. He raised his rifle, seeing the gunman clamber onto a horse and spur it towards a great mound of ancient stones. Guzmán fired and saw the dust as his shot hit the rocks beyond the rider. He ejected the cartridge and aimed again, though too late as the rider slipped away behind a rocky promontory near the skyline.

Silence returned to the ridge. Ochoa came running over to ask for orders.

'Bring the horses through the ravine,' Guzmán said. 'I'll get the men in position in case that bastard comes back.'

And he would come back, he thought as he listened to Ochoa relaying his orders to the men. Because if Guzmán was in his place, faced with a squad of incompetent civil guards, he would return again and again, cutting them down at every opportunity. He knew a lot, this Lobo. But there was one thing he didn't know, though he soon would. He didn't know who was coming after him.

The sun was starting to sink behind the distant mountains. Guzmán lay in the grass, moving the sniper scope over the harsh terrain. Behind him, the horses whinnied, unnerved by the mournful howling in the distance.

'Wolves,' Guzmán grunted. 'If the horses smell them, they'll start to panic. Make sure the boys keep them well guarded.'

'I will, sir.' Ochoa paused, seeing one of the sentries signalling from his position among the rocks. Guzmán was already moving, crouching low, and Ochoa followed, lying alongside Guzmán as he scanned the hillside with his binoculars.

'For fuck's sake,' Guzmán muttered to the sentry. 'What's that?'

Ochoa lifted his binoculars. 'It's those Frenchmen in the stupid hats again.'

'The Çubiry?' Guzmán peered through the scope. 'They're about to be dead brigands.' Angrily, he worked the bolt, putting another round in the breech.

The sentry grabbed his rifle. 'Don't shoot, *Comandante*. They'll kill us all.'

'You touched my rifle.' Guzmán stared wide-eyed at the man. 'And that's what it will say on your tombstone after the court-martial,' his eyes narrowed, 'assuming I don't kill you right here.'

'If you shoot at them, they'll attack.' The man's voice was trembling. 'And they can bring up more men. They say there's at least a hundred of them at their chateau in St Jean.'

Guzmán ground his teeth. Killing Frenchmen could attract unwanted attention. Particularly since Gutiérrez had explicitly told him to avoid an international incident. Perhaps he could compromise for once, kill them later.

'They've gone,' Ochoa said, lowering the binoculars.

Guzmán glared at the trooper. 'Your court-martial's postponed. Now fuck off.' He turned to Ochoa. 'What was that man's name, Corporal?'

'Santos, *jefe*.'

'Right,' Guzmán growled. 'Next time we need a volunteer, he's our man.'

It was still dark when Guzmán woke Ochoa, though a strip of light on the horizon signalled the coming dawn. He pointed to a wavering light in the distance 'Someone's lit a fire,' he whispered. 'Get two men, Corporal. I want to see who's camped over there.'

Quietly, they moved over the rocky terrain towards the fire. Guzmán signalled to the two troopers to stay a few metres behind. The last thing he needed was for one of those dunderheaded fools to trip and alert their quarry.

The camp was in a grassy hollow. The fire was almost burned out, its smoke a thin line stretched by the wind across the grey sky. Near the fire, Guzmán saw the shape of a man in a sleeping bag. Another man was standing near a patch of thick shrub, having a piss from the look of it. Guzman moved down the incline, taking cover behind a large boulder as he got nearer. He signalled to the troopers to move forward. As they began to advance, he saw the other man run into the bushes, his plumed hat outlined against the dawn light as he turned, raising a rifle to his shoulder. Before Guzmán could call a warning the shot shattered the thin air, sending the civil guards scrambling for cover.

As the echoes of the shot died away, the man in the sleeping bag sat bolt upright, struggling to get out. 'One of you go after that bastard in the bushes,' Guzmán yelled to the cowering troopers.

Reluctantly, one of them moved forward, into the dense foliage.

'*Manos arriba, coño.*' Guzmán aimed the rifle at the man's head as he climbed from the sleeping bag. 'Do you speak Spanish?'

The man narrowed his eyes. '*Inglés,*' he said. '*No hablo español.*'

'He says he's English,' Ochoa said. 'He doesn't speak Spanish.'

'Even I knew that,' Guzmán growled. He saw the civil guard watching. 'You, get over here and search his pockets.'

Guzmán waited as the trooper went through the prisoner's pockets. Finally, he brought the man's possessions over in his hat and Guzmán examined them, suddenly amused.

'*Me cago en la puta.* This is an ID card from 1938 that says he's a member of the International Brigade.' He turned to Ochoa. 'You speak English, do you, Corporal?'

'I had lessons in the press corps. What do you want me to say?'

'Start by asking who he is.'

Guzmán waited as Ochoa spoke to the man. It was clear he was not being helpful.

'He says he crossed the border by mistake,' said Ochoa. 'He wants a lawyer.'

Guzmán stared in disbelief. 'Tell him, if he says something as stupid as that again, the only person he'll be seeing is a priest.' He took his cigarettes from his pocket. 'And that will be posthumously.'

Ochoa translated the man's reply. 'He says you can't shoot him, he's American.'

Guzmán laughed out loud. Ochoa and the trooper joined in, nudging one another. 'Foreigners.'

'Right.' Guzmán looked the man in the eye. 'Tell him I want to know how—'

The American's chest erupted in a shower of blood. As he pitched forward into the damp grass, the shot echoed across the ridge. Guzmán stared at the horseman riding away in the distance. 'El fucking Lobo,' he muttered, raising his rifle. He had no clear shot and the rider vanished into the craggy landscape before he could fire.

'What happened to the man in those bushes?' Ochoa shouted, seeing the other *guardia* backing away from the gorse, ready to flee. Guzmán saw something hanging from a bush. 'What's that, trooper?' he yelled, panting.

Timidly, the *guardia* approached the gorse and lifted something from its spines. He turned, holding up the wide-brimmed hat. 'A Çubiry hat, sir.'

'So where's the fucking owner?' Guzmán shouted, raising the rifle towards the gorse.

The trooper hurled himself to one side as a horse burst from the bushes thirty metres away. Guzmán saw the rider pressed low, clinging to its mane, and fired twice. The rider tumbled from the saddle onto the rocky ground.

The troopers stared, white-faced. Guzmán glowered at them, incensed. 'What?'

'The Çubiry always avenge an injury, *Comandante*.'

'Shut up,' Guzmán snarled, distracted as he noticed Ochoa going through the American's pockets. He seemed to have found something.

'A word, Corporal.' Guzmán took Ochoa to one side. 'I hope that wasn't money you just found on the *Yanqui*,' he said quietly. 'I have rules about stealing from the dead and Rule One is that any money found on people I've killed belongs to me.'

'Actually, sir, you didn't kill him,' Ochoa said. 'El Lobo did.'

'My rules are very flexible, Corporal, and in any case, that's a technical distinction I don't intend to discuss with a fucking NCO. How much did you find?'

Ochoa held up a piece of paper. 'It's not money, sir. It's a letter.'

'Who's it from?'

Ochoa looked unhappily at the typewritten sheet. 'His brother. He looks forward to seeing him in San Sebastián in two days' time.'

Guzmán raised an eyebrow. 'Does it say why they're meeting?'

'No, sir, but it does say who his brother is.'

'Don't keep me waiting,' Guzmán snapped. 'Who is he?'

Ochoa turned the letter so Guzmán could see the letterhead.

Embassy of the United States of America

'His brother's the American Ambassador.'

CHAPTER 12

COLMENAR VIEJO, JULY 2010, FUENTES RESIDENCE

Galíndez accelerated and the countryside became an ochre blur in the shimmering afternoon heat. Twenty minutes later, a sprawl of tan-roofed houses and white apartment blocks began to emerge from the haze. She skirted the town to the south and headed out into the barren fields, following the road through an arid landscape wavering in the relentless heat.

A crossroads ahead. She sighed with relief, recognising where she was. A hundred metres further on, she saw the Fuentes house and turned into the sloping drive, the wheels crunching on the dry gravel as she came to a halt alongside the two cars parked there.

The burning air was thick with the scent of flowers as she walked towards the house, admiring the large shuttered windows and long veranda. To the front, the garden sloped up to a long stone wall that marked the boundary of the property. From somewhere behind the house, she heard the gentle sound of a stream.

The world intruded into her reverie. She heard pounding feet and the girls' breathless laughter as they came tumbling out to greet her. Clari stumbled, getting in the way as usual. Inés, being older, tried to adopt more demure behaviour and monitored Galíndez closely, looking for a gesture or a phrase she could imitate later.

'*Hola, chicas*,' Galíndez said, scooping Clari up into her arms.

'Babysitter,' Clari muttered, waving a DVD.

'It's a sleepover,' Inés told her little sister.

'Make yourself at home, Ana, I'm getting ready,' Mercedes called from indoors.

'*Dora.*' Clari tugged Galíndez's hand. 'Let's watch *Dora.*'

'I'll get my bag first, *querida.*' Galíndez knew how long a session with *Dora la Exploradora* could last once Clari took charge of the TV.

She strolled up the drive to her car. As she reached in to get her overnight bag, Galíndez sensed a shadow at the gate and looked up, seeing a metallic blue vehicle. Tinted windows obscured the occupants though she could just make out the pale shape of a face looking at her through the darkened glass. Probably lost, she guessed as she went up the drive, ready to offer directions.

The car's engine growled as it accelerated, leaving an amber cloud of dust hanging in its wake, the sun sparkling on the blue paintwork as the car went over the brow of the hill. *They must have found their map.* Galíndez gathered up her bags and went back to the house.

Inés was waiting on the porch. She looked at the box Galíndez was carrying. 'Did you bring your new boots, Ana?'

'I said I would, didn't I? Do you want to see them?' Inés nodded emphatically.

Galíndez sat on the porch to put on the boots. Carefully, she got up and took a few steps, the sound of her heels sharp on the wooden decking. 'What do you think?'

'Cool.' Inés reached into her pocket. 'Can I take a photo to show my friend Blanca?'

'OK, but do it quickly, I may fall over any minute.'

Inés took a photo, her thumbs playing over her phone as she sent the picture.

'Well, look at you, Ana María.' Mercedes Fuentes came out onto the porch in her bathrobe. 'Those boots look great, especially with that skirt. But don't wear them for work, will you? It might be bad for Luis's blood pressure.'

Galíndez looked round to make sure the girls weren't listening. She lowered her voice, 'The boss wouldn't notice. Last week I ran into him after I'd been on a vice operation; I was dressed as a hooker. He never even blinked.'

Mercedes shrugged. 'He told me he'd seen you but he didn't mention anything about your clothes.'

'Yes he did, *Mamá*,' Inés cut in. 'I heard him. He said you could have read a newspaper through her dress and that you could see her—'

'That's quite enough, señorita.' Mercedes drew a finger across her throat.

'And he said Ana's pants looked like a piece of string.'

Mercedes put a hand over her daughter's mouth. 'See, Ana? He never noticed a thing.'

Capitán and Señora Fuentes came out onto the porch, dressed for their evening at the theatre. Mercedes was wearing a black dress that looked like it had cost more than Galíndez earned in a month.

'I don't know which of you two is smarter,' Galíndez laughed.

'It had better be her, Ana María, given the time she's taken to get ready,' Fuentes said. 'I hope you've got the stamina for a night with these two?'

'Of course. I'm looking forward to it. Have a great time.'

Merche squeezed her arm. 'Thanks for coming at such short notice. We owe you.'

Galíndez lifted Clari so she could wave goodbye as her parents' car went up the drive.

'Ice cream,' Clari mumbled, absently twisting a strand of Galíndez's hair. 'Pizza.'

Once indoors, things went downhill fast. Clari put on one of her extensive collection of *Dora la Exploradora* DVDs. Loud. And then, from upstairs, Galíndez heard the unmistakable industrial barrage of Legions of Death. It took her back to her early days at university, crammed into a hot crowded bar, listening to Legions, though she didn't listen for long: they were crap. With any luck Inés would get over them. *Please God.*

The sudden blast of a ring tone. Woody Woodpecker, from the sound of it.

'Inés?' Galíndez called up the stairs. 'That was your phone.'

The heavy metal suddenly stopped. Inés came stamping down the stairs and snatched up her phone from the kitchen counter.

Galíndez peered into the fridge. 'So what do you want for dinner?' She noticed several items that didn't look like they'd fit into a microwave and ruled them out. 'We've got pizza, or there's different pizza. Do you want to choose, Inés?'

No reply.

'Inés?' Galíndez turned, sensing something was wrong.

Inés was staring at her phone. As Galíndez watched, a tear welled up and slid down her face. The phone trembled in her hand. Galíndez went across the kitchen to her. 'What's the matter, *mi vida*?' She took the phone from Inés's hand and held her close as she wept. Lifting the phone, she glanced at the message:

WE HATE INÉS

Inés Fuentes is a fat bitch.

Let her know if u agree & send her this text.

Do the world a favour Inés & die.

'Who sent you this, *querida*?'

Inés clung to her, her arms wrapped around Galíndez's waist, her face pressed against her chest, tears soaking her shirt. 'Don't tell anyone, Ana.' Her voice quivered. 'Please.'

Galíndez felt sweat on her palms. She knew how Inés felt. That was a part of her childhood she remembered very well. The part after *Papá* was killed. Clinging to Aunt Carmen, soaking her blouse with tears each day after school.

Why are you crying, Ana María?

No es nada, Tia.

Has someone been picking on you? Tell me, Ana. Remember what your father used to say? Tell the truth even if it hurts.

But that's just it: I don't remember Papá, Tia. I don't remember him and that's why they do it. At school, they call me Little Orphan Annie. Mad Annie. Loca Anita, can't even remember her papá. Why can't they like me?

'Please don't tell Mum, Ana María.' Inés's voice was painful to hear. 'Promise?'

Two days later, Aunt Carmen was waiting when Galíndez got home, her cheeks flushed from being chased.

I've booked you some lessons, mi amor.

What lessons, tia?

Something to make you more confident, mi alma. So you won't be bullied. I found this place in the local paper. Do it for me, cariña: I can't bear to see you like this.

Bueno, Tia Carmen. If that's what you want.

'Come outside.' Galíndez took Inés by the hand and led her outside to sit on the porch. Inés was still shaking as Galíndez stroked her hair. 'Tell me who's picking on you,' she said, still remembering.

A newspaper cutting. A small advertisement with a crescent moon in one corner:

LUNA NEGRA DOJO
Martial Arts training for women – Multi Discipline – Self-Confidence – Inner Strength

Your first lesson is on Saturday, Ana María. One thirty. The tone of Aunt Carmen's voice told her there was no backing out.

Sitting in Tia Carmen's car outside the dojo. The sign over the door with its black moon logo. Galíndez reluctantly gathered up her bag and trudged to the entrance, hearing Tia Carmen drive away as she went down the short flight of steps. A woman was waiting in the doorway. Tall, dark-skinned, high cheekbones, her curly hair bound in a tight knot.

You must be Ana María? Your aunt told me about you. My name's María Cristina but call me Mendez – everyone does.

'One of the girls at school,' Inés said, her voice wavering. 'She started calling me names and it just got worse. She hits me before class sometimes and everyone laughs – even people who were my friends…' Tears rolled down her cheeks. 'Now they're texting me…'

'It's not your fault,' Galíndez muttered, her fists clenched.

Inés snuffled. 'She calls me No-tits Fuentes.'

'She's just silly. You're twelve. Everyone's different. It's normal.'

'She's got big boobs. And she's taller than me. If I tell Dad, he'll say to hit her back. But she'll only hit me harder.'

Galíndez kicked off her shoes. 'OK, show me how she hits you. Do it slowly.'

Inés mimed a slow-motion punch to Galíndez's chest.

'*Bueno*, do it again, but this time try and hit me hard. Don't worry about hurting me.'

Inés drew her arm back and lashed out. Galíndez deflected the blow with her left arm and moved forward, her right foot hooking Inés's leg from under her, turning as she went sprawling onto the grass. Inés sat up, laughing as she brushed dirt and grass from her T-shirt.

'That was cool, Ana, I wish I could do that.'

'You're going to. We've an hour or two before dark. Now, hit me again slowly and I'll show you what I did. Then you can try it.'

As Inés began taking off her shoes, anxious to emulate her teacher, Galíndez did a few warm-ups, bending forward, touching the ground with her palms. As she straightened, her gaze wandered across the green sweep of the garden to the top of the drive. A blue four-by-four pulled away from the gate, the sun glinting on its tinted windows as it drove off. Troubled, Galíndez watched it go. She decided to mention it to Capitán Fuentes in the morning.

'I'm ready,' Inés called.

An hour and half later, Inés had got the basics: block, move and push. She'd even dumped Galíndez on her *culo* a couple of times.

'OK, that's enough for today,' Galíndez said, visualising a cold beer.

Inés twisted and feigned a punch, miming an attack on her. Annoyed, Galíndez remained motionless, facing her down. 'Hey, remember what I told you? What did I say?'

Inés sighed. A sigh that said Galíndez was really just another adult after all. 'Only for defence… blah blah… never use it to hurt anyone… and so on.'

'I mean it, Inés. Having the ability to hurt someone means you have to make sure you don't abuse that ability. If you do, you become a bully. Just remember that.'

'Whatever. Can I choose the pizza?'

'Go ahead. I'll see you in a few minutes, I'm off for my shower.'

The shower in the guest-room was almost as big as Galíndez's flat. Steam misted the mirrors and surfaces as she stepped under the powerful jet. After a few minutes, she turned off the shower and stepped out, looking round the bathroom for a towel. She didn't find one and padded out into the bedroom where she saw a pile of clean towels on the window sill, behind a small sofa. She walked across the carpet, leaving a trail of wet footprints as she went. As she reached the sofa, she looked out of the window at a sudden flash of blue as a car passed the gate. Suddenly uneasy, she knelt on the sofa and leaned forward to grab a towel from the window ledge.

A sudden noise behind her. She whirled round. Inés stood in the doorway, pushing her hands into her pockets. Her guilty look told Galíndez she'd been spying on her.

'*Dios mio*, you could have knocked, Inés. You made me jump.' Galíndez wrapped the towel around her, trying to be casual, deciding not to make a big thing out of it.

'The pizza's ready,' Inés said, staring.

'Do you want to go and slice it?' Galíndez said. 'I'll be down in a couple of minutes.'

Inés's face crumpled. 'I wish I looked like you, Ana.'

Galíndez smiled. 'Come on. We already talked about that. Don't take any notice of what some nasty girl at school says. You're an attractive young woman.'

'You think so? Really?'

'Of course. You'll have boys flocking around you in a year or two.'

Inés brightened at the thought. 'Is that what happened when you were my age?'

'Sort of.' Galíndez nodded, planting a kiss on her forehead. 'I'm going to get dressed now. See you downstairs.'

The introductory lesson in martial arts had left Inés exhausted and after three slices of pizza she was ready for bed. As they said goodnight, Galíndez remembered there were things she had to do. 'Inés, is there a computer I can use to check my mail?'

'It's in Dad's study, the room next to their bedroom. It's always switched on.'

'Thanks, see you in the morning.'

'Night, Ana María.'

Once she'd cleared the table and restored order to the kitchen, Galíndez opened a bottle of beer and went out onto the veranda. The night air was warm and soft, pulsing with the sound of crickets. She sat on the porch and drank the cold beer, staring into the darkness, half expecting to see the blue car drive past again. After a few minutes, the silence started to bother her and she went back inside to use the computer.

Capitán Fuentes' study was chaotic, a far cry from his spartan office at HQ. The computer was on a desk by the window. She slid into Fuentes' ergonomic chair, revelling in its structured comfort as she touched the mouse, bringing the screen to life. The computer desktop was neatly organised: just one folder labelled 'Work'. In the far corner of the desktop, she found a shortcut to the access screen of the *guardia* network and logged in. There was no mail apart from messages about server downtime, upgrades to the system and parking arrangements at HQ.

Outside, the darkness of the garden was suddenly broken by headlights. She heard the low grumble of an engine at the top of the drive and leaned over the desk, trying to catch a glimpse of the car as it drove away. Galíndez peered into the darkness, worried now. She took out her phone and walked up to the gate. If she could get the registration, she could call it in, get a patrol car to come over. She smiled to herself as she looked up and down the darkened road. It was empty. No sign of a car at all. She was being paranoid.

Galíndez logged off the *guardia* network. It was time to do a bit of quiet surfing. There was plenty of time and no one to disturb her. That was how she liked working: alone with her friend Señor Google. She wondered whether to trawl the net for any new mention of Guzmán, in the hope that someone somewhere, had come up with something that would throw new light on what little she already knew. But she did that so often that after five minutes she was bored. He operated long before the internet. Even if his deeds had been recorded, they weren't online.

Maybe it was time to go to bed. As she got to her feet, she recalled her conversation with Fuentes about Ramiro's kids. The family tragedy. She sat down again, tapping the desk with a finger, distracted. Remembering Aunt Carmen telling her never to mention it in the presence of Ramiro and his wife. There were some things time couldn't heal, Carmen said, and Ramiro's broken heart was one of those.

Galíndez stared at the screen. Naturally, she had never said a word to Ramiro. And Aunt Carmen only mentioned the tragedy obliquely. But Carmen was gone and Galíndez felt a sudden pang of curiosity as she looked at the computer screen. What good would it do to know more about it? But this was not just idle curiosity. Her amnesia erased so much of her memory of childhood that any new detail about the family took on added significance. It couldn't hurt to know a little more, surely?

Her fingers rattled on the keys as Galíndez went to the website of the daily newspaper *ABC* and checked their archive, searching for Ramiro's name. Nothing. She tried to think laterally. If the deaths weren't recorded, maybe the funerals were. She entered more search terms and got nothing. A better idea: who would attend the funeral? Definitely, there'd be Ramiro and Aunt Teresa, of course, and his sister Aunt Carmen, and Galíndez's parents, Miguel and Amaranta. The keyboard rattled again as she entered the words. Her eyes were dry and tired. If this didn't work, it was definitely bed for her. She waited as the hour glass turned on the screen. One hit. A small article tucked away deep in the paper.

Tragedy in San Sebastián de los Reyes
Madrid 15/3/1982

> Agents of the guardia civil found themselves dealing with a family tragedy on Tuesday evening when they attended an emergency call to a chalet in San Sebastián de Los Reyes. Inside the chalet, the agents found a baby and his sister aged 12, dead from carbon monoxide poisoning, the result of a malfunction in the boiler. No further details have been made available out of respect for the bereaved family.
>
> The two agents of the benemérita attending the scene were identified as Agents Luis Fuentes and Miguel Galíndez.

Galíndez realised she was holding her breath. She looked at the article again, reading it carefully for anything she might have overlooked. There was nothing. She felt a sudden rush of anger as she realised Fuentes had deliberately withheld this from her. As she got up, she saw her face reflected in the window, her deep frown accentuated by the darkness outside.

'*Buenos días.*' Fuentes looked up from his breakfast as Galíndez came into the kitchen, her hair wet from the shower.

'*Hola.*' She poured herself a glass of juice. 'How was the show?'

He shrugged. 'Went on too long. But don't tell Merche I said so, will you?'

'Promise.' Galíndez helped herself to a croissant.

'Did the girls behave themselves?'

'Of course. Clari fell asleep watching *Dora* and Inés and I went out in the garden – I showed her some martial arts moves.'

'Really? That's good.' Fuentes nodded. 'She should do more sport.' He glanced at his watch. 'Christ, look at the time, I'd better get off.' He excused himself and went into the hall. She heard the creak of the leather gunbelt as he fastened it round his waist. Collecting her briefcase and the new boots from the bedroom, she followed him into the garden, wondering whether to mention the article. Probably better not to, she decided. He must have had his reasons. Let sleeping dogs lie. As she got to her car, she threw her things onto the back seat and hurried up the drive after him.

Behind the wheel, Fuentes looked up and saw her in his mirror. He leaned out of the window. 'What's on your mind, Ana? That's your serious look.'

'You know when we talked about the deaths of Uncle Ramiro's children?'

Fuentes tensed. 'You didn't say anything to him?'

'Of course not, but I did find a piece in *ABC* about it.'

'There wasn't supposed to be any publicity.' A sudden edge in his voice.

'You could hardly stop the press reporting something like that,' Galíndez said.

'Oh yes, we could. I thought we had. What did the article say?'

'That two children had been found dead following an accident. It didn't name them.'

'That's good.'

'But it did name the officers attending the scene,' Galíndez said, her face dark with anger. '*Joder*, it was you and my father, *jefe*. Why didn't tell me?'

Fuentes sighed. 'We were ordered not to talk about it. Look, I'll tell you the rest, but promise me you'll forget about it after that? It was a long time ago.'

She gave him a curt nod.

'It was the start of a night shift,' Fuentes began. 'We were on a routine patrol that evening, your dad and me. We got a call to a summer house out at San Sebastián de los Reyes. When we got there, we had to break in by smashing a window. We turned off the gas and found two kids dead from carbon monoxide poisoning. It was the boiler, no doubt about that. But…'

'But what?'

'It wasn't an accident. The girl had put towels along the bottom of the doors and round the windows. Then she pulled the gas pipe from the wall. When we saw some correspondence on the table, we realised it was Ramiro's house. Since we didn't know where he was, we called his father, General Ortiz senior.'

'The one they called Iron Hand Ortiz?'

'That's right, and with good reason. Anyway, within twenty minutes, several cars full of plain-clothes men arrived along with General Ortiz. He said he'd find Ramiro and break the news. Then he took your father and me to one side and ordered us to keep quiet about the entire thing and let him and his staff officers clear things up.'

Galíndez narrowed her eyes. 'What did he mean by that?'

'He meant they'd deal with the press. That's why I was surprised when you said you'd found that article.'

'They censored the press?' Galíndez glared at him. 'And you helped?'

'I was young, Ana María. We were given a direct order to keep quiet. And we were rewarded for doing it. That was how things were done back then.'

'And what did you get for your silence?' She guessed maybe a hundred thousand pesetas, three months' wages back then.

Fuentes shrugged as he started the engine. A dry crunch of gravel as the big car rolled forward. He leaned through the window. 'You see this house?'

'Of course.'

'That's what I got.' Fuentes put his foot down and drove away.

CHAPTER 13

SAN SEBASTIÁN, OCTOBER 1954, LA ESCALERA DE MARI

'I must have killed a black cat,' Guzmán growled. 'Several, maybe.' He was sitting with Ochoa a few metres up the slope, waiting as the troopers got a fire going to brew coffee. 'What the fuck was that *Yanqui* doing here?'

'Maybe he was telling the truth when he said he got lost, sir?'

'Or maybe he was telling a fucking blatant lie, Corporal, since he was with that French degenerate.' Guzmán took a long pull on his cigarette and stared at the two civil guards idly chatting near the fire.

'Time you morons started pulling your weight.' He glared at them. 'You're from this part of the country, aren't you, Ruiz?'

'*Sí, mi Comandante.*'

'So tell me where you'd hide a body round here.' He glanced at the corpses sprawled nearby and corrected himself. 'Tell me where you'd hide two bodies.'

The men entered into a hurried discussion. 'La Cueva de Mari, *Comandante*,' Ruiz said finally.

'Her again?' Guzmán scoffed. '*Puta madre*, just how will the goddess help us this time?'

'La Cueva de Mari is a cave in the side of the mountain,' Diaz explained. 'Inside, there's a deep shaft, really deep. Someone climbed down into it sixty years ago and was never seen again. People don't go near for fear of making Mari angry.'

'Perhaps I was wrong about you two being complete imbeciles,' Guzmán said. 'Get those stiffs tied to their horses and we'll take them up to this cave.' He looked balefully at Diaz. 'It had better be deep, Private, because I don't want them found. Ever.'

The men went over to the bodies, pleased to be given a task that didn't involve a threat to their personal safety.

'*Imbéciles*,' Guzmán grunted. 'One day there'll be intelligent civil guards.' He spat into the grass. 'Not in our lifetime, though.'

The two men watched the troopers struggling to drape the bodies over the saddles of the dead men's horses. They were clumsy as well as stupid, Guzmán observed.

Ochoa offered Guzmán a cigarette and he took it, distracted. 'It's bad luck the *Yanqui* was the ambassador's brother,' Ochoa said.

'This was more than bad luck, Corporal,' Guzmán said. 'El Lobo shot that *Yanqui* deliberately. Why would he do that?'

'Maybe he was aiming at us?' Ochoa said. 'He was firing from a distance, after all.'

Guzmán shook his head. 'No, he's a crack shot. He meant to kill him, which means he knew who the *Yanqui* was.' His face set.

'Can't we call in some help?' Ochoa asked. 'General Mellado's got a whole division sitting in barracks. Couldn't we borrow a company or two? That would speed up the search for El Lobo's supplies. We might even flush him out.'

'No,' Guzmán said. 'The orders from the top are very clear: do nothing to attract attention. If Mellado gets involved he'll burn villages to the ground and shoot the inhabitants. And those will be the innocent ones. The *Yanquis* would turn faint if they got wind of something like that.' He had a sudden vision of Madrid, slowly moving out of his reach. 'We stick to my plan. We destroy his supplies and push him into going after the bank truck.'

'And then he walks into the trap.' Ochoa nodded.

'After which, we go back to Madrid.' Guzmán swung himself up into the saddle. He glared as he saw the two civil guards leading the horses carrying the bodies.

'Know how I can tell you're not used to carrying dead bodies, Diaz?'

'No, *Comandante*, how?'

'Because your fucking uniform's covered in blood.' Guzmán spurred his horse forward to catch up with Ochoa.

'Not far now, sir,' Ruiz called, pointing to the mountain looming above them.

Guzmán stared belligerently at the spectacular landscape. 'Know what our trouble is? Everything's different here. We know fuck all about what's going on.'

Ochoa nodded. 'Can't Gutierrez provide us with some intelligence?'

'I don't know, Corporal, because I haven't heard a word from him.' Guzmán swore as a gust of wind threatened to dislodge his hat. 'I can't get used to this fucking country.'

'It isn't Madrid, *jefe*.'

Guzmán sighed, almost nostalgic. 'True, in Madrid all you have to do is kick a few bootblacks, slap a barber or two and in no time we'd have a lead.'

'Proper police work,' Ochoa agreed. 'A drink in every bar and all of them on the house.'

Guzmán looked at him. 'Of course.' He called to the trooper ahead. 'Diaz, do they have taverns round here?'

Diaz nodded. 'See that dark shape on the hillside over there, sir? That's La Cueva.'

Guzmán reined in his horse. 'It's called The Cave?'

'No, it is a cave, *Comandante*,' Diaz said. 'It can get pretty rough sometimes.'

'So can I,' Guzmán said. 'Perhaps their customers know something about Señor Lobo. Let's get these bodies disposed of and then we'll have a quiet drink with the local peasants.'

OROITZ 1954, CUEVA DE MARI

Guzmán knelt by the edge of the shaft and looked down into the darkness. Dank air rose from the depths below. He took a stone from the floor of the cave and dropped it into the shaft, listening for the sound as it hit the bottom. 'That's deep enough.'

Behind him, in the mouth of the cave, the two *guardia* were pulling the bodies from the horses. They were taking their time about it, Guzmán noticed, watching the men carry the first corpse in. He groaned at the reverential way they laid the American's body by the edge of the shaft. 'For fuck's sake, you don't need to be so gentle. He's not going to wake up.'

'Shouldn't you say a few words, sir?' Diaz asked, wringing his hat in his hands.

Guzmán looked at him, wondering if he was mad. 'Of course, Private Diaz.'

Diaz and Ruiz doffed their tricornes and stood at attention, heads bowed.

Guzmán put his foot against the body of the dead American. 'Don't fucking come back, you Red bastard.' He rolled the body over the edge of the shaft and listened to the echoes as the corpse bounced off the stone walls as it fell. Moments later, a final muffled impact, satisfyingly distant. As Guzmán turned away, he saw the two troopers cross themselves. They paused in mid-genuflection, seeing his baleful look. 'Cut that out and toss that Çubiry in after him, *rapido*.' Guzmán gave Diaz a venomous look as he dragged the Frenchman's body towards the drop. 'No graveside weeping, Diaz. Throw him in and be quick about it. You're not a mourner.'

Diaz nodded unhappily, fumbling for a better grip on the corpse.

'*Puta madre*,' Guzmán sighed, 'He's dead, you can't hurt him now.' Irritated, he watched Diaz roll the body into the shaft. 'Amateurs.'

A cool wind ruffled the sparse grass outside the cave and Guzmán fastened his hunting jacket. 'I want the squad to start looking for El Lobo's supplies immediately. Anything he can use to store food or weapons is to be burned.'

'There are some drovers' shelters and old cattle sheds along the ridge,' Ochoa said. 'I'll tell Ruiz and Diaz to pass the order to the others.'

'Good.' Guzmán led the way back to the horses. As the two

guardia saluted, he stopped and towered over them, bristling with aggression. 'Where's the *Yanqui*'s body?'

Ruiz shuffled his feet and looked down. Diaz stared into the distance.

'At the bottom of Mari's Cave, *mi Comandante*,' Diaz said. He stumbled backwards as Guzmán jabbed him in the chest.

'Wrong. You never heard of any American, or that French bastard, for that matter. That goes for you too, Ruiz.' He put a foot into the stirrup and climbed into the saddle. 'We'll see you back here at sunset with the others.'

The two troopers saluted and rode off towards the ridge.

'Time for a drink then, Corporal,' Guzmán said.

OROITZ 1954, TABERNA LA CUEVA

'I thought they were exaggerating,' Guzmán said. 'But it really is a cave.'

La Cueva was a natural opening in the hillside, though the owner had built a rough wooden wall to protect its customers from the mountain winds. A man was standing outside as they tied their horses to a rail by the stone trough. He was bald, though his beard made up for that, reaching halfway down his barrel chest. He stared at them with virulent suspicion.

'*Muy buenas*,' Guzmán said, almost pleasantly.

The man's face became even more hostile. That took some doing.

'What do you Spaniards want?' he asked, his beard rising and falling as he spoke.

Guzmán shrugged. 'I want a drink. What the fuck do people normally come here for?'

'Why didn't you say so?' The man turned and pushed the door, though with some difficulty, since it was not fixed to its hinges. 'No need to be unpleasant.'

Guzmán and Ochoa followed him into the cave. Towards the

back was a bar hewn from a long boulder. The surface of the rock had been flattened and polished until it shone. Behind the bar, a series of shelves had been hacked out of the side of the cave, all crammed with bottles containing a diverse assortment of bright-coloured liquids, the likes of which Guzmán had never seen outside a pharmacy.

'This is fucking primitive.'

The bearded man gave him a dark look. 'It's not like you were invited, is it?'

At the far side of the cave, a fire blazed in a circle of large stones, sending pungent wood smoke into the soot-stained roof. A group of men sat near the fire, staring into the flames with the glazed expressions of the seriously inebriated.

Guzmán leaned against the bar, admiring the smoothly dressed surface of the stone. 'Bit quiet today then?'

'I never said it was quiet. What's it to you?' The barman went behind the bar, smoothing a wet cloth across the polished stone. 'I thought you came here to drink?'

Guzmán turned to Ochoa. 'What do you want?'

Ochoa looked at the array of bottles. 'I'll have a beer.'

The barman snorted. 'We don't sell it.'

'All right,' Ochoa said, 'give me a glass of water.'

'We don't have water.' The bald man narrowed his eyes. 'And we don't have glasses, either.' He slammed a battered metal tankard on the stone counter.

'If you don't have water, how do you wash those?' Ochoa asked.

'What? Are you two *maricónes* or something?'

'Why don't you tell us what you've got and we'll have some of that?' Guzmán said.

'All right.' The owner nodded. 'We have absinthe.'

'What else?'

A blank stare. '*Patxaran.*'

'I don't like *patxaran.*'

'Everyone likes *patxaran*,' the man said. 'But if you don't want that there's absinthe.'

'So what's in those bottles behind you?'

'Absinthe.'

'Why are there so many different colours?'

'The colour doesn't matter,' the bald man said. 'It's the strength that counts. In fact, it's a matter of life and death for some folk.'

'Why?'

The barman sighed as if it was obvious. 'If you have a couple of glasses of that yellow stuff there,' he pointed to a squat bottle on one of the upper shelves, 'you'd better not be walking home after dark. We've had people fall over cliffs, others froze to death, and don't get me started about the ones who ended up in the river.'

'So what do you recommend?'

'None of them. They all lead to trouble.'

'I come into a bar for a fucking drink and you try to talk me out of it. What kind of barman are you?' Guzmán said despairingly.

'Fuck you and your fancy ways.' The barman slammed another metal tankard onto the bar next to the first and splashed blue liquid into both. With a scowl, he pushed the tankards across the smooth stone counter. 'Get that down you.' It was less a friendly injunction and more a threat, Guzmán thought, taking a mouthful. '*Puta madre.*' He clutched at his throat.

Ochoa took a tentative sip, his eyes widening as he swallowed. He shrugged and lifted the tankard again, chugging half of it down in one gulp. Slowly, he lifted his left hand in front of his face and stared at it, entranced.

'What the fuck's up with you?' Guzmán grunted.

'My hand's on fire.' Ochoa grinned. He lifted his hand to admire the flames.

'I think you'd better take it easy with this stuff,' Guzmán suggested.

A man came in, though Guzmán smelled him before he got through the door. '*Kaixo*,' he said, leaning on the bar. Just another peasant, Guzmán deduced from his threadbare clothes and tattered *alpargatas*.

The barman looked up. '*Kaixo*, Aïtor. What will you have?'

'Absinthe.' He leaned against the bar. 'Nothing like a day's work to build up a thirst.'

The barman lifted his stone flagon above one of the rusty tankards. It was empty.

'Out of absinthe?' Aïtor said. 'I can always go somewhere else.'

The barman reached behind the bar for another flagon. 'Not unless you want a twenty-kilometre walk you can't.' He filled the tankard and pushed it across the counter. 'In any case, once you've drunk this you won't be capable of going outside for a piss, let alone to another bar.'

'Let's get a seat.' Guzmán led the way to a couple of chairs near the fire.

A few more customers drifted in. Few looked at Guzmán or Ochoa. This was clearly a place where men minded their own business and that business was drinking. Guzmán cast an eye over the clientele. Degenerate drovers, garrulous goatherds and shambling shepherds, all drinking home-made absinthe or *patxaran* as if their lives depended on it. Soon the rough stone walls of the cave echoed with drunken arguments and half-remembered jokes.

'I like it here,' Guzmán said, trying to focus as he looked at Ochoa. 'Though you're a bit of a misery.' When he got no answer, he decided to make small talk. 'So how's the wife?'

Ochoa peered at him, his pupils small dots in his pale eyes. 'I wouldn't know.'

'Why not?' Guzmán waved to the barman for a refill. 'Isn't she in Madrid?'

Ochoa took a swig of absinthe. 'She left me and took the kids with her.'

'Shame.' Guzmán held out his tankard as the barman brought more drink.

'When this is over, I'm going to take some leave and find her.'

'Good idea. You going to make it up, get her to see sense?'

'No.' Ochoa gave him a blank look. 'I want to find her so I can kill her.'

'So there's no chance of a reconciliation?' Guzmán had a sudden urge to laugh and changed the subject. 'How many kids have you got, Corporal?'

'Three,' said Ochoa. 'Two boys and a girl.'

'Which are the hardest to bring up?'

Ochoa's eyes rolled. 'They're all difficult to bring up. I can't say.'

'Try thinking about it then, Corporal, and I'll ignore the fact that you're habitually as miserable as fucking sin.'

Ochoa shrugged. 'Girls are more of a worry. And they cost more to keep.' His face creased into a lopsided grin. 'Why do you ask, *jefe*? Planning on having a few?'

'I ask you a perfectly serious question,' Guzmán snapped, 'and you turn into a fucking comedian. Any more of that and I'll take you outside.'

'Forget it.' Ochoa slumped back in his chair.

'Don't tell me what to do. I don't like someone having a laugh at my expense.'

'No one's doing that, boss. Christ, all I said was that I wanted to kill my wife.'

Never one for domestic issues, Guzmán got to his feet. 'I'm off for a piss.' He saw the barman by the door and walked towards him, a little unsteady. 'Where's the toilet?'

'The pissing rock is out there.' The barman stepped back to let Guzmán pass. 'You'll see it across the track.' He called after him as he reached the door. 'And don't get shy if the whore's watching. She's seen it all before.'

The pissing rock was a huge outcrop of sheer stone, uncovered when part of the hillside had collapsed at some time during the last millennium or so. It was clearly in heavy use, judging by the smell and the soggy texture of the soil. Guzmán noticed a sign nailed to a post.

FOR REASONS OF HYGIENE, DO NOT URINATE HERE

He shook his head. Living in the countryside was probably the worst punishment that could be inflicted on a man. To his right two goatherds, or possibly shepherds for all he cared, were talking about El Lobo as they pissed.

'Say what you like,' the first said, 'but El Lobo's had the army, the *guardia* and the police after him and no one's got near him. He vanishes like a ghost.'

'They say he was a Republican general,' the other said. 'If he can do it…'

'I know, imagine if there were ten like him. Things would start to change then.'

Guzmán buttoned up and walked back to the cave. To one side of the door he noticed a young woman, tall and slim, her brown hair tied back, revealing a pale face with dark tired eyes. Busy watching her, he stumbled and fell. When he got back to his feet, the woman was gone.

Inside the cave, he negotiated his way through the increasingly drunken clientele and sank back into his chair. 'I just heard two peasants idolising El Lobo,' he said to Ochoa. Exactly what Gutiérrez was afraid of.'

Ochoa stared into his tankard, struggling to focus. 'That's not good.'

'We should get back and see if the squad have found anything,' Guzmán said. As he tried to stand up, he looked up. 'Looks like the trouble's starting.'

A group of men were standing in the doorway. Plumed hats, spiked Prussian helmets and various other instances of eccentric headwear. A tall thin man led them into the bar. He had a narrow, chiselled face framed by long dark hair tied back with a ribbon. His big knee boots emphasised the piratical look as did his silk waistcoat and blue frock coat.

'I am Etienne Çubiry,' the young man announced.

The cave fell silent. Drovers and shepherds backed away, suddenly nervous.

'I'm looking for one of our men,' Etienne said. 'He should have met us up on the ridge this morning.' He looked round the smoky cave. 'Anyone seen him? No? He held up a coin. Guzmán couldn't see what it was, but it wasn't gold. Clearly Çubiry was a cheapskate.

'Any strangers passed through in the last two days?' Etienne's face darkened with frustration. 'I want to find my man,' he said, raising his voice. 'Someone must have seen him.'

That was unlikely, Guzmán thought, since he was at the bottom of the shaft in the mountain, keeping the American company. He leaned back in his chair, feeling the comforting weight of the Browning beneath his jacket. He was starting to feel irritated by the young Çubiry's behaviour. Despite his swagger, there was nothing brave about him – Guzmán saw that in his eyes and heard it in his voice. Etienne was a coward. The same couldn't be said for the three men standing behind him. Though their clothing was every bit as bizarre as Etienne's, they looked harder and more experienced. If things got rough, Guzmán decided to kill them first. Cheered by the thought of violence, he folded his arms across his chest.

Etienne saw the movement and stared at Guzmán. 'Do I know you, *monsieur*?'

Guzmán thumbed back the hammer of the Browning.

OROITZ 1954, LAUBURU FARM

Begoña put the tray of newly baked loaves on the window ledge to cool. Outside, she saw Nieves watching the clouds over the mountains and went to join her.

Nieves turned as she heard her aunt approaching. 'The weather's about to change.'

'It's going to be a hard winter, that's for sure,' Begoña agreed. 'There'll be snow before long.' She looked at the sky again. 'I think this winter could be as bad as nineteen thirty-nine, maybe worse. *Dios mio*, that was cold.'

'Perhaps you should invite Comandante Guzmán to spend the winter with you?' Nieves said with a cheeky smile. 'You could be snowed in with him.' She saw Begoña's colour rise. 'I don't know why you're blushing. You let him see you naked.'

'That's not true,' Begoña muttered. 'I didn't know he was going to ride into the glade.' She fidgeted with her shawl. 'He could just as easily have been watching you.'

'But I'm not the one who's been trying to attract him,' said Nieves. 'You've been lighting a candle at midnight. You're casting a spell.'

'Be quiet. It's only—'

'A love charm.'

'A bit of fun,' Begoña said, regaining her composure. '*Nada más.*'

Nieves linked arms with her as they walked back through the lilac bushes to the house. 'It has to be done for a full seven days, you know, otherwise it brings bad luck.'

'I've done it before,' Begoña said, with a vague shrug. 'It didn't work then either.'

'*Mira*, look up on the ridge,' Nieves said, pointing. 'To the left of Mari's Peak. It's the *guardia*. Perhaps Señor Guzmán's with them.'

Begoña saw the line of horsemen moving along the ridge in single file. Behind them, trails of bluish smoke curled into the wind. 'They're burning the old cattle byres. Another winter and most would have fallen down anyway.' She looked again at the horsemen. A long way behind the civil guards, she saw the silhouette of another rider moving more slowly, following rather than trying to catch up. At such a distance it was impossible to tell if it was Comandante Guzmán. Nieves called to her from the house and Begoña turned away from the mountain and went indoors.

OROITZ 1954, TABERNA LA CUEVA

'No.' Guzmán's curt answer hung in the sudden quiet.

'Then I want to know who you are, *mon ami*,' Etienne Çubiry said. 'The Çubiry are friends to all. That's right, no?' He looked at the crowd clustered by the bar. Their silence did nothing to suggest they agreed. 'You don't want to upset me,' Etienne added.

'Don't I?' Guzmán returned the Frenchman's stare until he looked away.

'You're starting to annoy me, *monsieur*,' Etienne said, resting his hand on the pommel of the cavalry sabre hanging from his belt.

Guzmán shrugged. He had thirteen bullets in the Browning. Fuck swords.

Ochoa raised his tankard to his mouth. 'Low profile,' he whispered.

He was right, Guzmán thought grudgingly. A fatal confrontation with the Çubiry wasn't in Gutierrez's orders. Which was a shame, because Etienne Çubiry was just asking for a bullet.

'We sell whisky,' Guzmán said, improvising. 'Scotch whisky.'

'Ah, businessmen?' Etienne said, less agitated now. 'What kind of whisky?'

'Single malt, aged in sherry casks,' Guzmán said, recalling the drinks at one of Franco's receptions. 'Stolen direct from Scotland.'

'We could do business,' Etienne said. 'Come see us in St Jean.'

'I'll do that.' Guzmán nodded.

Etienne turned to the barman. 'Hey, Iñaki, better not let your children outside today.'

'Why's that?' Iñaki asked.

'The Israelites are loose.' Etienne shook his hands in mock fear. 'After all these years, the crazy people are coming down from the peak.'

'So what?' Iñaki shrugged. 'They're harmless.'

'Don't say you weren't warned.' Etienne turned to the men behind him. '*Allons-y*.'

'Good luck finding your friend,' Guzmán called.

Etienne smiled. 'Maybe he's been delayed by a lady. *Agur*, gentlemen.' He swept off his hat in an elaborate gesture of farewell and left the cave, followed by his men.

With the Çubiry gone, the tension eased and the barman

wandered among the customers with a large earthenware pitcher, topping up their drinks. Guzmán watched the yellow liquid splash into his battered tankard. 'What was that the Frenchman said about Israelites?'

'They're a bunch of lunatics who've lived wild since the war,' the barman said. 'A shell hit the old asylum and blew a hole in the wall. The madmen escaped and took to the hills. That's why we call them the Israelites – lost in the wilderness and all that. They ended up at the abandoned convent near Mari's Peak.'

'And they don't usually leave the convent?'

'First I've heard of it. Why don't you ask them yourself if you're so interested?'

'I might just do that.' Guzmán got to his feet, somewhat unsteadily. He laid a hundred peseta note on the counter and waved away the change. As he stumbled to the door, pulling Ochoa along by his lapels, he heard the barman's voice behind him.

'Pair of lightweights. They could have stayed here till Easter for a hundred pesetas.'

The squad was waiting near Mari's Cave. From a distance, the troopers looked like strange birds, dark and angular in their oilskin capes. In front of them sat three wild-looking characters, their wrists bound with rope, glancing nervously at their captors.

'Who are these ugly bastards?' Guzmán asked as he got down from his horse.

'Israelites, *mi Comandante*, madmen from the mountain. The others got away.'

The prisoners were not a pretty sight. Weather-beaten faces, lined and tanned like ancient leather, matted shoulder-length hair, long stained beards, their clothes in rags. Boots held on by lengths of torn cloth. All were deep in conversation, though since it was with themselves, it was hard to understand.

'Any of you got a name?' Guzmán asked.

'Answer the *comandante*.' Ruiz poked the nearest lunatic with the butt of his rifle.

The madman stared at Guzmán through a fringe of greasy hair and grinned, exposing a row of rotten teeth. 'At first wolf says keep quiet, see nothing and you can stay. Now he says Israelites must go. We ask him let us stay, but no, he says, the wolf lives here now.' He paused, disturbed by his own incoherent rant. 'Leave now. Wolf eats Israelites.'

'You crazy *badulaque*.' Ruiz gave the man another blow with his rifle.

'Let him be,' Guzmán said. 'Has anyone got some food?'

One of the troopers produced a length of chorizo from his saddlebag. Guzmán cut a slice and held it up in front of the madmen. 'Hungry?'

Their reply was like a pack of rabid dogs.

Guzmán handed the chorizo to the nearest *guardia*. 'Cut them a few pieces of that.'

'But *Comandante*,' the trooper protested, 'they've got no teeth.'

'Then they can suck it,' Guzmán said. 'It'll will keep them going until the nineteen sixties.' He strode away towards the cave, calling for Ochoa to follow.

'I want you to take the squad back to the *cuartel*,' he said, keeping his voice low.

Ochoa nodded. 'What shall I do with them?'

'Light the fire, sit round it and sing a few songs. I don't know, Corporal. Improvise.'

'And what will you be doing, *Comandante*?'

Guzmán was torn between explaining his plan to Ochoa and telling him to mind his own fucking business.

'Mind your own fucking business.'

'Very good, sir.'

'When you ride down towards the valley, take it slowly,' Guzmán said. 'I want anyone watching to think we're all on our way back to the *cuartel*.'

'Those lunatics said they were driven out by wolves,' Ochoa said. 'What if there's a pack of them up there?'

217

'That madman didn't say wolves.' Guzmán smiled. 'He said *the* wolf. El Lobo.'

OROITZ 1954, ABADÍA DEL INMACULADO CORAZÓN DE MARÍA

It was hard work climbing such steep ground, weighed down by his haversack and rifle. Looking up the escarpment, Guzmán saw the grey stone convent perched on an outcrop of ancient rock. High above it, Mari's Peak rose up into the sky. As he looked up, something wet hit his face and he wiped it away. When it happened again, he realised this was something he had not factored into his sudden decision to inspect the nunnery. It was starting to rain.

As he climbed, the grim outline of the convent blurred as curtains of rain swept over the escarpment. Nearer now, he saw the broken ridgeline where part of the roof had collapsed. It was easy to imagine the dreary existence of the nuns who once lived here, beset by endless rain and bitter snows. Even bolstered by their faith, such a life must have rapidly lost its attraction. Isolated in the ceaseless cold, they must surely have wondered if God had abandoned them. Probably they realised he had, since they were long gone, their place taken by lunatics. That was appropriate, he thought. And now even the madmen had gone.

Which was not to say the convent was empty, he realised, peering through the rain at the pale glow of a lantern in one of the windows.

CHAPTER 14

MADRID, JULY 2010, CALLE DE MIRA EL RÍO BAJA

It was a quarter to ten as Galíndez turned off the Ronda de Toledo into a fractious line of traffic, horns blaring as exasperated drivers looked for parking spaces near the flea market. She drummed her fingers on the wheel, increasingly impatient as the temperature inside the car rose, her discomfort made worse by the smart black suit. Still, it would be worthwhile if Ochoa was so taken with her that he wanted to share a few reminiscences about the old days.

And even if Ochoa wasn't captivated by her appearance, there was something else that made it likely he would open up to her: he wanted his money. Her story was credible enough: administrative errors made it necessary to verify a few details before the payments could resume. Particularly details about his past. And then, some light conversation about his time in the *guardia*. All of it captured by the small digital recorder in her bag.

'*Hijo de puta*.' Galíndez slapped a hand to her forehead as a truck pulled out in front of her, forcing her to brake sharply. Her hand wavered over the horn, about to blast him until she saw the parking space he'd vacated. She parked quickly and checked the recorder was working before setting off for her appointment with Señor Ochoa.

Ochoa's building was located on an anonymous steep hill lined with shops, their metal shutters pulled down and locked, the walls covered in graffiti. Plastic sacks of garbage awaited collection in doorways. A few of the sacks had split open, spilling their contents onto the cobbles, and a ripe smell hung in the warm air.

As she passed a gift shop, Galíndez paused to read a sign

offering palm readings without an appointment. Tempting though it was, the shop was shuttered and had been for some time from the look of it. A sign on the door: *Closed Due to Unforeseen Circumstances.* The effects of the recession struck everywhere.

The building was halfway up the narrow hill, skulking beneath a patina of grime. Dirty windows, shutters askew, curls of paint peeling from the front door. Galíndez scanned the list of residents' names next to the doorbells. *Machado-Garcia... Barzon... Robles... Ochoa.* Flat three, fourth floor. It was a couple of minutes before ten. Perhaps Ochoa would be impressed by her punctuality. She pressed the bell and waited. There was no response from the speaker by the door and she rang again. And then again, this time with short angry stabs of her finger.

'Forgotten your key? I'll let you in.'

A young man was standing behind her, holding out his key. Galíndez thanked him and stepped back to let him open the door, following him into a dingy entrance hall that smelled of wet plaster. She paused by the row of mailboxes on the wall and waited as the young man went into one of the ground-floor apartments before she made a move.

There was no lift, she realised. That was a pain – literally. Ochoa's flat was four floors up: four flights of narrow stairs in these tight boots with their precarious heels. And when she got there, he might not even be in. The only way to find out was to go and knock on his door. Loudly. She walked to the stairs, wincing at the sharp tap of her heels on the tiles.

As Galíndez reached the next flight of stairs, she waited, hearing the footsteps of someone coming down. A figure emerged from the shadows, an elderly man in a fedora and a well-cut dark suit. He had been handsome once, she imagined, and though his face was creased by the years, his eyes were still sharp and alert. As he reached the bottom stair he saw her and with a charming smile swept off his hat, exposing his bald head as he held an arm towards the stairs and waited with old-fashioned courtesy for her to pass.

'*Muchísimas gracias*.' Galíndez stepped past him onto the stairs, trying hard to keep her balance. 'You wouldn't be Señor Ochoa by any chance?'

'I'm afraid not, I've been visiting my sister. I don't know anyone else in the building.'

'Thanks anyway.'

'*De nada. Adiós.*'

The fourth floor was depressingly familiar, the windows just as unwashed as those on the landings below. Three *pisos* on this floor. One on either side of the stairs, a third tucked down a small corridor. She saw the number on his door as she approached, grateful for the threadbare length of carpet that muffled the sound of her heels.

Ochoa's door was half-open and she paused, listening for the sound of someone inside, hearing only the faint drone of traffic from the street. She put her head round the door. 'Señor Ochoa?' No one answered and she called his name again. When there was no reply, she went in.

From the look of it, the flat hadn't changed its decor in sixty years. The hall had a sour odour of fried food and neglect. The first door she came to was open and she saw an ancient bathroom with a stained toilet and tiny bath. Further along the hall was a bedroom, the curtains tightly drawn, throwing the room into sepia half-light. Ochoa certainly wasn't house-proud. The bed was unmade, the sheets and blankets pulled back carelessly. He must have been searching for clean underwear, since his socks and pants were strewn haphazardly over the grimy carpet. Very haphazardly, she thought, suspicious now. This chaos wasn't an old man's untidiness. Someone had been searching the place.

Cautiously, Galíndez went down the hall into the shabby living room. Ochoa only had a few pieces of dilapidated furniture. A TV set on a fragile-looking stand at one end of the room, a tattered sofa by the window overlooking the street and an old armchair near the door to the kitchen. And sitting in the armchair was Señor Ochoa.

Or rather the late Señor Ochoa, his head tilted back, his mouth open in the rictus of sudden death, his dentures hanging from his mouth. Identifying the cause of death didn't need her expertise. She saw the loop of wire tight around his neck, the trickle of blood where it cut into his skin.

Galíndez noticed a smell of urine as she bent over to touch his hand. He was still warm. She swore, loudly. Someone had garrotted a man who probably worked with Guzmán on the morning of her visit. She doubted it was a coincidence. No one knew she was coming here and it seemed unlikely Ochoa had told anyone, since he thought she was his new handler coming to reinstate his special payments from the *guardia*.

Galíndez paused to take stock, knowing she should dial 062 and call the killing in. If she didn't make the call, she'd be breaking God knows how many sections of the Code of Conduct. But then, if she did call, they'd want to know what she was doing here posing as Teniente Galíndez. That would also prevent her searching the flat again, a course of action that was rather appealing now she couldn't question Ochoa. No, it was unthinkable not to notify the *guardia*. This was a clear-cut case of murder, for God's sake. She knew what she had to do.

Her mind made up, she went down the hall and used her elbow to close the front door. Back in the living room, she checked under the carpets and behind the sofa. When she found nothing, she rifled through Ochoa's pockets. Nothing there either: just a dirty handkerchief and a few coins. Somewhere in the building a door slammed, interrupting her fevered speculation about the motive behind Ochoa's killing. The wire round his neck was Guzmán's signature method. That suggested Ochoa's death could be linked to his time at Calle Robles, though she had no definite evidence to show Ochoa worked with the *comandante*. That was why she was here. Perhaps it was also why the killer had paid him a call. Her skin prickled as another thought occurred: what if the killer was Guzmán himself? What if he knew she was coming here and didn't want his ex colleague talking to her?

She looked round, desperately seeking some niche or alcove where Ochoa might have hidden something that would throw light on his relationship with Guzmán. After twenty minutes she groaned with frustration. She'd searched every room now and found nothing.

Every room but one, that was, Galíndez thought as she went into the kitchen. Rows of shelves teeming with ancient packets and boxes, jars of condiments that looked as if they dated back to the Civil War. It would be easy to hide something in one of those. There were an awful lot of them for a single man and she doubted Ochoa was much of a cook.

Twenty-five minutes later, the kitchen was in a state of Galíndez-induced chaos. Every jar of flour, coffee and all the other containers Ochoa had amassed over the years had been opened, their contents emptied over the shelves or into the sink. And she'd found nothing. Staying here any longer was just pushing her luck. She frowned at the noise of her footsteps on the stone tiles. *These fucking heels.*

She paused, suddenly aware of a change in sound as she neared the door. She went back into the kitchen and took a few steps, hearing the brittle timbre of the heels modulate as she stepped on the tile nearest the door. The other tiles produced a more muted sound. She tapped the suspect tile with her heel again, harder. The noise was deeper, more resonant. Hollow.

Ochoa's carving knife slipped into the thin gap between the edge of the tile and its neighbour. With a little encouragement, the tile lifted cleanly from its resting place. Galíndez prepared herself for the disappointment of seeing wooden joists below as she lifted the tile, a few pale strands of cobweb trailing from the underside. But something gleamed in the dark recess below and she reached down to lift out a small metal box, the kind used for camera accessories. Inside was a cardboard folder, contents bulging. She opened the folder and saw an unlabelled reel of 8mm film. So Ochoa made movies? She put the reel to one side. That would have to wait until she found a suitable projector. Underneath the folder was a sealed envelope and beneath that a few black and white photographs held together by a paper clip. She examined the envelope, seeing the short message written on the front:

In the event of my death, this is for the attention of
Señora Remedios Ochoa.
Segismundo Ochoa, 23 Abril, 1982

Ochoa's will, she guessed, wondering if Señora Ochoa was still alive. In any case, it wouldn't hurt to take a look. She slipped her finger under the flap of the envelope and opened it. Inside was a single sheet of paper bearing one sentence.

I never stopped looking for you.

Galíndez folded the paper and shoved it into her pocket, allowing herself a cynical smile. True love would have to wait, there were other things she needed to attend to. She reached for the wad of photographs and slipped off the paper clip keeping them together.

The first picture was strange. Almost entirely black but for a distorted grey rectangle. She peered at it, starting to recognise the unusual angle from which it had been taken, realising the cameraman was standing on a flight of stone steps leading down into what appeared to be a dungeon. As she looked closer, she realised it wasn't a dungeon at all.

It was a cellar. The cellar she had visited only a few days ago in Legutio. She felt a chill as she realised the difference between what she'd seen that day and this picture. What she'd seen a week ago had been the aftermath. Three long-dead people with no hope of identifying their remains. This photograph showed them alive.

Four chairs in a row, a metre or so between each. There were people tied to the chairs, the detail of their faces lost in deep shadow. Despite the warmth of the day, Galíndez's hands were cold as she turned the photograph and saw Ochoa's inscription: *Morning of March 10th 1937, Villarreal.* Steady, careful handwriting.

Unlike the word scrawled underneath: *Before.* The ink used to write the word was different from that used for the caption. Ochoa must have added this annotation at another time.

The next photograph lay face down. She looked at Ochoa's writing on the back. Now, his annotation read Evening of March 11th 1937. Once again, a word scrawled below: After. After what? she wondered, though only for the moment it took to turn the photograph over.

The camera flash spilled bleached light over a scene of carnage. Taken from a similar angle to the other, perhaps even on the same step. The four dark shapes were transformed into a tableau of savage horror. On the far left, a metal chair lay on its back, empty. Just as she would find it seventy-three years later. The occupant of the chair to its right was slumped forward, still bound in position, his long hair spilling forward over his face. Something gleamed on the chest and thighs, reflecting the flash of the camera. Something shiny. A similar gleam around the feet as well. Blood. Lots of it. Blood that one day would reveal itself, glinting with the blue light of her luminol spray.

Looking at the next prisoner, Galíndez saw a similar configuration: the slumped body, the gleaming blood-shadow. This one must have been bound tightly: the body was still upright, though it had no head, just a ragged stump of neck. And now, the final victim, half buried in rubble. Something strange about the head, it seemed too small for an adult. Then she remembered: the top of the skull had been sliced off. A skull that was now in a plastic bag in her cupboard at the lab. *What the fuck happened?* If she'd come here a day earlier, she might have asked Ochoa that question, might even have found out why Guzmán had carried out these killings. *Mierda*, Ochoa might have been able to identify these people.

This wasn't the time to sit round asking questions with a corpse just across the room from her, his dentures dangling from his mouth. It was best to get out while her luck held. And then, as she closed the box lid, she froze as she heard someone turn the handle of the front door.

Carrying the metal case under her arm, Galíndez crept towards the hall. She was four floors up with no way out other than the stairs. She cursed herself for trying to be too clever, dressing up to get Ochoa talking but neglecting other details like staying alive.

Something pushed against the front door, straining it against the hinges. Whoever it was had put their shoulder to the door, trying to see if it would open quietly. The door shook but held firm. They'd have to smash it open if they wanted to get in and that would carry a risk of alerting the neighbours. Another thought: what if it was the good guys, the *policía* or *guardia*? No matter who it was, she was in trouble. And then a faint rustle as a piece of paper slid under the door. Footsteps fading as the person went back downstairs. Galíndez went to the door and retrieved the paper. A handwritten note.

> _YOU_ asked me to come round, you prick.
> Where are you? Call me when you get back

Galíndez waited a few minutes before she left the apartment, wiping everything she remembered touching clean of prints before she went downstairs. She crossed the third-floor landing, hearing only the faint drone of traffic outside. Below, on the ground floor, the front door closed with a loud metallic crash and she heard footsteps as someone hurried up the stairs. She stepped back, hoping the shadowed landing would prevent the passing tenant from seeing her in any detail. As she moved, her heel dragged on the worn tiles, painfully loud. Below her, the footsteps stopped abruptly.

Galíndez didn't move, tense in the sudden silence. A sharp metallic click, like someone cocking a pistol. She felt a sudden burn of adrenalin. Quietly, she put the metal box on the floor and straightened up, ready to face the person now climbing the stairs towards her with slow cautious footsteps.

A door opened on the floor below. Loud angry voices: a man and a woman arguing. The approaching footsteps stopped and a few seconds later Galíndez heard them retreating downstairs. She picked up the metal box, waiting until she heard the street door bang as someone left the building before she hurried down past the couple on the landing. They ignored her and carried on arguing, from the sound of it, about money.

The door slammed behind her as Galíndez went into the street. Cautiously, she looked round, scanning the faces of passers-by, wondering if the mystery visitor was out here, watching. No one gave her a second glance and she relaxed a little. The midday sun felt bright and clean after the dank twilight of Ochoa's building and her mouth watered at the smell of frying potatoes from a nearby bar as she hurried past the shuttered windows of the fortune-teller's shop.

She pushed the metal box into the boot of her car and drove away, past the flea market, vaguely aware of the flocks of tourists clustering round the stalls. Traffic was slow and she watched the vehicles ahead without interest, wondering whether she would be able to identify the victims in Ochoa's photos. And something else troubled her about the executions in that ruined building. Why had the bodies been left and the cellar sealed with concrete during a major offensive?

Behind her, a huge refrigerated truck unleashed a violent blast from the multiple array of horns on the roof of the cab. Galíndez looked up, startled, and saw the truck driver gesticulating wildly. The traffic was moving again. She sighed and pressed the accelerator, still preoccupied by those black and white images of violent death. Everything linked to Guzmán seemed to throw up more questions. Whether she could get answers to any of them she had no idea.

And that, she suspected, was exactly how Guzmán wanted it.

CHAPTER 15

OROITZ, OCTOBER 1954, ABADÍA DEL INMACULADO
CORAZÓN DE MARÍA

Guzmán struggled to keep his balance as he stumbled along the last few metres of muddy track into the shelter of the ancient walls. He took a moment to catch his breath, examining the entrance, a low arched doorway with a small carved virgin in a niche above the lintel. It was clear there would be no problem getting inside. Though the door was reinforced with iron bands, the wood was rotten and the ornate bands hung from their fittings.

He pushed open the door with the toe of his boot, aiming the rifle as he stepped into a narrow arched passageway. With such limited room for manoeuvre, the pistol was better suited for close-quarter combat so he drew the Browning instead. To his right were three evenly spaced wooden doors and he checked them, one after another, kicking open the door and entering quickly, scanning the room, pistol held out. All were empty, though the air was thick with a faecal reek, testimony to the long occupation of the building by the escaped lunatics.

The stench followed him down the passageway. Through the arched doorway ahead he saw the walls of a small chapel. Near one of the narrow windows an old oil lantern flickered in the fierce draught. It was the light he had seen from the escarpment. At the far end of the chapel was the altar, its large stone cross wavering in the feeble light from the lantern. As another massive gust buffeted the building, the lantern sputtered, sending a wave of dancing shadows rippling over the chapel walls. Not exactly home from home, he thought, taking off his sodden hat and throwing it onto the lid of a nearby crate to dry.

Other than the cross, there were few signs this had once been a place of worship. The pews were gone, used long ago as firewood. Now, lines of boxes and crates were arranged on either side of the aisle. He looked at the crates, suddenly curious. Unlike every other piece of wood in this crumbling mausoleum, these were not on the verge of disintegration. He leaned forward to inspect one and removed the screws from the lid with his knife. He pushed the lid aside and peered in, seeing a dull metal sheen in the sallow light. Surprised by the contents, he opened another. Yet another surprise.

This was not the work of lunatics, Guzmán thought angrily. The madmen didn't have laces for their shoes, far less crates of rifles and grenades. Nor did they have sacks of banknotes bearing the stamp of the Banco de Bilbao like those propped against the mildewed chapel walls around him.

Guzmán had been right that El Lobo would have hiding places for his supplies hidden up in the hills. That was what enabled him to carry out his robberies at will, without the need to visit village stores or raid farms. Even so, he'd expected the bandit might have a few modest stashes of tinned food, maybe some hay for his horse and a few boxes of ammunition, not a fucking arms dump like this.

He looked round, wondering how one bandit got all these crates up here. Even using mules it would be difficult to avoid being seen. He knelt by one of the crates and read the label by the flame of his lighter.

ÇUBIRY PÈRE ET FILS, AGENTS D'EXPORTATION

26 RUE DE VICTOR HUGO,
ST JEAN PIED DE PORT, FRANCE

A difficult task all right, though not for experienced smugglers. Dark rage burned as he thought about those French bastards in their absurd feathered hats and antiquated clothing. Because they looked like fools, he had not taken them seriously. That had been a serious oversight. The Çubiry had long experience in shifting contraband around this region. That was all well and good if the merchandise was destined for the *estraperlo*, the black market that augmented Spain's feeble economy. It was something else if they were selling weapons to the resistance. The first was a minor crime the authorities could ignore. The second merited a death sentence no matter what country the bastards lived in.

He could forget about burning ancient byres and shepherds' huts. This was El Lobo's lair and Guzmán needed to destroy it immediately. That had been his plan all along. With no weapons and no money to replace them, El Lobo's only option would be to hit another bank truck – using insider information as he had before, not knowing that the only shipment of money in this region would be in a truck full of civil guards.

He reached down and took a grenade from the second crate. Brand new. He put it on the lid of one of the unopened crates and cursed as it rolled off and clattered onto the floor. He smiled to himself. At least the pin was still in.

He unfastened his hunting jacket and rummaged through his pockets in search of a cigarette. Along the corridor, he heard the sudden howl of the gale and then the muffled impact as the door closed again. And then, the sound of heavy footsteps coming down the stone passageway towards him. The metallic clinking of someone wearing spurs. More than one, from the sound of it.

OROITZ 1954, MENDIKO RIDGE

Ochoa watched the smoke rise into the wind as the squad set fire to the remains of another derelict byre.

'There's a storm getting up, *Cabo*,' Ruiz called.

Ochoa looked toward Mari's Peak where scrawls of lightning traced white fire across the darkening sky.

'Be nice to get back to the *cuartel*,' Ruiz muttered, climbing back into the saddle. 'We must have burned a dozen of these things today. You really think it will stop El Lobo?'

'All you need to worry about is who's doing the cooking when you get back to barracks,' Ochoa said. 'I'm going to stick around and wait for the boss. You take the men back down to the *cuartel*.'

'Me?' Ruiz grinned. '*A sus ordenes, Cabo.*'

'And post sentries before you eat,' Ochoa said. 'The *comandante* likes things done in a proper military manner.'

'Don't worry, we don't want to get on the wrong side of him.'

As the squad moved off down the track, Ochoa trained his binoculars on the mountain, trying to pick out the convent through the gusting rain. He watched the slope for a moment and then spurred his horse forward. The ground was slick and treacherous, but he kept the horse moving at a brisk pace, troubled by the dark figure he'd just seen on the escarpment, climbing up towards the convent. The *comandante* was not alone up there.

OROITZ 1954, ABADÍA DEL INMACULADO CORAZÓN DE MARÍA

Guzmán moved quickly, looking for cover. There was space behind the altar, a small alcove sheltered from the rest of the chapel, and he moved towards it, quietly. His foot connected with something and he gritted his teeth as the lost grenade rattled away into the shadows below the altar. The footsteps in the passageway stopped.

Quietly, he slipped behind the altar. It was a good hiding space, protected by solid walls on each side. Behind him, he noticed a rotting wooden door. His view of the chapel was restricted, to a view of the first row of crates near the window. That was enough. Once they reached those, his visitors would make a good target. All he need do was stay put and let them come into range. And, as he waited, he saw his hat, perched on the crate where he'd left it to dry.

Two men came into the chapel. Wide-brimmed plumed hats, bandoliers of ammunition slung across their chests. Cavalry boots fitted with elaborate spurs.

231

A low cautious voice. 'Lobo?'

Guzmán pressed himself against the wall. As long as he didn't move, he was invisible to them. For now, at least.

'Lobo? *Dónde estás*?' The other man's voice, worried now.

They were getting closer; Guzmán saw their approaching shadows on the worn tiles.

Sudden caution in the man's voice. '*Attention*, François, *regarde le chapeau*.'

Guzmán didn't understand his words but he could interpret their sudden caution: they had found his hat. He heard the sound of weapons being cocked and slowed his breathing, ready to make his move.

The outside door opened with a dull thud and a stream of cold air blew down the passage, almost extinguishing the lantern. Slow, heavy steps in the passageway.

One of the Frenchmen called out, his voice tense. '*Qui est-ce*?'

A deep sonorous voice. '*Soy yo*, Lobo.'

Guzmán eased his head around the edge of the wall and stared past the two Çubiry at the figure in the doorway of the chapel. A man in a dark overcoat and black slouch hat. A big man, taller than Guzmán, and broader too. But it was the man's face that concerned Guzmán most. He had the face of a wolf.

Some massive injury, Guzmán guessed. The right side of Lobo's face was almost normal. The left side was a huge expanse of ivory scar tissue running from above the left eye down to the jawbone. The crude lines of scars where the wound had been stitched pulled the left side of the man's face up, giving him a perpetual lopsided snarl.

'*El dinero*?' one of the Frenchmen asked, switching to Spanish.

'It's here. Help yourself,' Lobo said. 'Count it if you want.'

A rustling sound, grunts from one of the men as he picked up a sack of banknotes.

'It's hard to carry so much cash,' one of the Frenchmen laughed.

'Much easier to spend it, no?' There was no humour in Lobo's voice.

The other man grunted with exertion as he helped his comrade with the sack.

Now was the time, Guzmán decided. Leap out and kill them all. He was too slow.

Two shots, flat and percussive. The heavy clatter of men and weapons on the stone floor.

Guzmán stayed where he was behind the altar wall. He hadn't expected Lobo was about to kill the deliverymen. Not that he minded, since the odds of him killing Lobo had just gone up. He stepped out from behind the altar, the Browning raised in a two-handed grip. The Çubiry were not the only ones who were careless, Guzmán realised as he saw Lobo half-hidden behind a row of crates, a *Yanqui* M1 carbine at his shoulder.

As the firing started, Guzmán threw himself flat and the chapel rang with demented echoes as Lobo emptied the thirty-round magazine in his direction, the bullets whining off the walls around him.

There was no arguing with such firepower and Guzmán sheltered behind the altar, looking for a way out. He saw the ancient door behind him, though he had no idea where it led or even if it would open. He looked round for other options and in the shadows behind the altar, he saw the dark object on the floor.

Guzmán slid forward on his belly, stretching until his hand closed on the grenade. In the chapel, he heard sudden heavy footsteps moving towards the passageway. Guzmán hadn't anticipated Lobo making a run for it and he came out from behind the altar, furious as he realised his quarry was escaping.

A metre away, he saw the box of grenades he'd opened earlier. He pulled the pin from the grenade in his hand and lobbed it into the crate. Then he turned and charged at the ancient door, his shoulder lowered.

The rotten wood disintegrated under the impact and Guzmán plunged through it, briefly glimpsing the escarpment rushing up to meet him. The impact as he hit the muddy slope winded him, and he slid for several metres down the sodden hillside before he could bring himself to a halt. A moment later, the convent roof exploded in a shower of rotting timber and stone, quickly followed by a second explosion that brought down a section of the front wall in a cascade of rubble.

Sheltering on the escarpment, Guzmán crouched in the mud, the Browning raised as he looked for El Lobo through the drifting smoke.

And there he was, outlined against the lurid flames, a gaunt figure in a long black coat, the deformed face iridescent in the light of the burning building. The range was too great to hit him and a moment later he heard hoofbeats fade in the darkness. As he got to his feet, Guzmán smiled to himself. Lobo knew he had a fight on his hands now.

A faint noise behind him. A tense voice. 'Put your hands up.'

'Don't be so fucking stupid,' Guzmán snorted. He turned and glared as Ochoa lowered his pistol. 'What the fuck are you doing here?'

'I saw someone following you up the slope to the hermitage, so I rode back to help.'

'It was Lobo,' Guzmán said. 'The place was packed with guns and explosives.' He hawked and spat. 'He rode away over the far side of the ridge.'

'So it's not over?'

'No, but thanks for reminding me of that, Corporal.' Guzmán put a foot in the stirrup of his horse, suddenly exhausted.

Ochoa rode up alongside him. 'Did you get a good look at him, sir?'

Guzmán nodded. 'Something's wrong with his face. He really does look like a wolf.'

The rhythm of the horses' hooves was comforting and Guzmán stayed quiet for a while, lost in thought. As they reached the valley, he looked up. 'Did you book me into that *pensión* in the village?'

'Just as you ordered, sir. The men say the lady who runs it is the best cook for miles.'

'I'll let you know about that,' Guzmán grunted. 'In the meantime, there's a slight change of plan. All the munitions in the convent had Çubiry labels on the boxes. You know what that means?'

Ochoa shook his head.

'It means we're off to St Jean tomorrow. I want to know more about these Çubiry.'

Ochoa raised an eyebrow. 'A spot of diplomacy, sir?'

Guzmán patted his holster, feeling the weight of the Browning against his side. 'Something like that, Corporal.'

OROITZ 1954, PENSIÓN ARALAR

The door of the *pensión* opened. A large woman, wiping her hands on her apron.

'Señora Olibari?' Guzmán inhaled the smell of cooking with relish.

'I'm the widow Olibari. The gentleman must be Señor Ramirez? I hope you've an appetite, señor,' she said. 'I've done enough *pochas* for six and there's only three guests tonight.' She saw his puzzled expression. 'White beans, señor, cooked with a ham hock until the meat falls from the bone.'

Guzmán liked the sound of that and followed her up the narrow stairs to his small room. He threw his baggage onto the bed and took a look through the window at the precipitous drop below. As long as the house didn't collapse tonight, that wasn't something to worry about.

He washed with cold water in the small bathroom on the landing and put on clean clothes. On his way up from the *cuartel*, he'd thought about getting an early night. Now, smelling Señora Olibari's renowned cooking, sleep was off the agenda.

As he went downstairs, the smell of cooking grew stronger. Señora Olibari seated him in the dining room at a table set for eight. The furniture in the room seemed to date from a couple of centuries earlier while the walls were decorated with a collection of ancient yokes and other pieces of animal husbandry, interspersed with religious icons. In the vaults below his *comisaría* in Madrid, Guzmán had seen the tools of the Inquisition. Many had been far less intimidating than this collection of rusty agricultural equipment.

He heard footsteps in the hallway as the two other guests joined him for dinner. One was a salesman dealing in irrigation equipment. The other was a priest, on his way to deliver mass at an isolated church deep in the countryside. Both dealt in things in which Guzmán had no interest. His only interest tonight was in Señora Olibari's cooking.

OROITZ 1954, PENSION ARALAR

'Delicious,' Guzmán finished his second helping. 'I've never had *pochas* before.'

'Don't let this be the last time, señor,' Señora Olibari said, spooning more beans onto his plate. 'The gentleman may as well finish them.'

'I couldn't possibly,' Guzmán said, allowing her to fill his plate with beans and ham. 'You've had no problems with rationing here then?'

'We grow what we eat here. If we relied on *los de Madrid*, we'd be eating grass.'

Guzmán held out his glass for more wine. 'Really? Who are the ones from Madrid?'

She snorted. 'The government. Not the *caudillo*, of course, he's just one man, after all. No, it's the ones who surround him, the cronies, the city people and those who run the black market.' She paused. 'Many people round here supported Franco, you know. A lot of our men joined the *Requetés* when the war started. They went to war to fight for God and the King.'

'Spain gave them little in return once the war ended,' the priest muttered.

'Those *Requetés* were good men, warriors of Christ who always took mass before battle,' Señora Olibari murmured with a dreamy expression.

The priest sighed. 'Though they were betrayed after Franco's victory.'

Guzmán smiled to himself. Even a priest was capable of treachery after a few drinks.

'And look what's happened since,' the salesman said, suddenly animated. 'Basque language forbidden, wealthy businessmen building factories that pollute the countryside and getting rich while ordinary folk are left to struggle.' He took a breath. '*Perdón*, Señor Ramirez. I get a bit worked up sometimes. We're treated as second-class citizens.'

'Better times are coming,' Guzmán said diplomatically as the widow poured her guests large glasses of *patxaran*. 'Though they won't come any quicker with that bandit El Lobo around.' He sniffed the aniseed aroma of the *patxaran* with distaste. This was one drink he'd never have any truck with.

'A fearful character, from all accounts,' the salesmen said, though he was more interested in his *patxaran*. 'I'm sure the *guardia civil* will take care of him before long.'

Señora Olibari laughed. 'Those oafs? Look out of the door tomorrow, señor, and see what they're doing to keep order. It takes them all morning to have breakfast. They wander round, poking into people's bags, threatening the men and talking dirty to the women. They treat us like they treated the Reds. They won't catch El Lobo. He's too cunning.' She noticed Guzmán's empty glass. 'Would you care for a drop of *patxaran*, Señor Ramirez?'

He saw the empty bottles on the table. The wine had run out. 'Thank you, señora.' At least it contained alcohol.

'Are you working, or is this a holiday?' Señora Olibari asked.

'I'm here on business,' Guzmán said. 'But tomorrow I'm off to France to see some friends. It's about time I paid them a visit, so I'm going to turn up unannounced.'

Señora Olibari's face lit up at the idea. '*Qué sorpresa.*'

He sipped the *patxaran*. 'You're right, señora. It's going to come as a big surprise.'

'B*uenos días*, Ana María, how are—' Isabel stood in the doorway, looking round in surprise. Overnight, the office seemed to have shrunk. The tables and shelves were now filled with teetering stacks of letters, arranged in alphabetical order, each stack carefully labelled with coloured post-it notes.

'You've been busy,' Isabel said. 'Wherever you are.'

Galíndez appeared from behind one of the towers of paper. Her face was streaked with dust. '*Hola.* I came in early to get these letters sorted so we could start coding them.'

'Christ, how early was that? This must have taken you ages.'

Galíndez shrugged. 'Only a few hours.'

Isabel ran a finger over one of the letters and stared at the dust on her fingertip. 'So what do we do with them? They're a health hazard.'

'They're a bit dusty, I admit,' Galíndez said, stifling a sneeze. 'But the information we get from them is going to be really useful.'

Isabel took a letter from one of the stacks and studied it. 'And all these were written to the Church authorities by parents wanting help to trace their stolen baby?' She frowned. 'We can't investigate ten thousand missing children.'

'Of course not,' Galíndez said. 'We're going to analyse the letters and identify which clinics had the highest rates of child theft, so we can focus the investigation on them.'

'That makes sense,' Isabel said. 'But we still have to read all of these?'

'We read them and then code the information in them,' said Galíndez. 'Then I analyse the data and identify patterns in it.'

'It's not enough just to read them?'

'Could you remember everything you've read in over ten thousand letters?'

'I suppose not.'

'Exactly, so we identify particular pieces of information and give them a numeric code,' Galíndez said, animated. 'Then we create a data collection sheet with a list of the questions we want answered and work our way through the letters, recording the information as we go.'

'So it's like filling in a questionnaire?' Isabel said, looking happier. 'I can do that.' She glanced at the stacks of paper surrounding them. 'I think.'

'*Estupendo*. I've already prepared the questions.' Galíndez pushed a sheet of paper across the table. 'You read the letter and then it's just a matter of ticking boxes as you go.'

'We tick boxes?' Isabel sighed with relief. 'Why didn't you say so in the first place?'

'You have to tick the right boxes.' Galíndez frowned. 'That's why I've written guidelines for completing the sheets.' She saw the look Isabel gave her. 'Just so we're consistent in the way we complete them.'

Isabel shook her head slowly. 'I wonder what shaped your personality, Ana? Was your *mamá* frightened by a computer when you were a baby?'

'I'll ignore that,' Galíndez laughed. 'In any case, I don't know why you're worrying, we already agreed your skills should be used for carrying out interviews with the parents.'

'But there are thousands of letters. Isn't it going to take ages to code them?'

'That's why I got some help.' Galíndez looked at her watch. 'She should be here soon.'

Isabel groaned. 'Not one of Luisa's students? They all talk as if they were force-fed dictionaries when they were tots.'

'All I know is that she's called Claudia and she's studying for an MA. I don't know the title of her dissertation, but you can bet it's extremely long.' She turned, hearing a knock at the door. 'Speak of the devil.'

A tall blonde young woman looked down at her. 'Dr Galíndez? I'm Claudia Infante, your temporary assistant.'

'Have a seat.' Galíndez introduced Isabel and then filled Claudia in on her plans for the data collection. Claudia picked up a copy of the coding sheet and flicked through it.

Isabel watched her. 'Looks horrendous, doesn't it?'

'I worked on a few surveys in my vacations,' Claudia said. 'I think it's pretty straightforward.' She looked at Galíndez. 'But I'm not very familiar with quantitative methods of analysis, Profesora Ordoñez doesn't like that kind of approach.'

'Tell me about it,' Galíndez muttered. 'Don't worry, just code them and I'll take care of analysing the data.'

Isabel looked again at the piles of letters. 'It's going to take ages for two people to get through all these, especially since we've got a deadline. That's what your friend the minister of the interior said, no?'

'You're friends with Rosario Calderón?' Claudia asked, impressed.

'I wouldn't say we were friends.' Galíndez glanced at the towering stacks of paper. 'Isabel's right. We need more people to help with the coding. I'll ask Luisa if we can borrow a few more students.'

Claudia looked up from the questionnaire. 'Maybe you should ask Profesora Vasquez? She's head of the School of Applied Statistics. My friend Angelina is on her research methods course and she said the *profesora* is always looking for placements for her students.'

'Really? I'll go and see her,' Galíndez said, heading for the door.

'This is more like it,' Isabel said, watching Claudia and the fifteen newly arrived statistics students filling in the data collection sheets. 'They even brought their own computers.' She glanced at the students again. 'Notice anything about them, Ana?'

Galíndez looked at the students for a moment. She shook her head. 'No. Should I?'

Isabel lowered her voice. 'Look again. Studious, obsessive attention to detail, rigid concentration on the job in hand? See how neatly they put the letters and coding sheets to one side when they've completed them. Who does that remind you of?'

Galíndez gave her a puzzled look. 'Who were you thinking of?'

'Never mind.' Isabel smiled. 'When do I start interviewing some of the parents?'

'It's all arranged,' Galíndez said. 'I contacted a parents' support group who're willing to talk to you about their experiences.' She handed Isabel a piece of paper. 'Here's their details. Their next meeting is this evening. Sorry it's such short notice.'

'That's OK, I can make it,' Isabel said. 'In the meantime, I suppose I'd better show willing and code some of these letters.'

'That's a great idea. I have to see Luisa in a few minutes but I'll be back by twelve. Can I buy you lunch?'

'You certainly can. Reading always gives me an appetite.'

As Galíndez left for her meeting with Profesora Ordoñez, she paused in the doorway for a moment, looking back at the students as they worked on the piles of letters, wondering what Isabel was talking about. They didn't remind her of anyone.

Claudia looked across the table, noticing Isabel hunched over a letter as she tried to find an appropriate code on her sheet. 'Are you are OK there, Izzy?'

'I think I'm OK, thanks, I'll let you know.' Isabel picked up the letter and studied it again.

The letter was addressed to the Bishop of Madrid.

23/Febrero/1993

Estimado Señor Obispo

I write to humbly request your Excellency's assistance with a matter of terrible injustice. I gave birth to a little girl in February of this year in La Clinica Sanidad GL in Fuenlabrada. After the delivery, I saw my daughter for only a few minutes before one of the nuns took her away while the doctor put in some stitches. Half an hour later when I asked to see her, I was told she had died. My husband and I were terribly upset but we were even more distressed when the head of the clinic told us the child had already been buried in order to spare us any further pain.

When we insisted on seeing her grave we were told she was in an unmarked plot in the Almudena Cemetery. We were then asked to leave the clinic. I wrote several letters to Sanidad GL without them giving me the courtesy of a reply. We have seen similar things reported in the news and we now think our child didn't die at all but was stolen and given to someone else. As your Excellency will understand, every day we suffer the agonies of the Cross thinking of our baby being brought up by strangers.

We beg you, Señor Obispo, as a Christian, as a priest and as a fellow human being, for the love of God, help us find out what happened to our child.

Humbly,
Sonia & Jorge Luis Perez

'God, how awful,' Isabel muttered. 'Do you think they would ever get over it?'

Claudia shrugged. 'I can't imagine how you could get over something like that.'

'It's a shame we can't see how they're doing now. That's what we used to do on my radio show: try to look for the happy ending to show how people got over adversity.'

'That must happen sometimes,' Claudia agreed. 'Like if they won the lottery. It wouldn't bring the child back but it might brighten up their lives a little.'

Isabel looked at the letter in front of her, thinking Claudia was right. Maybe things did change for the better for some people, despite the tragedy of having their baby stolen. She imagined a headline: *After the Heartache: Life's Still Worth Living, Say Parents of Stolen Child*. A little clichéd maybe, but a few pieces of good news would at least add some warmth to what was likely to be a depressing report.

She entered the names of the parents into Google, adding some extra terms to narrow the search: *Fuenlabrada, Stolen Children, Perez, Sonia, Jorge Luis.* A string of hits with numerous references to Sonia and Jose Luis Perez. Headlines from local papers, one from a national daily.

Claudia looked up from her keyboard. 'Isabel?' She hurried over to put an arm around Isabel's shoulders. 'Izzy, *que te pasa*? Why are you crying?'

'I'm being silly,' Isabel said, dabbing her eyes. She pointed to the screen. 'It's just so unfair after losing their child like that.'

Claudia saw two pages from *ABC* dated 6 May 1996. The first carried a photograph of the swearing in of the new prime minister, José María Aznar. The second was a black and white picture of a burned-out apartment. Firefighters' ladders leaned against the walls beneath shattered windows with dark scorch marks on the brickwork above them.

Tragic Parents Die in Fire

Less than a year after the sad death of their newborn daughter, fate again struck a terrible blow as Sonia and Jorge Luis Perez perished in a fire in their apartment in Fuenlabrada, Madrid last night. Official sources say the fire started accidentally, probably the result of faulty wiring.

Neighbours said Señor Perez was a keen DIY enthusiast though they were not sure whether he had undertaken any electrical work recently. A municipal police spokesman said they were treating the deaths as a tragic accident.

'These things happen, Isabel,' Claudia said, trying to comfort her.

'It's the injustice of it,' Isabel sniffed. 'They'd already suffered so much.'

'Coincidence is pretty scary.'

'That's what it is, I know: coincidence,' Isabel agreed. 'I could take any other letter off that pile, look it up and there're be no mention of the parents dying.' She thought for a moment. 'Pass me another, will you?' She took the letter and glanced through it. 'Same thing, different hospital. Eduardo and Belén Castillo. Their son was born on the sixteenth of January 1982. He was taken out to be washed. An hour later, they were told he'd died and been buried in an unmarked plot.'

'Look them up, it'll put your mind at ease,' Claudia said. 'I bet there's nothing.'

Isabel entered the names into Google and watched as the list of hits appeared.

'I'll get you a coffee.' Claudia got up to go to the vending machine in the hall. She stopped. 'Isabel? You've gone white.'

Isabel stared at the screen. 'Twenty-ninth of June 1992,' she whispered, struggling to control her voice. 'The bodies of Eduardo and Belén Castillo were recovered from their car yesterday in the Sierra de Gredos. Both were killed instantly after their car left the road and plunged down the side of a steep hill. The accident was discovered by a passing...' She looked up. 'I think we've got some checking up to do, don't you?'

'OK.' Claudia shrugged. 'Let's look at some more and see.'

'There you are, Ana María. I thought you'd got lost.'

Galíndez closed the door behind her, smoothing her shirt. 'It can be a bit of a struggle talking to Luisa.' She noticed Isabel's red eyes. 'Look at that. You must be allergic to the dust on these letters. Why don't we go out for some fresh air?'

'It's not an allergy,' Isabel sniffed. 'There's something you need to see.'

'OK, go ahead.' Galíndez sat down next to her.

'It's bizarre,' Isabel began. 'I started thinking about how sad these letters are and wondered if something positive might have happened to the couples later on. A happy ending, you know?'

Galíndez nodded, keeping quiet as she realised how upset Isabel was.

244

'I searched the net for one couple.' Isabel's voice trembled. 'They died in a house fire.'

'That's tragic, but it's just random chance, Izzy.'

'After that I did a search for another couple and found they'd been killed when they drove over a cliff in broad daylight.'

'It's a big data set, you get those kind of results now and then. It doesn't mean there's a connection. Correlation isn't the same as causation.'

'Sometimes, Ana María, you sound like one of those talking weighing machines.'

'I know you're upset,' Galíndez said quietly, 'but this is common in research. If you compare the *guardia civil*'s use of horses over the last fifty years with the crime rate for the same period, you find the fewer horses they have, the more crime there is. But no one believes giving up mounted officers leads to more crime. We call it a spurious relationship.'

Isabel looked at her, red-eyed. 'You're telling me horses commit crimes?'

'I'm saying there's no connection between the two things, it just appears that way.' She put a hand on Isabel's arm. 'You found two cases. There are thousands of letters.'

'Don't be so dismissive,' Isabel snapped. 'After I noticed those first cases where the parents were killed, Claudia helped me check some more. 'Ana, I looked up thirty cases. In twenty-one, the parents died in accidents or as the result of violent crime.'

Galíndez's face clouded. 'You're right,' she said. 'That doesn't feel like coincidence.'

'So what now?'

Galíndez opened her laptop. 'Have you got all those cases together?'

Isabel pushed a pile of letters across the desk. 'What are you going to do?'

'We need to incorporate parental death into the data collection,' Galíndez said. 'Then we can use it as an outcome variable.'

'Translation please.' Isabel frowned.

'It's a piece of information that measures whether something happened or not,' Galíndez explained. 'In this case, whether the parents died or not. We can then calculate whether other items of data appear to influence the likelihood of dying. And you know what? I think that the hospital where they had their child stolen from is going to be a key predictor. Because if those deaths weren't accidental, who had most to gain from their deaths?'

'The thieves,' Isabel said. 'With the parents dead, there'd be no more complaints, no one making trouble with the authorities. Case closed.'

'Exactly. And it's likely that the thieves were working in those hospitals, so we'll ask the students to check each case online to identify any parents who died after their child was stolen. Then they can record it with the other information.'

'Sorry.' Isabel wiped her eyes. 'I don't usually let things get to me like this.'

'It's not surprising, Izzy. This whole thing is a tragedy. But look on the bright side, when we've identified the hospitals with the highest rate of thefts, maybe we'll have enough evidence to make arrests.' She glanced at her watch. 'How about some lunch?'

'We'll have to hurry,' Isabel said. 'I'm meeting that parents' support group later.'

'Would you mind if I came along? Maybe we could get a drink afterwards?'

'Good idea.' Isabel nodded. 'I've a feeling we're going to need one.'

MADRID 2010, SALA DE REUNIONES, CENTRO SOCIAL,
CALLE COLOMER

Galíndez sat in the meeting room of a chilly municipal building near Las Ventas bull ring, giving the parents an overview of her investigation. The parents listened politely. They'd met others like her over the years. They came and went, their interests changing in response to the availability of funding and shifting trends in academic interest. Many felt there was no reason to think Galíndez would be any different.

Before she introduced Isabel, Galíndez offered to answer any questions the parents might have about the project. Unexpectedly, one woman asked about the explosion at Guzmán's *comisaría* the previous year. Taken by surprise, Galíndez started to say she didn't like to talk about it but stopped herself, realising how ironic that would be when she was asking these people to share the most traumatic event of their lives. Instead, she described how her determination to uncover Guzmán's crimes had nearly got her killed. That broke the ice. These parents had been obstructed and fobbed off by officials for years. Hearing a researcher willing to put her life on the line to discover the truth got their respect. Now the parents were more receptive, Galíndez decided it was time to introduce Isabel.

Isabel was a revelation. Most of the people in the room were familiar with her radio show and were only too pleased to tell their stories. She handled each contribution with consummate skill, asking questions that frequently brought tears to her respondents' eyes yet left them feeling validated, grateful she'd touched on an aspect of their lives that had been ignored until now. When some of the parents got upset, Isabel consoled them with a perfectly judged comment that gave the right level of empathy and understanding without seeming patronising or dismissive. At the end of each contribution, Isabel reflected on the salient details of what they'd said, highlighting key points she thought the authorities ought to address and repeatedly emphasising the central issue: the need to bring to justice those who had taken part in the theft of thousands of children following the Civil War. At the back of the room, Galíndez sensed the audience bonding with Isabel as she raised new points and questions, quickly moving on if things became too painful.

And things were painful, because at the heart of this was the same ghastly story: parents going to a clinic or hospital, nervous and excited by the imminent arrival. Finally seeing an end to the waiting and false alarms as the baby was delivered. Tears of laughter, marvelling at the tiny bundle in the mother's arms as she rested, thinking dreamily about the future. Not knowing the ordeal was just beginning as nurses or nuns took her baby away to be cleaned up. Relaxing as she waited for the infant to be brought back, the afterglow turning to disquiet at the length of time it was taking. The sudden apprehension as a doctor or priest appeared to announce the baby was dead. The strange callousness as the heartbroken parents were ushered from the hospital, unable to understand why their child was already buried in an unmarked grave.

It went on for so long. Thousands of lives blighted by those they trusted: doctors and medical staff, nuns and priests, their crimes assisted by countless officials for whom corruption was a part of their organisational culture. In Spanish society, authority had been respected – feared even – following the Civil War. Calling the word of medical professionals into question was difficult and reporting them to the police a waste of time, since often they had been bribed. In such a moral vacuum, the risks were small and the profits enormous.

The demand for children was constant and to meet it, the child thefts evolved into an industry that would outlive Franco. It preyed on those least able to pursue the matter: the poor, unmarried mothers, or sometimes anyone about to give birth whose baby could be sold to someone willing to pay the price of a small apartment for an infant.

Niños robados – stolen children. A crime disguised by those involved as one of life's tragedies. Until the rumours began once democracy was re-established, fuelled by the mounting suspicion of bereaved parents. The slow emergence of cases where parents were reunited with a long-lost child, the news spreading disquiet as thousands of other parents realised what might have happened to them.

Hearing the testimonies at first hand was raw and brutal. The woman talking to Isabel broke down, unable to continue. In the shadows at the back of the room Galíndez found herself dabbing her eyes with a tissue as she listened to the woman's grief.

It was getting late. Isabel saw the janitor waiting by the door, ready to lock up the building, and brought the meeting to a close, thanking the parents for giving voice to their suffering, explaining how the investigation would make politicians aware of the issues and, hopefully, pressure them to act. It was a moving speech and the audience rose to their feet, cheering Isabel as their new champion. Many rushed forward to embrace her, others waited, more reserved, wanting to thank her with a few private words.

When all the parents had gone, Isabel strolled between the lines of chairs to the back of the hall, her eyes flashing, pleased at a job well done. She was beautiful, Galíndez thought, watching her. A beautiful person in every sense.

Isabel saw the tissues in her hand. 'Did it upset you, Ana?'

Galíndez looked down, composing herself. 'It makes me so angry.'

'You know what they say,' Isabel said. 'Don't get mad, get even. Find the people who stole those babies.'

'You were brilliant,' Galíndez said, getting to her feet. 'They loved you.'

'It made them feel better for now but the effect will soon wear off. I just hope we can track down some of the people responsible.'

'We will.' Galíndez glanced at her watch. 'It's getting late. Can I get a lift back to the university to get my car?'

'Why not come back with me and let me cook you something? We can drive in together in the morning.' Isabel slipped an arm around Galíndez's shoulders. 'You look like you could use some cheering up.'

Galíndez leaned against her, feeling the warmth of Isabel's breath on her hair, the soft weight of her hand on her shoulder. She closed her eyes, seeing an image of herself, buried in the smoking rubble of Guzmán's *comisaría*. She pulled away. 'Don't touch me.'

Isabel looked at her in surprise. 'What's wrong?'

'This,' Galíndez muttered. 'We're colleagues. It's not professional.'

'I didn't mean to offend you.' Isabel's voice was brittle. 'I'll drop you at the campus.'

They walked to the car without speaking. Around them, the city throbbed with the noise of traffic.

Isabel sat behind the wheel, staring ahead.

'Look, it's not you—' Galíndez began.

'God, don't talk to me in clichés,' Isabel cut in, 'I made a mistake.' She reached for the ignition key. 'I won't make it again.'

The university grounds were hidden in shadow as Isabel pulled up by the entrance to the faculty car park. As Galíndez got out, she leaned back into the window. 'The thing is—'

'No, Ana María, I got the message the first time,' Isabel said. 'Forget it.' She accelerated out of the car park, scattering loose gravel into the darkened shrubbery.

Slowly, Galíndez walked to her car. Behind her, she heard a screech of tyres and turned, thinking Isabel was coming back. But it wasn't her, just a pale blue people carrier heading towards the centre of the campus.

She climbed into her car and sat for a while, trying to think how she could explain things to Isabel. But these were things she couldn't explain to herself. It was best not to try. There was no room for anyone else in her life. She bore his mark now, that long pale scar down her left side: Guzmán's brand, indelible and contaminating.

She leaned forward and opened the glove compartment, reaching for the plastic tube of painkillers. She shook a couple of tablets into her hand and swallowed them. Slumping back in her seat, she looked out into the warm night, seeing the shadowy campus, its paths and kerbs illuminated by pale slanting light.

She sat quietly, resting her hands on the wheel, wondering if these feelings would ever pass. In the mirror, she saw the dark tower of the faculty building. The cleaners were turning out the lights and as she watched, the detail of the building was gradually erased, floor by floor, until only the small emergency lights in the stairwells were visible.

CHAPTER 17

FRANCE, OCTOBER 1954, ST JEAN DE PIED DE PORT

Guzmán slowed as the bend ahead revealed another vertical drop behind a flimsy wooden fence.

'That's the road to St Jean on the right,' Ochoa said, glancing at the map on his knee.

'About time.' Guzmán gave him a dark look. 'You're not still worrying about us crossing the border, I hope?'

'It was you who said we had to keep a low profile, *jefe.*'

'And we are,' Guzmán said. 'But since I'm in command, we're doing it my way.'

'Going into France after a bunch of smugglers isn't going to be low profile if the French authorities find out.'

Guzmán hunted in his jacket for a cigarette. 'I want to know why the Çubiry have been supplying arms to El Lobo. If that's all right with you, Corporal?'

Ochoa stayed quiet, looking at the passing sprawl of white houses, their red-tiled roofs glowing in the early morning sun. Soon the clusters of buildings grew more numerous and, in the distance, against the green mass of the foothills, they saw St Jean de Pied de Port, an uneven line of rooftops shrouded in mist.

'What's our plan for today, sir?'

Guzmán slowed, seeing a large crowd a couple of hundred metres further on, walking towards the village. 'I'll see what I can find out about the Çubiry from the locals. There's bound to be someone in need of a few pesetas.'

'They use francs here.' Ochoa saw Guzmán's expression and wished he'd kept quiet.

'Peasants are peasants, Corporal. They want money no matter where it comes from and if I want a lecture from you on the currency of effeminate European countries, I'll ask for it.'

'What do you want me to do in St Jean, sir?' Ochoa asked, changing the subject.

'I want you to take a look at the goods yards near the station. Look out for any merchandise with Çubiry labels that's bound for Spain and make a note of the address. Do you speak French?'

Ochoa nodded.

'Then tell me what that says.' Guzmán pulled to a halt by a large gaudily painted sign.

'There's a fiesta of Basque sport today,' Ochoa translated. 'Wood-chopping, stone lifting and ram fights.'

'*Jesús Cristo*, I'd rather shoot myself in the leg. I can throw stones any time.'

'The sign also says there's food and drink available all day, sir.'

'In that case, I'll start there. If there's drinking, it might make the locals more willing to chat about the Çubiry.'

'Let's hope so.'

'Fucking hell, cheer up, will you?' Guzmán snapped. 'We'll check out the Çubiry and then go back to Spain later tonight.' He slowed to a halt as they reached the crowd bustling to the village. 'Be back here at seven thirty, I'll park over there by the war memorial.'

Ochoa slammed the door behind him. In a few moments he caught up with the crowd and melted into the throng, turning up his coat collar, another country bumpkin come to town for the day. Ochoa was a useful man to have around, Guzmán thought, though his persistent melancholy was irritating. He was probably still pissed off at his wife for running away. He'd get over it, they always did. Apart from the ones who ended up blowing their brains out in a lonely hotel room, of course.

Guzmán parked by the war memorial. Making sure no one was watching, he slipped off the shoulder holster and hid it with the Browning under the driver's seat. If he was stopped by the French police, he didn't want the complications that would arise when they found he was armed. The French were prissy about things like that, especially if they involved members of the Spanish secret police. Still bearing a grudge about Franco's support for the Nazis, no doubt, the petty bastards.

He got out of the car, glad to stretch his legs after the long drive. The trees were starting to shed their leaves and the village had an autumnal feel. As he crossed the bridge over the river, he saw a bar on the far side, its terrace crowded with noisy customers, and decided a drink would be in order. Today was a fiesta, after all. Pushing his way through the scrum at the bar, he ordered beer and a sandwich packed with links of *txistorra*, the thin Basque sausage. The spicy meat was delicious and he wolfed it down and ordered another.

From the terrace, Guzmán noticed a stream of people heading up the road towards a field where large signs announced the Basque Sports Day. It was a popular event, judging from the number of people going in that direction. He finished his beer and followed them.

The field was crowded. A line of big canvas marquees ran along one side and he inhaled the aroma of meat cooking on charcoal braziers and improvised griddles. In the centre of the field, some sort of competition was about to begin. To make sure he was able to enjoy the spectacle fully, Guzmán wandered into one of the tents and bought a large beer before joining the crowd waiting for the start of the contest.

The contest involved several sturdy men lifting a large rock, the winner being the one with the most lifts. The rules were easy enough to grasp, though as entertainment Guzmán found it absurd. The other spectators, however, were entranced. Then again, watching paint dry was probably the highlight of these peasants' sporting calendar, he guessed.

After a couple more beers and some lamb chops, Guzmán found himself much better disposed towards watching two sweating yokels exert themselves to ridiculous levels of physical discomfort while the spectators ate and drank to excess around them.

Something nudged him in the ribs and he turned, annoyed to find a short, swarthy peasant huddling against him. The man gave him a smile consisting mostly of gums. Guzmán stared at him. 'Fuck off, you inbred bastard.'

'Ah, *Spanyol*?'

'No, I'm Napoleon, you moron,' Guzmán said evenly. '*Hablas Español*?'

The man nodded, not understanding a word. '*Spanyol très bien*.' He grinned. '*Les Espagnols sont forts, mais les basques sont plus forts*.' He pointed to the two men in the ring, grunting and straining as they raised vast stones above their heads. You had to give them credit, Guzmán thought magnanimously, they were strong. Strong and relentlessly boring.

Guzmán and his unwanted new friend abandoned their conversation, distracted by a commotion on the far side of the field where a raucous group of men were tramping across the grass. Guzmán thought they were gypsies at first but as they came nearer, he saw the gaudy waistcoats and tooled leather riding boots. The fashion sense of the Çubiry Clan was becoming annoyingly familiar.

The man at his side tugged his sleeve, suddenly alarmed. '*Allons-y*.'

'Get off my arm.' Guzmán spoke slowly in Spanish, raising his voice so the man could understand. Freed from his annoying company, he turned back to watch the stone lifting.

Someone touched his arm and he turned, thinking his toothless friend had returned.

'*Merde*, I thought so. It's my friend from La Cueva.' Etienne Çubiry gave Guzmán a yellow-toothed smile. 'Did you bring your whisky?'

'It's going to be about a month until we get another shipment,' Guzmán said. 'I'll bring a few barrels for you to try once I know the date of the delivery.'

Etienne nodded. '*C'est bon*. We have an office near the station, ask for me or my father.' One of his gang called out, beckoning him to the drinks tent. Etienne grinned, '*Excusez-moi*, I go now to get drunk, it's a fête, after all, no?'

Etienne hurried after his companions and Guzmán noticed their sudden animated conversation as he caught up with them. Some of the men looked back at him. Guzmán returned their sullen looks as he sipped his beer, deep in thought. And what he thought was that the first one of them to try anything would get his glass in their face.

'Excuse me, monsieur?'

Guzmán turned and saw a small, stocky Basque, sporting a long thick beard.

'*Perdón*,' the man said in a low voice. 'My name is Fermín Etxeberria. I couldn't help but notice you speaking to that French gentleman just now.'

'I wouldn't call him a gentleman,' Guzmán said as Etienne and his pals disappeared into one of the tents. 'What's it to you?'

The man glanced round, nervous. 'I can tell you a lot about him if you're interested.'

Guzmán realised he'd found an informant.

'That's very kind. You're a good Christian soul helping a stranger, is that it?'

'No one does something for nothing, I'm sure the gentleman understands?'

'Only too well,' Guzmán said. 'How much?'

'I could tell you plenty with a drink or two inside me,' Etxeberria said. Raucous laughter came from the drinks tent. Clearly the Çubiry were getting warmed up.

'We'll go over there.' Guzmán pointed to a tent where a man was basting lamb on a griddle. He was unsure about Etxeberria. If people sold information cheap, it was usually because it wasn't worth having. On the other hand, since it was cheap, he might as well hear it. And in any case, the lamb smelled so good it would be a crime not to try it.

The tent was crowded with farmers and shepherds, filling the air with the fug of black tobacco and the musky odour of their animals.

Etxeberria asked for *patxaran*, which pleased Guzmán enormously since it was dirt cheap. He ordered brandy and a plate of the lamb, beaming at the ruddy-faced cook as she gave him a large plate of roast meat, the skin brown and crisp, the meat pink and glistening, surrounded by soft roasted garlic cloves and red peppers.

Guzmán led his would-be informant to a corner of the tent, where seating was provided in the form of rough wooden crates. He balanced his plate on his knees while he tore open a piece of bread and filled it with roasted red peppers and garlic and several large chunks of seared meat. He held the sandwich in both hands as he raised it to his mouth, aware of the little Basque's avid attention.

'I bought you a drink,' Guzmán growled. 'Be grateful for what you've got.' He took a bite from the sandwich and chewed happily. 'So, tell me about the Çubiry.'

Etxeberria was nervous. 'They've lived here a long time, señor.' He paused. 'I'm sorry, I don't know your name.'

'That's right, you don't. Keep talking.'

'The Çubiry family settled here after the war with Germany,' Etxeberria began, eyeing the lamb on Guzmán's plate. 'I wonder if I could just have a small piece—'

'Which war?' Guzmán interrupted. 'The last one?' He took another slice of lamb and added it to his already well-filled sandwich.

Etxeberria shook his head.

'*Hombre*, this isn't a radio quiz,' Guzmán grunted. 'Be specific.'

'The one before that. The Franco-Prussian war of 1870.'

'Makes no difference.' Guzmán took another bite of sandwich. 'The French always lose.' He reached for his brandy. 'The meat here is excellent, I must say.'

'I live in Spain,' Etxeberria muttered. 'I've forgotten what meat tastes like.'

'They say it's bad for you.' Guzmán gestured to the woman behind the counter to bring more drinks. 'You'll be happier with *patxaran*.' He leaned forward menacingly. 'Though you won't be getting that if you don't tell me something useful.'

'Grandfather Çubiry was an ex-soldier, they say,' Etxeberria continued, anxious to please. 'When he settled here, he turned his hand to crime: stealing horses, cattle rustling, smuggling – you name it, if it's criminal, they're involved in it.'

'They sound like the Spanish government.' Guzmán paused to take their drinks from the ruddy-faced woman. 'Don't stop,' he told Etxeberria, 'but try to make it more interesting.'

'They say the Çubiry have links with organised crime in Paris. They have more armed men in their chateau than the local gendarmes and the *guardia civil* avoid them when they cross the border into Spain as well.'

'So who's the boss?' Guzmán asked. 'Grandfather Çubiry?'

'No, señor. He died long before the Civil War. Suicide, they say.'

'Really? How did he kill himself?'

'He stabbed himself in the back,' said Etxeberria. 'The clan leader now is Grandfather Çubiry's son, Abarron. That was his son Etienne who you were talking to.'

Guzmán drank more brandy. 'So really, you're saying they're an undesirable bunch?' He scowled at his would-be informant. 'I have to tell you, that's hardly a revelation.'

'They're dangerous,' Etxeberria muttered. 'The Baron had his own sister killed.'

'Now you're talking,' Guzmán mumbled through a mouthful of food. 'Why?'

'She wanted to marry a man from across the border, a schoolteacher,' Etxeberria went on. 'Even though he was a fellow Basque, Baron Çubiry forbade the marriage.' He swallowed a mouthful of *patxaran* – without wincing, Guzmán noted – before carrying on. 'She eloped and married him in Spain. They settled in San Sebastián and had three children. Fifteen years later the war broke out.'

'Fucking hell, you should pay me to listen to this,' Guzmán snorted. 'Get to the point.'

'It was fifteen years after they'd married,' Etxeberria continued. 'Baron Çubiry took advantage of the war to bribe some of the troops who'd captured San Sebastián. They shot his sister and two of the sons. The third son was injured but they left him alive so the schoolteacher would have a constant reminder of what he'd lost.' The little Basque sat back. 'They say the Çubiry never forget an insult and no insult ever goes unpunished.'

Guzmán took a handful of change from his pocket and put it on top of a nearby crate. 'Here, get yourself a plate of lamb.'

'Would the gentleman be offended if I kept the cash instead?'

'Not at all,' Guzmán said. 'The gentleman would be most impressed by your self-restraint.' He got up and left the humid atmosphere of the tent, hearing excited voices rattling in Basque as people hurried towards the centre of the field.

'Jesús is here,' someone shouted in Spanish.

Guzmán looked round, curious. He expected many things from these Basques, but the second coming certainly wasn't one of them.

A crowd had formed around the chalked circle where the contests took place. Inside the circle, Guzmán saw two lines of big logs arranged in parallel. He had no idea what they were about to do with those but at least it would be a change from stones.

The crowd was blocking Guzmán's view, but one thing was sure, whoever was about to take part in this contest wasn't popular with the Çubiry, judging from their jeers and catcalls. He looked over the rows of heads in front of him at the object of their derision, a giant of a man, a good half-metre taller than Guzmán and much broader and heavier. The giant looked at the crowd gathered around him with a vacant expression. A simpleton, Guzmán guessed, watching his face. Strong but stupid. He seemed to have the intelligence of a small child, judging from his uncertain demeanour, smiling when he discerned a friendly voice, frowning when he heard the jeers from the Çubiry. As he turned, Guzmán tensed, seeing a mass of scar tissue on the left side of the big man's face. He turned to a plump man next to him, his thick beard speckled with crumbs and pieces of food. 'Who's the big guy?'

'Jesús Barandiaran, señor. The poor lad's not good for much apart from these sports.'

'And that one?' He pointed to the other man in the ring.

'That's Javier Bidane. He's the best *aizkolari* in Vizcaya – many say in all the Basque country. Put your money on him, señor, you won't lose a *céntimo*.'

Guzmán didn't hear the man's advice. He was too busy thinking about how the scars on Jesús Barandiaran's face made him look like El Lobo. Not only that, the big man had a similar build to the bandit.

Bidane was swinging his axe now, loosening up for the contest. As he watched, Guzmán couldn't help noticing the axe seemed to pass awfully close to the spectators. Perhaps accidental decapitation was part of the contest, he thought, watching Bidane's balletic movement as he held the heavy axe in one hand, spun it dexterously into the air and then caught it as it fell.

Jesús Barandiaran had left his axe buried in one of the big logs and he wrenched it from the wood with one hand as his opponent finished his display. Guzmán realised the big man was about to attempt the same moves Bidane had just demonstrated. He decided to move back a few paces. As the vast Basque lifted the axe, the Çubiry burst into a renewed frenzy of insults. Guzmán could hardly blame them. This simple giant could hardly walk properly, never mind swing an axe with the same skill as his opponent. He would be better off in a circus, being booed and mocked for a living.

The crowd watched astonished as Jesús threw the axe above his head and caught it behind his back as it fell in a gleaming blur. After several more manoeuvres, he looked across at his opponent and nodded. It was time to begin.

There were roars of excitement as the two men jumped up onto their respective piles of logs and began chopping furiously, showering the spectators with wood chippings. It was skilful and artfully done, Guzmán observed, stifling a yawn. But it was a shame to watch men chop wood while there was still some excellent lamb to be had and he returned to the marquee.

Inside the tent, the lamb was being pulled from the brazier and Guzmán savoured the aroma as the cooks began cutting the meat.

His hungry anticipation was interrupted by a sudden commotion outside. Intrigued by the notion that something exciting or even interesting might be about to take place, he went to investigate.

The gang of *Çubiry had tired of watching the contest and* were now milling round Jesús Barandiaran, grunting and swinging their arms, calling him an ape. Distraught, Jesús let the axe fall to the ground, waving his huge hands at the men dancing around him in a fruitless attempt to keep them away. He was too slow, Guzmán saw, as the Çubiry took turns to run in and tap Jesús on the back, cackling as they ducked away before he could confront them.

It was unfair, but Guzmán was hardly going to get into a fight with the Çubiry just because they were bullying a simple wood-chopper. For all he knew, this might be part of the entertainment. On the point of going back into the tent, he paused as he saw the other wood-chopper throw down his axe and plunge into the gaudily dressed Çubiry. Finally, things were getting interesting.

Bidane moved with remarkable speed and Guzmán chuckled as Etienne Çubiry took a punch to the belly that dropped him as if he'd been shot. It was clear Bidane could handle this lot on his own and Guzmán glanced round, wondering if anyone was taking bets. Disappointingly, they were not.

Unexpectedly, Jesús Barandiaran made a move, delivering a wild but accurate punch that sent one of the Çubiry boys flying backwards onto the grass and then, without pausing, he seized another of the gang by the collar and threw him into the stack of half-chopped logs. It was obvious the Çubiry boys had no taste for a fight against someone able to defend themselves, Guzmán thought, watching them retreat across the field, yelling outraged threats at the two wood-choppers as they went.

With the excitement over, Guzmán returned to the tent where his plate of lamb waited on the counter. He paused, hearing a strange whistle followed by shouts and laughter as someone pushed through the crowd towards the wood-choppers. Guzmán sighed and left the lamb, anxious once more not to miss anything.

A man dressed in shepherd's clothing was slowly weaving his way through the spectators. As he neared the wood-choppers, he whistled once more before setting off across the field at a sprightly pace that was surprising for a man of his years. When he repeated the whistle, Jesús Barandiaran obediently ambled after him.

Realising the two men would pass him on their way to the gate, Guzmán stepped back under the awning of the marquee to avoid being seen. He watched, puzzled, as they went out into the lane leading back to town, wondering why an old shepherd like Mikel Aingeru was leading the giant Basque wood-chopper around like a tame bear.

FRANCE 1954, ST JEAN PIED DE PORT

It was seven thirty and the sky was dark with rain clouds as Guzmán walked through the deserted village to the station. There were no passengers on the platform and no sign of Ochoa. Slow drops of rain began to fall, and he returned to the car to have a cigarette. He was a little drowsy, possibly from the wine, beer and cognac he had drunk throughout the day together with a few tapas and, of course, a hearty lunch. In his pocket was a paper bag containing a half-eaten pig's cheek. Opening the door, he took the bag from his pocket and threw it onto the verge. You could go off things.

Guzmán had just started to doze when the sound of voices made him look up. A group of men were coming towards him, led by Etienne Çubiry. As the group passed the car, Guzmán pulled the brim of his hat down to hide his face, watching them in the rear-view mirror as they turned into a narrow street that led to the river. They were probably going home for dinner, he realised, with a pang of jealousy. And then it struck him: perhaps this was his chance to take a look at Chez Çubiry. He reached for the Browning under his seat but, once again, thought better of it. There was no love lost between the French and Spanish governments. It would cause a diplomatic incident if he was arrested carrying a weapon.

He climbed from the car and turned up the collar of his coat as he followed the gang down dark cobbled streets, the shops now shuttered and locked. In front of him, he heard the boisterous chatter of the Çubiry echoing in the autumn air as he trailed them along streets where pale lights glinted through chinks in the wooden shutters.

Ahead, across a narrow bridge, was an arched gate. Beyond it, a steep cobbled street rose past the shadowed outline of a church. Guzmán watched from the doorway of a pharmacy as the Çubiry crossed the bridge in a staccato clatter of boots and turned onto a path running along the riverbank. A moment later, he followed, guided by their noise through the dark trees and bushes. After ten minutes, the Çubiry rattled across a wooden bridge and Guzmán saw vague lights from a huddle of low buildings behind a wire fence. Beyond the fence, the sombre outline of a dilapidated chateau, its detail lost in shadow, a few stuttering candles in some of the windows the only sign of occupation. He heard a sharp voice give a command and saw a flicker of light as the gate opened. A moment later, it closed again.

Guzmán crossed the bridge and sheltered under a knot of dripping trees near the gate, listening for voices, though he heard only rain and the slap of the river against its banks.

A handwritten sign hung on the gate, the inked letters now streaked.

Exportation Çubiry, Accès Interdit

The fence was an ugly construction of wire strung between concrete posts about two metres high, topped here and there with rusted strands of barbed wire. The Çubiry seemed relaxed about their security, since there were several places where an intruder could be over the fence in a matter of seconds. An intruder like Guzmán, anyway.

The rain grew heavier. This was no night for standing around. He put a hand on the gate, testing it as he heaved himself up. Nothing stirred on the other side and he dropped down into the compound, listening carefully as he moved in the direction of the house. He tensed as he heard voices coming towards him. Men chatting, their boots splashing in the mud as they approached. Cautiously, he drifted into a thicket of bushes, grateful for the protection of their sodden leaves as the two men went by. They were not taking an evening stroll, that was clear: one carried a shotgun, the other wielded a large cudgel. The men continued their conversation under the trees for a few minutes before moving on, unaware of Guzmán's presence a couple of metres away.

His eyes growing accustomed to the darkness, Guzmán noticed the array of abandoned vehicles and equipment littered across the grounds as he worked his way closer, seeing the detail of Chateau Çubiry emerge from the rain. A sullen, cheerless building, exuding abandonment and neglect. Most of the windows were dark, suggesting the building was not fully occupied, though, occupied or not, he had already decided he was going in.

The ground-floor windows were tightly shuttered. But Guzmán was skilled in such things and soon forced one open. Behind the shutter the window pane was broken and he slipped his hand through the hole in the jagged glass and felt for the handle. The window creaked open and he climbed in, careful to close both window and shutter once he was inside.

The room was in total darkness, the air rich with a smell of neglect and decay. Guzmán winced at the creaking floorboards as he moved across the room, arms outstretched, feeling for obstacles in his path until he found a door and went out into a dimly lit hallway. To his left was a wide staircase leading up to a landing. To his right, the hall disappeared into shadow. Dimly lit was better than no light at all and he went upstairs, making for the door at the end of the landing.

He found himself staring into a long, narrow gallery, illuminated by a smoking oil lamp on a table near the fireplace. The gallery had once been elegant, that was clear. The elaborate gilt cornicing on the ceiling a reminder of the aristocratic chic and refined taste of a bygone age. But what remained of the room was now a mocking echo of what it had once been. And what remained was a nightmare.

The carefully decorated walls were marred by huge patches of damp, the wallpaper hanging loose, weighed down with green mould. To either side of the grand fireplace were armchairs, their faded damask upholstery marred by patches of mildew. Next to them, a rectangular walnut table, its legs warped with age, the sheen of the wood masked by a film of dust. Dry brown flowers slumped in a crystal vase of cloudy water. Everywhere, an air of decay and corruption. Slowly, he moved to the door at the far end of the gallery and stepped into the next room. As he turned away from the door, he stopped in his tracks, seeing the rows of men staring at him. Big men, their dark hooded eyes filled with violent intent. Innumerable Guzmáns, all scowling.

The room was filled with two parallel lines of mirrors arranged to form an aisle. Above, on soot-stained walls, huge vases of black feathers hung in terracotta vases, their rustling strange and unsettling as he advanced between the mirrors towards an old chaise longue by the window where a single candle flickered in an ancient candelabrum. Behind the couch, the shutters were open. All he need do was open the window and slip away from this bizarre labyrinth into the darkness. As Guzmán moved round the side of the chaise longue, the wavering light was so weak he failed to see the body lying beneath the window until he stumbled over it.

He knelt by the corpse and rolled it onto its back, examining the ragged cut across the man's throat. He had been killed elsewhere, since there was no blood on the floorboards. Even though the man's face was a contorted mask of fear, Guzmán recognised his cut-price informant from the sports day, Fermín Etxeberria.

Something creaked behind him and he turned, seeing vague figures filing into the room.

'A little demonstration of our hospitality, monsieur,' a deep voice said. 'And we treat uninvited guests in the same way we treat informers.'

Rapid footsteps behind him. Guzmán turned quickly, though too late to parry the cudgel as it cracked against his head in a sudden explosion of white light and pain. And then a strange darkness, filled with the rustling of feathers.

Guzmán felt the rough wooden floor against his face as he came to. Movement produced a sickening pain and it took a moment to drag himself into a sitting position. He was in the middle of a large room, dimly lit by a series of flickering candles arranged on the tables. As his vision cleared, he took a look at his surroundings.

He had company.

At least twenty of the Çubiry clan clustered round him. Many were holding cudgels, slapping them into their palms impatiently. It was not an encouraging sign.

'*Bonsoir*, monsieur.' A deep voice from outside the ring of candlelight.

Guzmán looked at the figure coming towards him. A hard-faced man, brown skin tanned by the sun and the mountain wind, topped by a thick mane of silver hair tied back in a ponytail. Riding boots, a velvet frock-coat and, beneath it, a crimson waistcoat. All had seen better days, though the pistol in the man's belt looked anything but dated.

'*Buenas noches*,' Guzmán grunted. 'I don't speak French.'

'No facility for languages, monsieur?' The man had a reasonable grasp of Spanish and Guzmán thought it best not to correct his mistakes. 'Allow me to introduce myself: I am Abarron Çubiry, though most round here call me the Baron.'

'Nice to meet you.' Guzmán ran a hand over his scalp and winced. 'This is my first visit to France.' He touched his scalp again. 'It's made quite an impression on me.'

'Visitors usually knock at the gate,' Baron Çubiry said. 'You broke in.'

Guzmán shrugged. 'I'll knock next time.'

'There'll be no next time. We'll feed you to the pigs, *Spanyol*.'

Guzmán saw Etienne Çubiry's sallow face a few metres away.

'There you are,' Guzmán said. 'I wanted to discuss that consignment of whisky.'

'You aren't a salesman of stolen whisky,' the Baron said. 'And we are not stupid.' He glanced at Etienne and shrugged. 'My son, maybe. But I must live with that.'

'Let me shoot him, Father.'

'Patience, *mon fils*. Let's hear what our guest has to say before we make a decision about his future.' The Baron stared at Guzmán. 'Why are you here, monsieur? And, please, the truth. If you lie to me, my son's pigs will eat well tonight.'

Guzmán had been preparing a string of lies and half-truths to explain his visit. That would only work if Çubiry knew nothing about him.

'My name is Comandante Leo Guzmán, from the *Brigada Especial*.' Guzmán listened to the frantic translation taking place around him.

'The secret police?' The Baron didn't seem surprised. 'Do continue.'

'I'm trying to find a notorious bandit known as El Lobo.'

'Then we have a problem,' Çubiry boomed. 'He's one of our most valued customers.'

'I noticed,' Guzmán said. 'I found a cache of weapons in an old convent near Mari's Peak.' He glared at Baron Çubiry. 'They all had your label on them.'

'No doubt.' The Baron smiled. 'And you took them from El Lobo?'

'They were destroyed.'

'Then he'll need to buy more guns from us. You're good for business, señor. The Baron's smile slipped. 'Too bad we have to kill you.'

'That would be a mistake,' said Guzmán. 'The Spanish government are already making a protest to the French authorities about your activities. You can expect a visit from your gendarmes very soon.'

'*Les flics* won't help you.' Çubiry's laugh exposed a line of yellow teeth. 'We pay them to mind their own business and they do it very well.' He narrowed his eyes. 'And don't try to threaten me with your government. You don't have one, just a bandy-legged general.'

'That's unfair,' Guzmán said. 'Even if it is true.'

'Any more questions before we say goodbye?'

'We arrested an ex-Republican in the hills. He was travelling with one of your men.'

Çubiry shrugged. 'Sometimes we provide guides for such people. They pay well to get over the border.'

'Are all of them are ex-soldiers like him?'

'*Bien sûr*, we're not a travel agency. Most are highly skilled in their trade. That's why they're coming home: to use their skills to demolish that chocolate-box soldier you call Generalísimo.' He rested his hands on his belt. 'They say war is hell, Monsieur Guzmán. Let me tell you, war is highly profitable.'

'It has to stop,' Guzmán said.

The Baron's thick eyebrows rose in mock surprise. 'You speak as if your pathetic country were a matter of any importance. You were ruled by the Arabs for five hundred years, and now you cling to memories of a golden age the rest of the world has long forgotten. You are inconsequential, you Spanish. We Basques listen to the voice of our land. It speaks our history in words unblemished by time, so know this, *Comandante*. I don't care what happens to Spain. Let it burn, and let the flames cleanse its filth.'

'You sound like a philosopher,' Guzmán said, glancing round in search of a weapon.

A Gallic shrug. '*Merci*.'

'It wasn't a compliment, I don't trust philosophers.'

'That doesn't surprise me. Suspicion always haunts a guilty mind. But philosophy is both a tool and a weapon. It's my greatest regret that I had to abandon my studies at the Sorbonne.' Another nonchalant shrug. 'I killed a man.'

'That must have disappointed your philosophy teacher.'

'Indeed it did. He was the man I killed.'

Guzmán got up, shaking his head as if to clear it. Checking the distance to the door. 'So you're helping the resistance?'

'Of course not. I'd betray them all in a heartbeat, for the right price. But seeing that our trade with them seems to have unsettled you so much, I think the resistance may become even more profitable in the future.'

'And what if you provoke another war?' Guzmán asked, buying time.

The Baron held out his hands in a helpless gesture. 'The forces of the market are like God: they move in mysterious ways.'

'Suppose we come to an arrangement?' Guzmán said. 'A fair price for El Lobo and an end to your gun-running.'

'That's almost acceptable,' Çubiry said. 'But you annoy me with your assumption that I'll accept your money like some bourgeois merchant.' He laughed. 'Others will come after you. They'll offer more than you can and they'll be much more inclined to bargain.'

'I'm authorised to make a bargain like that,' Guzmán lied.

Çubiry shook his head. 'There have to be casualties to show we're serious. You'll be the first, señor.' He bared his teeth again. 'Though not the last, I assure you. And each time we kill one of your kind, the price will rise. What else can your government do, declare war? Of course not, they'll pay up.'

Out of the corner of his eye, Guzmán noticed a burly man sidling towards him. Another moment or so and the entire crew would be on him, cudgels and all.

He swung his elbow back into the man's face, smashing his nose and sending him tumbling into the men behind. In the confused mêlée that followed, Guzmán leaped forward and seized the Baron's throat with his left hand, using his right to tug the pistol from the man's belt. Unbalanced, Çubiry fell back against the table holding the candles, knocking it to the floor and plunging the room into darkness. A chorus of furious shouts and threats, the deep voice of the Baron calling for order. A lighter flickered and a candle sputtered into life. Several more quickly followed, bathing the room with hesitant light.

Baron Çubiry struggled to his feet, dusting down his velvet coat. His eyes widened as he saw Guzmán with his back to the wall, one arm around Etienne's throat, the Baron's pistol pressed against his temple.

'Go ahead, shoot him,' the Baron said calmly. 'It's not loaded.'

'Let's see.' Guzmán thumbed the back the hammer, ignoring Etienne's choked protest.

'*Touché*,' Baron Çubiry said. There was no smile this time. 'But you can't get out of here, *Comandante*. Not unless I give the word.'

'Then you'd better give it,' Guzmán said. 'Blood's thicker than water.'

The Baron lowered his voice. 'I know a lot about blood, my friend.'

'Fuck with me and I'll show you just how thick it is right now.' Guzmán shoved the muzzle of the pistol against Etienne's temple, harder this time. 'We're going for a walk.'

The Baron's face remained impassive. 'Where are you taking him?'

'The border at Hendaya. I'll leave him on the French side for you to collect.'

'Very well.' Baron Çubiry nodded. 'But this insult will be avenged, rest assured.'

'Perhaps you'd show me the way out?' said Guzmán. 'And no surprises, I'd hate to pull the trigger by accident.'

'I'm sure you know how to handle a firearm, monsieur.' The Baron gestured to his men to back away. 'Please, follow me.'

They moved slowly through the decrepit house. Guzmán kept a tight grip on Etienne, keeping the pistol pressed to his temple as he waited while the Baron threw open the front doors with an elegant gesture and went out into the night. Cautiously, Guzmán followed.

The Çubiry clan were waiting. All of them. The crowd filled the space between the chateau and the perimeter fence. Many held burning torches, others brandished clubs and pitchforks. The Baron shouted a few sharp words and the mob fell back, clearing a path to the gate for Guzmán and his prisoner.

'Let me go, *Spanyol*.' Etienne struggled to get the words out with Guzmán's arm crushing his windpipe. 'Let me go and I'll ask my father to forgive you. What do you think?'

'I think if you say it again I'll blow your head off,' Guzmán said as the gate opened.

The walk to the car was painfully slow. As Guzmán expected, the Çubiry followed them along the riverbank and back through the village. As he neared the car, Guzmán noticed how the fields on either side offered the crowd room for manoeuvre. This was where they would make their move. If they did, he would shoot some, but the rest would certainly overpower him.

'You have to be clever now,' said Etienne. 'And it would be very clever to let me go.'

'I'm not clever,' Guzmán muttered. 'But I'm very good at killing people. So shut the fuck up.' He tightened his hold on Etienne as he saw the crowd edge closer.

A voice from the shadows. '*Vamos, Comandante, rapido*.'

Ochoa came out from behind the car, his service pistol aimed into the crowd. One of the Çubiry took a step towards him and Ochoa raised the pistol into the man's face. '*Vete, coño*.' The man backed away, snarling insults.

Guzmán pushed Etienne across the road and bundled him into the front passenger seat. 'Keep the gun at his head,' he ordered, as he went to the boot for a piece of rope. Once Etienne was bound securely to the seat, Guzmán got behind the wheel and reached down to retrieve the Browning. Ochoa climbed into the back seat behind Etienne and pressed his pistol against his head. As the crowd started to edge forward again, Guzmán floored the pedal.

FRONTERA INTERNACIONAL, ESPAÑA–FRANCIA 1954

It was just after two in the morning and Guzmán felt his eyes closing, despite the erratic motion of the car as he hurled it round another sharp bend. 'That's the French customs post coming up,'

Ochoa said. Two hundred metres ahead, the weatherboard shed was lit by a couple of oil lanterns that threw trembling light onto the French flag hanging limply above the wooden barrier between France and Spain.

'We'll stop here.' Guzmán slowed and pulled onto the grass verge.

'My father will be here soon,' Etienne said truculently. 'Better get over the border quick, *Spanyol*, or you're going to be sorry.'

Guzmán used his trench knife to cut the ropes holding Etienne to his seat. 'No tricks,' he warned, pushing Etienne in front of him as they walked across the grass towards the road. In the distance, faint headlights pierced the darkness. The sound of a car moving at speed.

'That's my father.' Etienne smirked. 'Better run, *Spanyol*, you're in the shit.' He peered at the approaching lights. 'Better keep running too; the Çubiry have a long reach and an even longer memory.'

'You're full of fucking hot air, just like your papa,' Guzmán muttered.

'I'm next in line as leader of this clan and I tell you if my father doesn't kill you, I will.'

'The successor?' Guzmán's face set with concentration. 'There's a thought.' He pushed Etienne forwards and clubbed him with the Browning, knocking him to the ground. Etienne lay half-stunned in the wet grass, moaning French obscenities.

The headlights were now large radiant circles of light racing towards them.

Guzmán tried to work the slide on the Browning. 'Fucking thing.'

Concerned, Ochoa got out of the car. 'What's up, *jefe*?'

'Jammed,' Guzmán grunted.

'What are you doing?' Etienne wailed. '*Allez*. Go before my father arrives.'

Guzmán struggled with the pistol. 'Keep quiet.'

Dazzling white light as the car roared down the road, closing fast.

'Do you want mine, *jefe*?'

'I've got it now.' Guzmán worked the slide and grunted with

satisfaction as he heard the round go into the chamber. He cocked the hammer.

'What are you doing?' Etienne struggled to his feet. 'I'm warning you—'

Guzmán moved behind him. 'I've got a warning of my own to deliver, *amigo*,' he said, his eyes on the approaching car. 'Kneel.'

'Why?' Etienne moaned as he sank to his knees.

'I want to be sure your father sees who's doing this.'

'What the fuck are you talking about?' Etienne's voice was sharp with fear.

'Sometimes there's a line to be drawn,' Guzmán said, raising the pistol. 'And you're next in the Çubiry line. You said so yourself.'

'You can't.' The white headlights illuminated Etienne as he knelt in the mud, wringing his hands. Behind him, Guzmán's dark silhouette, his arm pointing accusingly at Etienne's head.

A flat bitter report. The ejected cartridge rolling on the ground. Etienne pitched forward into the grass, dead before Guzmán's second shot hit him.

Guzmán strode past the twitching body and opened fire on Baron Çubiry's car. Behind him, Ochoa started shooting, the staccato muzzle flashes flickering over Etienne's crumpled body.

Sparks flew off the Çubiry vehicle, its tyres squealing as it veered into a shallow ditch on the far side of the road.

Ochoa ran back to the Buick and slid into the driver's seat. He waited until Guzmán was inside and then gunned the engine. The car raced forward past the French customs post, smashing through the wooden barrier, sending the flag falling in a limp heap onto the road.

Guzmán lit a cigarette. 'First time the Browning's ever jammed,' he said through a cloud of smoke. 'I must oil it more often.'

Guzmán and Ochoa were already three hundred metres across the border before the French police tumbled from the wooden guardhouse, seeing the remains of the shattered barrier strewn across the road. In the distance, the tail lights of Baron Çubiry's car were already fading into the night.

CHAPTER 18

MADRID, JULY 2010, CALLE DE LOS CUCHILLEROS

Dull noise growing louder. Men shouting, the low rumble of a truck making its way down the narrow street. Galíndez pushed her face into the pillow, trying to will herself back to sleep as the garbage collectors moved away towards Calle de Segovia. She focused on the steady rhythm of her breathing, imagining herself on a deserted island, the gentle sound of waves, warm sand beneath her feet.

An explosion of noise. Galíndez jerked upright, heart racing. '*Mierda.*'

The phone kept ringing.

Groaning, she slipped out of bed and padded into the living room. As she reached for the handset, the ringing stopped. She turned to go back to bed, angry now.

The phone went again and this time she snatched it up. 'What?'

'You fucked up. Thanks a lot.'

'Mendez?' Galíndez glared at the phone. 'Do you know what time it is?'

'It's time for work, Ana. Maybe it's different for you on that cushy secondment but the rest of us are working our butts off.'

'You rang me to tell me that?'

'No. I asked you to do one lousy DNA test and you fucked it up.'

'What's wrong?' Galíndez knew she'd done the test as she always did. By the book.

'Come and see for yourself. I've got to tell the coroner and the prosecutor that we can't present the evidence in court today. Guess what? They won't be pleased.'

'I don't understand, it's a simple procedure.'

'You're right, which is why I'm so pissed off. Because the case was going to the coroner, I had to have the sample taken by someone qualified who knew what they were doing. That was you, *amiga*. Only you didn't do it right, so now I'm going to get it in the neck because of you.'

'I'll come in,' Galíndez sighed.

'So you should. What are you wearing?'

'A Barcelona shirt. Why?'

'OK, I'll factor in an extra five minutes for you to get dressed. Be here in ten.'

'I'll be there as soon as I can.' Galíndez slammed the phone down. '*Mierda.*' She pulled the football shirt over her head and threw it at the wall as she stormed into the bathroom and turned on the shower. The day could only get better. At least she hoped so.

MADRID 2010, GUARDIA CIVIL, LABORATORIO FORENSE NO 5

Mendez listened as Galíndez described the procedure for taking the DNA sample.

'Excuses, Ana?' she grumbled. 'You came here to give me excuses?'

'No, I came to give you this.' Galíndez looked up from the dead girl's file and raised her index finger. 'There was no problem with that sample, for Christ's sake. Everything we sent to the central crime lab was in order.'

Mendez picked up the file and pointed to a sheet of paper bearing the *guardia* logo. 'So how did they come up with this?'

Galíndez looked down at the scrawled note at the top of the page. As a routine procedure, the lab had run the sample against their database and got a match. The result was conclusive but puzzling. Sixteen-year-old Zora Ivanova, a Bulgarian national, date of birth unknown, date of death 8 July 2010, had a perfect DNA match with one Leticia Solano, date of birth 2 February

1993, date of death 2 Feb 1993, who died in the Santa Rosa maternity clinic run by GL Sanidad. The cause of death was recorded as sudden infant death syndrome.

'Well?' Mendez asked, looking at Galíndez for an answer. 'Our dead hooker can't be both those people, can she?'

Galíndez looked again at the dead girl's details, remembering.

'*Hola*?' Mendez said, impatient now. 'I'm waiting.'

Galíndez rummaged in her jacket for her phone.

'Hey, I'm asking you, Ana, don't phone a friend.'

Galíndez narrowed her eyes. 'On the first day at the university, a woman came to see me. Her newborn daughter was supposed to have died at birth but she didn't believe it. She thought she was one of the *niños robados*. It destroyed her entire life, Sarge. I've never seen anyone look so haunted.'

'Well, sorry as I am to hear that, Ana, how does it help me?'

'These are her details.' Galíndez held out the phone.

Mendez looked at the names. Adelina Solano, 32,3a Calle Azcoitia, Madrid, 28004. Daughter's name: Leticia, born/died 2nd Feb 1993. She raised her hands, suddenly conciliatory. 'There's something strange here.'

'Isn't there,' Galíndez agreed, putting her phone away. 'I'd better talk to her. She asked me to help find her daughter. I should be the one to tell her.'

'Good luck with that,' Mendez said. 'Ever told anyone their kid's dead before?'

Galíndez shook her head. 'What should I say?'

'Don't beat about the bush. When she opens the door, come straight out with it. "I'm sorry ma'am. Bad news about your daughter: She's dead."'

'And then?'

'You stand back while she falls apart. From what you said about the state she's in, that could be spectacular.'

'Thanks.' As she got to her feet, Galíndez remembered the sun of a faded afternoon, her mother weeping in the kitchen, holding her dead father's leather tricorne in her hands. She pushed the memory away. Señora Solano's grief was going to be more than enough without revisiting her own tragic past.

As she reached the door, Mendez called after her. 'Seen where she lives? Better take your hubcaps with you after you've parked.'

MADRID 2010, CALLE AZCOITIA, CARABANCHEL

Galíndez got out of her car, beginning to think Mendez had been right. A soulless area of low-rise apartments, patches of scuffed grass strewn with dog shit. Anaemic-looking trees along the roadside, planted in an attempt to mask the featureless buildings hung with badly fitted TV and power cables, their small windows protected by metal blinds. Walls daubed with low-quality graffiti as if even the local taggers couldn't be bothered to exert themselves.

Señora Solano's apartment building was a squat three-storey construction, with a patch of grey concrete at the rear, housing a row of garbage skips. There was no one around as Galíndez walked to the entrance, though there was plenty of noise coming from inside the building: deep bass notes throbbed from a window, competing with a dozen TV channels all at full volume.

She climbed the stairs to the third floor and went along a narrow walkway that overlooked the building's evil twin thirty metres away. Señora Solano's door was at the far end of the walkway. A small window next to the door was broken. Someone had repaired it with a piece of tattered cardboard fixed in place with sticky tape. She knocked and waited, thinking it might have been easier if she'd just phoned. But Adelina Solano had helped her by bringing the cache of letters to the university. The least Galíndez could do was give her the news about her daughter face to face. She knocked again, louder this time.

'Looking for Adelina?' An elderly lady with an Andalucían accent peered at her from the doorway of the flat next door.

Galíndez decided not to reveal she was *guardia*. It might have a negative effect round here. 'Have you seen her?'

The woman shook her head. 'No, *querida*, she was in an accident a couple of days ago.' She shook her head slowly. 'They took her to the hospital but she was already dead.'

Galíndez looked at her in surprise. 'She's dead?'

'A traffic accident, I heard. Are you a relative?'

Galíndez decided she didn't want the woman asking any more questions and pulled her ID from her pocket. '*Guardia civil.*' The woman's face changed at once. 'How long did Señora Solano live here, ma'am?' Galíndez asked, icily formal now.

'About fifteen years. She moved here after her husband left her. Seems she had a daughter who died young and it sent her a bit funny. Far as I know, she spent most of her time writing letters.' As Galíndez expected, producing her badge had curtailed the woman's desire for small talk. 'I must go,' she muttered as she closed the door.

Galíndez looked round at the deserted streets of anonymous buildings with half-closed shutters and sagging electricity cables. *Adelina wrote letters?* She was willing to bet they were linked to the *niños robados*. Maybe she had an address book. It would be interesting to know who the recipients of her letters were.

Galíndez put her hands on the door of Adelina Solano's flat and pushed. That wasn't going to work. The door was in bad condition but it would need more than a push to open it. She sighed. Now she needed to call Mendez and ask for authorisation to get inside. They'd have to get a warrant, or contact Adelina's relatives. You could spend days doing stuff like that. She put her hands on the door and pushed again, harder this time. The door gave a little, clearly the lock was badly fitted. Galíndez pursed her lips, weighing things up. All that bureaucracy just because of a cheap lock that might blow open in a puff of wind. She glanced round. There was no one on the landing and the street below was deserted.

Galíndez kicked the door hard, just below the lock. She heard a dull crack as the door swung open, the ruined lock dangling from it. She slipped inside and closed the door behind her.

Adelina's flat had a sad air of neglect, the smell of cabbage and dust mixed with other more complex odours, none of them pleasant. A kitchen sink with a ring of well-established green mould. Beyond the kitchen was a living room, though Galíndez decided living might be too strong a word. Adelina Solano existed here, no more. A table and a single chair by the window, the metal blind drawn and locked. An electric fire by the wall, far too small to provide adequate warmth in a Madrid winter.

On the wall above the fire was a large photograph of a young woman. Galíndez stared, realising she'd seen her before, lying on a mortuary trolley at HQ. It was the young hooker, Zora Ivanova, the girl who shared a DNA profile with Adelina's dead – or not so dead – daughter, Leticia. Galíndez exhaled slowly. *Adelina knew this thin-faced prostitute was her daughter.* That was why she'd said she hoped to have more information for Galíndez. She'd been watching her daughter, photographing her. Galíndez's eyes widened. *She was collecting evidence.*

Next to the electric fire was a small heap of newspaper cuttings and Galíndez knelt to examine them. The first was from a Madrid daily, *La Razón*, a picture of a man outside an imposing building, holding his hand up in an unsuccessful attempt to block the cameras. She read the headline:

Husband of the Minister of the Interior Attended Sex Parties

Madrid 19 December 2009

Juan Luis Calderón, husband of the interior minister Rosario Calderón, admitted today under intense media pressure that he attended parties organised by disgraced financier Ricardo Castro despite earlier denials. The parties were held for foreign businessmen interested in investing in Castro's development projects. Witnesses have spoken of drunken affairs with prostitutes brought in to entertain prospective business partners.

'It is true that I denied attending these events,'

Calderón said in a statement drafted by his lawyer. 'I should have said I was present, though had I realised that these events involved call girls, lap dancers and, in some cases, the use of hard drugs, I would of course, have avoided them. My only wish was to help support a Spanish trade event aimed at creating jobs.'

Calderón refused to say how many of these parties he had attended. He also denied knowing the where-abouts of Ricardo Castro, who has not been seen in public since the Guardia Civil raided his business HQ earlier in the month. Unofficial sources suggest Castro may be in hiding in Bolivia where he has a number of business interests. A brief statement from Minister of the Interior Rosario Calderón said her husband had committed no crime and that his private life was no one's business but his. She herself had no knowledge of him attending these events.

Another piece taken from *El Mundo* carried a similar story, noting that the prime minister had expressed his confidence in the minister of the interior, emphasising that her integrity was beyond doubt no matter how 'unfortunate' her husband's actions had been. Galíndez hadn't heard about this, and no wonder, she realised, seeing the date. When this story had broken, she had still been in intensive care.

As she got up, she saw a photograph almost hidden beneath the cuttings and picked it up. The photo was of a party, taken through a blurred crowd of revellers. A young woman leaning on a bar, a glazed expression on her face, next to her a man, resting his face against the girl's hair, his arm wrapped around her waist.

'*Me cago en dios*,' Galíndez breathed. The girl was Zora Ivanova. And although the man's face was partly hidden, it wasn't enough to hide Señor Calderón's identity. She took a plastic evidence bag from her pocket and put the cuttings and photograph inside.

A jumble of letters lay on a cheap plastic table by the window and Galíndez leafed through them. All were dated some time during the past ten days. Adelina must have intended to post these in a batch, since alongside them was a packet of envelopes and a book of stamps. Galíndez took a look at a couple of letters. One was addressed to the King, Juan Carlos, the other to the president of Real Madrid Football Club. All were handwritten, beginning with the words 'May God bless you'. She could imagine the reception these got from the recipients.

In her letter to the King, Señora Solano noted his failure to reply to her previous correspondence, undoubtedly due to His Majesty's enormous workload, she was sure. Perhaps now, however, his Royal Highness would be considerate enough to consider the case of her daughter Leticia, a baby stolen from her mother at birth against the laws of man and God. For years Señora Solano had searched for her child, sensing with a mother's unerring instinct that she was still alive. And her persistence had finally paid off: she had found her, selling herself on the streets, the prisoner of a group of Bulgarian pimps. If His Majesty would only see fit to order the police to intervene…

Galíndez cringed as the letter became increasingly garbled. It would undoubtedly have been dismissed as the product of a disturbed mind. Adelina Solano repeatedly emphasised the vast wrong done to her, but each time omitted to mention the evidence she'd been collecting.

For fuck's sake. Galíndez shook her head. Adelina's suspicions had been right all along. Working alone, she'd somehow managed to find her daughter. And then, before she could give the information to the police, her daughter was dead. Galíndez looked down at her clenched fist. The bastards killed the girl because she crossed them in some way. Killed her as if she was nothing, gutting her like an animal in the slaughterhouse.

Galíndez continued her search in Adelina's bedroom. She imagined Adelina in this musty box, spending long nights agonising over who she could write to next for help. As if it mattered. No one was prepared to help her. No one except Galíndez, and she hadn't done much. *Why didn't she tell me about the girl?*

There were two cardboard shoeboxes by the wardrobe, one on

top of the other. Galíndez took the boxes and sat on the edge of the bed to examine them. Inside were more letters, with the letterheads of medical companies. The first was a sheet of thick vellum with a pale blue letterhead: *GL Medical Group, Caring for the Health of Spanish People since 1957*. Dated a few weeks earlier, the letter informed Señora Solano that GL intended to take legal action if she continued to sully their company's name. It was signed by the chief executive, Jesper Karlsson. There were other letters from different companies, but all carried the same message, spelled out in indignant and threatening tones. *We strongly deny your insinuations… a matter of conjecture… you provide no proof of your unfounded and libellous claims… your letter is now in the hands of our legal team… legal action… defamation… we must warn you…* None of the letters expressed sympathy or offered any sort of advice.

Galíndez checked the rest of the flat to make sure there was no more correspondence hidden amongst the few possessions Adelina Solano had possessed. She found only a few cheap pens and several pads of writing paper. Adelina had spent almost half her life writing letters to people who had never read them, Galíndez thought sadly. But she'd been right and she'd stuck to it. And in the end she'd found her daughter. Galíndez admired her for that. And then she'd died in an accident. How unlucky could you get?

Galíndez took a deep breath. You couldn't let cases like this get to you, that was what they told her when she first joined the *guardia*. You couldn't let them work their way under your skin until every spare moment was taken up agonising over minute aspects of the case. That way, you ended up like Adelina Solano: lonely and obsessed, pursuing a hopeless quest. But it wasn't hopeless. She knew she was right. Galíndez picked up the cardboard boxes and left the flat. Back in her car, she called Mendez at HQ.

'Hey, Ana, how did Señora Solano take the bad news?'

'She's dead.' Her voice was flat.

Mendez was as sarcastic as ever. 'What happened? Did the shock kill her?'

'She died a couple of days ago in a traffic accident,' Galíndez said, heading for the city centre. 'Will you do me a favour?'

'Under the circumstances.'

'Check out the report on her death for me? You've got her details there, haven't you?'

'Let me have a look. Yes, I've got them. Do you want me to email you the report or are you coming back to HQ?'

'Email it, will you?' Galíndez said. 'I'll work on it at home.'

'The luxury of secondment,' Mendez muttered. 'OK. It's on its way.'

Galíndez drove back, deep in thought about Adelina Solano. And the more she thought about it, the more she realised how much she and the late Señora Solano had in common. It was not something that cheered her.

MADRID 2010, CALLE DE LOS CUCHILLEROS

Galíndez paused in the entrance hall to check her mailbox, finding only circulars and junk mail. The projector she'd ordered from Amazon still hadn't arrived, so Ochoa's spool of film would have to wait. In any case, she knew it was almost certain to be a let-down, a movie of his family perhaps, or some ancient porn film. She ran up the stairs and opened the triple-locked door. Inside, she checked the answering-machine. No call from Isabel.

After she'd made a coffee, she sat at her desk by the window and opened her laptop. The screen flickered into life and a message told her she had mail. It was the report from Mendez. No comments, just a cryptic header: *Not quite what you thought?*

Laughter drifted up from the bar downstairs and she leaned forward to concentrate on the report into Señora Solano's death. The preamble said Adelina was forty-seven. That was a surprise, Galíndez would have guessed she was in her sixties. She was divorced and though her ex-husband had been located by the *guardia civil* in Zaragoza, he declined to have anything to do with the funeral arrangements. Even in death, no one wanted anything to do with Adelina.

She moved on to the main report. After a paragraph, she understood what Mendez meant in her cryptic header. Adelina Solano hadn't died in a traffic accident.

The report said that at 8.40 on the night of her death Señora Solano was walking along Calle Polvoranca at the junction with Calle Joaquin Turina. As she turned left, passing the Cooperativa Nueva Carabanchel, a car mounted the pavement, dragging her under the vehicle for about three metres. A passer-by, Señor Adebayo Olowanyi, ran to help. As he approached, the car reversed over Señora Solano. The witness said this seemed deliberate since the car then drove over her lifeless body again before speeding away down Calle Guitarra. The witness was traumatised and unable to give a description of the vehicle.

There was no other evidence. No traffic cameras, no CCTV in shops overlooking the site of the accident, no other witnesses. A patrol car reported seeing a light blue car driving fast down Calle de la Duquesa de Tamames coming from the direction of the church of San Pedro Apóstol. Since they were on their way to a domestic violence incident, the officers had not stopped the car and only later became aware of its involvement in the death of Señora Solano.

Galíndez finished her coffee, relishing the feel of caffeine in her system as she tried to picture the driver's escape route after he killed Adelina Solano. She closed the report and opened a map of Madrid, examining the location where Adelina was killed. These were narrow roads in the suburbs, and many were one way. For the car to be going along Calle de la Duquesa de Tamames away from San Pedro Apóstol, it had to have left the scene of Adelina's death down Calle Guitarra and then turned left into Carabanchel Alto before taking a right near San Pedro Apóstol. There was no other route that would place them at the point where the municipal police saw them at the time they did.

The bastards had planned this carefully, Galíndez thought

angrily. They ran down and killed Adelina Solano and then took a route as if heading for the city centre before they doubled back towards the suburbs. They must have thought they were smart, planning the escape route like that. But they didn't realise the drive down Carabanchel Alto would take them past the entrance to the Metro. And Metro stations were good things for people like Galíndez. Lots of people coming and going. Busy places. All those people needed a lot of management, you couldn't just rely on staff to keep an eye on thousands of passengers every day. That was why they had CCTV.

She picked up the phone and dialled. 'It's me,' she said when Mendez answered.

'Did you read the report, Ana? There's not much to go on.'

'It's a long shot, but is there a chance you can get access to the CCTV at Carabanchel Alto Metro station?'

A long sigh. 'I suppose you want it tonight? I'll make a call. Stay by the phone.'

An hour later, Mendez called back and instructed Galíndez to log into the *guardia* network. Mendez had been busy. She'd isolated the incident on the camera footage and made a copy, which was now on the forensics department's server. The rest was up to Galíndez. Once Mendez hung up, Galíndez made more coffee and returned to her laptop. She saw the blue hypertext: *CCTV Footage of suspect vehicle* and selected the link. The screen filled with a grainy image of the view from the station entrance to the road three metres away. Two red bands appeared on either side of the video, a warning the incident was coming up.

Galíndez saw a sudden blur of movement across the camera's limited viewpoint, gone in a second. She slowed the replay and watched again before slowing it some more, repeating the operation until the real-time trajectory of the vehicle was reduced to a block of imprecise detail crawling across the screen. She saw a dark stain along the front passenger door, possibly blood though it could just as easily have been shadow. There wasn't much to go on. The darkened glass windows hid the identity of the occupants and the angle of the camera made it impossible to get a glimpse of the licence plates.

She drank the last of her coffee, watching the slo-mo movement of the car until her eyes ached, seeing the same uncertain detail repeated again and again. There was only one thing she could be certain of and that was the colour of the vehicle, a light metallic blue, glinting in the garish light of the street lamps.

CHAPTER 19

SAN SEBASTIÁN, OCTOBER 1954, CALLE DE FERMÍN CALBETÓN

Dawn was a faint hint of light on the horizon as Guzmán knocked on the front door of Magdalena's apartment building. The bleary-eyed *sereno* scuttled to the entrance, his face dull with sleep as he peered at the identity card pressed against the smeared glass. One glance was enough and the door opened at once. Before the door closed, the nightwatchman was back in his dingy cubicle, wrapping his tattered blanket around his shoulders. If the police wanted to enter the building it was not for the likes of him to enquire about their reasons.

Magdalena opened the door, fastening the belt of her dressing gown. '*Dios mio*, you look terrible.' She stepped back to let him in.

'I've been to France,' he grunted as he slumped into a chair. 'It didn't agree with me.'

She went into the kitchen and Guzmán let his eyes close, hovering on the edge of sleep. From the kitchen, he heard her making coffee. Real coffee too, from the aroma.

Magdalena returned with two cups and sat across the table from him.

'What happened, Leo?'

He shrugged. 'A disagreement with the Çubiry.'

'It must have been serious. What was it about?'

He lifted the cup to his lips, savouring the smooth coffee. 'We had a difference of opinion on whether I should stay alive.'

She got to her feet and came to him, running her hand over his hair, a spontaneous gesture of affection that ended as she drew her hand away, staring at the blood on her palm.

'Don't worry about that, I have a hard head.'

'What were you doing with the Çubiry?' Magdalena watched him over the rim of her cup. Large blue eyes, a sleepy tendril of blonde hair hanging over her brow. It made him even more aware that he looked like shit.

'I was investigating their smuggling,' he said. 'We want to put a stop to it.'

She laughed. 'You'd ruin a large part of the economy in this region if you do.'

'Never mind them.' Guzmán took a cigarette from his pocket, careful to keep the black tobacco from spilling. 'I've been thinking about what you said about Mellado.'

'I don't want to make trouble for him, if that's what you're thinking, but it's a fact that Mellado kills women in those little games of his.' A slight shrug. 'But as you said, these things happen every day in this country.'

He kills women. An image of a bitter night. The relentless drumming of rain. He blinked, trying to concentrate.

'What if I take a look at the intelligence reports on those women?' Guzmán placed a hand on the table, noticing the broken skin on his knuckles. 'If I can prove to you they're traitors, would that set your mind at rest?'

'Well,' Magdalena said, cautiously, 'if they've been breaking the law, then clearly one couldn't object to him…' she paused, choosing her words, '…mistreating them.' She leaned forward, resting her elbows on the table. 'What would those files tell you?'

'They contain all the evidence that led to the arrest. It's collected very carefully,' Guzmán said, speaking from experience. 'Everything is recorded in detail.'

Magdalena breathed out a halo of smoke. 'Can you get access to his files?'

'Of course.' Guzmán nodded.

'I'd be much happier knowing the general was acting in the public interest rather than just gratifying his own desires.'

He looked at her, admiringly. When she talked like that, she sounded like a general's daughter.

Magdalena got to her feet. 'You really need to go to bed for a while.'

'I could use a couple of hours' sleep.'

She arched an eyebrow. 'That's not at all what I had in mind.'

Guzmán took the cigarette from her and inhaled deeply before letting his head fall back on the pillow. 'I could sleep for a week,' he muttered, watching the smoke rise into the light slanting in through the shutters.

'Only a man could say a thing like that after what we just did.'

He frowned. 'I am a man.'

Magdalena changed the subject. 'I'm having lunch with my godfather this afternoon – would you like to come? We're going to the Luna Negra near the harbour. The food's excellent.'

'Do you want me to come?'

'Don't look so worried, it doesn't mean you have to marry me. You must have met your other girlfriends' families in the past, surely?'

'Of course.' Though Guzmán recalled that most of his other girlfriends had expected him to leave ten pesetas on the bedside table and be out of the room before the next client arrived.

'You'll like him. He has an important job with the government.'

'Really? Have I heard of him?'

'Probably.' She nodded. 'But you'll have to be there at three if you want to find out.'

'Three o'clock it is.' *Meeting the family now.* An unfamiliar sense of respectability.

She rested her head on his chest, her breath soft and warm, on the verge of sleep.

But Guzmán was restless. An idea kept nagging him. 'Did you hear from Jiménez?'

'I think seeing my father killed terrified him so much he's gone into hiding.' She raised herself on her elbows and plucked the cigarette from his lips. 'I sent a note asking him to contact me but he hasn't. It's terribly inconvenient.'

'I'd like to have a word with him. Someone told El Lobo your father was going to be at the hunting lodge and I think it could have been Jiménez.'

'I can't believe that. But you're the policeman, naturally I'll give you his address.'

Guzmán noticed her look of sudden concentration. 'What is it?'

'You know I mentioned he was…'

'A *maricón*?'

'He has a gentleman friend,' she said, carefully.

'That's hardly surprising.'

'I suppose not, but it might be that Esteban's staying with him.'

Guzmán smiled. 'You'd make a good detective.'

'His friend's quite a bit older than Esteban. He's very respectable. I'm sure he wouldn't let him engage in any criminal activity.'

Guzmán scowled. 'On the contrary, they probably commit a criminal act every night. Sodomy's a criminal offence, as is being homosexual. If you were to read a few books on criminals you'd know that's how it works: they start with petty crimes and then work their way up to much more serious ones. For God's sake, Jiménez could be an accomplice to murder. That's hardly innocent, in my book.'

She looked down for a moment. 'Of course, one can't excuse his perversion. Though I have heard it can be cured these days.'

'It's a long process with drugs and electric shocks,' Guzmán said. 'Even then, there's no guarantee they'll live a respectable life after they leave prison.'

'But Esteban's friend works in a bank, Leo. You can't get more respectable than that.'

Guzmán stared at her. 'Which bank?'

'He's senior clerk at the Banco de Bilbao.' She saw his expression. 'Why?'

'Nothing. You're right, that is a respectable position.'

'I know you have a job to do, but could you not be too hard on Esteban until you have proof about him helping El Lobo?'

'Of course. I only want to have a quick word with him.' And it would be quick, Guzmán knew, because it wouldn't take him long to kick the truth out of a pair of *maricas* like Jiménez and his friend.

He slid from the bed, blinking in pain as a shaft of sunlight hit his eyes.

Magdalena watched him dress. 'Take a siesta later, you really do look bad.'

'I'll call at a barber's shop and get a shave, that will perk me up.' He went to the bed and kissed her. 'I'll see you at the Luna Negra. I won't forget about Mellado's files, either.'

He was halfway down the stairs when the door opened and Magdalena called his name. With the light behind her, her sheer dressing gown was transparent as she came down the stairs.

'There was something else I wanted to ask when you go to see General Mellado. There's a lady who works in the typing pool at our depot. Her daughter's missing. She's awfully worried, Leo. Could you check to see if she's been arrested?'

Magdalena was worried too, Guzmán heard it in her voice. 'Of course I will,' he said. 'What's her name?'

'María Vidal.' She held his arm for a moment. 'Her mother will be so grateful.' She paused. 'And so will I.'

Once in the street, Guzmán reached into his jacket pocket and fumbled for the note the girl in the cell gave him. The note he'd forgotten.

> *Mamá,*
>
> *I'm at the military governor's residence.*
> *I've been arrested. Please come and get me.*
> *Please hurry, I'm frightened.*
>
> *Your loving daughter, María*

He should never have taken this from her. The best thing to do was screw the letter into a ball and throw it into one of the reeking piles of garbage across the street. You couldn't get mixed up in other people's business, not with someone as volatile as Mellado.

He rubbed a hand across his face, feeling the thick stubble. In Madrid he could have pulled rank or bribed someone to let the girl go, as a favour to Magdalena, but not here. In any case, the girl claimed to be innocent, but guilty people always said that. It was only when you started getting rough that they told the truth. The motto of the Inquisition still held: *The truth through pain.* People were cunning creatures, go easy on them and they took advantage. This María Vidal had clearly been led astray by the excitement of the resistance. Excited to repeat their slogans and anti-government phrases. Criticising the natural order of things. They started out being clever in front of their friends, showing off, insulting Franco or the Church. As if they knew better. Some saw sense and stopped before they got into serious trouble. Others thought they could say what they liked, where they liked. Kids like Nieves Arestigui.

He reached for a cigarette, wondering what he would do if she had been the one in the general's cell instead of María Vidal. All it would take was for Nieves to shoot her mouth off in public as she had when Guzmán had visited the farm. She would have been arrested at once.

He knew from long experience the sequence the interrogators would follow. Strip her naked, shove her head into a bucket of water until she was pleading for it to stop. Then the beatings and abuse would begin. Petty tortures, such as forcing her to kneel for hours on dried lentils, following that with something darker and much more painful, depending on the whim of the interrogator. Electric shocks. Perhaps the use of a heated iron.

He wiped sweat from his face. He would have a word with Nieves, get her to be more careful about what she said for her own safety. He could imagine her response.

But it wasn't Nieves' voice he heard. *Work it out,* chico. *You're the smart one.*

Further down the street, he paused by the flyblown window of a souvenir shop. Through the dirty glass he saw lines of painted figures in Basque dress, paper flags on sticks, faded postcards and a few garishly coloured sweets. He went in and asked for directions.

The street was nearby, a narrow cobbled lane running up from the port to the side of the basilica. An old building, the shutters hanging loose, damaged by the sea air. Three storeys of faded, damp apartments. A smell of cooking hung in the air a nd from one of the upper windows he heard the sounds of a family meal.

He stepped into the dingy entrance hall. Worn tiles, a light that didn't work when he pressed the switch. The familiar odour of damp. A line of rusty mailboxes along the back wall. He found the box marked Vidal and pushed the girl's letter into it. He could do no more, he thought as he went back into the street. He wasn't sure why he was doing this at all.

Guzmán took a shower at his hotel and swallowed a couple of aspirin he'd bought for a fiercely contested price from the abrasive dwarf in reception. Somewhat refreshed, he left his room, heading for the exit. Heráclito was busy behind the reception desk and Guzmán slapped the key onto the counter as he went past.

'Where do you think you're going?' Heráclito called. 'There's a telegram here for you.' He pushed the envelope across the desk. 'Shall I read it to you or do you want to spend an hour struggling with the big words?'

'You know, it isn't illegal to kill dwarves.' Guzmán picked up the telegram.

'Only the secret police can do things like that,' Heráclito sneered.

Guzmán stopped and stared at him. There was a long silence, broken only by the ticking of the ancient clock behind the reception desk.

'I think I'll just go and polish something,' Heráclito said, getting down from his stool. 'Unless you'd like a coffee, or a French woman, perhaps? I can get either for a similar price.'

Guzmán left the hotel and went in search of a barber's shop. After an excellent shave from a pleasingly tight-lipped barber, he took a seat on a bench overlooking the beach and opened the telegram. It was from Gutiérrez. It took only a few minutes to decode and it was not good news.

CARRERO BLANCO COMING TO SAN SEB.
VERY CONCERNED BY LOCAL PROBLEM OF
MISSING PERSON. AS AM I.

Guzmán sighed. The last person he needed up here was Franco's second in command, not least because Carrero Blanco despised Guzmán with a passion. As to which missing person Carrero Blanco was concerned about, it was highly likely Gutiérrez was referring to the *Yanqui* now resting deep in Mari's Cave.

An idea struck him. Just because Carrero Blanco was in town it didn't mean Guzmán had to see him. It was an unannounced visit after all. He just needed to avoid Carrero Blanco and get on with the job of tracking down El Lobo. That thought cheered him immensely as he sauntered down to the port to meet Ochoa.

The corporal was waiting by the quay, smoking as he watched a fishing boat head out past the island into the Bahia de Vizcaya.

'We're going after two gentleman of a delicate persuasion today,' Guzmán said.

'*Maricones*?' Ochoa brightened a little. 'We might have a laugh if they resist arrest.'

'They always resist arrest. It usually adds a few years to the sentence.'

'So who're the lucky ladies?'

'One's called Esteban Jiménez, he was General Torres's warehouse manager. His boyfriend is a Señor Elias Cardoso, a senior clerk at the Banco de Bilbao.'

Ochoa gave a low whistle. 'The bank where someone's been tipping off El Lobo?'

'That's the one,' Guzmán agreed. 'Of course it could just be coincidence.' He took one last pull of the cigarette and flicked it into the dirty water of the harbour. 'But Jiménez arranged for

General Torres to sit by the window at his lodge shortly before El Lobo shot him. No one's seen either of them since.'

'Got an address, *jefe*?'

Guzmán held up a scrap of paper. 'Calle de la Pescadería. Let's pay them a call.'

SAN SEBASTIÁN 1954, CALLE DE LA PESCADERÍA

A dark cobbled street crammed with rundown shops and bars, echoing with the song of caged birds. On the floors above, people were closing their shutters against the fierce midday sun. The lower floors remained in shadow and in the street men smoked, or read a paper, as they waited for their wives to prepare lunch. Guzmán soon found himself distracted by the savoury smells emanating from some of the cafés and it took a great effort of will not to stop for a few tapas.

'*Cuarenta y très*, this is the one,' Guzmán said, pointing to the plain wooden door. He yanked the length of rusty wire that served as a bell pull. Nothing happened. When he tried the door, it swung open. That was a surprise: leave a door open and anyone could walk in and help themselves to whatever they could find. Even if burglars didn't seize the opportunity, there was always a chance the police might.

As they crossed the dingy lobby, a harsh voice from a radio on one of the upper floors relayed news about a phenomenal harvest due to advances made by Spanish science.

They reached the first floor and continued upwards. The radio was still crackling out a triumphant litany of Spain's achievements. Guzmán heard the words *Glorious Leader, Sentinel of the West praised by the Heads of Europe.* The same old shit. Spain had no new stories to tell, contenting itself by regurgitating past glories and triumphs, continually evoking the past in an attempt to convince itself – against a wealth of evidence to the contrary – of its greatness. This was a country sustained on lies and improvised fictions, though those alone did not maintain the balance of power. Men like Guzmán did that.

The fourth floor reeked of damp. Ancient doors with peeling paint and faded numbers. Bare floorboards that sagged beneath their feet. No professional man would live in such a place from choice, unless he had a secret he preferred to keep hidden. Which, of course, explained why Jiménez's boyfriend lived here.

They moved quietly along the corridor, looking for a door with the name *Cardoso*. It wasn't difficult to find. In fact, they couldn't have missed it. What was left of it. It looked as if it had been hit by a truck. The hinges were ripped from the doorframe, the shattered remnants of the door strewn around the entrance.

Guzmán aimed the Browning into the apartment while Ochoa stood by, ready to cover him. Together, they worked their way down the narrow hall, checking each room as they went. A bathroom, two bedrooms, a sitting room, all empty and apparently undisturbed. An expensive clock and some Venetian glass ornaments suggested the occupants were not poor.

At the far end of the hall, dim light came from a window overlooking an inner courtyard. Guzmán went in slowly, keeping the pistol raised. He stopped so abruptly Ochoa almost walked into him. He saw the object of Guzmán's attention and let out a low whistle.

'*Me cago en Dios.*'

The table was set for a meal. Two places, the food untouched on the plates. Shattered wine glasses on the floor, brittle under their feet. There hadn't been much of a struggle. Possibly the men had been too frightened to resist. And no wonder.

Esteban Jiménez was sitting in one chair, Elias Cardoso in the other. Both had their backs to the window, their faces rigid monochrome masks in the pale light. Death masks, since their heads had been twisted at an impossible angle to face the smeared glass.

'*Mierda,*' Guzmán said. He took hold of Esteban Jiménez's head, holding it with both hands as he rolled it about. 'They broke his neck like a chicken.' He turned to inspect Cardoso's corpse. 'This one's the same.'

'Looks like you were right, *jefe*,' Ochoa said. 'They did have something to hide.'

'And someone didn't want us talking to them.' Guzmán went into the small kitchen adjoining the dining room and returned, brandishing a bottle of brandy. 'Cheap stuff,' he said scornfully. He raised the bottle to his lips and took a long swig. '*Joder*, it's been a long time since I had anything that rough. Want some?'

Ochoa shook his head and then changed his mind. 'Just a swig.' Guzmán handed him the bottle and he took a pull. 'Fucking hell.' He wiped his mouth with his sleeve.

Guzmán took the bottle from him and drank again. 'You're right, this is shit.' He rummaged in his jacket for his cigarettes and gave one to Ochoa. The black tobacco tasted vile after the cheap brandy.

'What do we do now, *jefe*?'

'You'd better call the *comisaría* and get a wagon sent over for these two.'

Guzmán listened to Ochoa's footsteps as he went downstairs. Then he picked up the bottle and inhaled the sickly aroma. It was undrinkable even for him and he put the bottle down, annoyed. If these two *maricas* could afford Venetian glass birds, they could easily have got a better make of brandy.

SAN SEBASTIÁN 1954, RESTAURANTE LA LUNA NEGRA

Despite its name, the restaurant was lit by powerful spotlights that bathed the room in an unforgiving glare. Guzmán looked round, disapproving of this modern nonsense. He preferred more traditional establishments where the lack of adequate lighting gave customers an opportunity to skulk or intrigue in the shadows, which, as far as he was concerned, was why God made restaurants in the first place.

At a table overlooking the sea he saw Magdalena, looking like a movie star, the one whose name he'd forgotten, in an expensive off-the-shoulder dress. It was difficult to believe that only a few hours ago he had been in her bed. She looked up from the menu, her face lighting up as he made his way towards her. As Guzmán approached, Magdalena's godfather raised his head and stared at him, bemused, though no more so than Guzmán.

'Leo.' Magdalena smiled. 'This is my godfather, Almirante Carrero Blanco.'

Guzmán's face was impassive. 'We've met.'

'We have indeed,' Carrero Blanco agreed. His tone suggested he preferred not to be reminded of the fact.

A long, empty silence.

'For heaven's sake, do sit down, Leo.' Magdalena gestured to the chair next to her. 'I'm sorry, I didn't know you two were acquainted.'

'Very well acquainted,' Carrero Blanco muttered. While Magdalena examined the leather-bound menu, he leaned forward and mouthed a word to Guzmán. A question.

'*Leo?*'

Guzmán frowned and kept quiet. One day, it was said, Carrero Blanco would take over from Franco. Even Franco, who in his heart never truly believed he would have to relinquish power, said so. That was all the more reason for Guzmán to detest him.

Carrero Blanco was clearly taken aback by Magdalena's behaviour towards Guzmán. Her gestures, the tone in her voice, the light in her eyes all carried an unmistakable message about her feelings. It was a message that was probably burning Carrero Blanco's dour soul like a flame. That thought pleased Guzmán immensely.

As Guzmán expected, Carrero Blanco took charge of ordering, checking the provenance of each dish with the waiter with a string of pompous and increasingly awkward questions that encompassed not only the food but also the man's war record. Once the order was finally taken, the waiter hurried away, sweat dripping from his face as he picked his way through the admiral's bodyguards back to the kitchen.

Once the food was served, the meal took on the character of a particularly unpleasant visit to the dentist. Carrero Blanco and Magdalena made light conversation, with the admiral expressing his condolences about her father, extolling his virtues and praising his cruel and bloody war record. All of it delivered with practised, utterly bogus sincerity.

Guzmán was exhausted. His head was starting to throb again, and he let his eyes close for a moment, lulled and bored in equal measure by Carrero Blanco's bombastic drone. On the brink of sleep, he heard a monotonous buzz, like the bothersome sound of some persistent insect. He heard rain. The sudden clatter of safety catches. Muttered curses in Arabic. Someone screaming threats. His voice. Someone trying to hold him back.

'Leo?' Magdalena's voice brought him back to the present. She laid a hand on his wrist. 'I asked whether the *ajoarriero* was to your liking?'

He turned to look at her, aware of Carrero Blanco's expression as he saw how Magdalena was touching him. 'Sorry, I was miles away.'

'Perhaps the *comandante* isn't used to such a rich dish,' Carrero Blanco said with a sour smile. Guzmán restrained an urge to punch him.

If she was aware of Carrero Blanco's insinuation, Magdalena didn't show it. She crushed out her cigarette in the heavy brass ashtray and stood up with a soft rustle of silk. 'If you'll excuse me for a moment, I must visit the powder room.'

Carrero Blanco and Guzmán both leaped up to help her with her chair and watched as she weaved her way through the tables of the crowded restaurant, Carrero Blanco with a proud godfather's look of approval, while Guzmán's eyes followed the movement of her hips beneath the silk skirt, bringing back memories from a few hours earlier. As the red leather door of the powder room closed behind her, they took their seats, fumbling without success for a few polite words to break the silence.

'I didn't realise you knew my goddaughter.' Carrero Blanco poured himself a glass of water. He offered the carafe, but Guzmán refused. A man didn't go to restaurants to drink water when Carrero Blanco was paying the bill.

'We met at a charity ball in aid of the Falange,' Guzmán said, omitting the detail.

'You astound me,' Carrero Blanco said. 'I never saw you as a party man.'

'I've always liked parties.' Guzmán smiled, knowing humour was lost on the *almirante*. The Jesuit bastard.

'But you do like newspapers, *Comandante*?' the *almirante* asked, reaching under the table.

'I'm hardly going to read a paper in such pleasant company.'

'Oh, you'll want to read this.' Carrero Blanco slapped the paper onto the table and waited as Guzmán looked at the headline.

'I don't speak French,' Guzmán said, even though he knew enough to understand this.

'I'll read it to you,' Carrero Blanco said, struggling to contain his anger. 'It says "El Lobo Challenges Franco's Bloody Rule".' He put the paper down. 'The article says El Lobo's activities should be seen in the context of a bigger struggle by the growing resistance movement in the Basque country. It suggests the days of Franco's regime may be numbered.'

Guzmán took a mouthful of wine. 'Who wrote that shit?'

'Some French journalist called Jeanette Duclos.' Carrero Blanco shrugged. 'Is it true that this bandit is linked to the resistance?'

Fucking French bitch. There was a time for lying and a time to tell the truth, Guzmán knew. Sometimes you had to tell the truth no matter what the cost.

He lied. 'No,' he said firmly. 'In any case, by tomorrow night El Lobo will be dead.'

Carrero Blanco pursed his lips. 'Is that an opinion or is it based on something more solid?'

'It's a fact,' Guzmán growled. 'I guarantee it.'

'Then I leave it to you,' Carrero Blanco said, changing the subject. 'Incidentally, I hear the leader of the local branch of the Falange has gone missing. Have you heard anything about it?'

'Señor Bárcenas?' Guzmán said scornfully. 'He's an oily bastard with his fat fingers in the black market. When the auditors have finished with his accounts, I think it will be clear he's taken off with the funds.'

'He wouldn't be the first.' Carrero Blanco nodded. That just leaves one last question.'

Guzmán felt sweat run down under his collar. The man had been doing his homework.

'A woman wrote to Franco, saying someone shot her husband on the beach,' Carrero Blanco said, toying with his napkin. 'Naturally, Franco hasn't seen the letter yet. If I have my way he won't. Has there been a shooting?'

'The local police are dealing with it,' Guzmán said. 'A love triangle, I understand.'

Carrero Blanco took a sip of water. 'In that case, I have nothing to worry about. So all that's left is for you to resolve this El Lobo business satisfactorily.'

'It will be resolved,' Guzmán said. 'I've set up an ambush for him tomorrow. He's been getting inside information about the bank's shipments of cash. That's why he's been so successful in pulling off his robberies.'

Carrero Blanco looked up. 'Surely you're here to bury Caesar, *Comandante*?'

Guzmán frowned. No one had mentioned any Caesar to him. He ignored it. 'We've already destroyed his supplies up in the hills so he'll be keen to get his hands on some cash. When he attacks the truck, it will be full of *guardia civiles*. And me, of course.'

'Excellent. Then there's no more to be said.' Carrero Blanco brushed his hands together as if cleansing them of their contact with the French newspaper. 'You know, Magdalena will make the right man a wonderful wife.'

Guzmán noted his emphasis on the word 'right'. 'I imagine so.'

'I put that badly,' Carrero Blanco said, 'because it might have implied the right man could be you. That will never happen. But then you probably weren't even thinking of it.'

300

Guzmán gestured for the waiter to fill his glass. 'I imagine Señorita Torres is able to make up her own mind about her choice of men.' It was always a pleasure to annoy Carrero Blanco, because it was so easy. As a fanatical Catholic, little could annoy him more than the suggestion that a woman was able to make a decision without male advice.

'She's a respectable girl,' Carrero Blanco said. 'You don't have a chance.'

'I've always taken my chances.'

'I'm serious, she's not for the likes of you.' The admiral lowered his voice, seeing Magdalena returning. 'You and that woman would be married over my dead body.'

'I think that would be a very satisfactory arrangement.' Guzmán lifted his glass in a mock toast. *Smug fucking Jesuit. One day things will blow up in his face.*

Magdalena slid into her chair. 'Talking business, gentlemen?'

Guzmán breathed in her perfume, remembering her naked a few hours earlier.

'We were just finishing,' Carrero Blanco said. 'So, *Comandante*, I'd be very grateful if you could conclude the work we discussed on time, because we don't want anything to disturb the US Ambassador's visit.'

'Is he making an official visit?' asked Magdalena. 'I'll buy a hat.'

'No, my dear.' Carrero Blanco beamed. 'He was hoping to meet his brother, who's been on holiday in the French Pyrenees. Apparently, he hasn't been in contact for several days. I'll be meeting the ambassador to reassure him we're doing all we can to see if his brother has wandered over the border and had an accident.'

'Does the brother know the country?' Guzmán noticed his collar seemed a little tight.

Now it was Carrero Blanco's turn to look uncomfortable. 'He does, I'm afraid. He was…' He looked round furtively. 'He fought with the International Brigade during La Cruzada.'

'He's a criminal?' Guzmán adopted a suitably outraged tone. 'We should arrest him.'

'You know damned well we can't,' Carrero Blanco spluttered. 'We don't want to upset them now they're about to hand over the money for that trade deal. Franco's livid but he's agreed it's best if we just ignore it.'

'The mountains are treacherous,' Magdalena said. 'Is he used to such rough country?'

'Don't get me started about *Yanquis*, my dear. They think the world is their playground. It wouldn't surprise me if he's fallen and broken his neck somewhere.' He took a sip of water. 'Deal with it, will you, Guzmán? See if he got lost up in those hills. Organise a search party or something?'

'I'll attend to it,' Guzmán said, knowing no search would find the missing *Yanqui* because there wasn't going to be a search.

Carrero Blanco leaned back, relaxed now. 'Franco asked about you a couple of days ago.'

Guzmán put down his glass, trying not to seem too interested. 'How is the *caudillo*?'

'He's well, Guzmán.' Carrero Blanco smirked, taking pleasure at being able to demonstrate his close relationship with the *generalísimo*. 'I had the impression he's keen to have you back in the capital. He's concerned the Russians are spying on us.'

Guzmán took a sip of wine. 'Naturally, I'm at his service.'

'Has Comandante Guzmán told you he's an acquaintance of the *caudillo*, my dear?' Carrero Blanco asked, smiling at Magdalena.

'He did mention it,' she said coolly, 'when we came out of church after confession.'

'Church?' Carrero Blanco gave Guzmán a curious look.

'I apologise,' Guzmán said, glancing at his watch. 'I must go. I'm seeing General Mellado in half an hour about this operation.'

'Give him my regards, Guzmán. He's a rock of loyalty in this sea of traitors they call the Basque country. We have a great admiration for his firm stance.' He called to the waiter for the bill.

Guzmán made his way past the bodyguards at the front door and went down the street, almost happy. Everything was under control. For now, at least.

Faisán stumbled as he came through the door. 'You wanted to see me, General?'

Mellado was sitting in his favourite armchair, legs crossed, slapping the side of his boot with his riding crop. He looked up at Faisán as if surprised to see him. In the dull afternoon light, his ravaged features were even more disturbing than usual.

'You came in, you saluted and you nearly fell over,' he said, maintaining the same slow rhythm with his riding crop against his boot. 'Not entirely a success, but not entirely a failure either. Have you completed the arrangements for the harvest ball?'

'I have, General. The ladies have been rehearsing the tableaux and, as far as I can tell, they know what's expected of them.'

Mellado cackled. 'I doubt that, boy. But in any case, their role isn't complicated. They aren't auditioning for the Moulin Rouge or that other place in Paris, what's it called?'

'The Eiffel Tower?' Faisán was not well travelled.

'It doesn't matter,' Mellado said. 'All they have to do is stand holding jars of wine or trays of canapés.' He gazed up at the ceiling. 'And the rest, of course.'

'The rest?' Faisán glanced anxiously at his list. 'I didn't know there was a rest.'

'A huge party with unlimited food and drink being served by women in a state of undress, desperate to save themselves and their daughters from being charged with treason.' Mellado chuckled. 'Don't you think there might be a bit more happening than wine tasting?'

'And do you still want me to approach Corporal Ochoa about the photography?'

Mellado's one eye rolled in its socket as he glared at Faisán. 'An order was given, and acknowledged, thus making it unnecessary to seek further confirmation.'

'I'll see to it, sir. Is that the plan for Comandante Guzmán's operation over there?' He gestured towards a large map on the table.

'It is,' Mellado said, 'though it's secret. However, since I made it clear when you took this job that any breach of security will result in your immediate execution, I'm happy to show it to you.'

Faisán wiped a bead of sweat from his forehead. '*Gracias, mi General.*'

Mellado smoothed the map across the table. 'This the road from Hernani,' he said, tracing a road marked in a red pencil with his finger, 'and here's the road from Oroitz in green.' 'We expect El Lobo will attack just here, on this ridge.'

'The Mendiko ridge,' Faisán said.

'That's what the Basques call it.' Mellado frowned. 'We call it the hill of the Blessed Virgin, naturally, because we're not libidinous Marxist traitors.'

'Of course,' Faisán agreed.

'Look at the time,' Mellado barked. 'I'll be late for my meeting because of your chattering.' He slapped Faisán around the head as he headed for the door. Faisán lingered in the doorway in case the general had any final instructions.

'I'll be back in an hour or so,' Mellado called. 'Make sure the office is tidy by then.'

Faisán waited, listening as the sound of the general's boots died away. Only when he was certain Mellado was gone did he go back inside and slump into the general's chair.

A sudden knock at the door. Faisán leaped up, terrified Mellado had returned. If the general caught his assistant lounging in his favourite chair, there was no knowing what level of violence he might deploy. Faisán opened the door and stared at a burly *sargento*, dressed in the uniform of the catering corps, standing on the bottom step. 'Yes?'

'I've come for the general's lunch tray, sir.'

'Of course.' Faisán pointed to the table where Mellado's lunch lay untouched.

'Didn't the general like it?' the *sargento* asked, covering the food with a napkin.

'What do you care? Just take it away and clean up that mess in the corner,' Faisán snapped. 'It was the dessert that upset him. The general doesn't approve of anything with nutmeg in it. He thinks it's decadent.'

'Right you are, sir.'

'I'll be back in ten minutes,' Faisán said. 'Don't be here when I get back.'

'Certainly, sir.' The *sargento* watched Faisán hurry away, waiting until the door closed before giving him the finger. Quickly, he walked across the room, picked up the dessert from the floorboards and put it onto the tray, wiping his hands with the napkin. The map lay on the table and the *sargento* went over to examine it. Each coloured road was annotated with Mellado's surprisingly elegant handwriting: *(a) Route for Comandante Guzmán & Corporal Ochoa. (b) Route to be taken by bank vehicle. (c) Anticipated site of ambush (d) El Lobo.*

The *sargento* went to Mellado's desk and reached for the phone. He dialled a number, alert for the sound of anyone in the courtyard.

'*Oui?*' A woman's voice.

'It's me, León,' he said. 'I've got something for you.'

CHAPTER 20

MADRID JULY 2010, GUARDIA CIVIL CENTRO DE INVESTIGACIÓN,
UNIVERSIDAD COMPLUTENSE

I t was just after nine as Galíndez stepped into the office The room
was already crowded with her borrowed students, all diligently
coding the mass of old letters, barely noticing her presence as she
manoeuvred through the tightly packed clutter of tables to her
desk. From the faint odour of pizza and the heaped cardboard
takeaway boxes in the waste bins, the students had brought their
breakfast with them.

Claudia smiled at her as Galíndez took a seat.

'Have you seen Isabel?' Galíndez asked.

'She's doing some interviews with a group of women whose
children were stolen in the fifties,' said Claudia. 'You haven't got an
aspirin, have you, Ana?'

Galíndez noticed her pale face and bloodshot eyes. 'Big night
out, was it?' She rummaged in her bag for a wrap of soluble
aspirin.

'That's an understatement,' Claudia muttered as she dropped
the tablets into a plastic cup of water. 'It's the last time I go out on
the town with Isabel.'

'Sounds like you had a good time.'

'God, yes, it was the best. We went to a whole bunch of clubs
and got in free. I forget sometimes just how well known she is.'
Claudia emptied the water in one swallow. 'All the drinks were free
as well, unfortunately.'

'You should be careful if you're not used to drinking a lot.'
Galíndez frowned. *Mierda, I sound like her mother.*

'Tell me about it,' said Claudia. 'I was really out of it by the time we got in the taxi. Luckily, Isabel let me stay at her place. I couldn't have made it home on my own.'

'Really?' Galíndez gave her a curious glance before logging onto the university network. She navigated to the server where the data on the stolen children was stored and opened the file containing the information from the letters coded so far. The file was growing by the day, and no wonder: the students were working flat out, their faces glued to their screens, all of them determined to contribute to the investigation.

Galíndez noticed for the first time the Photoshopped poster on the back wall, a photograph of a line of children dressed in what looked like clothing from the fifties, led by a stern-faced nun. Wherever the children were being taken, they didn't look happy about it. A large caption above the picture: *Niños Robados: Queremos La Verdad.*

'Thirteen thousand letters done so far. We're almost finished,' Galíndez said.

'Cool. Does that mean you can you start your analysis soon?'

'It does, though first I'm going to check to see if there's any missing data. Then, if everything's in order, I'll start analysing it.'

'Isabel says you're brilliant with statistics.'

Galíndez frowned, about to point out that Isabel might not be the best qualified person to comment on her statistical abilities. She checked herself. 'I know what I'm doing, put it that way. My speciality is profiling, that relies heavily on stats.'

Claudia looked up, impressed. 'Do you do a lot of profiling in the *guardia*?'

Galíndez shook her head. 'I was about to transfer to the profiling unit last year but then I was injured and someone else got the post.'

'Can't you reapply when you've completed this project?'

'I'd like to.' Galíndez was suddenly uncomfortable recalling the events of the last year and went back to her computer. She immersed herself in the data, the rattle of keyboards around her fading as she focused on the familiar procedures of data analysis, losing herself in the manipulation and transformation of data, shaping it into meaningful tables and summaries, eliciting patterns and relationships that might answer her questions. People thought such things were complex. Galíndez found the rigour and precision of the work reassuring.

Claudia pulled her chair closer. 'Can I watch? I don't get to use these methods often. Profesora Ordoñez says it introduces a barrier between the researcher and her subject.'

'Of course you can,' Galíndez said. 'Luisa – I mean Profesora Ordoñez – has a very fixed view of how research should be carried out.'

'I've noticed,' Claudia said. 'Although she said much the same thing about you.'

Galíndez frowned. 'Luisa forgets we have to adapt our research methods to fit the situation. We can't interview a lot of these people because they're dead. If we didn't have these letters, the parents' complaints about their children being stolen would be lost for ever.' She took a deep breath. Luisa's rigid antagonism to scientific method always annoyed her.

'Don't get angry, Ana,' Claudia said. 'We're all really excited to be working on this project. Have you seen the posters some of the students put up?'

'The one saying, "We want the truth about the stolen kids"?' Galíndez nodded. 'I think it's great that you all see the value of this.'

'No, that one.' Claudia pointed to the wall above the sink.

Galíndez's eyes widened as she saw another home-made poster, though this time the photo was of her, wearing her dark suit, sunglasses pushed up into her hair as she completed the interview with RTVE. A caption in bold letters: *¡Forza Galíndez!*

'This isn't about me,' Galíndez said, suddenly self-conscious.

'It's about doing the right thing, getting justice for people who wouldn't get it otherwise,' Claudia said. 'It's great to be a part of your investigation. That's why we all come in early: we want to do a good job for you.'

Galíndez looked at her for a moment, lost for words. Then she changed the subject. 'Right, I'll show you how I analyse the data.' Claudia watched as she typed commands into the software. 'OK, here's a frequency table showing responses for question one. Let's see what type of obstetric unit had the highest rate of baby thefts.'

'OK,' Claudia muttered, concentrating on the tables.

Galíndez tapped the screen with her pen. 'This table shows where the thefts occurred. The column headed *n* is the number of responses and the column headed *per cent* is the percentage of all cases each response represents.'

Q1: Facility where Child stolen

	n	%
1. Public	682	5%
2. Private	7788	58%
3. Church	4832	36%
4. Other/Not Known	198	1%
	13,500	100%

'There!' Galíndez said, 'you can see at once where child thefts were most frequent.' She tapped the percentage column with the tip of her finger. 'Over half of all the kids reported as stolen in these letters were stolen from private obstetric facilities and thirty-six per cent of cases involved facilities run by the Church.'

'So why is the figure so high for private clinics?' Claudia asked.

'Probably it was easier for them to avoid scrutiny. If there were any complaints, they'd be investigated by their own staff.'

'But couldn't the parents have gone to the *policía*?'

'A lot did,' said Galíndez. 'But the police were often corrupt and didn't investigate. Some police officers were even involved in the thefts. In any case, doctors and medical staff back in Franco's day had very high social standing. It was hard to challenge their authority.'

Claudia glanced at her. 'Did you think life was really so bad during the dictatorship?'

'I wouldn't know.' Galíndez smiled. 'I was born eight years after Franco died.'

Claudia's expression suggested she wasn't sure when that was and Galíndez had the feeling she'd just been reclassified as old. She was still considering that when something touched the back of her neck. Startled, she turned, surprised to find the students crowded behind her, watching her impromptu demonstration of data analysis. Engrossed in her work, she hadn't even been aware of them leaving their seats. A few were holding up their phones, capturing on-screen events for later viewing.

One of the students raised her hand. 'May we ask questions now, Doctora Galíndez?'

'I suppose.' Galíndez nodded.

She spent the next ten minutes dealing with questions about methods, about using the software and discussing the problems researchers encountered with various types of data. As she got onto the topic of advanced data analysis techniques, she decided to call a halt to things.

'Will you be demonstrating those techniques later?' someone asked. It took Galíndez a moment to identify the source of the voice, finally realising it came from one of the students sitting cross-legged at her feet.

'We still have more letters to code first. When you've finished entering them, I'll take you through the analysis step by step if you want.'

The students' enthusiastic response told her the answer to that.

'You love your work, don't you?' Claudia said as the students went back to their desks and started work again. 'Not everyone likes to share their knowledge like you do.'

Galíndez looked at her, surprised. Knowledge was the only thing she was willing to share with anyone these days.

'Where is everybody?' Isabel asked, seeing the empty room.

Galíndez looked up from a desk filled with piles of printouts, the tables and figures circled and annotated in red ink. 'There's a compulsory lecture for the statistics students this afternoon,' she said. 'And Claudia went home, she felt ill.'

'No wonder, after the amount she drank last night.' Isabel smiled. 'She'll sleep it off, that's one of the great things about being young.'

'If you say so.' Galíndez's fingers rattled on the keyboard and the printer stuttered into life, spilling new sheets of graphs and tables across the desk.

Isabel came nearer. 'Looks like you've been busy.'

'So have you, I hear,' Galíndez said, without looking up.

'Are you still mad at me, Ana?'

'Since you ask, I don't think much of your behaviour,' Galíndez said. 'It was inappropriate.'

'I put my arm round you. No one died. Can't we move on?'

Galíndez finally looked up. 'I'm talking about you taking Claudia out, getting her drunk and then spending the night with her. She's a student. That's the sort of thing Luisa would do.'

'Claudia spent the night at my place because she was blind drunk.' Isabel laughed. 'I told her to slow down but you know what? She's twenty-two. That's what people do when they're at university.' She gave Galíndez a long look. 'Normally.'

Galíndez looked down at her screen. 'Even so.'

'What?' Isabel sighed, exasperated. 'I phoned her boyfriend this morning and he came over to pick her up.'

'Boyfriend?' Galíndez saved her file. 'You shouldn't have let her drink so much.'

'*Por Dios*, she's young. Didn't you ever get wasted when you were at uni?'

'Not really.' She frowned. 'Once or twice.' She saw Isabel's look. 'A few times, maybe.'

'Feel free to apologise.' Isabel pulled up a chair. 'I think you're jealous because I went out and had a good time while you were home poring over trichotomous outcomes.'

'Dichotomous actually,' Galíndez muttered.

'Come on, loosen up, Ana,' Isabel said. 'This investigation is depressing enough without us being miserable. You're usually happy when you're knee-deep in figures.'

'Someone's got to do it.' Galíndez gave her a reluctant smile. 'But you're right about not letting it get us down.' She pointed to one the papers on her desk, a set of tables, surrounded by scrawled notes in red ink and flurries of exclamation marks. 'We've got all the letters coded now, it's starting to get exciting.'

'Exciting?' Isabel looked dubiously at the printouts. 'You'd better explain it to me. Though without the numbers.' She noticed something lurking under one of Galíndez's printouts. 'And if you're leaving that sandwich, I'll have it.'

Galíndez retrieved the plate from under her papers and pushed it across the desk.

'So, what is it you've been doing?' Isabel asked.

'Logistic regression.' Galíndez pointed to the printout. 'It identifies items of data that predict a particular outcome like yes or no, buy or don't buy, that kind of thing. In our data the outcome is whether or not parents who made a complaint about their child's death were killed after the letter was sent.'

Isabel's eyes widened. 'Strangely, Ana, I understood that. Keep it at that level.'

Galíndez leaned forward, using her pen to point to the figures in the table. 'Out of all the factors we've got in our database, six things most accurately predict the subsequent death of the parents. The likelihood of getting these results by chance is about one in a hundred thousand. Since it's highly unlikely they occurred randomly, we can infer there's a relationship between the type of clinic and the death of the parents.'

Factors in Letters Increasing the Likelihood of Parental Death

	Sig.	Odds Ratio	Change in Likelihood of death
Private Clinic	***	2.0	+ 100%
Church-run Clinic	***	1.8	+80%
Single mother	***	1.7	+70%
Threat to complain to media	***	1.47	+47%
Complaint to Policía/Guardia	***	1.36	+36%
Working Class	***	1.25	+25%

*** $p < .0001$

'Which is good, right?'

'It suggests the deaths weren't random,' Galíndez agreed. 'It's not conclusive proof.'

'And what does that thing, the Odds Ratio mean?'

'It's an indication of how much a particular factor affects the likelihood of the outcome,' said Galíndez. 'If the Odds Ratio is one, there's no change in outcome. If it's less than one, the likelihood of the outcome is reduced and an Odds Ratio greater than one indicates an increase in the likelihood of the outcome.'

Galíndez saw Isabel's dazed expression. 'OK, look at the column on the far right. It shows the percentage change in the likelihood of parental death. See what I mean? If someone's baby was stolen in a private clinic, the odds of them being killed goes up by a hundred per cent; in a clinic run by the Church, the odds are increased by eighty per cent. Parents who threatened to complain to the media also had a forty-seven per cent increased likelihood of dying and those who complained to the police or *guardia civil* increased their chances of death by thirty-six per cent. Lastly, working-class parents had a twenty-five per cent greater increase in the odds of the parents dying.'

'*Jesús Cristo*,' Isabel muttered. 'You can explain all that from a set of numbers?'

'It's not proof, but it shows we should focus our investigation on private clinics.'

Isabel peered at the screen. 'So why are single mothers more likely to be killed?'

Galíndez shrugged. 'It's just conjecture, but I'd say because it's because they'd be more vulnerable and easier to get at.'

'Can we use these to get the people running the clinics arrested?'

'It will take too long,' Galíndez said. 'We have to make the case to the prosecutor. Then we'd have to obtain warrants to examine their records.' She chewed her lip. 'Rosario Calderón wants our findings before the election.'

'But that's only a few weeks away,' said Isabel. 'We can't check out all the clinics and hospitals in Madrid in that time.'

'We won't need to. Calderón wants something to illustrate what happened. As long as we can present clear-cut evidence about our findings, she'll have to set up an inquiry or send in the police. Then she'll get her wish – it will make her look good.'

'Can you do that?' Isabel wondered. 'Give her clear-cut evidence, I mean.'

Galíndez searched through her papers. 'It would be a good start if we focused on the hospital with the highest rate of child thefts and took it from there.'

Isabel nodded. 'No time like the present. Shall we get started?'

'I already have.' Galíndez pushed a sheet of paper across the desk. 'This shows the differences in the likelihood of parental death for different obstetric units in the Madrid area. These results are highly unlikely to have occurred by chance. Look at the figure I've circled.'

Obstetric Favility & Likelihood of Parental Death

	Sig.	Odds Ratio	Increase in Likelihood of Parental death
GL Sanidad	***	2.90	+ 190%
Hospital Santa Clara	***	1.80	+80%
Clínica de La Virgen	***	1.60	+60%
Hospital San Antonio	***	1.56	+56%
Grupo Salud	***	1.20	+20%
Hospital Manzanares	***	1.13	+13%

*** $p < .0001$

'*Mierda*,' Isabel muttered. 'So anyone complaining about a child theft to GL Sanidad had an increased risk of being killed?'

'*Absolutamente*. Complaining to GL increased the likelihood of them dying by one hundred and ninety per cent. And these figures only relate to GL's clinics in Madrid. Imagine if we could get hold of the figures for the entire country.'

'So how many deaths are we talking about for GL's Madrid operation?'

'Of those who complained to GL between 1957 and 1994,

314

around one thousand five hundred died,' said Galíndez. 'And don't forget our data is based on people who complained. There could be others who had a child stolen but didn't complain.'

'Surely this is enough to call in the *policía*?' Isabel asked.

'First, I want to know more about GL Sanidad.' Galíndez bent over her laptop and searched for the GL website. 'Here they are. Their HQ is in an industrial park in San Fernando de Henares. And look.' She pointed to a colour photo on the website. 'The chief executive is someone called Jesper Karlsson.'

Isabel leaned over her shoulder to look at the photograph. 'Why is he orange?'

Galíndez laughed as she took her phone from her pocket and called GL Sanidad. 'I'll ask him, shall I?' She stopped laughing as someone answered. '*Hola*, may I speak to Señor Karlsson, please? This is Agent Galíndez of the *guardia civil*. Yes, it's extremely urgent.' She looked up at Isabel and winked as the receptionist put her through. 'Good afternoon, Señor Karlsson.'

MADRID 2010, AVENIDA DE ASTRONOMÍA, SAN FERNANDO DE HENARES

The industrial park was a wasteland of barren fields crosscut by wide roads serving clusters of industrial buildings, warehouses and offices separated by wide open spaces where building work had stopped overnight when the economy nosedived. Immobile cranes next to half-completed buildings in the distance, dark skeletal outlines against the bright sky, more casualties of the recession. Galíndez slowed at an intersection, waiting as a large tanker rattled past, shrouding her car in a greasy haze of exhaust fumes. Ahead, isolated among the squares of unused land, she saw a gleaming white building, with black glass windows. A large sign across the front: *GL Sanidad (España)*.

She parked near the GL building and walked across the car park, seeing the distant cranes wavering in the burning air. As she approached, the entrance doors glided open, closing with a gentle whisper behind her. Inside, the air-conditioned building was cool and quiet, occasionally disturbed by the ringing of a phone. Even the staff talked in hushed voices, she noticed as the receptionist directed her to an expensive black leather chair in the lobby. Minutes later, she heard footsteps as the chief executive came to greet her.

'Dr Galíndez? Jesper Karlsson.'

Karlsson was tall, in his mid-forties, Galíndez guessed as she shook his hand. He had a tan that was either fake or the result of some serious sunbathing. From his name, she guessed he was Swedish, though there was barely a hint of an accent in his voice. He led her to an elaborate lift constructed entirely from glass and gleaming steel, showcasing the movement of the winch mechanism as they glided up to the second floor.

Karlsson showed her into his office. The outer wall was made of dark glass, giving an eerie, shadowed view out over the strange post-nuclear landscape of the industrial park. Once she was seated, Karlsson reclined in his designer chair, anxious to get down to business. As she explained the purpose of her investigation, she noticed he wasn't good on eye contact.

'So how can I help, Doctora Galíndez?' Karlsson asked.

His attitude soon changed as Galíndez told him about the letters of complaint and the high rate of death among the parents. He made the right noises, but said nothing to suggest he was going to assist in any way.

'Complaints are usually dealt with by individual clinics,' Karlsson said. 'It's rare we need to deal with them here, unless they involve litigation.'

Galíndez leaned forward a little. 'Why would anyone take legal action against you?'

Karlsson gave her a tight smile. 'On rare occasions, staff might not handle a procedure as well as they might: putting in stitches after an episiotomy, for example. Patients are frequently nervous in childbirth so even the smallest error takes on great significance and for some people their first reaction is to sue.'

'I presume you keep records of your correspondence?'

He shook his head. 'Not for very long. Unless the correspondence involves legal action, we only keep it for a year or two.'

'What about parents complaining their child has been stolen?'

Karlsson's face showed the first sign of discomfort since she'd arrived. 'I imagine you're referring to the stolen children of the Franco era?' An irritated tone to his voice now. 'I don't know anything about what happened during the dictatorship. I've been CEO here for three years and we haven't had a single complaint relating to babies going missing from our clinics during that time. It was a long time ago, Dr Galíndez. We live in different times now, thank goodness. Frankly, it's ancient history.'

'You don't seem concerned that your predecessors may have been involved in a major crime, Señor Karlsson.'

'I don't like your insinuation,' Karlsson said. 'Those things happened before you were even born. Quite frankly, I can't see much point to your investigation. You've looked at some old data, misinterpreted the results and then blundered in here to see what you can find to back up your mistaken ideas.'

'So you won't cooperate?' She went to the water cooler to get a drink. 'That won't look good in the press.' An innocent smile. 'It's funny how they hear about these things so quickly.'

Karlsson sighed. 'Why don't you go back to your investigation and carry on wasting your time on a spurious theory about parents dying because they wrote a letter years ago. You do that and I won't complain to your bosses at the *guardia civil*.' He leaned towards her. 'Just so you know, young lady, I'm a personal friend of General Ramiro Ortiz. Piss me off any more and I'll make a call and you can explain to him what you're doing here. How would you like that?'

Galíndez stared at him. *Young lady? Hijo de puta.* 'Go ahead.'

'OK, but remember, you brought this on yourself.' Karlsson reached for his phone and pressed a quick dial number. Galíndez heard a gruff bark as Ramiro answered.

'Ramiro? It's Jesper Karlsson. Karlsson, remember? Jesper Karlsson, GL Sanidad?'

Galíndez listened to Karlsson denouncing her. Mainly he was correct, though she thought he exaggerated her lack of courtesy somewhat.

Karlsson finished his list of grievances against her and she watched his smile vanish as he listened to the barrage of invective coming down the line. By the time Ramiro was done, Karlsson was sweating. He managed a stammered *adiós* and handed her the phone.

'*Buenas tardes, mi General*,' Galíndez said.

'Don't be so bloody formal, Ana María,' Ramiro bellowed. 'I don't know why you're threatening the head of the biggest medical group in Spain, but you'll find he's willing to cooperate now.'

'I haven't threatened him.'

'No? Well, I just did. I told the oily bastard if he obstructs you in any way, you're taking him to HQ in handcuffs. You can Taser him if you like.'

'I see.' Galíndez noticed Karlsson wiping his face with a hand-kerchief. 'Is there a reason for that assessment?'

'He's listening, is he?' Ramiro growled. 'There's a very good reason, which is why I'm giving you permission to beat the crap out of him if he resists.'

'Why is that?' Galíndez asked, giving Karlsson a cheery smile.

'He's a big contributor to Rosario Calderón's election campaign. Trying to buy favours, I reckon.'

'Interesting,' Galíndez muttered, watching Karlsson squirm as he wondered what Ramiro was saying. 'I'll let you know how things progress, General.'

'Progress your boot up his arse. That should get his attention. *Hasta pronto*.'

'*A sus ordenes, mi General*,' Galíndez said. By then, Ramiro had hung up. She handed Karlsson's phone back. 'General Ortiz says you'll cooperate?'

'Of course,' Karlsson muttered. 'There's been a misunder-standing, that's all.'

'Good, I'll email you a list of the information I want later today,' Galíndez said. 'I'd also like details of the owners of this company.'

His face fell. 'Not without a court order.'

'No problem. I can have one issued and delivered here within the hour and I'll make sure it's accompanied by a team of forensic accountants. It shouldn't take them more than a couple of months to check your financial records.'

Karlsson's jaw sagged. 'That would send our share price into a nosedive.'

'I'm sure it will recover,' Galíndez said. 'Eventually.'

He backed off. 'I'm not trying to be difficult. The truth is, I don't know who owns GL Sanidad. I take my instructions from a holding company.'

Galíndez took out her notebook. 'What's their address?'

'They're based in the Cayman Islands,' said Karlsson. 'They communicate with me through our chairman.'

Her eyes narrowed. 'So, effectively, no one knows who the owners are?'

'I can ask the chairman of the board if you want?'

'*Bueno*. Can you speak to him as a matter of urgency?'

'Of course. I'll contact him this afternoon,' Karlsson said, eager to cooperate now.

'Thanks for your help.' When she went to the door, he didn't offer to see her out. 'By the way,' she said, turning back. 'Can you tell me the chairman's name?'

'Of course.' Karlsson nodded. 'His name is Jose Luis Calderón.'

CHAPTER 21

SAN SEBASTIÁN, OCTOBER 1954, BANCO DE BILBAO

Señor Cifuentes unlocked another door and ushered Guzmán into a badly lit chamber. 'This is the door to our strongroom.' Guzmán watched as the heavy door swung open. The bank manager pointed at a line of sacks inside the vault. 'There it is, *Comandante*. Twenty sacks of notes, worth—'

'Five million pesetas,' Guzmán cut in. 'Don't look so worried, no one will steal it.'

'Of course,' Cifuentes agreed. 'And, since the *caudillo* guaranteed to reimburse us for any losses, our only concern is for the safety of you and the brave men of the *benemérita*.'

Guzmán nodded, relieved that Cifuentes had swallowed the lie about Franco so completely. 'I'll pass on your good wishes to the civil guards in due course.'

'And may I add, I have every confidence in the success of your operation, *Comandante*. It's well known the Spanish police are the best in the world.'

Guzmán stifled a laugh. 'That's what we tell people,' he agreed. 'Did you make arrangements for my men?'

'Billeted in the church, as you instructed. The nuns are providing refreshments.'

'Excellent.' Guzmán gave the bank manager an encouraging slap on the back, forcing Cifuentes to clutch the vault door in order to stay on his feet. 'You've handled the arrangements very well,' he said. 'So well, I'm going to inform the *caudillo* of your cooperation once this operation is over.' He cut short Cifuentes' obsequious thanks with an impatient gesture and hurried up the stairs, wondering how anyone so gullible could reach such an elevated position in the bank.

The church was three hundred metres away, tucked down a quiet side street of shabby offices with dark windows and lowered blinds. Guzmán went up the steps and pushed open the doors. The church shimmered with whispering echoes. Absently, he dipped his hand in the font and crossed himself. As his eyes became accustomed to the unsteady glimmer of votive candles around the altar he saw the civil guards slumped on the pews, resting their heads on their rucksacks, rifles at their sides. He recognised some of the men from the Oroitz garrison, tense and anxious.

The lance corporal leaped to his feet. '*Buenos días, Comandante*.'

Guzmán was not there to exchange pleasantries. 'How's the squad?'

'In good spirits, sir, and looking forward to tomorrow.'

Guzmán doubted that as he looked the men over. 'Any of these men seen combat?'

'Of course, sir.' The lance corporal's tone was too confident for Guzmán's liking.

'Are they clear about what they have to do?'

The lance corporal nodded. 'When we come under attack, the squad take up position around the vehicle and begin suppression fire at the target. We keep him pinned down while you and the corporal attack from the flank.'

'That's it. I'm relying on you to do a good job.'

'Don't worry, *mi Comandante*. El Lobo will be hanging by his heels tomorrow night.'

'I hope so.' Guzmán nodded. 'Are the nuns looking after you?'

'Yes sir, they cook our meals, just like in a hotel.' He frowned. 'I imagine.'

Guzmán ignored his salute as he went to the door. Outside, the street was bright in the midday sun. He turned back to the troopers. 'Good luck for tomorrow, señores.'

The civil guards responded with a barrage of jokes and threats to El Lobo's manhood. Their boisterous shouts were still echoing round the church as Guzmán left. Deep in thought, he scarcely noticed the warmth of the sun. He was disappointed. Not one of the men had bellowed *Arriba España*, as they did in the War. Not even a *Viva Franco*.

Times were changing.

SAN SEBASTIÁN 1954, PENSIÓN EUROPA

Ochoa watched the fishing boats rise and fall as they left harbour and ploughed into the heavy swell. It had been some time since he photographed anything as mundane as this and it felt strange taking pictures that were not of dead bodies, or prisoners undergoing torture. Not that those were his favourite subjects. There was one picture he wanted to take more than any. Not for the first time, he imagined himself looking at his wife down the barrel of his Astra 400 pistol, saying the words he'd rehearsed so many times during long sleepless nights. *I never stopped looking for you.* He would leave a moment for that to sink in and then kill her and photograph her body. A memory of vengeance.

'Corporal Ochoa?' Ochoa turned to see a young man, well wrapped in a thick lambswool overcoat, his wide-brimmed hat jammed tightly down to his ears. He looked like one of the men who sold stolen nylons on the black market. 'Rafael Faisán, General Mellado's assistant.' He held out his hand.

Ochoa thought he would trust a gypsy with his wages before he trusted this man. He stared at Faisán's outstretched hand without taking it. 'What do you want?'

'The general asked me to see you,' Faisán said. 'He wants you to take some pictures. He said he'd square things with the *comandante*.'

'All right. What kind of photos?'

'We'll pay two hundred US dollars. For your discretion as well as your time.'

Ochoa's expression didn't change. 'What am I taking pictures of?'

Faisán gave him the details. It was not what Ochoa was

expecting and he thought about it for a moment, slightly disappointed because it was so vile.

'I'll do it, but a job like that is worth five hundred.'

'I must say, Señor Ochoa, you know the value of your work.' Faisán reached into his thick coat and took out a thick envelope. 'There's five hundred dollars here, the two hundred I offered, plus three hundred I was going to steal.'

Ochoa put the money into an inside pocket. 'When do you want it done?'

'Right now, Corporal,' Faisán said, smiling.

Ochoa liked him even less when he smiled.

SAN SEBASTIÁN 1954, RESIDENCIA DEL GOBERNADOR MILITAR

'Don't fucking knock, come in.'

Guzmán came in and closed the door behind him. '*Buenas tardes, mi General.*'

'Have a seat, Leo.' Mellado waved at one of the armchairs near his desk.

Guzmán noticed the pile of paperwork on Mellado's desk. 'If you're busy, General, I can come back another time?'

'I won't be a minute.' Mellado looked up from the papers in front of him. 'These are intelligence reports from our agents. Bad news, too. More people are getting involved with the resistance. Can you imagine, after all we sacrificed?'

'Dreadful,' Guzmán agreed, thinking that any sacrifices he'd made during the war had always been for his own benefit. 'A few arrests will put a stop to that.'

'I wish it was that simple. It's going to take a lot of blood to stop this, I'd say.'

'Be careful,' Guzmán said. 'You know Franco's forbidden anything that could upset the *Yanquis* until he's got their money in his pocket.'

'Is that a threat, Leo?' Mellado growled. 'Did Gutiérrez tell you to threaten me?'

'It's what Franco ordered.'

'Franco?' Mellado sneered. 'I'm sick of hearing about him. Anyone would think he won the war.' He put down his pen and gathered the reports in front of him together. 'That's enough of these traitors for one day. Time for a brandy.'

Guzmán watched as Mellado opened the drawer on the right-hand side of his desk. A deep drawer, full of red-covered intelligence reports. He shoved the reports on top of the others and went to the drinks cabinet to pour two large glasses of Carlos Primero.

Mellado sighed as he put down his glass, 'First drink of the day's always the best.'

'I had lunch with a girlfriend yesterday,' Guzmán said casually.

'*Joder*, got yourself a *novia*, have you? You always were one for the ladies. How much does this one charge?'

'She's General Torres's daughter, actually,' Guzmán said, irritated.

'Fucking hell, little Magdalena?' Mellado whistled. 'She's gorgeous, what does she see in you?' He saw Guzmán's expression.

'Only joking.' Mellado picked up his glass and went for a refill. 'A talented woman, Magdalena, and that's with her clothes on.'

Guzmán stayed silent.

'By the way, I sent Faisán to hire your corporal this afternoon. I need some photos taken. We always get a few pictures of the girls who pass through the cells. A little reminder.' He winked. With his one eye, the effect was disconcerting. 'I paid him well, don't worry.'

'Fine,' Guzmán said, wondering how much he was talking about.

Mellado looked at his watch. 'Christ, I've got a briefing with my watch commanders.'

'I'll be off then,' Guzmán said, getting to his feet.

'No, *hombre*, you stay here, I'll only be half an hour at most.' Mellado pointed unsteadily at the drinks cabinet. 'Help yourself.' He gave a wave of his riding crop as he left.

Guzmán waited until the general's footsteps died away across the courtyard. The drawer where the intelligence reports were kept was locked and he cursed himself for not watching Mellado more carefully when he closed it. He examined the desk, seeing the drawer underneath, thin and flat, designed for storing blotting paper and other items of office equipment. He opened it and looked down at a tangled mess of rubber bands, pencils and rusty nibbed pens. A key lay on top of some sheets of blotting paper and he tried it in the lock. The big drawer opened and he reached in for the bundle of reports, all bearing the crest of the Military Governor's office.

Opening the first folder, he smoothed its pages with the palm of his hand. It was a similar format to the one used by his men at Calle Robles: a series of printed forms with neatly laid-out sections for the different entries. Entries recording the place of surveillance and the time the suspect was observed. The telephone numbers of people called by the suspect, the names of friends, relatives and acquaintances and their addresses. A section indicating if the behaviour of the friend, relative or acquaintance merited a new file being opened on them. This evidence carried a lot of weight: people were imprisoned and tortured on the basis of these files. Sometimes they went to the firing squad.

Guzmán put the file to one side and reached for another. He skimmed it quickly and went on to the next, working fast, the pile of files growing on the general's desk. Finally, he found the name he was looking for: *María Vidal.* He opened the file and flicked through the pages, checking each one, wanting to know exactly what the girl had done so he could give Magdalena a detailed account later. He reached the last page and put the file with the others. Things were much worse than he'd imagined.

In his *comisaría* in Madrid, Guzmán always made sure his men kept these files updated and ensured each section was completed properly. They worked long into the night compiling those dossiers, and with good reason: they were the memory of the regime and the contents were used to calculate the retribution necessary for those who defied it.

The files in front of him were different. Apart from the name and address on the cover, each was as pristine as the day it had left the printer. Whatever reason Mellado had for keeping these women prisoner, none of it was recorded in the reports. He looked up and saw the door to Mellado's inner sanctum ajar. It was possible there was information in there, waiting to be entered into the reports. There had to be an explanation.

He went to the door and fumbled with the light switch. The solitary bulb glowed, weak and ineffectual, though there was enough light to see the rows of shelves, the boxes of filing piled high. And then he stopped, staring at the stark apparatus in the middle of the room and the naked body strapped into it.

Mellado had put María Vidal in the garrotte.

She had been dead for some time. Her wrists and ankles were secured by the leather cuffs attached to the machine and he saw the marks on her skin where she'd struggled. It had not been a quick death, he guessed. Her face was congested and mottled, her dead staring eyes bulged from their sockets. As he turned to leave, he heard Mellado's voice booming across the courtyard as he returned from his meeting.

Guzmán ran back into the office, trying to keep the folders aligned as he bundled them into the drawer and closed it. He stepped back, checking there was nothing out of place on the desk. The middle drawer under the desk was still slightly open. When he pushed it, the drawer didn't move.

Outside the door, Mellado was dressing someone down for being sloppily dressed,

Guzmán pushed the drawer again. When it still wouldn't close, he pulled it open a little, trying to clear whatever was catching in the metal runners at the side. That didn't work either. On the other side of the door, the general was now expounding on the need for sartorial propriety. Guzmán pulled the drawer further out, and felt it start to move smoothly again on the metal runners. He heard the soft impact of something on the carpet beneath the desk and saw a brown cardboard envelope, slightly chewed up on one side where it had been caught in the runners. He bent down and retrieved the envelope. There was folded paper inside, possibly banknotes. He pushed the envelope into his jacket pocket and closed the drawer.

Sargento León's boots clattered on the ceramic tiles as he stepped into the house. Jeannette Duclos shut the door behind him.

'Nice place you've got here, mademoiselle,' León said. 'Did your father buy it?'

'None of your business, *Sargento*, just stick to the matter in hand.'

She was a bitch, he thought, though he kept his opinion to himself since there were a number of reasons why she commanded respect and it was sensible not to forget any of them.

She opened a door at the end of the hall. 'This is the library. We'll talk in here.'

León went in and took a seat by the desk. He noticed a bottle of Napoleon brandy on the cocktail cabinet. 'Any chance of a drink, mademoiselle?'

'No. This isn't a social visit.'

'As short as you like,' he said, 'just so long as I get paid.'

Jeanette smiled. 'You'll be paid all right.'

'I give you the map and you give me the money?'

'*Bien sûr*. Did you think we were having this conversation because I like you?' She leaned forward, suddenly conspiratorial. 'We want you to go with the truck, *Sargento*. Make sure it stops in the right place.'

He hadn't expected that. 'They'll suspect something. I'm in the catering corps now.'

'Ah, you're scared? Traitors often are.'

'Given the help your family gave the Nazis, that's a bit rich,' León muttered.

Her expression didn't alter, but the tone in her voice disturbed him. 'Is that something you wish me to convey to my father?'

'No, mademoiselle. If you want me to go in the truck, I'm happy to do it.' It was best to lie. Her father had a long memory for those who slighted him.

'Don't worry, our men know you. You can slip away while we do what's needed.'

327

'What if I'm recognised? One witness and I'd be in front of the firing squad.'

She tilted her head, almost coquettish. 'There'll be no witnesses, *Sargento*.'

'All right.'

'A present for you.' She pushed a book across the table. 'My latest work. Shall I sign it?'

León picked it up and frowned. 'It's in French.'

'Clever of you to notice.' She got up. 'We're done. Don't forget your book, will you?'

León reluctantly picked up the book and looked at her photograph on the fly leaf. 'Why do you still use your married name? Your husband's been dead for years.'

'I can assure you, it's not from affection. It just makes things easier. People can be so prejudiced about my family's name.'

SAN SEBASTIÁN 1954, RESIDENCIA DEL GOBERNADOR MILITAR

The door crashed open as Mellado staggered in. 'Still here, Leo?' He threw his hat across the room, missing the peg by a metre.

'I like it here,' Guzmán said as he watched Mellado pour them a drink. 'By the way, I saw Carrero Blanco yesterday.'

'I know,' Mellado said. 'He called here to see me, the Jesuit fuck. Thinks he's a cut above the likes of me. What did say?'

'He's worried about El Lobo. He also heard something about dead women,' Guzmán said, stony-faced. 'At a party, apparently. We were with Señorita Torres so I wasn't listening.'

Mellado smirked. 'Keeping an eye on little Magda's assets, were you, Leo?'

Guzmán forced a smile. 'Carrero Blanco said something about a ball?'

'The harvest ball.' Mellado nodded. 'It's a big event. I invite party members, the great, the good and the fucking rubbish – anyone who's worth influencing. I send the women prisoners up there for entertainment.' He grinned. 'Not their entertainment, though. Sometimes a guest gets a bit excited and one of the women dies. It's no great loss, they're fucking Reds, for God's sake.'

'He must have got the wrong idea,' Guzmán said. 'He never listens to people.'

'I might have known that God-bothering *cabrón* would be worried about protocol,' Mellado said angrily. 'I'm not doing anything I didn't do in the war, for Christ's sake. Franco and the rest were fucking grateful back then. Things haven't changed. People have to fear us: without fear, there's no law and no order.'

'I don't think Carrero Blanco understands the ball is properly organised.'

Mellado sighed. 'Pious bastard. Of course it's organised, using rules and regulations. My rules and my regulations, anyway.'

'You're a man who always does things by the book.'

Mellado poured himself more brandy. 'It's all down to my records, Leo. I keep track of everything. Someone changes their socks, one of my operatives will make a note of the time, the place and the colour.' He leaned forward, peering uncertainly at Guzmán with his bloodshot eye. 'That was an exaggeration, by the way.'

'Even so, you've always been known for your record keeping.'

'It's almost perfect,' Mellado agreed with drunken modesty.

'Which reminds me,' Guzmán continued. 'Señorita Torres wondered if you were holding the daughter of one of her employees, a María Vidal. I said I'd ask you.'

'María Vidal?' Mellado rolled his eye, deep in thought. 'We do have a girl by that name. She's still being questioned.'

'What did she do?'

Mellado's eyes narrowed. 'The silly bitch attended meetings of a resistance group. We raided their meeting place and she was arrested. Do you want to see her file?'

Guzmán stared. 'What?'

'The intelligence file, Leo. It's all in there, naturally.'

'Naturally,' Guzmán agreed, uncomfortable now.

'The key's in that middle drawer and the files are in the drawer

329

to your right. Help yourself.' Mellado watched Guzmán carefully. 'Open it and have a look, Leo. Go on.' His voice was low, threatening.

Guzmán shook his head. 'I don't need to. Your word's always been good enough for me.' He glanced at his watch. 'Better get moving. I'm driving up to Oroitz tonight.'

They shook hands. 'Good luck for tomorrow, *chico*,' Mellado said.

Guzmán scowled as he went to the door. If he wanted luck he'd see a gypsy.

'Leo?' Mellado called. 'Drop in at the harvest ball on Saturday night if you can. Starts at nine. It'll be just like the old days.'

GETARIA 1954

A pale sun muffled by clouds, the sea the colour of lead. Sitting up front with the driver, Ochoa watched gulls wheeling over a small boat as the nets were drawn in. He sat quietly, his camera on his lap. From time to time, he glanced in the mirror, watching the couple sitting in the back with Faisán. The glass partition made it impossible to hear what was being said but it was clear they were upset. The woman was weeping into a crumpled handkerchief while the man appeared to be struggling to contain his emotions, though without much success. It was best not to dwell on such things and he looked away towards the sea.

Faisán knocked on the glass partition and the driver slowed. In the distance, Ochoa saw houses clinging to the hillside and below them, the rocky cliff face reaching down into the sea. The car halted on a patch of yellowing grass. Faisán jumped out, still talking to the couple, patting them on the arm, giving them some sort of reassurance. He saw Ochoa waiting and called for him to photograph the pair, backing away to keep himself out of the shot. Ochoa took several pictures and then Faisán began to direct the couple, instructing them to walk towards the camera, to look up at the hillside, stand together, now apart. To link arms. Each time, Ochoa waited as Faisán gave them new instructions and then

330

aimed the camera again, dazzling them with the sudden light of the flash.

Faisán drifted away, engaging in conversation with the driver, and Ochoa found himself standing with the couple, not even knowing who they were, let alone why they were so upset. It was the woman who broke the silence.

'Why do you have to take so many pictures?' Her voice cracked with grief. She gestured at Faisán. 'That gentleman said you had to take a couple of photographs for the newspapers, but you've never stopped. It's not fair.'

The man was more reticent. 'My wife is right,' he said cautiously, unused to arguing with authority figures. 'Can't you just take us to where it happened?'

'All I know,' Ochoa said, 'is that I was told to take photographs.' He had been told other things as well. It was not for him to reveal those.

The man looked back down the slope towards Faisán, suddenly uncertain.

'Who are you, señor?' Ochoa asked, annoyed at Faisán. Clearly the kid didn't know how these things should be done. That, or there was something seriously wrong with him.

'I'm sorry, I should have said,' the man spluttered, absurdly apologetic under the circumstances. 'I'm Luis Vidal and this is my wife María Carmen.'

'It's our daughter, María,' Señora Vidal said, suddenly choked by grief.

'Killed by a madman,' Faisán added as he came up behind Ochoa.

Señora Vidal began weeping again.

Ochoa looked up the hill. Shrub, a few stunted trees. Heaps of soil. Some freshly dug, others sprouting grass. A number completely grassed over.

'You have to identify the body,' said Faisán. 'It's important Corporal Ochoa takes as many photographs as possible because we need a complete set for General Mellado. He has to see everything. I'm sure you understand.'

The couple understood nothing. That was clear as Faisán gave them instructions to proceed up the windswept hillside, accompanied by the sudden bursts of light from Ochoa's flash. The ground flattened out and Ochoa saw more heaps of soil by a line of gorse bushes. They were not a natural phenomenon.

Looking back down the hill, Ochoa noticed a dark car pull up. Several burly men in fatigues got out, lifting a white-wrapped bundle from the back seat. He saw the men coming up the hill, obscured by a row of stunted trees a hundred metres away. He understood now why Faisán was keeping the couple talking.

'Stand over there,' Faisán told the couple. 'Keep going, Corporal.' His voice was sharp and petulant.

As Ochoa raised the camera, he saw the men coming through the trees.

Flash: The couple looking at Faisán.

Flash: Faisán walking to the bushes. The couple watching him.

Flash: Faisán, obscured by branches, heaving something from the bushes. A strange smile on his fleshy lips.

Flash: Faisán dragging the bundle towards them. The couple staring, apprehensive.

Flash: The couple staring at the pale shape as Faisán unwrapped the single sheet, revealing the naked body inside.

Flash: The woman's hand over her mouth.

Flash: A young woman's face, her eyes wide, her mouth wide open in a last attempt to draw breath on the garrotte. Her tongue lolling from her mouth, swollen and black.

Flash: The woman on her knees. The man pathetically trying to comfort her. Faisal behind them, pistol raised.

Flash: Two bodies, face down by their daughter's corpse.

Ochoa spat bile into the soil. He watched the driver come up the hillside, carrying a shovel. A metre away, Señor and Señora Vidal were still bleeding into the coarse grass.

Faisán came towards him. He was smiling. 'I did it,' he said, as if he had surprised himself. 'The general said I could do it if I tried. He had faith in me.'

332

'Why did you kill them?' Ochoa asked, spitting again.

'Their daughter managed to smuggle out a letter from her cell and they came to the mansion, asking after her,' Faisán said. 'The general was mightily displeased.' He took out a gold cigarette case and put a Turkish cigarette between his fleshy lips. 'Can I buy that camera?'

'You can if you've got the cash.' Ochoa shrugged. 'It's expensive, mind.'

'Tell me when to stop,' Faisán said, counting out the notes into Ochoa's hand.

Ochoa kept him waiting.

SAN SEBASTIÁN 1954, CALLE DE FERMÍN CALBETÓN

As Guzmán stepped into the room, Magdalena came to him and he put his arms around her, feeling the warmth of her body crushed against his. He felt her breath against his chest, the beating of her heart as she raised her face to kiss him. He delayed it. It was best to tell her first.

She felt him tense. 'What's wrong, Leo?'

'Mellado arrested María Vidal.'

'Heavens, what's she done?'

'I'm not sure. All I know is that she's dead.'

Magdalena raised a hand to her mouth for a moment. 'Did she try to escape, is that it?'

He pulled her close in a clumsy embrace. 'I don't know what happened yet.'

'She must have done something dreadful.' Her blue eyes were wide.

'She must have,' Guzmán agreed.

Magdalena pulled away and went across the room to her record player. Guzmán saw the HMV badge, a small dog peering into the trumpet of a wind-up gramophone. He watched as she shuffled through a pile of records. He had never had such a beautiful woman, not even the ones he'd paid in *Yanqui* dollars. For once,

Carrero Blanco had been right: a woman like her wasn't for the likes of him. That made him want her all the more.

She put a record on the turntable. The speaker hissed for a moment and he heard a woman's voice, the French words slow and smoky.

'Who's that?' He stood behind her, unaware she was crying.

'Juliette Gréco,' she said quietly. 'It's called "Autumn Leaves".'

'It's beautiful,' Guzmán said, hoping it was.

'You'd better go, you must have a lot to do preparing for your operation.' Her back still turned to him.

He nodded. 'I'll see you tomorrow night. We'll talk then.'

She turned to face him and he saw her tears for the first time. 'You will come back to me, won't you?'

'Of course.' And then he left, closing the door behind him. He went down the stairs into the street, troubled.

No one had ever worried about him on a job before.

SAN SEBASTIÁN 1954, CALLE SAN JUAN

The narrow streets were empty, their cobbles black and slick with rain as he wandered past the basilica, following a narrow alley deep into the old town. Finally, he stopped to look at a handwritten sign in a shop window. The window was almost empty but for a shelf covered with a piece of ancient black velvet. In the middle of the velvet was a large glass ball. A handwritten card was propped against the ball and Guzmán stared at the words through the smeared glass:

Amaya, Genuine Gypsy from Jerez – Fortunes told –
Tarot and palm readings.
Love potions
Husbands and Wives found – Luck restored

The room was dark, lit only by the dubious light of a paraffin lantern hanging from a nail on one side of the room. The walls were draped in dark cloth embroidered with the moon and stars in silver thread. As his eyes grew accustomed to the gloom, he saw a woman dressed in black, sitting at a table. A smell of smoke and roses. Rain hammered against the window.

'*Buenas tardes*.' He put his dripping hat on the table. Then he stared. 'You again?'

'The gentleman is surprised?' the gypsy asked.

'I thought you were a whore?' He frowned. 'Or a man.'

'Those are merely labels, señor. How can Amaya help?'

'When I have problems, I always consult a gypsy.'

'Quite right.' She held out her hand. 'Let me see your palm.'

Her touch was like ice as she traced the lines on his palm with a broken fingernail. 'I see bad things,' she muttered. 'Any woman who follows you…' A slow intake of breath.

'What?'

'I see footsteps following yours. They end in…' She stopped.

'They end in what? In Madrid?'

'No, señor, they end in shadow. *The* shadow.'

'Death?'

'That's one interpretation. Nothing is ever certain.'

'I'm certain you're full of shit,' Guzmán growled, reaching for his hat.

'I see what I see,' the gypsy said. 'And I see the shadow round you.'

'Most likely you've got the clap, that's why you're raving.' Guzmán threw down a couple of banknotes. As he stood up, his hat fell to the floor and he reached down to retrieve it. 'Get yourself some penicillin on the black market before your mind goes completely.'

The gypsy watched him stamp off down the street before she picked up the money and pushed it into the folds of her dress. And then her mouth sagged open as she saw his wallet on the table. She opened it and saw his identity card and behind it a thick wad of money, much of it American dollars. And there was something else, folded neatly behind the identity card. She unfolded the mimeographed document and struggled to read the text requiring all personnel below the rank of *coronel* to obey his orders and to give any assistance he might request. The paper was signed by the head of state.

When she finished reading, her hands were shaking. Her client was in the *policía secreta*. And, as if that wasn't bad enough, he had the shadow around him: he was cursed. Death walked beside him.

She thought quickly. The smart thing would be to leave town with the money. That was the gypsy in her. The survivor in her realised it would go badly if she did that and he found her. And how hard would it be for someone so powerful to track her down? She went to the door and peered out into the rain. At the end of the street, she saw his dark shape, walking towards the seafront. She ran down the street after him.

SAN SEBASTIÁN 1954, CATEDRAL DEL BUEN PASTOR

Jeanette Duclos sat in an empty pew behind a row of soberly dressed women waiting for confession. The cathedral fluttered with soft echoes, bathed in a trembling light from several large candles illuminating a painfully graphic carving of the Crucifixion near the altar. Jeanette waited patiently until the last of the penitents left the confessional. She heard the priest's spluttering cough and the faint slap of his feet on the stone floor as he walked to the sacristy. And then the sound of another taking his place.

She stepped into the cramped black box and knelt by the grille, inhaling the sweat and stale breath of the penitents who had passed through before her. The grille slid to one side. She saw dark flashing eyes beneath his cowl, a sudden movement of silver hair. A deep sonorous voice.

'*Ave María Purísima.*'

'*Sin pecado concebida.*'

'How long since your last confession, my child?'

'About twenty-eight years.'

A muffled laugh. 'Do you still drink?'

'Frequently.'

'Men?'

'Constantly.'

A deep chuckle. 'Shameless, just like your mother. May she rest in peace.'

'I have something for you, Papa. That thing you said you wanted.'

'You always were a thoughtful girl.'

Jeanette took a scroll of paper from her bag and pushed it though the opening.

She heard his grunt of satisfaction. 'How much did León ask for this?'

'He left that to us, Father. But he expects a lot.'

'People with expectations are usually disappointed. What do you think he deserves?'

Jeanette began fastening her coat. 'I leave that to you, *mon père*,' she whispered. 'But don't they say the wages of sin are death?'

'How very true.' A deep chuckle. 'I'll see he's paid in full.'

The grille closed. Jeanette crossed herself and went out into the shadows.

SAN SEBASTIÁN 1954, HOTEL INGLÉS

The lights of the city glimmered through the dismal night as he watched a couple strolling by the harbour. And then another shape by the quay, emerging from the shadows of the old town. It was Guzmán. The target he'd been hoping for. He pressed the rifle stock to his cheek, ready to take the shot. Breathing slowly, easily, letting the weapon become an extension of his body. And then something came out of the darkened street behind Guzmán, its coat inflating in the wind like a bat. Viana frowned as he saw the gypsy's turban, the high cheekbones and missing teeth. As Guzmán turned, Viana fired.

Behind him, Guzmán heard footsteps on the wet cobbles. He turned and saw the gypsy, her soaking dress and cloak flapping around her. He watched her carefully, suspecting an attempt to extract more money from him.

'Your wallet, señor,' she panted. 'You left it on the table. I didn't touch any of the money, see for yourself.'

He took the wallet from her. 'You knew I'd come after you if you stole it,' he grunted, handing her a hundred pesetas. He begrudged her this reward, but it was best to be careful. The last thing he needed was to be cursed the night before a job. Once was enough in any man's lifetime.

The gypsy continued protesting her innocence. He had no time to waste listening to her attempt to increase the reward for her uncharacteristic honesty and he turned away to go to his hotel. A sharp torrent of rain rattled against his back, the noise almost drowning out the sudden noise of the shot.

The gypsy crumpled like a broken doll, folding into the wet pavement, blood welling from the hole in her forehead. Guzmán knelt and plucked the wet hundred peseta note from her hand. It was wasted on her now. There was nothing more he could do for her and he hurried up the boulevard to his hotel where Ochoa was waiting.

SAN SEBASTIÁN 1954, HOTEL INGLÉS

Through the rifle sight he saw the gypsy fall, dead before she hit the ground. He cursed her for ruining his shot. Still, he would get another chance at Guzmán, he knew. And next time there would be no gypsy to save him. He was cold now, soaked by the rain as he left the eyrie where he kept these deadly vigils. He hid the rifle in its waterproof case in a small recess by the chimney before climbing down the wooden fire escape. Back in his hotel room, he made a call to Madrid. Gutiérrez answered at once.

'Carrero Blanco had lunch with Guzmán and General Torres's daughter,' Viana said.

'That's a strange trinity.' Gutiérrez's voice was faint down the crackling line. 'Did you deliver the message?'

'I did but he still hasn't made contact.'

'I need to think about this,' Gutiérrez grunted. 'Keep me informed if anything else happens, *Capitán*.'

The office was empty, though the waste baskets overflowing with Styrofoam cups and empty bottles of sports drinks hinted there had recently been life here.

Galíndez sat on a table, surrounded by the cardboard boxes full of letters. The pain of thousands of parents now transformed into numerical data on her laptop.

No one would ever know how many children were stolen over the years, she thought, staring at the boxes. She had been right to give Jesper Karlsson a hard time. The smug bastard hadn't been vaguely interested when she'd confronted him with her findings.

She got up and went over to the small kitchen area at the back of the office, relieved to find no one had used her last few spoonfuls of Colombian roast. A few minutes later, the smell of fresh coffee filled the room.

The phone vibrated in her pocket. It was Capitán Fuentes.

'*Hola, jefe*, what can I do for you?'

'Ana, this is very short notice but I've got a favour to ask.' He sounded embarrassed.

'Are you in need of a sitter again, by any chance, *jefe*?'

'You got it in one. Can you do tomorrow night? Merche's mother is going into hospital for a minor operation and she wants to be there when her mama wakes from the anaesthetic.'

'No problem. What time?'

'Could you get over here by six?'

'Of course.'

'You're a star,' Fuentes said. 'We really appreciate it.'

'*Hasta mañana.*' She took a mouthful of her coffee. It was far too strong, just how she liked it, and she lifted the cup to her nose and inhaled the dark aroma.

'You're supposed to drink it, not sniff it.' Isabel was standing in the doorway.

'*Dios mio*, Izzy. You made me jump.'

Isabel looked round at the empty room. 'Isn't it quiet without the students?'

'Very quiet,' Galíndez agreed, 'although I think I could get used to it. Now they're gone, could you order some proper office furniture? Let's spend some of that budget.'

'I'll be happy to,' Isabel said. 'What happened with GL yesterday?'

Galíndez wrinkled her nose. 'The CEO didn't want to know. He even claims not to know who the company's owners are.'

'So he won't cooperate?' Isabel frowned. 'That's a pain.'

'I think he'll be more cooperative now the pressure's on.'

'By the way, this package arrived for you yesterday, special delivery.' Isabel took a thick envelope from a shelf and handed it to her.

Galíndez saw the crest of *guardia* HQ on the envelope. 'These are the photographs of the Luminol spray I did in the Basque country.'

Isabel wrinkled her nose. 'Luminol sounds like something our students drink.'

'It's a chemical we use to identify the presence of blood. You mix it with an oxidising agent and spray it over the crime scene. Any traces of blood glow in the dark.'

'Nice.' Isabel sat down and opened her laptop.

Galíndez tore open the cardboard envelope and slid the photos onto her desk, though without much interest. What could they tell her that she didn't know already? The only reasonable conclusion was that the killings were carried out by Guzmán, since his name was on the sword. The same old story: he killed with impunity and then erased the traces, obscuring his own bloody role as he went. Just as *Papá*'s murderer had.

Her phone rang and she glanced at the screen as she answered. An unknown number.

'*Buenos días.*' A cold humourless voice, immediately recognisable.

'*Hola*, Señora Calderón.'

'There's something we need to discuss.'

'Go ahead.'

'I mean face to face.'

'By all means. Where do you want to meet?'

'The Retiro Park this afternoon at one thirty. You know the Palacio de Cristal?'

'Of course,' Galíndez said, wondering why the minister wanted to meet outdoors. She was left wondering: Calderón hung up.

Galíndez twisted a lock of hair around her finger. Something in Calderón's voice troubled her. 'That was the Minister of the Interior,' she told Isabel.

'I never realised you were so important.'

'I must be,' said Galíndez. 'Because I didn't give her my mobile number.'

She turned to the photographs from Legutio, undecided what to do with them. One last look wouldn't hurt. She pushed her papers to one side and arranged the photographs on her desk.

The first picture was taken before she applied the spray. The darkness of the cellar, grainy stone steps descending into shadow, four chairs arranged in a line from left to right, the one on the far left overturned, empty. Pale scattered bones around the other three. She could have sketched all this from memory. She slid the photograph to one side, replacing it with the next in the sequence, taken after she applied the spray.

Glimmering blue light glowed in the darkness, marking traces of blood invisible to the naked eye. More blood than she remembered. Much more. Luminous filigrees of intricate lines, thick trails and isolated splashes illuminating Guzmán's butchery in all its ghastly detail. Long streaks from severed arteries, wide pools around the chairs where the victims' lifeblood spilled into the rubble as Guzmán continued his gruesome work with the sword.

She wiped a hand across her brow, trying to imagine it: the helplessness of being tied, the smell of fear. The realisation of what was about to happen as they saw Guzmán coming towards them, holding the sword. And, judging from the decapitations and scattered limbs, they died in a savage frenzy as Guzmán turned the cellar into a charnel house.

She turned to the last photo. Similar to the others, taken from lower down the stairs. Her eyes narrowed. Something was different, something she hadn't noticed at the time. There had been so many blue trails glittering in the cellar that day. And, of course, she'd been distracted, angered by the Basque construction worker. Because of that, she'd failed to give these blood patterns the attention they deserved.

She leaned closer, peering at a glittering blue smear on the far wall, behind the row of bodies. Almost horizontal, running along the wall towards the pile of debris on the far side. The pattern didn't appear to be spatter from a severed artery. It was a contact smear, made by someone whose wound had touched the bricks, the slight undulations indicating the person had been unsteady, undoubtedly injured. Here and there, small irregularly spaced patches above and below the smear. She opened a drawer and took out a magnifying glass.

Lost in concentration, she peered through the glass at the trail of blood along the wall, seeing the small marks clearly now. Seventy years old and still discernible thanks to the Luminol. Their shape unmistakable through the magnifying lens. They were handprints.

Now she understood. When Guzmán had killed the prisoners, his murderous rampage must have been interrupted when the shell had exploded outside, blowing a hole in the wall above the cellar, half burying the nearest prisoner in rubble. By then it was possible the three prisoners were already dead. But the prisoner on the far left wasn't. In the confusion of the blast, the chair had fallen backwards and, somehow, he'd managed to get loose and then, staggering and bleeding badly, he'd placed a steadying hand on the wall as he'd made his way to the sloping pile of debris and climbed up through the gaping shell hole, escaping Guzmán's slaughter.

Isabel's voice broke her concentration. 'Did you find something, Ana? You look like you've seen a ghost.'

Galíndez looked up, still deep in thought. 'One got away.'

'Very cryptic.' Isabel nodded. She went back to her work.

Galíndez felt suddenly elated. Guzmán operated in total secrecy, and yet she'd discovered something he wanted kept hidden. Wanted it so badly he'd had the cellar sealed up in the middle of an offensive. She put her hand on the back of her neck, kneading the tense muscles, trying to think why these prisoners could be so important they'd had to be killed and entombed like this. Guzmán had even discarded his sword, presumably thinking no one would ever find it. He thought sealing up the cellar was enough to hide his monstrous crime. But he was wrong, there was something he hadn't anticipated: her.

She glanced at her watch. 'I'd better get going, I'm meeting the minister at one thirty.'

'Maybe she'll offer you a job in the government,' Isabel said, without looking up.

Galíndez went over to Isabel's desk. 'Listen…'

Isabel looked up. 'Why the long face?'

'The other night…' Galíndez began.

'I thought we agreed to forget it?'

Galíndez hesitated. 'I overreacted.'

'Well, you're allowed to.'

'The thing is,' Galíndez said quietly, 'I've had a lot of stuff going on this last year.'

'That's an understatement.'

'I don't like talking about it,' Galíndez went on. 'I just wanted you to know why I reacted that way.' She looked down. 'It's hard for me to talk about stuff like this.'

'There's no need to tell me anything, Ana. You almost died in an explosion, you were in hospital three months, spent several more on sick leave and then you worked in Vice, pretending to be a prostitute.' Isabel's smile faded. 'And you're still grieving for Natalia.'

Galíndez looked at her, wide-eyed. 'What are you, psychic?'

'It doesn't take much figuring out.' Isabel shrugged. 'In any case, from 2000 to 2002 I had a late night show, *Tell it to Isabel*. If you ever want an agony aunt, here I am.'

'It's not easy. The thing with Natalia was more complex than you think.'

'Well, if you want to talk about it, I'm here for you,' Isabel said. 'Meanwhile, you'd better get going, you don't want to keep the minister waiting.' She turned back to her laptop.

Galíndez picked up her bag and went to the door. '*Hasta luego*.' She opened the door and turned, seeing the top of Isabel's head as she ordered their new desks. 'You give up too easily,' she said and hurried out into the corridor.

Isabel looked up sharply. 'Ana?' She jumped to her feet. 'Ana, wait.' As she passed Galíndez's desk she saw a yellow plastic tube of pills on the floor and snatched it up before continuing her pursuit.

Isabel came out of the faculty building just in time to see Galíndez's car reach the gate, waiting to edge into the city-bound traffic. She waved the container above her head, trying to catch Galíndez's attention in the mirror, but her view was suddenly blocked as a blue Nissan pulled out from the visitors' car park and followed Galíndez into the heavy traffic.

MADRID 2010, PALACIO DE CRISTAL, PARQUE DEL BUEN RETIRO

The afternoon was humid and ominous dark clouds were gathering over the city as Galíndez walked along the gravel drive of Paseo Ferrian Nuñez towards the elegant nineteenth-century *palacio*. As she approached, she saw Rosario Calderón waiting near the palace, watching the fountain. The minister was smoking, moving her cigarette in impatient gestures as she watched Galíndez approach.

Rosario didn't waste time with pleasantries. 'You were going to arrest Jesper Karlsson?' Her pale eyes were as cold as her voice. 'Are you out of your mind?'

'I still might arrest him,' Galíndez said, immediately defensive. 'I also notice the chairman of the GL Board just happens to be your husband. I want to speak to him too.'

'You have been busy.' Calderón scowled. 'What led to you to GL Sanidad?'

'There was a high incidence of child theft at clinics owned by GL during the dictatorship. When I told Karlsson about it, he wasn't interested and tried to go over my head. I think he knows more than he's letting on.'

Calderón gave a contemptuous wave of her hand. 'Coincidence.'

'There was also a high death rate amongst complaining parents,' Galíndez said. 'Far too high to have occurred by chance. Señor Karlsson didn't seem to take it seriously. He will now.'

'This isn't what I asked you to do,' Calderón said, staring at her.

Galíndez felt her anger growing. 'I did exactly what you asked. I've uncovered large-scale homicide linked to the theft of children.'

'I say a lot of things,' Calderón snapped, 'I'm a politician. It doesn't necessarily follow that I mean any of them.'

'I did everything I could to complete the brief you gave me,' Galíndez muttered, trying to keep her anger in check. 'Just what did you expect?'

Calderón smiled. 'I expected you to fail, Ana. Just like you did last year.' She threw the cigarette to the ground and crushed it with her heel. 'Everyone would have been happy then.'

'You thought I'd fail?' Galíndez asked, incredulous.

Calderón looked straight through her. 'It's time I told you the facts of life.'

'I think I've got a grasp of those, thanks.'

'I'm sure, from what our background checks turned up.'

'You ran checks on me?' Galíndez's dark eyes flashed, furious.

'The secret service is part of my little empire,' Calderón said. 'I always like to be sure I know who I'm dealing with. Though, to be honest, all those one-night stands and broken relationships don't make exciting reading.'

The humid air was suddenly oppressive. 'Fuck you,' Galíndez said, angry.

Calderón glanced round, suspiciously. 'You have to drop the investigation.'

'Drop it?' Galíndez echoed. 'Why?'

'You've pissed off people who take a great deal of interest in the fortunes of GL Sanidad. They'd rather no one went poking around in their archives. Leave the skeletons in the closet, so to speak.' She smiled, maliciously. 'No offence there, *querida*.'

'Who are these people?'

Calderón pursed her lips. 'You might call them an interest group, I suppose. They have a simple aim: to get on in life without worrying about some young *guardia civil* like you rummaging around in their secrets.'

Galíndez stared at her. 'Does this group have a name?'

Rosario Calderón snorted with impatience. 'Haven't you ever heard that old saying, "Speak of the devil and he'll appear"? You really don't want to know, señorita, believe me.'

'Tell me who you're talking about.'

'I'm not talking about anyone, because this conversation never took place,' Calderón said, lowering her voice. 'Let me give you a little background. I became a Member of Parliament at thirty-six. I was hard-working with a reputation for attention to detail. Despite that, I was passed over for promotion for the next four years, no matter how much I worked. Eventually, I realised the only way I could make any impression on my party was on my back.' She laughed. 'Not always on my back, but you get the idea.'

'Too much information.'

Calderón ignored her. 'I only focused on people who could help my career.'

Galíndez looked at her with disdain. 'You know what that makes you?'

'Pots and kettles. You haven't exactly lived the life of a nun,' Calderón sneered. 'Anyway, back to the story, one day I was approached by the group I mentioned.'

'Don't tell me. They made you an offer you couldn't refuse?'

'They made me an offer all right. One that I didn't want to refuse. They saw my drive and ambition. I was—'

'Corrupt?'

'Open to new ideas.' Calderón frowned. 'I did things for them in Parliament, made sure votes went in certain ways, introduced new legislation, weakened resistance to their projects.'

'And you were paid, no doubt?'

'Money was only part of it,' Calderón said, lighting another cigarette. 'Suddenly, doors started opening for me. Before I knew it, the Prime Minister wanted me as Minister of the Interior.' A brittle laugh. 'I have control of the police and civil guard.' She looked straight at Galíndez. 'You work for me, *querida*. How's that for irony?'

Galíndez didn't speak.

'When I asked you to investigate the *niños robados*,' Calderón went on, 'you had those great ratings in popularity polls despite that air of being so fucking holier-than-thou. The public like their experts to be good looking, so those big brown eyes made you ideal for my purpose. Or would have, if you hadn't done such a good job.'

'So what happens now?'

Calderón shrugged. 'We're in trouble. My friends aren't happy about you drawing attention to GL. That medical group is important to them.'

'Why?' Galíndez frowned. 'They aren't stealing babies any more.'

'A great deal of money passes through GL,' Calderón said. 'It makes it easy to shift money from EU grants, channel it into research funds and then transfer it around the system until it reaches a point where it disappears into a Swiss bank account.' She saw the look on Galíndez's face and mistook it for bewilderment. 'Don't worry, Ana. I'll still help you. As long as you do the right thing, of course. You do want to do the right thing, don't you?'

'Oh yes,' Galíndez agreed, thinking hard.

'Think strategically,' Calderón advised. 'Just think of this moment in your life as a battle. You're surrounded and outnumbered. No chance of reinforcements. What do you do?'

It was a good question. One Galíndez had heard before. She saw herself twelve years earlier in the dojo. Barefoot, in her white karate tunic and trousers, holding a long wooden stick. A couple of metres away, her friend Fran, also armed with a stick. Watching them was their instructor, Mendez, alert and ready. *This is a battle*, she told them. *Just me against your army. Two against one. Good odds, no?*

And every time, a flurry of sticks, flailing hands and kicking feet resonating through the dojo as Mendez dumped them on their *culos* yet again.

'You surrender, that's what,' Calderón said, answering her own question. 'And I'm going to tell you the terms of surrender, Ana María.'

Galíndez remembered cold rain slanting through the street lights as she waited outside the dojo. Waiting to ask Mendez for the secret that enabled her to beat her and Fran week after week, without them ever landing a blow. *You said I could ask any question I like, Mendez.*

'Destroy all those letters you got from Adelina Solano,' Calderón continued. 'And all your computer files.' Her voice was confident. 'That will save your life.' She gave Galíndez a penetrating look. 'And mine as well. Are you listening?'

Galíndez didn't speak. In her mind she was sixteen, standing in a dark side street in Lavapiés with Mendez towering over her, her Afro glistening with rain. *Why would I tell you that, niña?* Her eyes bored into hers. *I need to learn if I'm going to get better, and I can't learn alone.* Mendez nodded, weighing up her response. *Good answer, kid.*

'*Hola?*' Calderón's tone was mocking. 'Pay attention. You don't want to end up like Adelina Solano, do you? Drop the investigation, Ana, or they'll kill you. You and that bimbo who used to be on the radio, the one with the big tits and perfect teeth.'

Mendez's words came back to her. *Strike where the enemy least expects it. Fast.*

'*Puta madre*, listen to me, will you?' Calderón was shouting now. 'Are you stupid?'

She waited for a response. 'Tell me you know what you've got to do, will you?'

Galíndez took her phone from her pocket and scrolled to her contacts. She looked at Rosario without speaking. When she did, her voice was icy. 'I know exactly what to do.'

'What are you doing?' Calderón asked, suddenly uneasy.

'I'm calling Uncle Ramiro. You probably refer to him as General Ortiz, I imagine.'

'Ramiro Ortiz?' Rosario's eyes bulged. 'Are you insane?' She snatched at the phone but Galíndez moved back out of reach. 'Don't do that, Ana. Just tell me what you want.'

'Publish the report you commissioned from me,' Galíndez said. 'In full.'

The blood drained from Calderón's face. 'Be reasonable. I said we'd fund your research centre for the next five years. Why don't we say ten?'

'Five will be fine,' Galíndez said coolly. She glanced at the screen of her phone.

'We could pay the funds straight into your account if you like?'

'Publish the report,' Galíndez said. 'And pay the funds to the university, not me.'

Calderón's eyes flickered. 'That's all you want?'

'It is. But go back on your word and the *guardia* will pay you a visit, I promise.'

They stood facing one another, both imagining it. All those specialist officers assiduously collecting details of phone calls, bank transfers, credit-card statements, phone calls and emails. All those transactions with Swiss banks.

'Deal?' Galíndez asked. *Game, set and fucking match.*

Rosario stared at her. 'Everything has a hidden cost, Ana.

You really think Ramiro's the guy in the white hat who saves the day in movies?'

'He is what he is. A policeman and a good one at that.'

'Is he?' Calderón reached inside her raincoat and took out a cardboard envelope. 'Investigate this then, you smug little dyke. Though don't do it on my time, will you?'

Galíndez took the envelope from her, puzzled. 'What's this?'

'I told you,' Calderón said. 'Everything has a hidden cost. I think it's only fair I spoil your day, since you've spoiled mine.'

As Calderón walked away, Galíndez suddenly became aware of the immense silence around her. The trees and shrubbery were lifeless and still. Even the drone of the city had faded. She ran a hand over her face. Her palm was damp with sweat.

Lightning flickered through the black clouds. A moment later, a deep roll of thunder shook the air. As the first drops of rain fell, she hurried into the Crystal Palace, sheltering under the elaborate wrought-iron and glass canopy as the rain drummed down. Cautiously, she opened the envelope and slid out the sheet of paper inside. Yellowing paper, the ink of the signatures slightly smudged. An adoption certificate, dated 11 August 1970.

The adoptive father was Teniente Ramiro Ortiz, occupation: *Guardia Civil*. The adoptive mother, Teresa Ortiz, occupation: Housewife. The space for the name of the child's biological mother was marked *desconocida*, unknown. And the child: Estrella Lucia, aged one month.

She stared at the certificate. Ramiro's daughter was adopted. Estrella Lucia, the little girl who twelve years later would pull the gas pipe from the wall and kill her and her baby brother.

At the bottom of the certificate was the signature of the authorising officer. A broad script in big angry letters. Galíndez had seen that writing before, in his diary. She had never forgotten it.

Comandante Leopoldo Guzmán,
Brigada Especial, Comisaría de Policía,
Calle de Robles, Vallecas, Madrid

CHAPTER 23

OROITZ, OCTOBER 1954, CUARTEL DE LA GUARDIA CIVIL

Guzmán's footsteps echoed down the dimly lit corridor as he followed the smell of coffee. Ahead of him, a patch of squalid light spilled from the door of the mess room. Inside the mess, Ochoa was sitting at the table, stirring a pot of coffee.

'It's been a long time since I slept in a barracks,' Guzmán said as he joined Ochoa at the table. 'I'd forgotten how much they stink.' He reached for the chipped mug Ochoa pushed towards him. 'On the other hand, that smells very good.'

'It should, I bought it on the black market yesterday,' Ochoa said. 'I got some bread and ham as well. No point fighting a bandit on an empty stomach.'

'Not fighting: killing a bandit,' Guzmán said. 'He has to die.'

Ochoa's expression didn't change. 'That was what I meant, *jefe*.'

Guzmán looked at the slices of ham Ochoa produced from a greasy paper package. 'Fuck, Corporal,' he said, tearing open a piece of bread and filling it with ham, 'if this is how you make breakfast, perhaps I should marry you.'

Ochoa almost smiled. 'You wouldn't want to be married to me, sir.'

'That's true. Because if I walked out, you'd spend the rest of your life tracking me down so you could kill me.'

'It says "Till death us do part" in the marriage vows, *jefe*.'

Guzmán gave him a long look. 'I'm just guessing, but I don't think they meant shooting your señora dead when they wrote that. You're not a Jesuit, are you?'

Ochoa carried on slicing chorizo.

'Did the squad leave anyone to man the radio?' Guzmán asked.

'They did, sir, a lance corporal called Rosales. I just looked in on him and he was sitting by the radio, waiting for messages. He seems keen.'

'That's unusual for a *guardia civil*.' Guzmán snorted.

Ochoa cocked his head, hearing footsteps outside. 'That sounds like him now.'

The lance corporal appeared in the doorway. '*Muy buenas, Comandante*. A message for you.' He handed Guzmán a piece of notepaper bearing a few scrawled sentences.

'Give me a pencil,' Guzmán ordered. He leaned forward and started to decode the message. The lance corporal waited at the door. 'Go,' Guzmán said, without looking up.

Ochoa waited patiently until Guzmán had finished.

'Listen to this,' Guzmán said. He didn't look happy.

LACK OF RESPONSE TO EARLIER CONTACTS MOST
UNSATISFACTORY. CONSIDERING ALTERNATIVE ACTION
UNLESS INFORMED OF SUCCESSFUL
OUTCOME IN NEXT 24 HOURS.

'Lack of contact?' Ochoa said. 'We sent several messages.'

'I know.' Guzmán scowled. 'Fuck knows what's going on, Gutiérrez has his fingers in so many pies. 'But he says he's expecting a successful outcome and that's what we'll give him.' He reached for his coffee. 'I don't have to remind you how important this job is, do I?'

Ochoa shook his head. 'It's your ticket back to Madrid, boss.'

'Our ticket,' Guzmán said. 'When we get back, you'll be the new *sargento*.'

'Thanks,' Ochoa said, though without much enthusiasm, Guzmán noticed.

'And you'll get a month off with pay and full use of the archives to track down your wife,' Guzmán added generously.

Ochoa smiled. 'Lobo's a dead man.'

'That's better. I like my men to enjoy their work.'

A sudden shout echoed down the corridor from the radio room. The truck containing five million pesetas from the coffers of the Banco de Bilbao had just left San Sebastián.

OROITZ 1954, LAUBURU FARM

Begoña was pulling weeds from the flower bed as Patxi Gabilondo came strolling up the track past Lauburu Farm. She smiled as she saw the thin young man with his buck-toothed smile and the vague fuzz on his jaw he hoped would one day be a thick Basque beard.

'*Kaixo*, Señorita Begoña,' Patxi called. 'It rained a lot last night.'

The Arestiguis were Patxi's favourite employers. They were kind and patient and he had learned much from them: how the colours of the clouds signalled changes in the weather, the best way to kill a chicken and the names of the old gods that inhabited the vast countryside.

As a child, Patxi had listened entranced to their stories, sitting before their fire, seeing the flames reflected in their dark luminous eyes as Begoña told of how the French Emperor Charlemagne came to Euskadi with his hordes of French knights and how the Basques had repelled the enemy, falling upon them from the heights with battleaxes, screaming the *irrintzi*, the shrill war cry of their people, as they slaughtered the invaders until only the French knight Roldán was still alive, riddled with arrows that pinned him to a tree like St Sebastian.

Begoña had looked deep into Patxi's eyes as she told that tale, ensuring her words were inscribed in his memory for ever. Roldán was brave, she told him, very brave, but he died because his cause was not just.

Begoña wiped her hands on her apron. '*Dios mio*, Patxi, you seem taller every time I see you. You're a man now.'

Patxi's face lit up at her words. 'Thank you, señorita.'

'Is that the crucifix we got you last Christmas?'

Patxi nodded. He lifted the cross to his lips and kissed it. 'It brings me luck, señorita.'

'So it should, Patxi.' Begoña smiled. 'You deserve it.'

'Is Señorita Nieves around?' Patxi had yet to learn about unrequited love.

'She's gone to the village. Where are you off to?'

'The ridge by the old road. Mikel Aingeru asked me to mend a fence.'

'Be sure he pays you. Mikel forgets things sometimes.'

'I will, señorita,' Patxi agreed. 'I'd better go.'

'Just a minute.' Begoña went into the house and returned with a *bocadillo* filled with links of thin *txistorra* sausage. 'Take this, it'll keep your strength up.' She gave him a stern look. 'Don't eat it all at once, do you hear?'

'*Eskerrik asko.*' Patxi started up the path, clutching the sandwich. She knew he would eat it long before he reached the village.

'You be careful on that ridge,' Begoña called after him. 'There'll be snow today and you know what it's like up there when it snows.'

'I'll be careful,' Patxi shouted, waving goodbye. '*Agur.*'

'*Agur*, Patxi Gabilondo.' Begoña returned to her work, idly wondering what it would have been like to have had a husband and a son. But then, some things were not meant to be.

Something touched her cheek. She looked up, seeing a dark quilt of cloud moving over the mountain. Around her, scattered snowflakes danced on the wind, growing thicker, the flakes clinging to her hair and eyelashes. She hurried back into the house.

SAN SEBASTIÁN 1954, IGLESIA DE LA ASUNCIÓN

The door to the church opened. A big man stood outlined against the light.

'Is that you, *Sargento*?'

355

'Course it is, you blind bastard,' León said, propping his rifle against a pew.

'What are you doing here? We heard you'd been transferred.'

'So I have,' León said. 'But they said you could use another gun, so I volunteered.'

One of the men laughed. 'That's not like you, Sarge.'

León shrugged. 'We'll all be famous when El Lobo's dead. And there's also the reward, I don't want to miss out on that.'

The men were cheered by the prospect of more money. Such things were rare. 'Glad to have you along, Sarge.'

'Me too.' León grinned. 'I wouldn't miss this for the world.'

Ten minutes later, they heard the low rumble of the truck as it pulled up outside.

'*Vamos*,' León shouted as the men filed out to the waiting truck. 'The sooner we get this done, the sooner we can spend that reward money.'

OROITZ 1954

'I don't fucking believe it.' Guzmán peered through the smeared arcs of the wipers at the snow settling over the countryside. 'If it's not raining, it's snowing. What a fucking country.'

'There's something you should know about yesterday,' Ochoa muttered, preoccupied.

'The job you did for Mellado?' Guzmán listened as Ochoa related the events of the previous afternoon with Faisán and the Vidals.

'That means he sent the girl's body up to Guetaria the moment I left him,' Guzmán said. 'And Faisán shot them both? I wouldn't have thought he was capable.'

'Seemed to enjoy it, sir. He said the general would be pleased with him.'

'That's not all,' Guzmán said. 'The intel reports on the women he's arrested are all empty. He's been arresting them for his own ends and once he's done with them, he kills them.'

Ochoa frowned. 'That's pushing things, even for someone in his position. How would he explain it away?'

'He wouldn't,' Guzmán said. 'Because he's mad, Corporal. Fucking mad.'

OROITZ 1954, LA CARRERA VIEJA

Inside the truck there was no light and little ventilation. Within half an hour the vehicle stank of sweat and black tobacco. The sacks of banknotes already took up a fair amount of space, obliging the men to cram themselves in as best they could. The only communication between the troopers and the driver was through a small hatchway in the partition separating the cab from the interior of the truck. Most of it consisted of muffled shouts from the back, complaining about the state of the road, and León's obscene responses.

The truck slowed and halted on the brow of the hill. Ahead, the road descended into the valley, narrowing as it passed between steep ridges to either side. Perfect bandit country, especially with the snow now blurring the slopes.

'Fucking weather,' the driver said. 'How long do we wait here?'

León looked at his watch. 'Ten minutes. Guzmán said he'd be in position by then.'

'You want to let the boys out to stretch their legs then, Sarge?'

'No, they can stay put.' León put a cigarette between his thick lips. 'If El Lobo sees them, he'll disappear and so will our chance of the reward money. Anyway, all that bellyaching will make them more aggressive.'

The driver peered into the snow. 'Are you sure this will work?' he asked, noticing how the road disappeared into thick woods beneath high, overhanging cliffs. 'If anything goes wrong, there's no one to help us within miles.'

'You know what it's like here.' León laughed. 'It might all blow over in a minute. I tell you, this will be a walk in the park, *amigo*.

And you never know, there might be a medal in it.' He threw the butt of his cigarette into the snow.

'You can't eat medals,' the driver grumbled. 'It's the reward I'm interested in.'

'First things first.' León crushed his cigarette into the snow. 'We've got to get the bastard before we see any money.' He went to the back of the truck and pounded on the doors.

A muffled voice. 'Who is it?'

'*Coño*, who do you think? Open up.'

The handle inside the vehicle creaked and the doors swung open. León stepped back to avoid a stream of stinking air. A row of pale-faced troopers blinked in the wintry light.

'Can we get out for a bit, *Sargento*?'

'Stay where you are, Private Ortega, we'll be off in a couple of minutes,' León snapped. 'We'll give the *comandante* time to get in position and then we'll get moving.'

'And we can fire at will if we're attacked, Sarge?'

'Just be sure you shoot straight.' León slammed the doors and waited until the men had locked them from the inside before he climbed back into the cab.

The driver frowned as he watched the wipers struggling to clear the windscreen of snow. 'I hope you know what you're doing, Sarge.'

'I know exactly what I'm doing,' León said.

OROITZ 1954

It was midday when Patxi Gabilondo reached the village. He peered through the snow at the *guardia cuartel*, despite the warnings Señorita Nieves had given him about staring at civil guards. Though he never said so, Patxi would have liked to join the *guardia*. They had nice uniforms, smart tricorne hats and he was mightily impressed by the long rifles they carried. His real motivation, however, was more mundane: three meals a day and accommodation. That luxury was hard for him to imagine.

358

He finished his *bocadillo* and wiped his mouth on his sleeve. Up the narrow street, near Señora Olibari's *pensión*, he caught a glimpse of Nieves Arestigui carrying her wicker basket and his heart pounded as he watched her laughing and chatting with the villagers clustered around the vegetable stall. Nieves didn't see him and Patxi was far too shy to approach her in public. He continued on his way.

OROITZ 1954, LA CARRERA VIEJA

The snow was falling faster, its endless continuity disrupted by sudden gusts of wind. 'What's that noise?' the driver asked.

León shrugged. 'I didn't hear anything.'

'We should drive straight to Oroitz,' the driver grumbled. 'Lobo won't try anything now. Even if he does, the *comandante* won't see him in this.'

'Tell you what, we'll drive halfway and see if it starts to clear. If it doesn't, that's it.'

The weather got worse. The road was already soaked from the previous day's rain and the wheels were losing their grip in the mud. León glared through the repetitive arcs of the wipers, seeing only mist and slanting gusts of snow in the headlights.

'It's a big reward,' he grunted.

'Doesn't matter how big it is,' the driver said. 'We can't catch him if we can't see him.'

The road began to slope to one side, causing the wheels to slip on the half-melted snow. The truck began sliding towards the verge.

'*Joder.*' The driver twisted the wheel as he tried to fight the skid. The truck didn't obey and León grabbed the dashboard as the vehicle slid down the sloping section of road, miring itself in the muddy ground.

'That's all we need.' León pulled his oilskin cape round his shoulders and got down from the cab. The driver heard a sudden flurry of oaths as León saw how deeply the wheels were embedded in the mud. 'We're going nowhere,' he muttered. 'Better let the lads out.'

The driver went round to the back doors and pounded on them with his fist. The cramped troopers climbed out unhappily, forming a semicircle around the stranded vehicle.

'I don't believe it,' the driver groaned.

A sudden sharp whistle, fading in the thin air.

'What the fuck was that?' the driver asked, suddenly uneasy.

'How do I know?' León said. 'A bird maybe.'

'Are we going to walk back, *Sargento*?' one of the men asked.

León shook his head. 'Not with all this money in the truck. We'll stick together. If Lobo makes a move, we're more than a match for him.'

Another piercing whistle in the wintry air. Louder this time.

'I don't know what that is but it's too close for my liking,' the driver said, unfastening the flap of his holster.

Snow dripped from the trees in heavy grey drops. The men looked at one another. Several had drawn their revolvers.

'Fuck's sake,' León said, 'put those guns away. If that bird suddenly flies past, you lot are going to panic and shoot one another.'

Sheepishly, the men holstered their weapons.

Several loud whistles. All around them.

'Shepherds,' León said. 'They'll be moving their flocks because of the weather.'

'You sure about that?' the driver asked, staring into the snow.

'Dead sure.' León leaned his rifle against the side of the cab. 'I'll go and have a word. They can help push us out of this mud.' He gestured towards the open doors of the truck. 'You wait inside, lads. No point all of us getting soaked.'

Anything was better than standing around knee-deep in mud and the men trudged back to the vehicle as León splashed across the road and disappeared into the mist-shrouded trees. The civil guards heard him calling to the shepherds to show themselves. And then his calls faded and all they heard was the dripping of melting snow.

Patxi Gabilondo followed the narrow trail into the valley. He had decided to take a short cut. If he got Mikel's fence finished quickly, he might be able to do some chores for Begoña on his way home in return for the sandwich she'd given him. With luck Nieves would be there too.

Below him, beyond the trees, was the old road. Patxi would follow that until he came to Mikel Aingeru's pastures. Despite being soaked, he was happy. This snow should have stopped by the time he was ready to make his way home.

He paused, hearing the muffled pounding of hooves coming towards him.

A dark shape emerged from the mist, towering above him. Patxi's eyes widened as he recalled the litany of gods and spirits who dwelled in the mountains. But this was no spirit or demon but a man on horseback wearing a wide-brimmed hat and a long oilskin coat.

Patxi saw the Winchester rifle in the man's hand, the high knee boots, the intricate spurs and ornate stirrups. He knew who this was. When he had still attended school, he had seen a picture in the only book the school possessed, showing one of Spain's greatest enemies, the pirate and heretic Francis Drake. And now here he was in front of him.

'Who are you, boy?' Francis Drake asked, in Basque. He raised the muzzle of the Winchester, resting the stock on his thigh.

'Patxi Gabilondo, your worship.'

'And where does Patxi Gabilondo live?'

'Past Oroitz, your worship, beyond Lauburu Farm in the house near the bridge.'

'Then go back there, young man. This is no place for you today.'

'I have to mend a fence, your worship,' Patxi stammered, 'for Mikel Aingeru.'

The rider laughed. 'There are no fences that can be mended for that old man.' Resting his rifle on the pommel of his saddle, he dug into one of the pockets of his coat. 'Here.' He flipped a coin towards Patxi, spinning a silver trail through the damp air.

Patxi retrieved the coin from the wet grass, his eyes wide.

'A *Yanqui* dollar,' Baron Çubiry said, as he wheeled the horse about. 'Spend it wisely.'

'Yes, your worship,' Patxi gasped, scuttling away up the trail.

OROITZ 1954, LA CARRERA VIEJA

'I'll tell you another thing,' Guzmán said, staring out of the window as the car slid on the sodden road, 'I'm never coming back to this fucking country again.' He pulled his cigarette case from his pocket. 'There's too much weather for my liking.'

'It was bad last time we were here,' Ochoa said. 'In the war, I mean.'

'I know what you mean,' Guzmán snapped. 'Although we agreed not to talk about it.'

Ochoa wisely changed the subject. 'I appreciate the time off to find my wife, sir. Especially since you know what I'm going to do.'

'For fuck's sake.' Guzmán breathed out a mouthful of smoke. 'I'm a policeman. What do I care if you kill someone? It's none of my business.'

Ochoa slowed to a crawl. 'Do you know where we are, *jefe*?'

Guzmán looked at the bleak landscape. 'Not really. But we can't miss the truck, it's coming down this road towards us.' He peered into the whirling snow again. 'Eventually.'

'Daylight at last.' Ochoa pointed ahead, where a long shaft of sunlight slanted down onto the craggy hillside, glittering on the snow.

'Pull over,' Guzmán said. 'I'm going up that ridge to take a look round.' He got out of the car and pulled his rifle from the back seat. 'You wait here. Keep me covered from behind the car, just in case.'

Ochoa took his rifle and rested it on the car roof, watching the hillside through the sight as Guzmán started working his way up the rocky gradient.

It was slow going. The snow fell steadily, imposing a muffled silence over the slope, a silence broken only by the sound of his laboured breathing. As he reached the top of the ridge, he heard a noise. Muted footsteps running towards him. He lifted the rifle and aimed as the figure appeared out of the snow. An adolescent boy, hair the colour of straw, his eyes wide as he saw the rifle pointed at him.

'*Joder.*' Guzmán lowered the rifle. 'Where are you going, *chico*?'

'To mend a fence in the lower pasture, your worship,' Patxi stammered.

'Go back home,' Guzmán said. 'Don't hang around here, it's not safe.' He put his hand in his pocket and pulled out a twenty peseta note. 'You know what this is, don't you?'

Patxi nodded. He knew what it was though he had never touched one.

'Take it,' Guzmán said, 'and get lost.'

Patxi scooted back the way he had come, his skinny figure soon lost in the mist and snow.

Guzmán started back down the hillside. There was nothing to be seen from up here, the visibility was appalling.

OROITZ 1954, LA CARRERA VIEJA

León moved across the road into a thicket of trees and tangled clumps of scrub. Behind him, he could just make out the dark shape of the truck where the lads would be smoking and joshing as they waited for his return. He grinned, pleased with himself. It was true what they said about having the last laugh.

'If you move, monsieur, I will surely kill you.' A suave French voice, disembodied in the swirling mist.

León saw the dark bulk of Baron Çubiry's horse as it edged towards him. The Baron was not alone. From where León was standing, the Çubiry were like an army bearing down on him, dark horses with coloured war ribbons plaited in their manes, sallow-

363

faced men with rifles, cutlasses and automatic pistols. An insane collection of headgear. León staggered, struggling to stay on his feet as Çubiry's horse pushed him aside. The Baron leaned from the saddle, baring his teeth. A metre away, León could smell his breath.

'You've done well, *Sargento*.'

'I'm glad you think so.'

'Where are they?' His voice thick, menacing.

'Over there,' León said, pointing. 'They're all in the truck, just as I told Jeanette.'

'Ah, my dear Jeannette.' Baron Çubiry smiled. 'You know what she said about you?'

León shrugged. Women's opinions counted for nothing as far as he was concerned. 'I imagine she said how helpful I've been.'

'Jeanette said there was no one on this earth the likes of you would not betray.'

León frowned. Things weren't going to plan. His plan, at least. 'She said we had a deal.'

Amused, Çubiry twisted in his saddle to address the riders behind him. '*Mes amis*, you ride as Çubiry, you die as Çubiry. When you meet the enemy there can be no mercy. As the Good Book says, "I will not listen to their cry; though they offer burnt offerings, I will not accept them. Instead, I will destroy them with the sword."'

The Baron leaned out of the saddle and stared at León, tightening his grip on the horse's reins. 'You think you're the only one who knows about treachery?' He pointed towards the road. '*Allez*, Çubiry.'

The pack of riders moved forward, picking up speed, the dull pounding of their hooves exploding into an agitated rhythm as they raced across the soaked ground, swords flashing as they left the scabbards. As he followed, the Baron called to one of the men behind him. 'Kill him, Jean-Claude.'

León saw the rider gallop towards him, his pistol extended over the horse's head. He heard the percussive blast of the shot and then the ground whirled around him as he pitched backwards into the sodden scrub.

Guzmán stood with Ochoa, listening intently to the silence. 'I'd swear I heard a horse.'

'I can't hear anything,' Ochoa said. He started walking back to the car.

Guzmán glanced around at the desolate landscape. He heard the horse again and raised his hand. Ochoa stopped, alert now.

'Get back in the car,' Guzmán said quietly. 'Don't hurry and don't look round.'

Ochoa walked slowly, his boots crunching on the snow. He paused as he opened the car door, still listening. Then he slid behind the wheel and started the engine.

Guzmán ran his eye over the hillside again before hurrying back to the car. 'Put your foot down,' he said. 'Fast as you can without killing us.'

Ochoa felt the wheel jar his hands as the car bounced over the rough road, accelerating in a shower of mud and snow, the engine rising in pitch as it picked up speed. A few hundred metres ahead, the road went down a slight incline. On either side the ground fell away steeply into groves of dark pines.

'Once we're past this wood, pull over and we'll take another look,' Guzmán said.

The windscreen exploded in a storm of stinging glass.

The car veered off the road, smashing through the remains of an old wall as it plunged down the slope, shedding pieces of wreckage as it went. The two men were hurled forward as the chassis hit a tree stump that ripped the exhaust from the vehicle in a howl of tortured metal. The wrecked car careered on down the hill until it smashed into a large boulder at the bottom of the incline, throwing Guzmán and Ochoa forward into the dashboard.

Inside the mangled Buick there was a sudden silence.

An abrupt clatter as the bonnet jerked up from its broken fittings; the sound of glass falling from shattered windows; the creaking of battered bodywork; steam spluttering from under the crumpled bonnet; a stench of gasoline.

Ochoa clutched his head. Guzmán saw blood running through his fingers. He pushed him to the door. 'Try and get behind those rocks over there.'

Ochoa threw open the battered door, and ran towards the shelter of the boulders. On the road above, Guzmán saw the mounted rifleman looking down at him. And then the horseman jumped down from the saddle, taking shelter behind a lip of rock that gave him an excellent field of fire while making it almost impossible for Guzmán to get a decent shot at him.

Guzmán kicked open the door and slid out, firing. He crouched behind the car, waiting for the response. A moment later the driver's seat exploded in a flurry of shredded leather as the report of the rifle echoed around the barren hillside. The gunman fired again and the nearside headlight disintegrated.

Guzmán smelled oil as a bullet shuddered into the engine block. The offside headlight went next, blasted apart in such a spectacular manner Guzmán suspected the bastard was using armour-piercing bullets. He spat angrily into the soil as he reloaded the Browning and got to his feet, holding the pistol in a two-handed grip as he crept along the side of the car.

Keeping low, he pulled at the handle of the rear door, hoping to retrieve the rifle from the back seat. The battered door didn't move. Guzmán raised his head slowly, looking through the shattered window for the rifle. The seething bee-whine of a bullet fizzed past him, forcing him to take cover again. The rifle would have to stay where it was.

The rifleman fired again and the car sagged as the front offside tyre exploded. Guzmán dashed from behind the rear of the car and ran towards the rocks, scrambling behind the boulder where Ochoa was sheltering.

'At least we're safe here,' Ochoa said.

Guzmán narrowed his eyes. 'Unfortunately, we're also trapped, Corporal.'

The rifleman turned his attention to the car. Within minutes the remaining tyres had been shot out. Another flurry of bullets sent shards of metal and broken glass flying. A sharp hiss of steam signalled the radiator had been hit.

'What the fuck's going on?' Guzmán said angrily. 'The *guardia* must have heard the shooting by now. They were supposed to support us.'

As suddenly as it had begun, the confrontation ended as they heard the muffled hoofbeats as the rifleman rode away.

Guzmán retrieved the rifles from the wrecked car and forced open the boot to get at the ammunition. He pointed down the road in the direction the horseman had taken. 'Let's find out.'

SAN SEBASTIÁN 1954, HOTEL INGLÉS

'What the fuck do you mean, you don't know where Guzmán is?' Gutiérrez barked. 'All week I've been telling you to get him to make contact and you say you can't reach him?'

'I've tried everything, sir,' Viana said. 'He's been lying low, I don't know why. The only time he showed himself was when he met with Carrero Blanco. I don't understand that.'

'I think I do,' Gutiérrez said. 'I thought Guzmán was loyal, but there are degrees of loyalty and his greatest loyalty has always been to himself. It's just possible Guzmán has decided to work for Carrero Blanco.'

'Shall I take action?' Viana asked.

'No. You'd have to find him. He may have a good reason for going to ground. I'll wait a little longer. In the meantime, I want you to keep looking for him, just tell him to get in touch. I'm arranging for a file to be sent to him. There are things he needs to know.'

'And you're going to send the file to me to pass on to him, sir?'

'Not at all. It will be sent by courier to one of my agents. Guzmán can collect it from them. Just in case, I'll telegraph you the address once it has been sent. You can phone to see if it has been collected. Understood?'

'Perfectly, sir. You can rely on me.'

'I hope so,' Gutiérrez muttered, 'because if Guzmán doesn't complete this operation successfully it won't just be him who's fucked, it'll be me as well.' The line crackled as he hung up.

Viana sat on the bed staring at the big Bakelite phone on the night table. 'Then you're both fucked, *mi General.*' He smiled.

OROITZ 1954, LA CARRERA VIEJA

The civil guards sat inside the truck, wet and miserable. Sitting by the doors, Diaz lifted his head, suddenly curious. 'What the fuck is that noise?'

The men exchanged glances, uneasy as the sound grew louder. A rolling noise, like distant thunder. But this was not thunder, nor was it distant, and it was coming towards them.

'Fuck this.' Diaz snatched up his rifle and climbed out, his boots splashing in the mud as he looked round, trying to locate the source of the noise.

The tension was becoming unbearable and Ortega quickly followed. Suddenly, no one wanted to stay in the truck and the others hurried after their comrades, jostling out into the open.

'Form a line,' the lance corporal shouted, realising he was in charge now. The men glanced at one another, grim-faced as they formed an irregular line by the rear of the vehicle, rifles lifted as they peered into the mist, trying to gauge where the noise was coming from.

'What the fuck is it?' yelled Quintana, his eyes flitting over the dark bushes across the road as the ground trembled beneath his feet. He saw vague movement in the trees and stepped forward, raising the rifle to his shoulder, trying to identify a target. The noise stopped.

Quintana lowered the rifle, puzzled.

A hoarse voice screamed a single word: 'Çubiry.' A chill colder than any winter as dozens of voices joined the chorus, howling the name again and again as the pounding of hooves swelled like an oncoming storm.

The rider exploded from the bushes, his long cavalry sabre sparkling like white fire in the autumn mist. Quintana screamed as the blade entered his back, and his rifle clattered to the ground as he clutched at the bloody point sticking from his chest.

Horsemen erupted from the trees on all sides, their great swords swinging in glittering arcs as they cut down those troopers who attempted to flee, splattering the churned snow with their blood. A few *guardia* tried to make a stand and the snow-swept escarpment echoed to the sound of gunfire as the Çubiry opened up with their automatic pistols.

'Kill them all.' Baron Çubiry's voice rose above the sound of fighting as he rode among his enemies, a thin smile on his face, a broomhandle Mauser in his hand. Private Ruiz was propped against the side of the truck, clutching a sabre wound in his side. As the Baron's horse wheeled in front of him, Ruiz pulled his bayonet from his belt and got to his feet. The Baron reined in his horse, aiming as Ruiz staggered towards him. As the shot echoed around the trees, Private Ruiz crumpled into the mud, leaving only a spatter of bloody tissue on the side of the truck to mark the one act of bravery in his short and unremarkable career.

That was enough for those who still lived. They fled, trying to dodge the massive horses as the Çubiry plunged after them into the undergrowth, charging down the fleeing men, hacking with sabres and cutlasses, cackling as they fell. For a time, the trees echoed to the sound of drumming hooves and screams of terror, punctuated by the crackle of small-arms fire. Finally, a chill silence fell, broken only by the whinny of a horse or a sudden scream as the Çubiry discovered a wounded trooper hiding in the bushes and dragged him out to face execution in front of the baying riders.

'*C'est fini*,' Baron Çubiry bellowed. 'God favours the Çubiry.

Our rage blazes forth like fire, and the mountains crumble to dust in our presence.'

Around him, the riders roared their defiance to the Spanish, to the police and to God himself, as they dragged the sacks of banknotes from the truck and tied them to their saddles. Once the vehicle was empty, they rode away in line, leaving the bodies of the Oroitz garrison strewn over the bloody snow amid a clutter of discarded weapons and equipment.

OROITZ 1954, CARRERA VIEJA

Guzmán and Ochoa made their way along the road, alert for any sign of the rifleman returning. Guzmán was having difficulty speaking, so great was his anger.

'Was it El Lobo, boss?' Ochoa asked, hoping Guzmán had cooled down.

Guzmán stared as if he didn't understand. 'Yes, it fucking was. Didn't you see him?'

Ochoa shook his head. 'I was behind the rocks, remember?'

Guzmán had nothing more to say and they pressed on through the fading afternoon in silence until his anger resurfaced. 'Twelve armed *guardia* should be a match for a bandit,' he said. 'All I expected was for them to pin him down.'

'Maybe that's what happened,' Ochoa said. 'Perhaps the lads drove him off.'

'You're right. They could be sitting in that truck right now, on top of five million pesetas, bellyaching about what a hard life they have.'

'Could be, *jefe*.'

'They'd better be, Corporal,' Guzmán said, 'because if anything happens to that money, it will be the end of my career.' He spat into the snow. 'It might be the end of me, come to that.'

As the snow died away, the details of the surrounding country-side began to emerge with increasing clarity. Ahead, the road sloped down to a glade of skeletal trees. Guzmán swore as he saw the angular shape of the truck protruding from the verge into the road, its wheels mired deep in the soft mud, the words on the side clearly visible: *Banco de Bilbao*.

'Look at that,' he said. 'The clumsy bastards ran it off the road. What did I tell you? I bet they're taking a nap in the back.'

As they got closer, he realised he was wrong. Angrily, he raised his rifle, looking for a target. 'I don't fucking believe it,' he said finally, lowering the rifle. There was no one to shoot. No one alive, that was.

Guzmán stared at the sprawled bodies, the equipment and weapons strewn around them on the wet snow. All dead. Even the wounded had been executed. Their bodies lay face down in the mud with a bullet in the back of the head. He saw Ortega, his face a frozen mask of surprise. And no wonder, Guzmán thought, seeing the sword sticking from his chest.

The truck was empty, the back doors open, just a few damp banknotes stuck to the floor. It was worse than he could have imagined. Far worse. Five million pesetas. Gone.

Ochoa called out to him. Guzmán turned and saw the line of horsemen on the distant ridge, silhouetted against the autumn sky, sacks of money hanging from their saddles, their bizarre headgear stark against the light as they headed back along the smugglers' trail to France.

It took León a moment to realise he was not dead. Lying dazed in the narrow ditch, hidden by soaking gorse, he listened to the slaughter taking place two hundred metres away. Warily, he got to his feet and made his way along the side of the escarpment. His thoughts echoed with bitter hindsight. Who but a fool would trust the Çubiry? Their fluctuating loyalty was legendary. Only a man driven by greed would involve himself in a scheme like this.

León was a big man and was soon out of breath as the escarpment grew steeper. As he climbed, the sodden ground crumbled under his boots and he was gasping by the time he reached the steep gradient near the top. Clutching at the wet turf, he dragged himself over the brow of the hill onto the flat track at the top of the ridge and lay motionless, gulping air like a drowning man.

As his breathing slowed, he realised he was not alone. He got to his knees, his eyes fixed on the tallow-haired youth standing a couple of metres away.

The lad smiled. '*Kaixo*, Sargento León.'

'Who the fuck are you?' León wiped sweat from his eyes with a muddy hand.

'Patxi Gabilondo, your worship.'

'And you know who I am?'

'Yes, sir, you're the *sargento* from the *cuartel* at Oroitz.'

'And where are you going?' León asked in a low voice.

'I'm going home, your worship.'

'No, you're not,' León said, reaching for his pistol. 'You're a witness.'

CHAPTER 24

COLMENAR VIEJO, JULY 2010, FUENTES RESIDENCE

Galíndez left her overnight bag in the spare room and wandered downstairs onto the veranda. Along the hall, she heard the girls' excited chatter as they trailed after their mother, ignoring her harassed requests to leave her in peace.

She heard their voices like someone listening to rain. Even the subtle colours of the garden were lost on her as she stared across the lawn, brooding on the hand grenade Rosario Calderón had tossed into her lap the day before.

Calderón knew exactly what she was doing, Galíndez realised. She'd gone to a lot of trouble to get that adoption certificate, knowing the effect it would have if Galíndez refused to close down her investigation. Knowing it would fuck her up. And she'd been right, it had. The evidence was clear-cut. The certificate showed Ramiro and Teresa had adopted a stolen child. Worse, the adoption had been authorised by Guzmán, the man Galíndez had turned into front-page-news. The media would have a field day reporting that ironic detail.

As well as Calderón's scheming, there was also the question of why Uncle Ramiro had never told her he knew Guzmán when she'd started her investigation. Hadn't it occurred to him she might unearth the details of the adoption? She lifted a hand to her mouth, chewing her knuckle in frustration, torn between anger at Ramiro and sympathy for his tragic loss.

Calderón's action had thrown her ethical principles into turmoil. If this had involved any other high-profile figure, her sense of justice would have overridden all arguments, Christ, there would have been no argument. Galíndez would have made it public as a matter of course. But this was different. Ramiro was family.

Driving up the motorway earlier, she'd wondered if perhaps Ramiro might welcome a chance to talk about what had happened. After all, his adopted child had been dead for twenty-eight years, maybe talking about it might give him a sense of closure? It would never happen. What would he do, appear on *Oprah*? He didn't do emotion, much less discuss it. And when Ramiro didn't want to do something, it didn't get done.

That left her with the option of making the adoption public by including it in her report – the report Calderón had just agreed to publish. If the report named him, Ramiro would complain vociferously, although complaint would be too slight a term to describe his volcanic fury. Her defence would be simple: the brief from Calderón was to compile information on the *niños robados* scandal and to highlight Guzmán's involvement. Worthy aims, she knew, though Calderón's words still haunted her: everything came with a hidden cost.

And what a cost it would be. Going public would ruin Ramiro's career and his life. He and Aunt Teresa were the only family she had. If she did this, they would never speak to her again. What was more, she wouldn't blame them. Galíndez was still little Ana María to Ramiro. He'd never understand why she'd betrayed him. Certainly he'd never forgive her.

Two choices then. Destroy her remaining family ties or lie and conceal the evidence.

She stared into the lush colours of the Fuenteses' garden, torn between truth and family loyalty, knowing there was no contest. She would destroy the adoption certificate. Her way of repaying Ramiro for his kindness over the years. But betraying her principles hurt, it hurt a lot, and she clenched her fists, remembering Calderón's eyes the previous afternoon, pale and staring.

A hand closed on her arm. Galíndez spun round, fists raised defensively.

'Sorry, I didn't mean to scare you,' Merche said, shaken by her reaction. 'Are you OK?'

Galíndez gave her an embarrassed smile. 'I was miles away.'

'I asked if you wanted a drink.'

'*Agua con gas*, please.'

Merche went into the kitchen and returned with a glass of sparkling water, the ice clinking against the rim. She turned, hearing a sudden bang inside the kitchen. 'Clari, you nearly smashed my best plates. Where did you get that ball?'

Clari kicked the football out onto the porch. 'Ana gave it to me.'

'Perhaps Ana will take you to play with it on the lawn.' Merche winked at Galíndez. 'Damage limitation.'

'Point taken.' Galíndez picked up the ball and punted it across the grass. Clari raced after it, squealing happily.

'We really appreciate you looking after the girls tonight, Ana María.'

'It's no trouble, Merche, I enjoy it.'

'You know what? Inés always said she wanted a big sister. I think she's got one now.'

'That's a nice thing to say.' Galíndez gave her a shy smile. 'I'll do my best.'

'Before we go, there's something I need to show you,' Merche said. 'The gas.'

Galíndez had a sudden image of Ramiro's children and the boiler.

'It's not dangerous.' Merche smiled, misreading her expression. 'Just one of the disadvantages of living in the country, I'm afraid. Come on, I'll show you.'

Galíndez followed her into the kitchen and saw the row of fat metal gas cylinders, arranged by the door to the veranda.

'There's not much left in the current cylinder,' Merche explained. 'If it runs out, you need to replace it with one of these. It's that blue nozzle on top, see? But be careful, they're really heavy.'

'No problem,' Galíndez said. She was going to use the microwave.

A car horn sounded outside and Merche snatched up her things. 'God, Luis is so impatient. See you later, Ana. *Hasta pronto, niñas.*'

The girls ran up the drive, chasing their parents' car, waving until it disappeared over the brow of the hill.

Galíndez was waiting when they came back. She was holding a package. 'Clari already got her present, so here's yours, Inés.'

'*Gracias*, Ana.' Inés weighed the package in her hands. 'It's heavy.'

'Too heavy for summer,' Galíndez agreed, 'but it was a such a bargain I couldn't resist.' She watched as Inés tore open the wrapping.

'*Madre mía*, a leather jacket?'

'It's from the flea market. I get mine at the same place.'

'It's totally cool,' Inés said, pulling it on. '*Muchísimas gracias*.'

'*De nada*. Come on, let's take Clari outside and play with her ball.' Galíndez paused. 'Maybe you should leave the jacket here, Inés, it's pretty warm out there.'

She followed the girls into the garden. Around them, the warm air pulsed with the sound of crickets. Near the boundary of the garden, the shadows of the cypress trees were slowly extending towards the house. She thought about getting a cold beer and sitting on the veranda to watch the sun go down. And then Inés screamed.

'I'll throw you in the stream if you do that again, Clarisa Fuentes. Tell her, Ana María, she kicked the ball at me.'

'Come on, girls,' Galíndez called. 'Let's walk up to the top of the garden. Inés, let Clari have the ball and we'll kick it all the way up and then all the way back down again.' *And then back again, until it's time for dinner. And after that, you'll be ready for bed. I have a plan.*

She glanced around the garden. Long shadows and bright pools of light, the murmur of crickets somewhere in a patch of tangled shrubs. Once the kids were in bed, she'd definitely slip out on the porch and have that beer.

The girls had almost reached the top of the garden and were kicking the ball, bored as they waited for Galíndez. She looked back down the garden towards the long lazy curve of the stream that disappeared into a knot of trees and bushes behind the house. She saw her car on the drive, the sparkle of sunlight on metal and glass and closed her eyes, enjoying the sun on her face. She opened them again. Near the top of the drive something glinted with shards of brilliant light. A metallic blue four-by-four was parked by the gate. She stared, remembering the car passing the Fuenteses' gate the night she gave Inés her martial arts lesson. Returning again and again. And she remembered the CCTV footage of the car passing Carabanchel Metro after running down Adelina Solano. Her stomach tightened.

'*Niñas.*' The girls didn't hear so she raised her voice. 'Come on, let's go back and get a drink.' Flushed and excited, the girls ignored her and carried on playing with the ball.

Galíndez looked back to the gate. The car was gone. Puzzled, she peered down the ochre strip of road into the distance and saw nothing. She realised she was holding her breath, listening for the sound of an engine.

Inés and Clari were waiting by the perimeter of the garden where the hedge met the ramshackle stone wall that marked the upper boundary of the property. Galíndez suddenly felt vulnerable at being so far from the house. *I'm probably being stupid. But still…*

A sudden flash of light. A car coming along the road. Light blue, metallic paint. Tinted windows. She frowned. People didn't just drive up and down like that. Didn't keep parking across the drive of the only house for several kilometres. But there were plenty of blue cars in the world, for fuck's sake. Perhaps someone was trying to spook her? If they were, it was working. She reached into her pocket, fumbling for her phone. Then she remembered. The phone was in her bag in the house.

'*Niñas*, time for a pizza.' Trying to sound authoritative.

The car was getting nearer, slowing.

'*Niñas, por favor*,' Galíndez yelled. And then much louder, '*Vamos, señoritas.*' She turned towards the house, hurrying them along, feeling like their teacher.

She wondered how many were in the car. If it was one guy she could probably handle him, two even. But what if they were armed? She breathed slowly, considering the alternative, that they were joyriders or kids from one of the houses along the road. They hadn't done anything, for God's sake, she thought, brushing her hair away from her face. Yet.

Something was eroding her usual confidence and she realised what it was. The girls. If she was alone, she could just take off into the countryside if she had to. She had no doubt she could outrun anyone in this terrain. But running wasn't an option. She was responsible for the children. If anything happened to them, she would have to explain to their parents. That responsibility felt strange and uncomfortable.

'Why are you walking so fast?' Inés asked, panting for breath.

Galíndez pointed. 'See that car?'

'Yes?' Inés nodded, her voice suddenly uncertain.

'I'm worried about it.'

'You think they might be, like, crooks or something?'

'I'm probably wrong,' said Galíndez. 'Does your papa keep a gun in the house?'

Inés nodded. 'It's in his wardrobe but we're not allowed to go near it, ever. We can't even open the door or we'd be in big trouble.'

'Don't worry, *chica*, I'm *guardia*, like your papa. I know how to use a gun.'

'Yeah,' Inés said. 'But you're a girl.'

The car would reach the gate in a minute at most.

'Let's run,' Galíndez said. 'First prize is two slices of pizza.' She kicked the ball, sending it flying towards the house. 'I said run.' The girls hesitated but Galíndez's next shout left no room for argument. 'Run when I tell you, for God's sake.'

Clari was too small to keep up and Galíndez scooped her into her arms and sprinted down the slope with Inés racing after her as they ran full tilt across the sun-scorched grass, past Galíndez's car, clattering over the wooden veranda into the kitchen.

Galíndez turned the key in the door. 'Go and lock the back door, Inés,' she gasped, trying to catch her breath. Inés hesitated. 'Now,' Galíndez shouted.

Inés scuttled away. She returned a few moments later, pale-faced. 'It's locked, Ana.'

'Good girl. Now, let's look in your dad's wardrobe.'

'Can't.' Clari was sitting on the floor. She shook her head. 'Gun.'

'*Vamos.*' Galíndez picked up Clari and carried her upstairs. Inés sighed and followed them to her parents' bedroom.

Capitán Fuentes had clearly taught his daughters about the danger of firearms since the girls stood on the far side of the room, watching unhappily as Galíndez opened the wardrobe door and rummaged inside. The pistol was in a cardboard box behind some shoes. Inside was an Star BM 9mm semi-automatic in a scuffed leather holster. Fuentes must have been issued this back in the day, she guessed. Despite its age, the pistol was solid and reassuring. She went to the window and looked up the drive.

'Is it there, Ana?' Inés asked.

'I can't see it,' Galíndez said. 'Maybe they've gone.' She ruffled Clari's hair in a clumsy attempt at reassurance. When she turned back to the window, the car was about forty metres up the road, nestled against the hedge, the setting sun glinting on the metallic paint.

Inés fidgeted nervously. 'Do you need Dad's big gun, Ana María?'

'His big gun?' Galíndez turned to look at her. 'What's that?'

'The one he uses for rabbits.' Inés pointed to the wardrobe. Galíndez leaned in and saw a long metal box set flush into the rear panel. She tugged at the handle. 'Where's the key?'

Inés retrieved a key from a drawer in the bedside table. Galíndez took it from her and unlocked the box. Inside was a shotgun, glistening with dark threat in the faint light. She lifted it out, checking it was unloaded. '*Joder,*' she muttered, weighing it in her hands. This was real firepower.

'If Dad says a rude word, it's a euro in the swear box,' Inés said.

'Rude,' Clari echoed.

'Sue me,' Galíndez muttered. In the bottom of the wardrobe she found ammunition for the pistol and a carton of shotgun cartridges. She took another peek out the window. The sun was setting, dazzling her with a few last shards of light. The car hadn't moved.

'Inés, take Clari, put some pizza in the microwave and then bring it back up here.'

Once the children were downstairs, Galíndez loaded both weapons. A few minutes later, the girls returned and sat on the bed, eating while she stood guard at the window, watching the car slowly blend into the shadows along the hedge.

Inés watched her intently, the slice of pizza never quite reaching her mouth. She was scared, Galíndez realised. It was time to do something.

'Eat your pizza, Inés,' she said firmly. She went along the landing, retrieved her phone from the spare room and dialled 062. There'd be an instant response to an Officer in Trouble call. If it turned out to be a false alarm, they could put it down to nerves or her hormones, she didn't care. Fuck them.

She glared at the phone as she went into the bedroom. '*Mierda*, there's no signal.'

Inés shook her head. 'You can't always get one out here.'

Galíndez went to the bedside table and tried the landline. No dial tone. She felt her stomach tighten. That was too much of a coincidence.

The girls watched, waiting for her to make things right, knowing that was what adults did. The kids needed calm and reassurance and here she was, clutching a pump-action shotgun. The girls' faces were already pale and tense. If things kicked off, they would be hysterical. She couldn't deal with the men in that car with the girls at her side. It was time to make a decision. Be the grown-up. She needed a plan.

'Do you two have a hiding place when you're playing?' Galíndez asked.

'Tree house,' Clari said, sucking a string of cheese from the end of her pizza.

'It's not really a house,' Inés said. 'You cross the stream and there are some thick bushes growing near the trees. Underneath them, there's a space where no one can see you.'

Galíndez glanced out of the window, seeing the detail of the car melding with the darkness. She made her decision. 'I want you to go to your tree house and stay there. You have to be quiet, no matter what you hear. If anything frightens you, put your fingers in your ears. And whatever happens, Inés, don't come out until I tell you it's OK.' She saw Inés's lip quiver. 'Be brave, Inés. Please.'

'I'll try.' Inés put a protective arm round her sister.

'*Vamos.*' Galíndez led them downstairs and shepherded them out of the back door. She helped them across the stream, gave them a last quick hug and then watched as they wriggled into the narrow gap in the bushes that led to their hiding place. She took out her phone and tried the *guardia* again. Still no signal. She was on her own. She shrugged that thought away. This wasn't the time to feel sorry for herself.

She went into the house and locked the back door again. As she went along the hall, she pumped the slide of the shotgun, putting a round into the breech. Babysitting was over.

She searched the kitchen, looking for the main power switch. If anyone broke in, the darkness would be to her advantage. Near the door to the veranda, she saw the row of gas cylinders, waist high, and heavy. Very heavy. Laying the shotgun on the table, she wrestled the cylinders against the door, one after another, a solid barrier against anyone who tried to force the door open.

She found the power switch on the wall near the sink and flipped it, filling the house with the night. Cautiously, she made her way back upstairs to the bedroom. Through the window a thin band of light on the horizon signalled the end of the day.

Galíndez stared into the garden. She could no longer see the car. For all she knew, it might have driven away. Maybe in half an hour she'd be laughing about this.

Something moved in the shadows by the hedge and Galíndez watched the dark shapes come stealthily across the lawn fifty metres from the house. Five men, dressed in black, two carrying sub-machine guns. She took the pistol from the window ledge and pushed it into the waistband of her jeans, wishing more than ever she had a plan. Through the window, she glimpsed the men with sub-machine guns crouching several metres apart, peering towards the house. No sign of the others. *They've got a plan.*

A sudden noise downstairs. Someone trying the handle of the back door. And then the sound of glass breaking. Galíndez turned from the window and ran across the landing to the stairs. Below, she saw pale shards of glass scattered on the floor, the jagged hole in the pane and, as she took another step down, she saw a gloved hand reach through the broken pane, fumbling for the key. Galíndez groaned, wishing she'd taken it from the lock. She sat on the stairs and aimed the shotgun, wondering whether to shout a warning as the key turned.

The shotgun blast was deafening. Ears ringing, Galíndez stared at the ragged hole in the door. Without thinking, she ejected the cartridge and raised the shotgun again.

'*Da eba.*' A man's shout outside. Angry.

Galíndez saw him, outlined in the doorway, swearing as he tried to drag the wounded man away. She went down a couple more stairs, the shotgun at her shoulder. The stair creaked and the man looked up, raising his pistol. She saw the sudden muzzle flash. Heard the muffled impact of the bullet somewhere behind her. She pulled the trigger.

There was no door left now, only shredded fragments of wood clinging to the hinges. Galíndez ran forward, pumping the shotgun, scanning for movement. There was no need, she realised, seeing the bodies. Neither of these men would move again. She turned and raced back upstairs to the bedroom, hoping to get a shot at the men in the garden before they came to investigate the shooting. But she was too eager. As she reached the window, the men were already raising their weapons, seeing her pale silhouette through the dark glass.

Galíndez dived for cover as the window atomised in a white mist of fragmented glass. She lay, protecting her head with her hands as bullets impacted on metal and brick in wild flurries of sparks; pillows exploding in demented snow-bursts of feathers, the doors of the wardrobe swinging crazily on broken hinges, shredded by the rattling waves of gunfire.

The house echoed with the sound of random destruction as she crawled on her belly out onto the landing. She sat on the top stair and eased herself down, one stair at a time, raising a hand to protect her face as a mirror exploded, sending a stream of jagged silver shards tumbling noisily down the stairs. She kept going, manoeuvring over the broken glass as the firing continued, a clamorous staccato hammer punctuated by the agonised sounds of the bedroom being torn apart. The gunmen clearly thought she was still up there, since only a few stray bullets hit the ground floor, tearing into the walls with a sibilant whine, ricochets veering along erratic trajectories of destruction through the darkened rooms.

At the foot of the stairs, she paused, seeing the ruined door and the crumpled bodies on the step. It was time to get outside, before the others came in after her. Outside, she could hide in the shadows and plan her next move.

Holding the shotgun upright, she checked the hall, peering through the gloom into the kitchen, seeing the door to the veranda wedged firmly shut by the line of gas cylinders. The important thing now was to get away from the house and she hurried to the back door, ready to dash outside. A slight movement in the shadows made her glance back. The tips of a man's shoes, protruding from the lounge doorway a metre away.

He came flying at her, big and heavy, eyes glinting in white fury through the holes of his black ski mask as he slammed her back against the wall, the air exploding from her lungs. She struggled to keep her grip on the shotgun as he wrestled it sideways, forcing the stock towards her, hammering her against the wall as he tried to push the weapon against her throat.

Galíndez's fighting was based on pitting skill and guile against brute force. For that, she needed to keep him at a distance. He was too close to kick so she tried to put pressure on his knee but there was no room for that in such brutal proximity as she fought for breath, feeling his massive strength forcing the cold metal of the shotgun against her throat. Her feet flailed against the sides of his legs as he pressed harder, pinning her against the wall. Strange noises, a feeling her eyes were about to burst. Thoughts jumbled, fleeting and random. *Should have had a plan.*

Her right hand scrabbled at her waistband, her fingers closing around Fuentes' semi-automatic. Strange lights burst across her vision. She was starting to lose consciousness. She tugged the pistol from her belt, pressed the muzzle into the man's side and pulled the trigger.

The gun didn't fire.

Galíndez felt the world around her dissolving. Soon she would sense nothing, just the sound of her own death rattle in the growing darkness. Her thumb moved over the rigid contours of the pistol, fumbling with the safety, pressing the hammer back. She made a final attempt to breathe and failed. Her left hand lost its grip on the shotgun and she sagged limply against the wall. Sensing victory, the man stepped back to let her fall, easing the pressure on her throat. She didn't fall.

Galíndez raised the pistol to his belly and fired. A sudden crack, the smell of scorched cloth. The clatter of the shotgun on the floor. She fired again, sending him lurching backwards, clutching the smoking holes in his combat jacket as he fell against the wall behind him and slid to the floor, his left hand clutching the wounds in his gut. Galíndez raised the pistol in a two-handed grip, shaking as she gulped air, trying to contain the rage surging through her. Wondering what happened now.

The man looked up. Seeing the uncertainty in her face, he reached into his jacket, scrabbling with bloody fingers for the pistol under his left arm. She pulled the trigger. A dry percussive report. His head rolled back, the hole in his forehead leaking blood. A mess on the wall behind him. And then, above her rasping breathing, she heard another noise. They were trying to force open the door to the kitchen.

She picked up the shotgun and stumbled down the hall. As she reached the kitchen, she heard the men outside swearing as they threw their weight against the door, trying to push the heavy cylinders back. Galíndez raised the shotgun and fired, blowing a hole through the door at chest height. The swearing stopped. A moment later, a vicious spray of sub-machine gun bullets swept the kitchen, raking the shelves of crockery on the wall in a deafening wave of destruction.

Galíndez pumped the shotgun, sending the spent cartridge rattling away across the tiles. And then the kitchen table erupted in a storm of ragged splinters as automatic fire raked across it. She threw herself to the floor, pressing herself flat as bullets ricocheted off the gas cylinders, embedding themselves in the wall above her head in violent staccato impacts, spilling plaster into her hair.

The shooting stopped abruptly and Galíndez looked up, dazed by the fragile silence. Despite the ringing in her ears, she heard another sound, a strange hissing. By the door, she saw a mist of liquid gas spouting from the damaged nozzle of one of the cylinders. She pulled the pistol from her waistband.

The kitchen window smashed and Galíndez saw a gloved hand clutch the window frame as a man started to climb in. Movement in the doorway, another man forcing back one of the gas cylinders, using his weight against the ruined doorframe as he pushed his way in, his dark shape blurred by the pale gas fumes. He glanced round, saw her lying outside the kitchen door, holding the pistol in both hands. Aiming.

Galíndez fired into the escaping gas. The bullet hit the cylinder in a flurry of sparks. And then the world exploded in fire.

She rolled away from the door, her hair scorching in a shower of sparks and embers as the fireball raged down the hall. And then a second deafening blast as another cylinder exploded, bringing down large sections of the ceiling in a rain of plaster and shattered tiles.

Beating at her smouldering clothes, she crawled down the hall, keeping her head beneath the dark choking smoke until she reached the back door and dashed out past the dead men to take cover in a patch of ornamental shrubs.

Inside the house, the remaining gas cylinders exploded and Galíndez pressed herself to the ground as the massive incendiary fury of the blast erupted up through the roof, launching an angry column of fire into the night sky, souring the air with the stench of gas. Within moments, the house was enveloped in flames, illuminating the surrounding garden with wavering red light.

The heat was intense, and Galíndez moved away, sneaking through the shadows back to her car. She opened the boot and found her hi-vis vest, feeling a renewed sense of authority as she pulled it on. She tried her mobile again but there was still no signal. Cautiously, she crept further up the drive towards the gate and tried again. This time, she got a signal and dialled 062.

'*Guardia civil*. How can I help?'

'*Emergencia*, officer in trouble, requesting immediate assistance.' Her voice was hoarse as she gave the operator the address. 'I've been attacked by a gang of armed men. There are fatalities and the house is on fire. We need the fire service.' When she tried to swallow, the pain made her wince. 'There are children here.'

The operator took her details and reassured her that help was on the way. Drained, Galíndez leaned against her car, shaking with cold as the adrenalin rush faded. And then, sirens in the distance, growing louder. Pushing the pistol into her waistband, she went out into the road to wait for the *guardia* and police units to arrive. Ten minutes later, she heard the rumble of approaching vehicles.

The white dazzle of a searchlight blinded her and she turned away, shielding her eyes. A loud voice from behind the light, a man with a loudhailer. 'Identify yourself.'

'Galíndez. *Guardia civil*.' She kept her hands raised as she turned to let him see the reflective lettering on her vest.

'Put the gun on the ground and raise your hands.'

She knew what to do. Slowly, she laid the pistol on the ground, straightening up with her hands open and high. Shadows moved towards her through the headlights. No half-measures here, she

386

realised, seeing the dark-clad figures of the UEI. They'd responded to her call for help by sending in an elite special ops team.

The men frisked her and confirmed her ID before listening to her description of events. When asked about casualties, she estimated there were probably five dead. Distracted, she didn't notice the expressions on their faces.

The special ops commander patted Galíndez on the shoulder. 'Go and get yourself checked out, señorita. There's an ambulance over there.'

Galíndez glared at him, her dark eyes reflecting the light of the burning house. 'I left Capitán Fuentes' daughters hidden in some bushes down by the stream,' she said, straining to make her injured voice heard. 'I need to go and get them.'

He nodded. 'OK. Machado, you and Tolosa go with her to get the children.'

The two men followed her, taking a detour around the blazing house before making for the dark outline of the trees where the children were hiding. 'Call them,' Machado said, gripping his machine pistol.

Galíndez paused by the stream with the two special ops men on either side of her, weapons raised. '*Niñas? Soy, Ana María.*' The pain in her throat was getting worse.

She stepped into the stream and splashed across. *I told them to stay put no matter what. God damn it.* The two special ops men followed. Machado was talking into his radio mike. 'Command, this is *Alpha Dos*, no sign of the children. We're going into the bushes after them now. *Cambio.*'

A hiss of static. '*Alpha Dos*, this is Command. Go ahead, but keep me informed. *Cambio.*'

Galíndez knelt, fumbling in the bushes for the entrance to the girls' tree house.

Machado came after her. 'Hold on, where do you think you're going?' He moved forward and grabbed her arm, trying to pull her back. Galíndez spun round and flew at him, hitting him under the chin with a blow from her forearm, unbalancing him. She was a good six inches shorter than Machado and less half his weight, which probably accounted for his surprise at being sent sprawling into the grass.

As Machado struggled to his feet, Tolosa came up behind her. Exhausted, Galíndez didn't resist as he grabbed her in an arm lock. 'Those girls are my responsibility,' she croaked. 'Help me or get out of my way. I can't leave them there.' She put her free hand to her throat, hoping swallowing would ease the pain. It didn't. 'I've got to find them.'

'For fuck's sake,' Machado said as he got to his feet. 'Calm down, will you? We're on your side.' He turned to Tolosa. 'Let her go.'

'Let's get on with it,' Machado said. 'You crawl in that way, we'll see if we can push our way through those trees over there.'

'OK.' Galíndez dropped to her knees and began working her way into the narrow tunnel the girls had burrowed through the bushes.

'Wait,' Machado called. 'Take this.' He handed her his pistol.

Galíndez gave him a vague smile, though it was so dark the gesture was lost on him. She pushed forward, squirming along the narrow tunnel. After about ten metres the sides of the tunnel opened out below a thick canopy of leaves and branches and she struggled to her knees, trying to get her bearings in the dark. She felt hard flattened soil under her hand. This was it: the children's hiding place.

'I've found it,' she called, her voice cracking.

Machado shouted in acknowledgement and distorted patterns of light from their torches danced through the branches as they forced their way through to her.

'*Niñas?*' Galíndez looked around, seeing only deep shadow broken by the wavering light of the torches. 'Inés?' she rasped. 'Clari? *Dónde estáis, niñas?*'

She held the pistol in one hand, feeling her way with the other. The ground was uneven and her foot caught on something, sending her tumbling forward onto the damp soil, fumbling blindly, trying to find what had tripped her. One touch told her all she needed to know.

She had found the first body.

CHAPTER 25

OROITZ, OCTOBER 1954, CUARTEL DE LA GUARDIA CIVIL

Guzmán stared at the mess room wall as if the answer to his problems lay in the black patches of mould staining the ancient paint.

'I'm finished,' he muttered. 'Finished by a fucking bandit.'

Ochoa saw no point offering sympathy. If Guzmán was finished, so was he.

'It's my fault,' Guzmán said, grinding out his cigarette on the greasy tabletop. 'I should have realised the Çubiry were helping him.' He pulled a crumpled pack of Bisontes from his top pocket and lit another. 'Remember we couldn't understand why that *Yanqui* was carrying his ID card from the International Brigade?'

'He was stupid to do that,' Ochoa said. 'It was no use to him after all these years.'

'I think it was,' Guzmán said, 'because he used it to identify himself to El Lobo. He'd come over the border to meet the bastard. When Lobo saw we'd got our hands on the *Yanqui*, he shot him.'

'To stop him talking?'

'I thought so.' Guzmán nodded. 'Or maybe he knew who the American's brother was.'

'If he knew that, why would he kill him?'

Guzmán snorted. 'Because he knew it would fuck us up, of course.'

'He did that all right, boss.'

'We need to think about this,' Guzmán grunted. 'Take stock about what we know.'

'I know we're in the shit,' Ochoa said, thinking of his pension.

Guzmán ignored that. 'Esteban Jiménez's boyfriend Cardoso leaked information about the shipments of money to El Lobo. And Jiménez set up General Torres at his hunting lodge. El Lobo was ready and waiting on the hillside, ready to shoot the moment he opened the shutters.'

'That was a big risk, *jefe*. Those *maricones* had a lot to lose if they were caught.'

'Didn't they just,' Guzmán agreed. 'Just being queer would have put them behind bars for years, that was reason enough for them to stay out of trouble. But instead they were accomplices to armed robbery and murder.'

'They must have been well paid. No one takes risks like that for nothing.'

'Neither was desperate for money. I think they did it for a cause.'

'The resistance, you mean?'

'Of course. It keeps coming back to them. I think they're trying to rebuild the cell, that's why the *Yanqui* came to meet with El Lobo.'

'But, *jefe*, you wiped out the entire resistance cell in this region.'

'Not quite,' Guzmán said. 'I thought I'd destroyed the cell but Gutiérrez said there were three who got away. Two members didn't turn up and there's an anonymous quartermaster who purchases their equipment. The two missing members that night must have been Jiménez and Cardoso. They were the last people anyone would suspect. For fuck's sake, Jiménez worked for one of Franco's best-known generals.' He poured himself more coffee. 'It all makes sense now.'

'So who's the secret quartermaster, *jefe*?'

Guzmán sighed. 'No wonder your wife left you, Corporal. For fuck's sake, It was El Lobo, you moron.' He gulped down the coffee. 'He's helping them rebuild the cell.'

Ochoa frowned, deep in thought. 'So who killed the two queers?'

'El Lobo, of course,' Guzmán snapped. 'To cover his tracks. If you paid attention you'd have realised that by now. If we can find him, our problems are solved.'

'We don't have long, *jefe*. You'll have to report the ambush soon.'

'I'll be the judge of that,' Guzmán said. 'What time is it?'

'Four thirty. It won't be light for two hours.'

Guzman poured himself the last of the coffee. 'I want you to go into San Sebastian. Take one of the jeeps out the back.'

'Yes, sir. What do you want me to do there?'

Guzmán took Magdalena's card from his wallet and slid it across the table. 'Go to this address and tell Magda to leave town for the day, in case El Lobo tries to go after her.'

Ochoa peered at the card through his thick lenses. 'Magda?'

'Señorita Magdalena Torres,' Guzmán said. 'She's General Torres's daughter.'

Ochoa raised an eyebrow. 'Sounds like you know her well, sir.'

'Is that a topic you want to pursue further, Corporal, bearing in mind that you're already annoying me intensely?'

'No, sir. I'll deliver the message as soon as I arrive.'

'After that, I want you see Capitán Viana at the local *comisaría*. That bastard is our link with Gutiérrez. Find out what's happened to our intelligence and then phone me at the Torres hunting lodge, the number's on that card.'

Ochoa nodded. 'What are you going to do there, sir?'

'Jiménez had an office at the lodge. I'm going to search it, there may be something that will lead us to El Lobo.'

'Good luck,' Ochoa said.

Guzmán scowled at him. 'Coming from someone whose face registers perpetual disappointment, Corporal, I have to say I find that comment less than encouraging.'

SAN SEBASTIÁN 1954, CALLE DE FERMÍN CALBETÓN

Viana stood in a doorway, watching the door to Magdalena Torres's apartment building. He saw the *portero* holding open the door for residents, probably in the hope of a tip. If that was the case, Viana observed, he must be sorely disappointed.

His hand tightened on the knife in his pocket. It was only a small blade, though very sharp. Certainly sharp enough to kill Señorita Torres. It would have been more enjoyable to pick her off with the rifle, but the buildings along this street were too tall and populous to risk wandering around trying to get access to the roof. Besides, the knife was messy, just the thing to send Guzmán a personal message.

Viana tensed as he saw the porter emerge from the building and set off down the street, clearly running an errand for someone. Quickly, he crossed the street and tried the door. He swore under his breath. The door was locked. The last thing he wanted to do was ring Magdalena's bell. Passers-by would remember seeing a good-looking woman like her, which meant they might also remember him. He pushed the handle again, harder.

'Are you going in or not?' Viana turned and saw a short, sad-faced man with thick round glasses. He recognised him at once. 'No, I'm just on my way out.' He brushed past Ochoa and set off down the street, careful not to look back. That was a shame. There would be no time to come back to finish this. Things would start happening soon, things much more important than cutting Señorita Torres's throat. She would never know just how lucky she'd been.

OROITZ 1954, MENDIKO RIDGE

From his hiding place on the ridge, Sargento León had a good view of the village below. Not that he was interested in the view. He had more serious things to worry about, staying alive being the most important. By now, the security services throughout the Basque region would be looking for him. Even if he tried to surrender to the *guardia* or *policía* they would probably shoot him on sight to save the paperwork. That narrowed his options to dying or fleeing to France. To León, those things seemed to be equivalent. He decided on France. He would sneak closer to the village, wait until dark and then steal a horse. He would be away before anyone was aware of him. Sweating from the effort, he eased himself through the bushes and began working his way down the slope. Sharp thorns pierced his clothes and tore at his scalp, though he ignored the pain. He had a plan.

OROITZ 1954, TORRES PABELLÓN DE CASA

Guzmán left the jeep outside the hunting lodge. Out of respect for Magdalena he decided not to kick down the front door and went round the back of the house. He was raging, tormented by hindsight, wondering why he hadn't noticed anything suspicious about Jiménez when he'd first met him. After all, homosexuals were notoriously accomplished liars. That had been established as a scientific fact by none other than Franco's chief psychiatrist Dr Vallejo-Nájera and his assistants from the Gestapo. There was no arguing with science.

He took out his set of picks and examined the lock on the back door before inserting one of the thin metal rods into the keyhole. He worked by touch, twisting the pick with gentle precision until he heard the dull click as the mechanism responded to his movements. He opened the door and went inside.

SAN SEBASTIÁN 1954, CALLE DE FERMÍN CALBETÓN

Magdalena opened the door of her apartment and looked at the man standing outside in the hall. A dour pale face, his eyes magnified by the thick lenses of his wire-rimmed glasses, much like those worn by the German officers her father used to invite to the house.

'Señorita Torres?' He took an identity card from his jacket pocket. 'Corporal Ochoa, I work with Comandante Guzmán.'

She stepped back to let him in. 'Nothing wrong, I hope?'

Ochoa stood awkwardly, holding his hat with both hands. 'The *comandante*'s operation didn't go very well, señorita.'

Magdalena's eyes widened. 'Is he…'

'No, miss, he's fine. But the entire squad were wiped out. El Lobo got away with five million pesetas.'

'That's terrible,' Magdalena said. 'So why are you here?'

'I've got a message for you. The *comandante* wants you to leave San Sebastián for the day. There's a chance you might be in danger.' He saw the sudden concern on her face. 'It's only a possibility, señorita, he just wants to be sure you're safe.'

'I understand.' She offered him a cigarette from a lacquered box. He took one and leaned forward as she gave him a light.

'Tell the *comandante* not to worry,' Magdalena said. 'I'll be out doing my monthly collection from local artisans today.'

Ochoa looked down, embarrassed. 'The *comandante* says he'd like to meet you later.'

'By all means. Would you tell him I'll finish my collection at Lauburu Farm around seven this evening? Perhaps he could meet me there?'

'Of course, señorita.' Ochoa got to his feet, anxious to leave.

'May I ask you a question before you go, Corporal?'

Reluctantly, Ochoa sat down, trying not to watch as she crossed her legs again.

'You and the *comandante* were in Villarreal during the war, I believe?'

He wiped a bead of sweat from his forehead. 'Why do you ask, señorita?'

'I hear things when he's asleep,' she said quietly. 'About Villarreal. What happened?'

When he's asleep. She was a whore then. He'd wondered if she might be something special and it cheered him to know that she was no different from the rest.

'Please tell me.' She sat back in her chair, rearranging her skirt. Ochoa caught a glimpse of her slip and looked away, swallowing hard. 'Someone was killed,' Magdalena said. 'I know that much.'

Ochoa looked at the curve of the expensive pearl necklace around her neck. 'Someone was killed, you're right.' He nodded, fighting an urge to look at her cleavage. 'A woman.'

'And she was killed by the *comandante*?'

'That's right.' Ochoa wiped his face with his hand.

Magdalena looked across the room, unaware of his furtive appraisal.

Ochoa got to his feet. 'He wouldn't like me talking to you like this.'

'No, I suppose not.' Magdalena ground out her cigarette in the ashtray. She glanced at her watch. 'If you'll excuse me, I have to get ready.' She got up and went to the door with him.

Ochoa paused. 'Thing is, señorita, we all have secrets that are best left alone.'

'I couldn't agree more, Corporal.' Magdalena smiled.

Ochoa hurried downstairs, aware of her watching him until he went out into the street and the heavy door clanged to behind him.

OROITZ 1954, TORRES PABELLÓN DE CAZA

Guzmán moved along the hall. The walls were adorned with weapons, though he doubted any had ever been used by General Torres. The house was furnished entirely in shades of brown, plain masculine tables and chairs. A smell of leather and polished wood. No sense of warmth or comfort. He quite liked it.

On the far side of the house he came to a large salon, perfumed by a sad air of tobacco. More austere furnishings. An oak door on the far wall with a gilt plaque: *Oficina*. The door was unlocked and he went in. In front of him was a large desk. The walls were filled by shelves piled with files and ledgers. He checked the desk and found nothing of interest. On one of the shelves by the far wall were several bottles of Carlos Primero. He could always make time for an expensive brandy, especially at someone else's expense, and went over to get a quick one.

He poured a couple of fingers into a glass, splashing some onto a pile of papers. As the ink on the papers began to run, he reached into his pocket for a clean handkerchief to mop up the drink and felt the thick envelope he'd taken from Mellado's drawer. Domestic cleanliness was suddenly forgotten. He took a seat and tipped the contents of the envelope onto the desk. He looked at the first picture. General Mellado, slightly younger, posing for the camera. Behind him, a pile of black shapes. The photo was not of good quality and it took a moment for Guzmán to realise they were dead tribesmen, the bodies heaped together, ready to be burned.

The second picture was of Mellado again, in the uniform of the legion, standing with two soldiers. All had cheery grins on their faces, and each was holding a Moor's head by the hair. Guzmán sighed. None of this was a surprise. Mellado's bloody antics in the legion were well known. Idly, he flicked to the third photograph.

He reached for the tumbler of brandy and took a sip. He'd thought nothing that Mellado could do would shock him. He'd been wrong. He looked at the photograph again and then swallowed the rest of the drink. Putting down his glass, Guzmán stared at the picture of a grinning Mellado, his arm wrapped around a soldier's shoulders. No heads, no burned corpses. The only horrific thing in the photograph was the soldier's face. Pale, shiny scar tissue, lines of stitch marks where the doctors had failed to put his face back together properly. The lopsided snarling mouth. Like a wolf.

Guzmán flipped the photo over. It was dated August 1947. So, Mellado knew El Lobo. Not only did he know him, he'd served with him. It made no sense. Impatient, he got up and went to get another brandy. As he did, his foot caught on the carpet and he stumbled. Furious, he pulled his foot from the rucked carpet, staring at the wooden floorboards exposed by his clumsiness. And not just floorboards, he saw as he pulled the carpet back further.

'*Puta madre.*' Guzmán examined the trapdoor carefully. At one end, a metal ring lay flat in a shallow recess. He flicked it up and heaved the trap open. Below, a short flight of wooden stairs descended into shadow. He drew the Browning and went down into the darkness, seeing only vague outlines from the meagre light coming through the trapdoor. Stretching his arms in front of him, he examined his surroundings as best he could. By the far wall was a small desk cluttered with paper and, next to it, two wooden chairs. A secret room, hidden under Jiménez's workplace. Guzmán smiled with grim satisfaction. He'd been right: Jiménez was hiding something.

A breath of air drifted down from above, filling the room with a strange dry rustling. Guzmán ran his hand along the wall, feeling papers, lots of them, though it was too dark to see what they were. And then his fingers closed on a light switch and a solitary bulb in the ceiling threw sallow light across the room. As the light grew stronger, he looked round in growing disbelief. Whatever he had been expecting, it was not this.

OROITZ 1954, LAUBURU FARM

Begoña Arestigui finished her ironing and put the ancient iron to cool on the same flat stone it had rested on since Grandmother Arestigui had arrived at the farm in the mid nineteenth century. She pressed a hand on the small of her back. That was annoying – despite the poultice she'd applied a few days before, the pain still hadn't gone. Back pain and she wasn't yet forty. It was depressing. One day, when Nieves married, Begoña would have to run the farm alone. It would be hard work if she was fit. Far harder if she suffered with her back. She dismissed the thought. She'd worked hard all her life, little point complaining now.

She went into Grandpa Arestigui's study and swivelled the big brass telescope up towards the mountain, peering through the eyepiece at the upper pastures, seeing the faint plume of smoke rising into the mountain air from the old fortress. That was unusual, since the crumbling structure was unsound. None of the villagers went near it. But someone was up there.

The old grandfather clock chimed the hour and Begoña frowned as she saw the time. Nieves had set off at seven that morning, taking a sack of flour to trade at the market in the village. She was over an hour late. But she had been late before, the rhythms of country life were like that. On these lonely paths through the hills there was always the possibility of running across some distant acquaintance or relative and such encounters always required an exchange of news and gossip. Begoña sighed. Perhaps she was just being foolish.

Or perhaps not. It had been a long time since she had experienced such a sense of foreboding. Some called these things premonitions or second sight, others even called it witchcraft. Begoña had no name for them since the feelings came naturally. And what she felt now was that something bad was coming.

She went to the front door and stepped outside. A faint breath of wind stirred the remaining leaves on the trees and she shivered. Something was coming all right, something dark and destructive. If it was a storm, it would be a big one. Begoña Arestigui had lived at Lauburu Farm for thirty-five winters. Had walked through this wood every day of her life. Had even had her first kiss among these gnarled trees. She had never been afraid here. She was afraid now.

SAN SEBASTIÁN 1954, COMISARÍA DE LA POLICÍA ARMADA

Ochoa hurried up the steps into the police station.

'*Buenos días.*' The officer behind the desk had a mouthful of stale roll and spluttered soggy crumbs onto the desk as he greeted the visitor. When he saw the name of Ochoa's unit on his ID card, he dropped the pleasantries and hurried away in search of his boss, a red-faced *sargento*.

'So you're from the Special Brigade?' The *sargento* saluted. '*A sus órdenes.*'

'Where's Capitán Viana?' Ochoa asked.

'It's a shame you didn't come earlier,' the *sargento* said. 'The *capitán* got a telegram a couple of hours ago. He's gone to collect a file sent by special courier.'

'Really? Where from?'

'The capitán said a courier was delivering the material to the pensión at Oroitz.'

'Show me his office.' Ochoa followed the *sargento* down the hall to a small drab room. 'You can go now,' he said. 'Close the door after you.' Once the *sargento* had left the room, he locked the door.

An envelope bearing the crest of the Spanish post office lay on the table. It had been opened with a neat cut along the top of the flap. There was no sign of the telegram and Ochoa rifled through the desk drawers without finding it. Annoyed, he knelt and ran his hands under the narrow gap between desk and floor. His fingers brushed something and he slid it out, his eyes widening as he recognised it. He had one of these in his pocket. The identification card of a member of the *Brigada Especial*. He opened it and looked at the details below the photograph. It was Viana's card.

Puzzled, he sat in the *capitán*'s chair, running through the things he would tell Guzmán when he phoned him. He stretched out his leg and heard a sharp clatter as his boot hit the metal waste-paper bin. Reaching down, he lifted the bin and inspected it. It was empty, apart from a heap of roughly torn scraps of paper. Ochoa upended the pieces of telegram onto the desk and started to rearrange them.

OROITZ 1954, LAUBURU FARM

As she heard footsteps running towards her, Begoña thought about hiding but decided that was ridiculous. Her ancestors had slain Charlemagne's rearguard, they were not frightened by an autumn breeze. She stood her ground as the noise grew louder.

'Nieves?' Begoña stared as her niece came running out of the trees. Her hair was tangled with burrs and pieces of leaves. '*Por Dios*, what happened?'

Nieves fell into her arms and Begoña held her, feeling her slight body pressed against hers, wracked by violent sobs. When Nieves calmed down, Begoña took her back to the house and poured a glass of *patxaran*.

Nieves drank it, holding Begoña's hand tight. 'I saw him, there was blood everywhere.'

'Saw who? What's happened?'

'Patxi Gabilondo. El Lobo shot him after robbing a truck on the old road yesterday.'

Begoña stared at her. 'Is he badly hurt?'

Nieves lowered her face, her tears falling into the lap of her dark skirt. 'He's dead.'

Begoña took a deep breath. 'I know where the killer is.'

Nieves looked up, her face streaked with tears. 'How do you know?'

Begoña pressed a hand to her breast. 'I know,' she said simply. 'He's in the old fortress.'

'So what shall we do?' Nieves asked.

Begoña knew there was only one response to the murder of an innocent like Patxi. She went to the fireplace and took down a battered short sword hanging beneath Grandfather Arestigui's portrait, a sword allegedly pulled from the body of one of Charlemagne's knights after the massacre at Roncesvalles. She went to the window and raised the blade towards the old fortress. Her voice trembled with the power of the storm and the ice of ancient winters as she invoked the power of the goddess. 'I curse the man who did this,' she said, going on to enunciate a list of torments that would befall Patxi's killer. She finished the incantation and turned back to Nieves. 'He walks as a dead man now.'

OROITZ 1954, CUARTEL DE LA GUARDIA CIVIL

Capitán Viana parked his car near the *cuartel*. A woman was walking up towards the village and he called to her, asking for the location of the Pensión Aralar. The woman looked at him, puzzled. She didn't speak Spanish. He glanced round, hoping to find someone who spoke a Christian tongue. As he did, he saw the name he was looking for on the painted sign hanging above the door of a large house further up the street. Pensión Aralar.

'*Buenos días*.' Viana smiled as Señora Olibari opened the door. He held up his ID. 'I've come to collect a file. I believe it was delivered recently?'

'That depends who you are, señor,' Señora Olibari said, keeping the door half-closed.

'My name's Guzmán. Comandante Leopoldo Guzmán.'

'Of course.' Señora Olibari beamed. 'I've been expecting you.'

She ushered Viana into the living room and offered him a seat in her best armchair. He sat, ill at ease, surrounded by horse brasses and cow bells. 'Has the gentleman come far?'

'Far enough.' Viana had no intention of being questioned by a peasant.

When Señora Olibari made another tentative attempt at conversation, he cut her short. 'The file, please, señora. I'm in a hurry.'

'I'll get it.' She nodded. 'If you'd like to use the telephone, señor, you're very welcome. It's the only one in the village, apart from the one at the cuartel.'

She bustled down the hall to the small sitting room at the back of the house. Double windows gave a spectacular view of the valley. In the distance, she saw the white smudge of Lauburu Farm where the witches lived. She paused, listening for the sound of her guest moving. When she heard nothing, she went to one of several large paintings on the wall, portraying rustic scenes from Basque life a century earlier. Taking hold of a gloomy depiction of cattle crossing a river with their ruddy-faced drovers, she lifted the painting from its hook, revealing a small safe set into the wall. She entered the combination: 18071936. A number she had chosen with care: the date the Civil War began. But though the war was long over, her work continued.

The safe door swung open on well-greased hinges. Somewhere along the hall she heard a creak. She froze, alert for further sounds of movement, and exhaled quietly, hearing none. This was an old house. It creaked all the time. She took a pair of shears from the safe. In contrast to the ancient farming gear in her living room, these were practically brand new, given to her when the telephone was installed. Quickly, she used them to cut the phone cable. Whoever her visitor was, it had never occurred to him that she would be able to recognise Comandante Guzmán. But then, Guzmán hadn't known that either.

Her orders for a situation like this were very specific. Reaching into the safe, she took out the file with its typed label: *Cdte L. Guzmán. Alto Secreto.* She placed the file on a stool and reached back into the safe for the Luger. It had been some time since she had used it, though not so long that she'd forgotten how to kill a man.

She heard a faint metallic sound in the hall. Quickly, she reached for the file, deciding to lock it in the safe before she dealt with her problem visitor. A sudden noise at the door made her look up. Capitán Viana was standing in the doorway. The sound she'd heard had been him fitting the silencer on his pistol.

OROITZ 1954, TORRES PABELLÓN DE CAZA

Guzmán looked in astonishment at the chaos of papers on the walls around him. Almost every available surface had something pinned or glued to it. Papers of all sizes, from large posters to the small pages of notebooks. Some handwritten in various-coloured inks, some typed. Pen and ink drawings, etchings, several small watercolours. Many depicted the *ikurriña*, the prohibited Basque flag. Among the items in the bizarre montage around him he saw a newspaper cutting from *ABC* dated 9 March 1951 announcing the death of *the glorious and celebrated Lieutenant General Gonzalo Queipo de Llano*. Above the picture someone had scrawled

Drunken murderer in red ink. A fair assessment, though one that would put the writer in jail nonetheless.

Guzmán shook his head, admiring Jiménez's cunning. The man had worked for Torres, posing as a loyal employee, while at the same time, down here, he was scrawling these messages of hate and treachery. And planning the general's murder. It was not just Jiménez's treachery that infuriated him: it was that Magdalena had trusted him.

He continued his examination of the walls. More sketches: cars being machine-gunned, blown up, *guardia civiles* being shot down by men and women in Basque berets. Next to the drawings was a series of small photographs. He moved closer to examine them, his smile fading as he saw the first.

OROITZ 1954, CUARTEL DE LA GUARDIA CIVIL

Viana went down the track to the barracks. As he approached, an old man came out from behind the building and started up the path towards him. Dressed in rough sheepskins, his rope-soled sandals tied with long laces wound round his calves, the man looked like the shepherds in Señora Olibari's paintings.

'*Buenas días,*' Viana grunted.

'*Muy buenas,*' the old man said, politely. 'Is the señor going to the *cuartel*?'

'That's none of your business,' Viana snapped.

'No offence to the gentleman,' the old man said, 'but something terrible has happened. The garrison were all killed yesterday, trying to stop a robbery by that bandit El Lobo. The entire village is in a state of shock.'

Viana glowered at him. 'That's why I'm here, you old fool. I'm a police officer, so stop wasting my time, I want to use the telephone.'

'Naturally, sir.' The shepherd swept off his cap with a servile gesture and watched as Viana continued down the path towards the building.

Viana walked fast, annoyed by the shepherd's unwelcome familiarity. These inbreds needed to be taught a lesson. They had clearly forgotten the last one.

Behind him, the old man let out a whistle, high and discordant like the sound of a madman's flute. Viana spun round, wondering if the unkempt peasant was mocking him, but the old man was slowly making his way up the track to the village. Viana snorted. The old man wasn't a problem, though it was always best to be cautious here. He was sick of this region. Once this job was completed, there would be a new challenge waiting, as there always was. Another new identity to acquire once the original owner had been disposed of. Just as he'd done with the late Capitán Viana. The thought of it made him smile. There was no point in killing people if you didn't enjoy it.

Something else amused him. By now, Guzmán was probably starting to realise he wasn't going to see the file Gutiérrez had sent him. It might take a while longer before he realised he was finished. And with any luck Viana might be the one to finish the *comandante*. He reached the *cuartel* and hammered on the door. There was no response and he went inside.

OROITZ 1954, TORRES PABELLÓN DE CAZA

Black and white images. Some framed, others pinned or glued to the wall. The cover of a local newspaper, *El Diario Vasco*, dated Saturday, 27 June 1936. The headline was far from exciting: *Local Sports Day a Great Success, Say Organisers.* It must have been, since most of the page was taken up with a photograph of the event. It was a familiar sight after his trip to St Jean: the huge stones for the weightlifters, the logs with axes buried in them, ready for the wood-chopping contest. Further away, tents, tables and chairs, women with parasols. A local fiesta, with the war only three weeks away. And in the foreground, smiling, eyes narrowed against the brilliant sun, a posed group of children and an adult. He recognised one face immediately.

Magdalena smiled at the camera, aged maybe nine or ten, Guzmán guessed. She was holding a scroll tied with a ribbon, pressing it to her chest. She wore Basque costume, a white blouse and black waistcoat, a dark skirt and white knee-socks with the laces of her *alpargatas* bound around her calves. Next to her was a smartly dressed man in white with a sash knotted round his waist. He seemed vaguely familiar. Seeing him like this, clean-shaven, his hair combed and oiled, made him difficult to recognise, since whenever Guzmán had seen him, Mikel Aingeru had been dressed in stinking sheepskins. He read the caption beneath the photograph:

1936 Festival Of Basque Culture a Great Success!

The Annual Festival of Basque Culture has once more been pronounced a huge success. As always, the festival was organised by Mikel Aingeru, the local school-teacher and renowned scholar of Basque Culture. He is seen here with his sons Jesús (13), Iker (15) and Xavier (17). With them is the winner of the under-twelve prize for the best poem in Basque, Señorita Magdalena Torres (9), daughter of General Torres, that loyal servant and faithful military protector of the Republic.

Guzmán smiled at the description of Magdalena's father. The man had been as loyal as a snake, changing sides without a second thought.

Mikel Aingeru and two of his boys were dressed in white, red sashes tied round their waists. Good-looking lads. But what puzzled Guzmán was the young boy standing behind them, holding an axe, ready for the wood-chopping contest. He didn't resemble his brothers – his face was broader and he lacked their easy smiles. It was his height and bulk that gave it away. That and the large scar on the side of his head. It was Jesús Barandiaran, the wood-chopper, and from his expression he wasn't a part of the happy family gathering.

Guzmán sat brooding amid the rustling papers around him. All these Basques seemed to know one another or were related in some way. Not for the first time, he reminded himself this was not Madrid. He looked again at the photograph, feeling his skin prickle as he saw two young women on one side of the picture, almost out of shot. Clearly sisters, though it was the older of the two that held his attention. The room grew quiet as he stared at her.

It was Nieves Arestigui. Or rather someone who bore a resemblance to her. Someone made from the same flesh: her mother, Arantxa. Chilled, he stared at her dark beauty. Even in this sepia photo she stood out, just as she had when she'd worked in the whorehouse. By her side, Begoña seemed plain, diminished by her sister's compelling looks.

The phone rang in the office above and Guzmán ran to answer it. It was Ochoa.

'Did you get Viana?' Guzmán asked, straight to the point.

'No,' said Ochoa. 'He's gone to collect a file Gutiérrez sent you by special courier.' He paused, listening to Guzmán's stream of obscenities for a moment before he interrupted. 'There's some good news, *jefe*.'

'I doubt that.' Guzmán scowled into the mouthpiece.

'He tore up the telegram. I found the pieces and rearranged them.'

'Good work,' Guzmán said, grudgingly. 'So where's he going?'

'That's the good news, he's headed for Oroitz,' Ochoa said. 'The document was sent to an agent called Skylark at the Pensión Aralar.'

'Fuck me, Señora Olibari's an agent? I'll get over there before he can collect it.'

'There's something else, *jefe*. He left his ID card in the office.'

'For fuck's sake, Corporal, he might not have worn his dress uniform either. We're the Secret Police, after all. Does it matter?'

'What does Viana look like, sir?'

'Tall, thinning dark hair, miserable face and a crappy little pencil moustache. Why? Do you want me to draw you a picture?'

'So he hasn't got thick blond hair like the photo on his ID?' Ochoa looked again at the card, and read from it, '"Colour of eyes, blue".'

'I'd fucking know if…' Guzmán stopped. He remembered the body being dragged from the dirty water of the harbour into a boat. The cries of the crowd watching from the quayside as they saw the dead man's staring blue eyes, his shock of pale hair laced with seaweed.

'Viana's dead,' he barked. 'They've replaced him with someone else.' His face darkened with anger. 'No fucking wonder we haven't heard from Gutiérrez. Viana hasn't been passing on our messages.' He slammed his hand down onto the desk. 'You said he's on his way to Oroitz? I'll get over there and find out who he really is.'

'Another thing, *jefe*,' Ochoa said, 'I gave Señorita Torres your message. She said she'd meet you at Lauburu Farm around seven. And something else.' His voice grew serious. 'Someone's reported finding the bank truck and the dead *guardia* to the local *policía*.'

'That should keep them busy. Call me at the *cuartel* in a couple of hours.'

Guzmán went back into the underground room and took the photo of young Magdalena from the wall as a keepsake. As he put it into his pocket, he saw a folded piece of paper that had been pinned to the wall behind it. He flattened out the paper on the desk. A large-scale map, covered in spiralling contour lines. Here was the village of Oroitz, the paths and roads all clearly marked. Just a regular map but for one thing. A smudged pencil line followed the smugglers' trail from France, curving round Mari's Peak up to the old convent. Another line led down through the cliffs, ending in a spot overlooking Oroitz half a kilometre or so below at a rectilinear shape imposed on the contours overlooking the road.

Guzmán stared at the map, wondering why anyone would plan a route from France that went via the convent and ended at the abandoned fortress. He realised he already knew. The weapons and ammunition were imported from France along the ridge and stockpiled at the convent. No one wanted to be caught carrying weapons around the countryside, they needed a distribution point where they could leave the cargo for the resistance to collect. He turned the paper over, seeing the handwritten list on the back:

25/6/1954 $1,850 ✓
30/7/1954 $1,200 ✓
23/8/1954 $1,750 ✓
15/9/1954 $1,950 ✓
8/10/1954 $5,500

This was Jiménez's work, without doubt. The little *marica* had been carefully logging the cost of weapons – what else could those sums represent? Certainly nothing legitimate, since he had gone to some trouble to keep this list and the map hidden. And how typical that the little faggot had used Magdalena's photo to hide it. Guzmán looked at the last date on the list. Yesterday's date. And the sum hadn't been ticked off. If El Lobo was delivering weapons to the old fortress he might still be there, waiting for someone to turn up and pay him. It would be a shame to leave the bastard alone up there. Guzmán shoved the map into an inside pocket as he made for the stairs. Above him, a shadow moved across the rectangle of light through the open trapdoor.

The shot whined past his head, impacting into the far wall in a storm of flying paper. Guzmán raised the Browning and fired through the trapdoor, flinching as a bullet ricocheted away to his left. He jumped to his feet. That had been too close for his liking. No one was going to use him for target practice.

He sprang up the stairs, firing at the office door as he scrambled behind the heavy desk. Brandy splashed onto the floor behind him as a bullet ripped through the door and shattered one of the bottles of Carlos Primero. Rising from behind the desk, Guzmán fired two rapid shots and dropped behind the desk again. On the other side of the door he heard a harsh, metallic rasp. The sound of an automatic weapon being readied.

Guzmán rolled away from the desk as a blast of machine-gun fire ripped pieces from the veneered desktop, filling the air around him with needle-sharp splinters. The firing stopped, leaving an abrupt silence, broken only by the shrill ringing in his ears and the dripping of brandy from the shattered bottles. Guzmán crouched by the doorway. Attack was always better than defence and he kicked aside the shattered remains of the door, scanning the room beyond with the Browning. The machine-gunner had gone, though his weapon lay on the floor, a Thompson, Guzmán noted, seeing the round magazine.

Cautiously, he made his way outside. As he crossed the lawn, he noticed General Torres's elegant Hispano Suiza parked by the fruit trees. There seemed little point driving a decrepit *guardia* jeep when he could borrow an expensive vehicle like that. He found the keys on top of the driver's sun visor and started the engine. Viana would have to wait. If El Lobo was up at that fortress, there was still a chance Guzmán could complete this operation. And a chance was all Guzmán needed.

OROITZ 1954, COMISARÍA DE LA GUARDIA CIVIL

Viana went down the corridor to the radio room. The air was thick with the stale smell of sweat. All the rooms he passed were empty, their doors open. A barracks with only ghosts to man it now. He smiled, thinking of Guzmán's failed attempt to kill El Lobo. The *comandante* had bet everything on that operation and lost. The fool didn't know how much he'd lost. He soon would.

Viana sat at the table and opened Guzmán's file, leafing through the typed sheets. After the first few pages he stopped and began reading again, more carefully this time.

'*Mierda.*' Viana smoothed his oiled hair with his hand, exasperated. It was just as well Guzmán hadn't read this. If he had, he could have spoiled everything. But there were others who needed to know and he looked round for a telephone, seeing the big Bakelite phone on a desk by the far wall. Cluttered with papers and boxes, he'd hardly noticed the desk when he'd come in. But from this angle he saw it differently. Very differently. Because now he saw the body on the floor, behind the desk. The green uniform and boots of a *guardia civil*.

A lance corporal, Viana saw as he examined the corpse. Someone had stabbed him in the chest, though it was like no stab wound Viana had ever seen. The upper chest was split in a great bloody gash of torn flesh and shards of bone. Afterwards, the killer had thrown a couple of blankets onto the body to soak up the blood. Without that, there would have been blood everywhere and Viana would been alerted the moment he'd entered the room. Ignoring the dead man, he pulled the phone towards him and lifted the receiver.

'*Me cago en la puta.*' He stared at the cable dangling from the phone, the jagged cut at the end of it.

A muffled sound reverberated along the corridor. Suddenly tense, Viana drew his pistol and walked down the corridor to the entrance, glancing into the rooms on either side of him. When he came to the front door, he stopped. The door was closed. He had left it open when he'd come in. As he reached for the handle, something moved in the room behind him. A faint sound, someone hoping to hide from him, no doubt. Viana spun round, aiming through the open door of the laundry. He'd got the bastard. There was no hiding in there. He took a step forward, his pistol held at arm's length. Ahead was a great stone washtub and a battered mangle draped with filthy sheets waiting to be washed. Beyond them, a large locker, big enough to hide a man.

He grabbed the locker door and yanked it open, aiming into the musty empty space. As he heard the noise behind him, he realised his mistake and started to turn. The blow hit him in the back, sending him crashing into the locker. Viana struggled to stay on his feet, wondering why he could no longer feel his legs as he twisted, trying to aim the pistol at his attacker. He heard shots, distant and faint. Then the axe struck him again and after that he heard nothing.

Magdalena Torres brought the Pegaso to a halt up near the gate of the isolated farmhouse. She got out and lit a cigarette as she looked round at the towering landscape, smelling autumn in the air. Her friends thought she was foolish to make these collections from such remote farms when she could easily have employed someone to do it. That was not the point. These monthly journeys let her experience her native land in all its massive beauty.

It was hard for her to imagine living anywhere else, though the *comandante* had hinted she might like to visit Madrid. She had no intention of leaping into anything since she was only too aware that men were always on their best behaviour at the start. But once that first flush of romance faded, they wanted to tame her, to get her down the aisle and say *Sí, quiero* as they put the ring on her finger as if branding a steer. She had seen it happen to her friends too many times to let it happen to her. And yet it was strange how well suited she and Comandante Guzmán seemed, despite everything. He could be obstinate and pig-headed, but then so could she. He had his secrets, she had hers. No one was perfect.

She crushed the cigarette underfoot and strolled to the gate. A sack was propped against the gatepost next to an old biscuit tin. She paused and pulled a slip of paper from the string round the top of the sack. A childish scrawl told her there were thirty this month. She took some change from her pocket and left it in the tin. As she lifted the heavy sack, she looked over to the farmhouse, hoping someone might come out to exchange a few words. But country folk felt uncomfortable talking to a rich señorita like her and they were embarrassed if she made the first move. She'd tried often enough.

Once the sack was stowed safely in the boot, Magdalena got behind the wheel and started the engine. Two more stops and she was done for the day.

CHAPTER 26

COLMENAR VIEJO 2010, FUENTES RESIDENCE

'*S*he's found a body. *Cambio.*' Frantic radio chatter crackled in the darkness as the special ops team pushed through the bushes towards the tree house. Abrupt shouts, flashlights glinting on the stream as a medical team splashed across, carrying stretchers. Ahead, men were already hacking furiously at the dense foliage.

From the darkness of the tree house, Galíndez saw the approaching lights and called out, trying to stop the men contaminating the crime scene. Her rasping call went unheard, and she covered her head under a shower of severed branches and leaves as the men cut their way through, crowding round her in the confined space. After so long in the dark, the flashlights were painful and she shielded her eyes with her hand.

'You OK, Galíndez?' Machado asked.

'I'm fine.' She pointed to the two crumpled shapes sprawled on the damp soil. 'The bodies are over there.'

Machado knelt to examine them. 'Any idea who they are?'

Galíndez crawled to the body nearest to her and rolled him onto his back. Even in the semi-darkness she could see the face was a mess. What was left of it. 'White male, forties maybe, hands tied behind his back. Killed by a single shot to the back of the head. Massive damage to the face.' She kept her injured voice flat and detached, trying to be professional, though it was hard to concentrate, tormented by her concern for the girls. But this was work and Galíndez knew better than to show emotion if she wanted to keep their respect.

Listening to her, Machado thought she was a cold bitch. 'This one's the same. Hands tied, shot in the back of the head.'

Galíndez moved away from the bodies and got to her feet.

Machado saw her get up. 'Where are you going?'

'To find the kids.' She turned to one of the firemen. 'Can I borrow your torch?'

Taking the flashlight, she went back through the opening the firemen had cut through the trees, looking for some sign of the girls. It wasn't easy. Between them, the special ops teams and the firemen had churned up the grass with their boots, obscuring any tracks the children might have left. As she swept the flashlight over the lawn, something glinted on the grass and she knelt to retrieve it. A red enamel badge with black lettering: LEGIONS OF DEATH WORLD TOUR 1996. Inés's favourite band.

She groaned. For some reason, despite her strict instructions to stay hidden, the girls had abandoned the tree house and come this way, probably terrified by the sound of gunfire and exploding gas cylinders. One thing was certain: they hadn't gone back towards the house, someone would have seen them by now. It was more likely they'd headed for the top of the garden, away from the noise and flames. Galíndez decided not to go back and get the special ops guys to accompany her. Whoever was up there would hear them coming from a hundred metres away. She started up the sloping lawn, heading for the wall that marked the limit of the Fuenteses' garden. In the darkness ahead she saw a brief flicker of light as someone lit a cigarette. She turned off the flashlight and started running.

Thirty metres from the wall she stopped, listening intently as she moved towards the wall, keeping low. A faint odour of cigarette smoke hung in the warm air as Galíndez paused, thinking of her options. If she went over the wall shooting she might hit the kids. But she had to take him by surprise, otherwise he would pick her off the moment she appeared. Assuming it was one guy and not several. She wondered for a moment about shouting for back-up and realised that wasn't an option. She could hardly speak.

Galíndez crouched like a sprinter on the block. *Uno.*

Her cracked voice, harsh in the night air: '*Niñas*? Where are you?' *Dos.*

A trembling voice to her right. '*Aquí*, Ana María.' It was Inés.

'*Callate.*' A man's voice silenced the child. Straight ahead. *Tres.*

Galíndez sprinted across the grass to the wall, her speed sending her flying up over the ragged stones, dropping down onto the parched grass, rolling quickly and scrambling to her feet, raising the pistol as she turned, looking for him. Something cold pressed against the back of her neck. 'Don't even think about it.' A familiar voice, thick with the threat of violence.

'Sancho?' She let the pistol fall to the grass. 'What are you doing here?'

'I missed you.' He laughed. 'What's wrong with your voice?'

'Someone took a dislike to me.'

'I'm not surprised.' He pressed the pistol harder. 'Kneel.'

She sank to her knees. 'Where are the girls?'

He shoved the muzzle of his gun against her back, hard. 'Face down in the grass. Hands out in front of you.'

She slid forward, flattening herself on the ground, arms outstretched. Dry grass pressed against her face. 'You've got me, you don't have to hurt the girls.'

He stepped back a couple of paces and retrieved her pistol. 'I don't have to do anything, Galíndez. Least of all listen to you talking like Donald fucking Duck.'

He knelt by her side. She struggled to control her breathing as he reached forward and lifted the hem of her shirt with the barrel of his pistol and pushed the muzzle against the small of her back. She clamped her teeth together, feeling the cold metal against her skin.

'One shot,' Sancho whispered. 'Just one and you'd be paralysed.' He pressed the pistol harder. 'If you lived.'

Sweat trickled into her eye. 'Let the girls go.'

'I like it when you breathe heavy, Galíndez.'

'I'm faking. I'm sure most women do with you.'

A sharp click as he thumbed back the hammer. Her body shook with an involuntary spasm as she imagined the damage the shot would inflict.

'Push your face into the dirt,' Sancho said. She sensed he was grinning.

She turned her face to the grass.

'Now, say something,' Sancho hissed.

'Like what?' Her words were muffled by the grass pressing into her mouth.

'It doesn't matter. I just wanted to hear how scared you are.'

He got to his feet, and moved away. 'See you later, Galíndez.'

She smelled his cigarette and heard his coarse breathing. She waited for her chance.

'Come on, you two,' Sancho said to the girls, as if they were on a day out. The tone of his voice was infuriating.

Faint snuffling, sounds of movement. Galíndez raised her face from the grass.

'Careful, Galíndez,' Sancho growled. 'You already look a mess without me putting a bullet in your head. That would make this your worst bad-hair day ever.'

'That's rich, coming from you.' She saw his bulky shape, imprecise in the darkness, the pale shaved head, the glitter of his piercings. 'If you hurt them...' Her voice faltered. Her throat was too painful to speak.

'Yeah, yeah, you'll track me to the ends of the earth.' He chuckled. 'If I was you, I'd stick to babysitting. You're good at that. Isn't that right, girls?'

Inés nodded. Clari clung to her sister, eyes tightly closed.

'*Vámonos*, señoritas,' he said. 'Over that wall with you, Ana's taking you home.'

Galíndez exhaled slowly, wondering what Sancho was up to. *It's got to be a trick.*

The girls were over the wall now. 'Wait there, *niñas*,' Sancho said. He came back towards Galíndez and she tensed, seeing him standing two metres from her, keeping enough distance between them to make it impossible for her to reach him without being shot.

He lowered his voice. 'Has anyone ever told you you're a fucking idiot?'

'Now and again,' Galíndez rasped. 'But I'm still going to put you behind bars.'

'Call me naive, but I always think it's best not to piss off someone who's pointing a gun at you.' Sancho moved backwards into the trees, still aiming the pistol at her. 'Now you've had a little rest, why don't you take those kids and get out of here?'

She heard his voice receding as he backed away into the trees. Beyond that wood were thousands of acres of farmland. She started to get up, wondering about pursuing him.

'Ana…' Inés called.

'*Momentito.*' If she let Sancho go now, he would come after her again, she knew that. Even so, the girls had to come first. She couldn't risk leaving them alone again.

She backed away, keeping her eyes on the dark clump of trees until she felt the wall press against the backs of her legs. As she turned, she saw her pistol lying on the wall. Furious, she pushed it into her belt.

'Right, let's get you two back to *Mamá* and *Papá.*' Galíndez lifted Clari into her arms. Inés stood immobile, waiting for instructions. 'Hold on to my belt, *querida,*' Galíndez told her as she set off back down the garden. 'Are you OK?' she asked Clari. The little girl didn't speak. She was staring at the burning house. 'Inés? *Qué tal?*'

Inés said nothing. Probably in shock, Galíndez guessed.

As they neared the pool of light around the house, figures came towards them. Galíndez saw Machado among them and returned his pistol. 'There was a guy with them,' she said. 'Big guy with a shaved head and facial piercings, armed with a pistol. He ran off through the trees.'

Machado started talking into his radio. '*Alpha Dos,* we have an armed suspect on the perimeter of the property, up near the woods. Request back-up. *Cambio.*'

Galíndez left him and continued towards the crowd of police and firefighters gathered by the gate. As she got nearer, the men parted to let her through, all of them staring. Galíndez wondered when someone was going to help her.

'I'll take the little one, you stay here, Ana.'

It was Mendez, wearing a Kevlar vest over her uniform. Galíndez watched her take the girls over to where Mercedes and Capitán Fuentes were waiting by their car, faces pale and drawn in the glare of the fire.

Galíndez watched the reunion from a distance. *I'm fine, just a sore throat.*

Mendez came back with a plastic bottle of water. 'You need to give a statement.'

'The boss,' Galíndez croaked, her throat raw. 'I want him to know I tried my best to protect the girls.' She swallowed the cold water, hoping it would ease the pain in her throat. It didn't. 'I need to tell them.'

Mendez grabbed her arm and pulled her back. 'Don't, not now.' Dazed, Galíndez tried to push past but Mendez stood in her way and took Galíndez's face in her hands. 'Listen to me, Ana, they don't want to talk to you.'

'I understand.' Galíndez blinked, not understanding. 'Maybe later?'

Mendez steered her to the patrol car and pushed her into the passenger seat.

'Why are they looking at me like that?' Galíndez asked as Mendez started the engine.

'The body count, Ana. There's at least seven dead. Guys don't expect this from a woman. Especially not a *forense* like you.'

'I did my best,' Galíndez muttered.

'You did something.' Mendez hit the siren to clear their way to the gate.

As they went up the drive, Galíndez saw the Fuentes family, still standing by their car, staring at her, their faces blank. As if she was a stranger.

CHAPTER 27

OROITZ, OCTOBER 1954

The mid-morning sun patterned the mountainside as Guzmán parked the Hispano Suiza near the village. Overnight, much of the snow had melted and the trees and bushes glittered. He scowled, furious at the unpredictable weather as he slung the sniper rifle over his shoulder and drew the Browning to check the action. Together with the big trench knife strapped to his leg, he had all he needed to deal with El Lobo. He'd killed men with less.

He left the village behind, following the dirt path that meandered through dense thickets of gorse and broom up to the fortress. The bright sun forced him to squint and, because of that, he almost failed to see the sudden flicker of light near one of the derelict buildings in the distance. He saw it again, a brief repetitive sequence of stuttering flashes. Morse code directed to an unseen observer in the valley below. He'd been right, then. There was someone up there.

As he continued up the steep path, Guzmán thought once again about Nieves Arestigui, and once again his thoughts troubled him. When he looked at her, it was as if Arantxa had come back to haunt him in the flesh, just as she'd haunted his dreams after the war. It was not the manner of her death that disturbed him, too many people had died around him – or because of him – for death to have any great importance. It was the question she planted that still troubled him seventeen years later.

Maybe she wanted to fuck him up. You could never tell with her. Volatile, that was what one of her clients had called her.

Guzmán had called her many things, depending on his mood – and hers. After all this time, he still remembered her words after they'd captured her. Standing with her amid the shattered buildings of the village, each recovering from this mutually surprising encounter. Wondering how it might affect them.

You're the smart one, chico. *You work it out.* The question tossed to him like a grenade.

Work it out. For all he knew, she'd said that to many of the men who'd been her clients. But she had shared something more with Guzmán than those furtive transactions in the field brothel. Arantxa had been many things but she had not been a liar. And smart or not, it was easy enough to calculate the time between his last visit to her bed and the child's birth. Though Arantxa hadn't confirmed it one way or the other. She'd just planted the question and left his imagination to do the rest. Not that it had changed anything. She'd died anyway.

And even if Nieves was his daughter, so what? Seventeen years on, what could he do, claim her as his long-lost child and take her back to Madrid? As if she would welcome having a father who worked in the *Policía Secreta*. He'd already heard the way she talked about 'fascists'. She meant people like him. He couldn't even talk to her about her mother. What could he say? *Your mama was a whore. She let me have credit when I was broke.* Nieves would hardly thank him for that posthumous revelation.

But there were other, better things he could tell her. *She could have betrayed me when she was captured but didn't. She fought and died for a cause she believed in.* Those were things Nieves would be proud of, no doubt. He would certainly omit the worst thing of all, the memory that still stalked his dreams. *She asked for my help and I let her down.* His breathing grew faster at the memory of it. Seventeen years on and the memory of it still burned inside him. He hadn't let her down. General Torres had moved the execution forward, wanting to show he was in command. Whoever had carried out the killings even used the sword the Moors engraved with Guzmán's name. He remembered walking towards the building when he returned from patrol, seeing his sword lying in the grass, smeared with blood. Reaching down for it. And then the sound of footsteps as Ochoa came running up from the cellar, clutching his camera, pale-faced, his eyes widening as he saw Guzmán holding the sword. His scream ringing in the chill air before he fled, spewing. *You fucking murderer.*

Things had happened fast that night. No sooner had he left that dank cellar, strewn with the corpses of the anarchists, than Torres announced his posting had been brought forward: he was to leave immediately for General Mellado's column in the south. There was no arguing: the papers came from Franco's HQ. Twenty minutes later, Guzmán was in a staff car, driving past the labourers sealing up the cellar to conceal the slaughter from the visiting journalists.

Guzmán had been powerless to help Arantxa. He'd tried and yet everything had seemed to conspire against him. What hurt most was that his plan to free her and the child failed. He had grown too used to having his own way. Not that he had seen fit to share any of that with Ochoa back then and he had no intention of doing so now. Enlisted men had no right to challenge their superiors.

He paused to light another Bisonte. It was time to put aside his tainted memories. Very likely El Lobo was up in that ruined fortress. If he was, Guzmán had to kill him. There wouldn't be another chance, not after losing five million of someone else's money. Even if he wasn't shot, the price of failure would be professional and social obliteration as he fell through the net of patronage and reciprocal dependencies that held the establishment together. He would fall so far that for the rest of his life he would be something else, something unspeakable. He would be poor.

He threw down his cigarette and ground the butt into the earth with his heel, disturbed by this line of thought. The dead were dead, little use worrying about them now. As for him, he was Guzmán. He was what he always had been. A survivor. So far at least.

Sargento León lay hidden in the gorse, angrily chewing a stalk of grass. This enforced inactivity left him with nothing to do but think and his thoughts were disturbing at the best of times. The more he brooded, the more angry he became, reflecting on a catalogue of grievances both serious and trivial, visualising diverse forms of revenge on those who had offended him. And of those, there were many.

Throughout the morning, León had worked his way down the hillside, crawling through the sharp scrub, tormented by the flies swarming over the cow pats scattered in the grass. Once night fell, he planned to slip into the village and steal a horse. Then he would ride to the border, though with a long diversion south to avoid Çubiry territory. Once across, he would make for Lourdes or Tarbes. He could find work there, he was sure. Maybe he would learn French. It had to be easy: even the children could speak it.

León held his breath, suddenly aware of rustling grass and the sound of rapid breathing. Someone was coming up the dirt path towards him. Just one person, walking fast, from the sound of it. That was good. Someone alone was not a problem for a man with his violent skills. He raised his pistol, peering through the shrubs at the trail as the footsteps came nearer and passed within two metres of his hiding place. He saw a swinging black skirt and white, rope-soled *alpargatas*, their red laces tied around firm tanned calves. As the woman continued up the hill, León rose from the bushes, his eyes glinting with malice as he weighed things up, balancing the risk to himself against other, more base desires. The calculation took only a second. Carefully, he made his way through the gorse and started up the trail, following Nieves Arestigui.

OROITZ 1954, FORTALEZA DE ZUMALACÁRREGUI

The trail petered out a hundred metres from the old fortress.

Ahead, lines of crumbling defence works sprawled across the hillside. At the centre of the ramparts was an arched gateway, its wooden gates long gone, the great fallen stones of the arch lying shattered on the ground nearby. He passed through the ruined portal and paused by a large opening in the rocks, edged with brick and smooth carved stone. A long tunnel stretched away into darkness. At the far end he saw an oblique patch of faint light

He unslung the rifle and went into the tunnel, making for the light at the far end. He emerged on a long gun terrace cut into the hillside, where rusting cannons stared out across the lonely countryside as they had for the last hundred years. Along the rear of the terrace several regularly spaced supply tunnels led to the arsenal deep inside the mountain, guaranteeing a steady supply of ammunition to the guns. Or would have if this isolated stronghold had ever been attacked. But no enemy ever had need to lay siege to it. Instead, it had been ignored and bypassed, making it a vain and futile monument to bad planning, worthy of Franco himself.

Guzmán took out his Zippo and snapped it into flame as he entered a tunnel halfway along the terrace. Along the walls, a long row of iron rings had been set into the stone just above head height, for the ropes of ammunition carts, he guessed. Bats fluttered out of the darkness, dark whispers whirling past his face. He walked cautiously through the strange, muffled silence, sensing the vast weight of the mountain overhead. And then, behind him, a sudden creaking followed by the sound of falling stones and debris rattling down onto the floor of the tunnel. He turned and lifted the lighter. Though a vague cloud of dust he saw scattered debris along the floor of the passage. Above the debris the curved ceiling sagged, spilling thin streams of dirt and powdered rock through growing cracks in the rough-hewn stone.

He continued down the tunnel, feeling cold air on his face, a silent chill draught that troubled the flame of his lighter, forcing him to pause and shield it with his cupped hand. That pause was fortunate, he realised as he looked down at the gaping drop a few paces ahead. A length of the tunnel floor had collapsed, opening up a deep chasm some twenty metres long between him and the next section of the tunnel. When he leaned forward, in an attempt to see the bottom of the crevasse, a stream of cold air from below extinguished the flame.

Behind him, he heard again the sound of grating rock and flurries of pulverised stone. From the sound of it, the tunnel roof might come down at any moment. That left him no choice but to continue on into the mountain towards the arsenal.

Guzmán looked again at the chasm in front of him. The collapse of the tunnel floor had left nothing, no slight ledge at either side where he might gain a foothold. He stared at the smooth curved stone walls, his eyes settling on the line of rusted iron rings extending along the tunnel. It was possible, he supposed. Possible, though not desirable. There was no guarantee the rings would take the weight of a man. His deliberations were cut short as a further small avalanche of broken stones tumbled down into the tunnel behind him.

Guzmán reached up and seized an iron ring with each hand. He hung from them, making sure they could bear his weight. When both rings survived that test, he launched himself to one side, grabbing a ring further to his left, then bringing his right over to grab the next before reaching out with his left hand again.

It was laborious work, made worse by the weight of the rifle. Within minutes, his fingers knotted from grasping the rusty iron, and soon after, the muscles of his forearms began tightening in painful spasms. If his arms cramped, he might not reach the far side of the crevasse. He was carrying too much weight, he realised. The rifle would have to go.

Guzmán let go of one of the rings. Sweat stung his eyes and he grunted at the effort of supporting his weight with one hand as he tried to shake the rifle strap from his shoulder without sending himself plunging into the chasm.

Finally, the rifle slipped from his shoulder and moments later he heard a sharp clatter as it hit the rocks below. He took a deep breath and continued. He was perhaps ten metres away from the next section of the tunnel, he guessed. That spurred him on as he grasped the next ring and continued his painful journey. And then, as he swung himself along, his outstretched foot hit stone. He shook sweat from his eyes, cursing the pain in his arms and wrists. Another two more rings and he would be across. He reached out, teeth clenched as he extended his arm, running his fingers over the stone, searching for the next handhold. Cramp burned across his shoulders as he hung by one hand, trying to find the iron ring with the other. Something was wrong, he realised as his fingers touched the rough holes where the bolts holding the ring in place had once been. There was only so long a man could support his own weight like this and he twisted and turned, swinging back and forth, creating new geometries of pain in his tortured muscles as he built up the momentum to fling himself forward towards the broken lip of the gaping hole, digging his fingers into the stone as he dragged himself up into the tunnel. A flurry of obscenities followed as he kneaded his forearms, forcing blood through the muscles. And then his cursing was interrupted as a distant sound cut through the darkness, resonating in brittle echoes off the stone walls around him. The sound of footsteps.

OROITZ 1954, MENDIKO RIDGE

The oil lamp swung in her hand as Nieves approached the fortress. High above, the pinnacle of Mari's Peak towered into a hazy sky as she whispered the name of the goddess, invoking her protection, confident Mari would come to her aid, because her cause was just. She came seeking justice for Patxi Gabilondo.

Nieves made for the entrance, negotiating her way over irregular piles of fallen stones. The carved gateway loomed over her, its lintel cracked and sagging under the eternal weight of the mountain. She took a box of wax *cerillas* from her pocket and lit the lantern before entering the tunnel. She walked slowly, distracted, as she planned what she would say to El Lobo when she confronted him. It had seemed a good plan when she'd left home. She was less sure of that now.

A few metres further on, she stopped as she heard faint echoes, growing louder as they reverberated down the tunnel towards her. Even a country girl like Nieves could recognise the sound of gunfire and she slowed to avoid making a noise, wondering who was doing the shooting. She was still wondering that as the man came out of the shadows behind her, clamping his hand over her mouth, his other arm wrapping around her body, pulling her close against him. The lamp clattered to the ground

'Keep quiet.' León's breath stank of garlic and sour wine. Her heart pounding, Nieves fought desperately to break free, though against León's strength there was never much chance of that. As she struggled, she called for help, the repetitive cadences of her voice echoing around her in the tunnel as León wrestled her to the ground.

Once León had pinned her down, it was easy to twist her arm behind her back, securing his hold on her. By way of emphasis, he pressed the muzzle of his service revolver against her head, muttering dark threats.

'Don't try anything,' he muttered, 'just walk. Try to get away and you'll suffer.'

Nieves obeyed. His grip was so tight there was no chance of her breaking away. She would have to wait. Perhaps there would be a way out of this. The thought there might not be made her shiver.

'Cold, Niña?' León muttered. 'I'll warm you up soon, don't you worry. Now, let's get moving.'

Nieves had no choice. She began walking down the tunnel, wincing at León's fierce grip on her arm.

OROITZ 1954, FORTALEZA DE ZUMALACÁRREGUI

Guzmán listened as the echoes of Nieves' cries receded into silence. He glowered, angry that she had put herself in danger and angry

425

that he had no way of finding her in the warren of tunnels running through the fortress. He continued along the tunnel, aware of soft echoes ahead, like the sound of autumn leaves. Ten metres away, the tunnel ended. Beyond that, he saw the pale wavering light of torches. Someone was expecting company. Crouching in the mouth of the tunnel, he peered into the huge cavern that had once served as the fort's arsenal. He had no idea who might be in there along with El Lobo. Dozens of heavily armed Çubiry, for all he knew. One thing he did know: if he had to get out of the cavern in a hurry, he didn't want to use this tunnel again. He reached down, picked up a stone and scratched a large X on the wall as a reminder to avoid this route.

He stepped out into a dank silence, broken by the rustle of bats and the slow drip of water from the cavern roof. At the far side of this vast stone chamber he saw a stack of long wooden crates stacked in neat rows. New crates too. Brand new. A delivery from the Çubiry to El Lobo, without doubt. Cautiously, he went over to examine them. The labels all carried the crest of the Military Governor. The weapons were from General Mellado's armoury. At the other side of the cavern he saw a cluster of great carved stone tables heaped with pyramids of cannon balls, their bulbous outline now muted by a century of cobwebs. Above the tables a long gallery had been carved into the wall of the cavern and from it burning torches threw a fitful, disorienting light over the cavern floor, picking out the large well at its centre, the buckets and pulleys hanging lopsided and rotten from a crooked gantry.

Guzmán paused, listening intently to the silence. A funereal quiet that amplified his cautious steps into shimmering Judas sounds, each ready to betray his presence. Slowly, he turned, scanning the cavern for signs of life. The bleak light from the gallery created long shadows over the skeletal framework of the well, almost hiding the man sitting with his back to the rough stone parapet, a rifle across his knee.

Guzmán crept forwards, keeping the Browning raised. It was unlikely El Lobo would take a nap here, in the centre of this dank grotto. More likely this was one of his men, taking a furtive break.

That was fine. No matter how many men Lobo had with him here, Guzmán would kill them one by one if he had to. Flexibility in combat was necessary to survive in fluctuating circumstances. There was only thing Guzmán would not change now: El Lobo had to die.

The man gave no sign of movement as Guzmán worked his way closer. Slowly, he holstered the Browning and drew his knife. This man would die without his sleep being disturbed.

Holding the knife ready, he moved in for the kill, aware now of a thick odour, both repugnant and familiar. The stench of putrefaction. The pallid torchlight from the gallery played over the man's features as Guzmán spat onto the rough stone floor, clearing the taste of death from his mouth as he glared at the bloated face. In death, the late Señor Bárcenas was no less ugly than in life, though he smelled much worse.

A sudden flash. Powdered stone stung Guzmán's face as he threw himself flat, hearing the rippling cadences of the shot hammer through the dark silence of the cavern.

He lay by the well, trying to see where the shot had come from. A noise to his left as Bárcenas's corpse slid across the stone wall towards him. Guzmán inhaled the stench of rotting flesh as he glowered at the corpulent face half a metre from his. Accurate shooting, Guzmán thought, realising the bullet had not been meant for him. Someone was playing games.

'I knew you'd come.' A deep, resonant voice from somewhere on the gallery. Guzmán glanced across to the stone tables. There was good cover behind those, enhanced by the heaps of cannon balls piled on them. If he could get among the tables, Lobo would need to lean over the balcony to get a shot at him. And that would make him a target.

Guzmán leaped up and fired, aiming at the sound of the voice. Harsh sharp cracks, the cartridges rattling onto the ground as he ran to the stone tables, firing again as he saw a dark shape rear up behind the balcony. He hurled himself into the shelter of one of the big stone tables as a rapid series of bullets exploded around him, whining away in clamorous ricochets. Sweat trickled down his face as he sheltered under the ancient carved stonework, planning his next move. He was safe for now, but the moment he moved, Lobo was in a prime position to pick him off.

'You lack finesse, *Comandante*,' the voice said. 'Men like you have no time for thought, you rely on your brute instincts.'

'I didn't come here for flattery,' Guzmán grunted, squirming through the space below the table towards the wall of the cavern.

'You came here to die.' The words bounced around the gallery, low and threatening. 'Perhaps you didn't realise it before. I'm sure you do now.'

Guzmán rolled onto his back and looked up through a lattice of cobwebs. He still had no clear shot at the gallery, so he twisted and slid forward under the next table.

'There's no escape from here.' The voice rolled around the walls of the cavern.

'Not for you, there isn't.' Guzmán scanned the balcony with his pistol. 'So far, every time I got near you, you ran. You won't do it again.'

A strange noise from above. The sound of cold laughter. 'Guerrilla warfare.'

Guzmán peered up at the gallery. The echoes made it hard to locate where the voice was coming from. He had to keep Lobo talking. 'You call running away guerrilla warfare?'

'Of course. You were so sure I'd walk into your trap, you never thought about other possibilities.' A mirthless laugh. 'Not until it was too late, anyway.'

Guzmán felt sweat trickle down his back as he struggled to control his anger. 'What's Bárcenas doing here?'

'It would have spoiled my plans if you'd been arrested for his murder, so I took him while you spent the night with General Torres's daughter.'

'I'd say I got the better deal.'

'I could have killed both of you any time I chose.' Lobo's voice had a sour edge to it. 'But I don't kill innocent women.' The words rebounded in muted echoes. 'How does it feel now? Are you afraid like we were, tied to those chairs? Or have you forgotten that night?'

Guzmán wiped a hand across his brow, beginning to understand now. 'You were at Villarreal?' He tried to remember the faces in that cellar. There was only one he recalled in any detail and that was Arantxa's. 'Did you think we'd send you home with a warning? It was war.'

A dark figure appeared on the balcony. Guzmán brought the pistol up fast, the bullets glancing off the stone balcony in eccentric patterns of fleeting sparks as the staccato bark of the Browning echoed up into the roof of the cavern, provoking a frenzy of startled bats.

'You had no need to kill her.' The deep voice was calm, almost thoughtful. Lobo fired again and another bullet exploded into the stone table above Guzmán's head. 'You said she could live and then you killed her in front of me.'

'I wasn't even there,' Guzmán snapped. 'And at least her child lived.'

The torches outlined Lobo in wavering fire. 'You'd say anything to stay alive. All of them died. All but me. I cheated death and now I've come for you, *Comandante*.'

'You're wrong – the child didn't die,' Guzmán said. 'A drover took her to Arantxa's farm. He was supposed to take both of them. For some reason Arantxa stayed with you.'

'No. I was there. I know what you did.'

'You couldn't have been, I'd never forget a face as ugly as yours.'

'This was your handiwork with that sword.' Lobo's voice pulsed with anger. 'You should have killed me. Vengeance has a long memory – as you're going to find out.'

'You talk like a poet,' Guzmán snorted. 'And that's not a compliment.'

'That was what they called me. But my poetry ended that night. Poetry comes from love. I have darker inspirations now.'

Guzmán remembered the lantern light, the row of chairs. 'The Englishman.' A statement, not a question. 'Was Arantxa your woman?'

'In a way. Though I had no time for whores. It was her mind I valued, not her body.'

'No wonder you lost the war,' Guzmán sneered. 'You sound more like a fucking Jesuit than an anarchist.'

'I believed in what I fought for, *Comandante*.'

'Really? I found photos of you and Mellado in his office. You make a strange couple.' 'I joined the Legion after the war. As long as a man could fight, Mellado didn't care about his past. I enjoyed my time in the desert. They say the hardest steel goes through the fire.'

'And you changed your politics as well while you were there, did you?'

'A marriage of convenience,' Lobo said. 'The general and I have similar aims.'

'And what would those be?'

'We want this region to burn, *Comandante*.'

Guzmán frowned. That was not the answer he'd expected. 'Why would you want that?'

'He wants an uprising so he can put it down. And so do I, though for different reasons.'

'That's why he supplied you with those rifles over there, is it?'

'Exactly. He wants the resistance to be well armed so he can slaughter them.'

'And he's got no idea of what your plans are?'

'Of course not, he's half-crazy. He doesn't realise the damage it will do to the economy. There'll be no foreign investment, just war, Guzmán. And this time it will be a war you won't win. No Germans or Italians to bail you out now.'

'You're the one who's fucking crazy,' Guzmán growled.

Lobo's voice throbbed with sudden passion. 'People here are too accustomed to defeat. They need blood to be spilled, their homes burned and their children murdered. That way, they'll realise fighting is their only option. Once the people rise up in arms none of you fascists will be able to stop them.'

Guzmán saw furtive movement on the balcony as Lobo shifted

position. 'You're still an anarchist, then?' he asked, hoping Lobo would move again. He raised the pistol.

'I believe in perpetual conflict, *Comandante*. Fire and revolution, constant upheaval.'

'But you've no interest in Arantxa's daughter? Some comrade you were.'

'Why should I care about her bastard child? When we were captured, Arantxa said you were the father. That was why she believed you'd help her escape.'

So it was true. Sweat ran into Guzmán's eye and he blinked it away. He began to raise himself from cover, ready to empty the magazine into Lobo's scarred face. But for that he needed the bandit to show himself. 'She's the image of her mother,' he called. 'If you saw her, you'd think it was Arantxa back from the grave.'

'I'd put a bullet in her,' Lobo said in a hoarse whisper. 'Let the child join her mother.'

Furious, Guzmán stepped out from behind the tables, aiming up at the gallery. 'Why the fuck would you do that, you crazy bastard?'

Standing in the mouth of the tunnel, Nieves sensed León's grip slacken as he leaned forward, preoccupied with Guzmán and Lobo's confrontation. With a sudden twist of her body she broke away from him and ran back into the tunnel. In the darkness it was impossible to see the uneven stone floor and she tripped, falling full length onto the ground. Before she could get up, León was on her, driving the air from her lungs as he pinned her down with his great weight, his big clammy hands clamped around her wrists, his legs clasping hers. Cold stone pressed against her cheek as he pressed himself against her, breathing into her ear. 'Not yet, *niña*. But soon now.'

She gasped as he grabbed a handful of her hair and dragged her to her feet.

Up on the gallery, Lobo stepped out of the shadows, a tall, bulky outline against the glow of the torches. 'Death has a strange symmetry, *Comandante*. Let the girl join her mother. If she knew who her father is – what he is – she'd welcome death.'

The bitter crack of the rifle. Harsh shimmering echoes. White, searing pain.

The bullet struck Guzmán high in the left arm, knocking him to the ground. He clutched the wound, looking up at the gallery as El Lobo slid over the balcony and dropped down into the chamber. He landed lightly on his feet and came sprinting forwards, the rifle held like a club.

Guzmán struggled to his feet, gripping the Browning with both hands. As Lobo closed on him, he aimed and pulled the trigger.

A hollow metal click.

Before he could even think about clearing the jam, Lobo was on him, and Guzmán grunted in pain as he blocked the rifle blow with his forearms. Desperate to get at him, Lobo dropped the rifle and launched a frenzied onslaught with his fists, driving Guzmán back towards the well, Guzmán's head snapping back as the bandit's punches struck home.

This close, El Lobo was even more monstrous, his ravaged face a taut mask of pale shiny flesh crossed by the marks of inept stitching. A dead face devoid of expression apart from his dark eyes, glittering with violent intent as he rained a flurry of blows at Guzmán, picking his spot now, hitting the side of his head, the chest, hammering into his ribs.

And Lobo was taller and stronger, Guzmán realised as he raised his fists, defending against the furious barrage of punches to his head. A sharp blow above the eye rocked him and he staggered back, blinking away the flickering lights dancing across his vision, feeling a trickle of blood from a cut.

Lobo had done this before, that was for sure. The punches were well timed and varied, one moment smacking against the side of his

432

head, the next hammering into his body with savage force, knocking the breath from him in noisy grunts. Even when Guzmán used his good arm to try and land a blow, Lobo moved fast, blocking it and then returning to the attack, striking with fast one-twos, forcing Guzmán slowly back, step by step, forcing him to block with his wounded arm while trying to hit back with the other.

Sensing Guzmán's disadvantage, Lobo slowed, striking with greater precision, picking his spots as he looked for the opportunity to finish him. Guzmán reeled as a heavy punch hit him full in the chest. For a moment, time slowed, as if his heart had stopped. He stood, gulping in air as Lobo squared up for his next attack. He raised his head, shaking sweat from his face, his fists clenched as he saw the pitiless eyes staring at him, glazed with fury. A killer's eyes. A reflection of his own.

And then Lobo moved in again, unleashing sharp, explosive punches, driving Guzmán back towards the well.

The pain was brutal. Nothing existed outside this grunting, spluttering world of fists and sweat and blood. It was not going well. Guzmán landed a punch here and there, but for every blow, Lobo landed three or four in return. Guzmán aimed a kick at Lobo's knee but the bandit danced back out of range before attacking again, confident now as he saw the damage he was inflicting.

Guzmán felt thick blood in his nose and spat, watching Lobo's fists as he prepared to hit him again. A succession of darting thoughts flashed through the pain. The feeling of being helpless when he was a kid, as his father bore down on him. The feeling when he saw Arantxa's body, deep furrows of bloody flesh bulging through her clothes where the sword had struck. *Helpless*. And now, wondering if this might be the day he'd always thought would come. The day he lost control of his destiny. His future no longer in his hands but those of his killer.

The blow caught him on the side of his head, above his ear. Lights flashed before his eyes. *Helpless*. Ironic for a man who earlier had congratulated himself on being a winner. *Helpless*. A man who had always thought he had what it took to survive in this world. Though not for much longer: he was thinking like a loser.

A voice in his head. *You're the smart one* chico. *You work it out.* Her voice. Arantxa.

The next punch caught him on the temple, sending him reeling against the crumbling parapet around the well. The ancient wall trembled under the impact, sending shards of ancient brick rattling down into the depths. Struggling to stay on his feet, Guzman put a hand on the wall to steady himself, feeling a sharp stone protruding from the rough surface, loosening from the ancient mortar as his grip tightened on it. Breaking away in his hand. He looked up and met Lobo's eye as he came towards him, ready to finish him. As Lobo swung his fist, Guzmán lifted his injured arm to deflect the blow, knocking the bandit's arm to one side.

Guzmán head-butted him in the face.

Lobo staggered back and Guzmán saw the long bloody gash above the bandit's eye where the flesh had torn open along the ragged scar lines. Lobo blinked as a rivulet of blood ran into his eyes and lifted his hand to wipe it away. As he did, Guzmán leaped forward and seized his throat with his left hand. Instinctively, Lobo clutched the hand on his throat, trying to break the choking grip. That was a mistake.

Guzmán smashed the jagged stone in his right hand into the open wound, ripping open more of the old scar tissue. With a howl of pain, Lobo broke away, clutching at the ragged flap of bloody flesh drooping over his left eye. A wound like that would distract any man and as Lobo hesitated, Guzmán struck again, tearing open more of the scarred flesh as he pounded the stone into the bandit's face again and again, feeling the blood splattering him with each blow.

Lobo staggered back, clumsily trying to push the fold of skin away from his eyes, which were filling with blood. In that one faltering moment, Guzmán was on him, his fingers tearing into the gaping wound as he gripped the tangle of muscle and sinew and brought all his strength to bear as he spun round, ripping part

434

of the bandit's face away as he hurled El Lobo into the parapet of the well. With a dry crack the ancient brickwork disintegrated, spilling into the well in an avalanche of tan dust, taking Lobo with it. Moments later, the huge stone chamber echoed to the sound of his body as it hit the rocks below. A few desultory flurries of loose stones and dirt followed before the silence closed in once more.

Gasping for air, Guzmán went over to the ragged gap in the parapet and looked down, seeing nothing but shadow. He wiped sweat from his face, grunting at the pain coursing through his battered body. He put a hand to his shoulder. The bullet wound was not the worst injury he'd ever had but he was alone here. If he lost too much blood and passed out, it was unlikely anyone would come looking for him. He needed to bind the wound quickly and doing that would make him vulnerable, especially if Lobo had brought men up here with him.

He looked round for somewhere he could attend to his injury without being surprised by Lobo's gunmen. In a corner of the cavern, he saw a cluster of boulders, each of them taller than a man. He staggered over and slipped into a gap between the rocks.

Hidden from view, he sat with his back to one of the ancient stones and tore a strip of canvas from the lining of his hunting jacket. Slowly, he looped the canvas strip around the wound. It was not easy working one-handed: he needed to be patient. But after two days of exertion and combat with little sleep, his patience was almost exhausted.

Sweat stung his eyes and the end of the canvas slipped from his fingers again and again. Cursing, he forced himself to work slowly, taking more care. This time he managed to work the strip around his arm into a half-knot and leaned back against the rock for a moment, almost comfortable. If he closed his eyes, he would sleep at once, he could tell. That was an attractive option. Just let sleep overtake him and abandon this running battle. Fuck Franco's secrecy, his need for *Yanqui* money. He was tired of all of it. He closed his eyes and felt the darkness calling to him, a siren song promising oblivion.

His head rolled back and hit the rock with a sudden jolt. His eyes snapped open and he looked up at the vast cavern above him and shook his head, dismissing the ideas spinning through his exhausted brain. When had he ever abandoned a job? He stuck with things, pursued them to the end. That was what brought him his rewards. And his reward for completing this job would be a return to Madrid, not sitting slowly bleeding to death in a fucking antiquated fortress. He would complete his mission, not out of a sense of duty but because he was – and always had been – a winner. There would be no lying back and sleeping, no resigning himself to fate or the whims of others. His fate lay in his hands, those big powerful hands now encrusted with the blood of a dead bandit.

He grasped one of the ends of the cloth tourniquet and held it tight as he leaned forward to grip the other end in his teeth, pulling the knot tighter, staunching the blood. When it was done, he slumped back, listening to his laboured breathing as he tried to gather his strength. As he struggled to his feet, he heard footsteps echoing around the cavern. The sound of voices.

'You're hurting me,' Nieves shouted as León dragged her towards the well, gripping her hair tight in his hand, forcing her to walk almost doubled.

'I haven't even started, señorita.' León's head swam with dark thoughts and intentions. 'I've wanted to get you alone for a long time.' He grinned. 'Don't worry, I'll take it slow.'

He saw the damaged section of the parapet of the well and dragged her to it.

'From what I heard back there in the tunnel, it sounded like Guzmán's your papa?'

'Ask him,' Nieves said, wincing at his iron grip on her hair.

León paused to look down into the shaft of the well. 'Whether he was or not, it looks like they both went down there.' Without warning, he pushed Nieves to the ground and knelt astride her.

436

She raised her head, her dark eyes glittering with anger and fear as he drew the skinning knife from his belt.

'Keep still.' León gloated as he slid the blade of the knife under one of the buttons on her blouse, enjoying her fear as he sliced though the fabric, cutting away the button. 'It's up to you,' he said. An almost casual aside. 'You can take your clothes off or I cut them off.'

'I'd rather die than let you touch me.'

León chuckled. 'You're going to die *after* I've touched you, *niña*. I'm going to carve you up like I did your mama.'

Her face froze. 'What do you mean?'

León was smirking now he'd got her attention. 'She was a spy. Guzmán was a bit too friendly with her, so the general ordered me to do the execution. And now I'm going to do the same to you. By the time I'm done, you'll beg me to kill you.'

Guzmán listened to León's taunts, feeling the anger burn in his veins. *He killed her?* He struggled to his feet. *He killed her.* As he prepared to slip out through the gap between the big stones, he reached for the Browning. His hand touched leather. The holster was empty. Wearily, he paused, resting a hand on the cold stone. He would have to rely on his fists then. Carefully, he pushed through the big stones and stepped out into the cavern.

Near the well, he saw León's dark bulk pinning Nieves to the ground. Heard his threats, his curses. Nieves's sudden protests as he touched her, mocking her helpless outrage.

Guzmán walked slowly, his breathing slow and controlled, as the Moors had taught him, heel first, rolling the foot forward, eyes scouring the ground for potential obstructions, his mind focused on maintaining his silent progress. As if from a great distance, he heard León's greasy chuckle as he sliced another button from Nieves' blouse. Guzmán ignored it, distracted as he stared at El Lobo's rifle, lying a metre or so ahead of him on the dirt floor.

León was breathing heavily. He'd imagined this moment for a long time. A thin string of drool hung from his mouth as he brushed the knife over Nieves' throat. 'Let's see what we've got in here shall we, *niña*?' He reached down with his free hand to open her blouse.

'Die on your feet or on your knees, León, it's your choice.' The metallic rasp of the rifle bolt echoed round the cavern as Guzmán put a round into the breech.

León moved fast, stumbling away from Nieves as he looked for an escape route. Desperately, he turned back, intending to use her as a shield, but she had moved beyond his reach now, holding her blouse closed as she hurried to put more distance between them. León stared at Guzmán, open-mouthed.

'This must be the only time in your fucking life you've got nothing to say, *Sargento*.'

'We can talk,' León said. 'It should be simple to sort this out.'

Guzmán kept the rifle aimed. 'You're dead. How's that for simple?'

'I'll tell you where the money is. All five million.'

'Makes no difference.' Guzmán took a step closer.

'*Comandante*?' Nieves' voice rang in the silence. 'I don't want you to shoot him.'

'He was going to rape you,' Guzmán said. 'And he killed your mother. He dies.'

She stood, arms folded tightly across her chest. 'I said let him go. Please.'

'Why?' Guzmán asked, suddenly belligerent.

'Because shooting him in cold blood isn't right.'

'She's right.' León nodded, his small eyes flickering around the cave.

Guzmán went to him. 'Turn round and walk towards that tunnel.'

León moved sideways, suspecting if he turned his back Guzmán would shoot.

'Tell me again why I'm not going to kill this dough-faced bastard?' Guzmán asked.

'It's not his destiny, *Comandante*,' said Nieves.

León stopped at the mouth of the tunnel, keeping his hands raised. Behind him, the light of the torches played on the rough stone walls, illuminating the first few metres of the tunnel.

Guzmán's gaze moved beyond León, focusing on the big X scratched on the wall behind him.

'Nieves is right,' he said. 'Get going. I don't want to see you again.'

León turned, unable to believe his luck.

'Fucking run.' Guzmán fired a shot past him into the darkened tunnel. As the echoes died away, León disappeared into the darkness, his hobnailed boots clattering as he ran.

Nieves came closer to Guzman. The colour was returning to her face. She was a brave girl, he thought.

'Thank you for not killing him, *Comandante*.'

He shrugged. From inside the tunnel they could still hear the sound of León's boots.

Nieves turned her head as León's scream came echoing toward them.

A scream of surprise, perhaps a tinge of disappointment too, Guzmán thought. 'I think León's destiny just caught up with him. Shall I take you home?'

She looked at him hard. 'Is that all you've got to say?'

'What do you mean?'

'You knew who my mother was all along and you never said a word.'

Guzmán wiped blood from the cut above his eye. 'It was difficult.'

'What was difficult?' Nieves snapped. 'Telling me my mother was a prostitute or that you were my father?' She tossed her hair from her face and he saw the dark anger in her eyes. Her mother's eyes.

'Both.'

'Why didn't you help her escape?' Nieves' voice was strained. 'You'd been lovers, she'd had your child. What sort of man are you?'

'She was supposed to go back to Lauburu Farm with you,' Guzmán muttered. 'I paid a local drover to take you both. Something went wrong. In the end, she stayed with her comrades and the drover took you.' He shook his head. 'There was nothing I could do. I wasn't there when they were killed or perhaps I could have stopped it.'

Her dark witch's eyes were radiant with fury. 'Maybe you didn't want to stop it?'

Guzman scowled. 'Of course I did. Why do you say that?'

An impenetrable silence. He saw her face darken, as if the shadows were growing around her. Her mouth a thin, tight line, stretched into a vicious smile.

'I'm just thinking, *Comandante*,' Nieves said. 'My mother was your prisoner.'

'I think we established that.'

'And yet you met her in the army camp where she was working?' Her eyes flashed. 'So that was the Republican Army.'

'So what?' Guzmán grunted, disturbed by her expression.

'When you captured her, she was an enemy agent and you were a Nationalist officer. That means you changed sides.' Her eyes glowed, triumphant. 'You were a traitor.'

'Things like that happen in wartime.'

'I doubt they happened to people who end up as secret policemen with credentials from Franco giving them all sorts of privileges. 'If I report it to the *policía* in San Sebastián, do you think they'll take notice?'

His face hardened. Better people than her had tried to use his secrets against him. 'No, of course not. They'll think you're a little farm girl with a grudge.'

'But I bet there'd be someone who'd do some checking, just because it seems so odd.'

That was true, Guzmán thought. There was always some busybody who might follow up something like that just for the hell of it, hoping that maybe it would make a name for them. He tried to stay calm. He had to, because otherwise it would be too easy to let the voice in his head guide him. It was loud now, urging him to do what he'd done to the few people who'd discovered his secret over the years. *Kill her.*

'You should go,' he said quietly. 'For your own good.'

'You won't hurt me, *Comandante*.' She tossed her hair from her face. 'Don't they say blood's thicker than water?'

'Don't be too sure of that,' Guzmán grunted. 'Go now.'

She looked him in the face, sensing the threat. 'All right. I'll go.'

He watched her walk towards one of the tunnels. She stopped and turned back.

'You came to our house as a guest and never said a word to me about my mother. I never knew how she died. You could have told me.' Her eyes shone. 'You should have told me.'

Guzmán was accustomed to having the last word. He had no words now.

Nieves gestured at the cavern walls. 'Mari punishes liars.' Shaking, she lifted her hand and pointed at him. '*Betiko madarikatua zara*. You are forever cursed. May those you care about die, and may you live long in solitude and despair.' She hurried away into the tunnel, her slight figure soon lost in shadow.

He listened as her footsteps faded into the darkness and then went over to the gallery and took down one of the torches to guide him back.

He emerged near the derelict fortifications on the hillside. Below, he saw Nieves, walking quickly into the valley, suddenly obscured by the great boulders and gnarled trees littering the hillside.

He walked back to the village alone, sullen and angry. Everything in this region was complicated. Even with El Lobo dead, he still had problems. He'd realised that as soon as he'd examined the crates of weapons in the old fortress. He'd expected to see the Çubiry label on them, not the crest of the fucking Military Governor. For his own lunatic reasons, Mellado had supplied arms to the resistance. That was something that needed to be dealt very quickly, before Mellado could do some real damage.

But now, as he neared the village, there was one last task to carry out. Gutiérrez had sent him a file to the *pensión*. He needed to read that to see if there were further orders for him. And there was a bonus: Capitán Viana – or whoever he really was – was coming after the file.

He was in for a surprise.

CHAPTER 28

'Here we are.' Isabel slowed the car as they approached headquarters.

Outside the building, several uniformed men in dark sunglasses stared at the passing traffic, sub-machine guns held at the ready.

'Don't pull up here,' Galíndez warned, 'they're worried about suicide bombers.'

Isabel found a parking space further along the road. She turned to Galíndez. 'How are you feeling, Ana?'

'I just wish it was over,' Galíndez said. 'And I'd be a lot happier if I could speak to Capitán Fuentes and Mercedes. I don't understand why they haven't been in touch.'

'It must have been a shock,' Isabel said. 'It's not every day you come home to find your house looking like a war zone.'

'That's what everyone says.' Galíndez nodded. Her face clouded for a moment. 'But a thank-you card from the boss wouldn't have hurt.'

'It's the least they could do, since you saved the girls' lives. And you're suspended again. It's not fair.'

Galíndez shrugged. 'A temporary suspension is routine after an incident involving fatalities. Once this meeting's over, I should be reinstated automatically.' She changed the subject. 'How do I look?'

'Very professional. That suit makes a change from a leather jacket and jeans.'

Galíndez smiled. 'Thanks, *Mamá*.'

'Good luck.' Isabel leaned forward to kiss her cheek. 'Do your ribs still hurt?'

'They're fine. If I get any pain, I'll take a tablet.'

'Maybe you should see the doctor again? If those tablets are as weak as you say, you might need something stronger.'

'No, I don't want to take medication all the time.'

'That's typical of you, Ana María.' Isabel laughed. 'Always taking the hard route.'

'Remember you said I could talk to you about what happened last year?'

'Of course. The offer still stands.'

'Could we do it soon? Like in a couple of days?' She looked away, suddenly awkward.

'If that's what you want.'

'It could take a while.'

'Take all the time you need, *querida*. Hey, do you want to go out for dinner tonight?'

'I'd like that.' Galíndez opened the door. 'I'd better go, I don't want to be late.'

Isabel put a hand on her arm. 'Remember you said I give up too easily?'

Galíndez nodded.

'I haven't given up.'

'Good.'

'Let me know how it goes, won't you?' Isabel called as Galíndez got out of the car.

'It might be a while, I expect they'll want to go through everything in detail.'

'I just hope your voice doesn't give out.'

'I'll try not to talk too much.' Galíndez laughed.

Inside the lobby, she took a deep breath, remembering what she had to do: *tell the truth, give them the facts.* That was simple enough. For once she had nothing to hide. The lift doors slid open and she stepped in. When the doors opened at the second floor, she saw the sign immediately, *Asuntos Internos.* As the lift doors closed, she caught a glimpse of the curious faces watching her, relieved that they weren't going into Internal Affairs for a grilling.

The corridor was empty and Galíndez tidied her hair before she went down the drab green corridor to reception. She put a hand in her jacket pocket, checking for the tube of painkillers. A couple of those would get her through the meeting nicely. As she looked round for the women's toilets, the receptionist came out of a room a few metres down the corridor.

'Dr Galíndez?' The woman extended her arm towards the open door. 'Everyone's ready if you'd like to come in.'

Reluctantly, Galíndez put the tablets back in her pocket and followed the receptionist into the conference room.

There were five people at the table. She already knew the meeting would be conducted by Comandante Del Rio and Capitán Rodriguez from Internal Affairs, and she was expecting Mendez to be there in her role as union representative, but it was a surprise to see Capitán and Señora Fuentes at the table, both staring at her as if she'd just crawled out from under a rock.

'Have a seat, Dr Galíndez,' Del Rio said, writing in his notebook.

Galíndez went towards an empty chair next to Mendez. Before she could sit down, Mercedes leaped up, her face contorted with anger. 'We invite you into our home and this is how you repay us?' Her eyes narrowed. 'You twisted bitch.'

Galíndez struggled for words. '*Qué pasa*?' Her voice was still gruff.

Mercedes slapped her across the face, hard. The sound of the blow seemed ridiculously loud in the small room.

Galíndez raised a hand to her cheek, bewildered. Mendez looked on, even more surprised. She'd seen the blow coming, just as she knew Galíndez must have, yet she hadn't blocked it.

Capitán Fuentes pulled his wife away. 'Leave it, *mi amor*. She's not worth it.'

'You know, *Capitán*, it would be better if you'd leave this to us,' Del Rio said.

'He's right. Let's get out of here,' Fuentes said, pushing Mercedes towards the door.

Mercedes looked back at her. 'How could you, Ana María?'

'How could I do what?' Galíndez asked. 'I don't understand what you're so mad about.' She lifted her hand to the angry red mark on her cheek.

Capitán Fuentes took a step towards her, his fists clenched, the veins in his neck bulging. 'You don't understand how taking advantage of a child's trust is the lowest thing you could stoop to?' He punched his fist into his palm.

'I had to protect the girls. I couldn't do anything about the fire.'

Fuentes shook his head in disbelief. 'No one's talking about the fire.'

'Then what's the matter?'

'I can't bear to look at you.' He turned and pulled open the door, standing aside to let Mercedes leave. He stared at Galíndez. 'The next time I see you, I hope you'll be wearing prison uniform.'

Fuentes stormed out, leaving the door open. Galíndez heard Mercedes crying as they went down the corridor to the lift.

Del Rio got up and shut the door. 'You want a glass of water, Galíndez?'

'No, *gracias*.' Her mouth was dry and her throat burned but she refused, knowing if she took a drink they'd see her hand shake as she held the glass. She slumped back in her seat.

Del Rio took a long breath. 'I'll make this as quick as I can.'

'Thank you.'

'Don't thank me yet,' Del Rio said, picking up a large cardboard envelope. He leaned towards the microphone in the centre of the table. 'For the record, Dr Galíndez is being shown the photographic evidence labelled as item A1.'

'Just a second,' Mendez cut in. 'She has a right to know what's happening.'

Del Rio looked up, annoyed at being interrupted. 'Go ahead.'

Galíndez saw Mendez's expression and felt a sudden weight in her stomach. *She thinks I did something wrong.*

'Ana,' Mendez said, 'this meeting is about a charge being brought against you. Comandante del Rio will go through it and you can comment or not, it's up to you. You have the right to have a lawyer present, so if you want legal representation we'll stop now and reschedule the meeting for a later date.'

Galíndez looked across the table at the two men, confused. She'd known they'd want to review events at the Fuentes house, but had assumed it would be a formality since she'd risked her life to protect the children. No one had even mentioned that. *Merche hit me. She hated me.* That was what hurt most: not the slap but the anger behind it. *What was she angry about?*

'OK.' Rodríguez looked down at the paper in front of him. 'First, we have a few questions about the incident at the Fuentes house.'

'Are the *capitán* and his wife angry because of all the damage?' Galíndez asked.

'No,' Rodríguez said, avoiding eye contact. 'And there's no problem about the men you killed in self-defence. We've spoken to the Fuentes girls and they corroborated your story.' He met her eye. 'To a point. But this is just a preliminary session. You don't have to say anything until you've seen a lawyer.'

'I've got nothing to hide.'

Rodríguez shrugged. 'I need to inform you of your rights first.'

Galíndez felt the blood drain from her face. 'I know my rights.'

'Just listen,' Mendez said. 'He has to read your rights in case they decide to arrest you.'

Galíndez stared at Mendez, her heart pounding. Mendez looked away.

'According to the *Ley de Enjuiciamiento Criminal* article 520.2 the detainee must be informed of the charges resulting in his detention,' Del Rio began.

'*Her* detention,' Mendez cut in.

'Whatever.' Del Rio shrugged. 'Dr Galíndez, you have the right to remain silent, to refuse to answer questions and you may choose to speak only to a *juez de instrucción*.'

'I don't need an examining magistrate,' Galíndez said. 'I'll answer your questions.'

Del Rio glanced at his wad of papers. 'You have the right not to incriminate yourself, the right to legal representation and the right to inform a family member of your arrest.'

'I know all of that. Can we just get to the part where you tell me what I'm supposed to have done?' She felt her temper rising.

'In a moment.' Del Rio nodded. 'First, there's the matter of the two dead men who were found in the bushes where the Fuentes girls were hiding.'

'I didn't shoot them.' She swallowed, trying to ease the pain of speaking.

'No one's saying you did,' Del Rio said, impassive.

Rodriguez slid two photographs across the table. 'You recognise these men?'

'They're the two corpses I found in the girls' hideaway,' Galíndez said, looking him in the eye. 'I already said I didn't shoot them.'

'Want to know who these two are?' Rodriguez asked.

'Go ahead.'

'This first one is Juan Luis Calderón, the husband of the Minister of the Interior,' Rodríguez said, watching as her expression changed. 'You know anything about him?'

'I certainly do,' Galíndez said, recovering from the surprise. 'He's been linked to a number of very questionable financial dealings, he's also been under fiscal investigation in at least three European countries and the *guardia civil* have arrested him several times over the last two years on suspicion of corporate fraud. There's also stuff about him attending parties with prostitutes but that didn't constitute a criminal action.'

'He was never formally charged with any of those things,' Del Rio said.

'What are you, his lawyer?' She felt Mendez kick her leg.

'How come you know all that stuff about him?' Rodriguez asked.

'I did some background checks.'

'You must have done a lot of checking?'

Galíndez gave him a sharp look. 'He had a lot of background.'

'So talk us through why you checked him out.'

'I was carrying out my investigation into the *niños robados*,' Galíndez began. 'That led me to a health-care company called GL Sanidad. The chief executive wasn't helpful when I questioned him so I asked to speak to the chairman of the board. It turned out the chairman was Juan Luis Calderón. So then I ran his name through our system.' She looked at them defiantly. 'I guess you don't remember what real police work is like when you work on this floor?'

Rodriguez smiled to himself.

'What?' Galíndez snapped. 'I'm answering your questions and you're being a smart-arse. What's your problem?' She closed her eyes, wishing she'd taken the tablets before she'd come in.

'You're answering the questions, Ana. But are you answering them truthfully?'

'So I'm a liar now?' She clenched her fists.

Del Rio cut in. 'You said you met the chief executive of GL Sanidad, Jesper Karlsson?'

'That's what I said.'

Del Rio tapped one of the photos lying on the table. 'But you don't recognise him?'

She looked again at the picture of the dead man. The gaping wounds to his face. 'This is Karlsson?' She sat back, twirling a strand of hair in her fingers.

Mendez remembered the gesture from when Galíndez was sixteen, training at the dojo. A sign she was under pressure.

Rodríguez sensed he'd got her rattled. 'So what was your opinion of Karlsson?'

'My opinion of both these men was very low. Frankly, Karlsson was a complete shit, as far as I'm concerned.'

Mendez groaned and leaned forward, resting her face in her hands.

'*Joder*, you think I shot them, is that it?' Galíndez glared across the table at Rodríguez. 'For fuck's sake, it's just a question of

448

ballistics. I was armed with Capitán Fuentes's pistol. Compare a bullet fired from his weapon to the bullets in those guys' heads. It's not difficult. Or is that something else you've forgotten since you moved to this floor?'

'Calm down,' Rodriguez said, 'and don't swear at us, please, we're not swearing at you.'

'*Jesús Cristo*.' Galíndez slammed the table with her fist. 'Don't talk to me like a cop talking to a drunk on the street corner.'

'You've got a temper, Ana,' Rodriguez said, locking eyes with her. 'And by the way, I am a cop and I'll thank you to remember it. I don't have to justify myself to people like you.'

Galíndez leaned forward so quickly Mendez grabbed her arm, thinking she was about to attack him. 'What do you mean, "people like you"?'

Del Rio tried to calm things down. 'Just help us here, Ana María. You have no idea why those two were at the Fuentes house?'

Galíndez thought about it, remembering Rosario Calderón's threats in the Retiro. 'Maybe they were killed to send out a warning.'

'That's a lot of trouble just to warn someone like you,' Rodríguez scoffed. He saw her expression and gave her a curt smile. 'By which I mean a lowly *forense* like you. '

'It could have been a warning to someone else.' Galíndez twisted the tendril of hair again. 'Perhaps they decided to kill me after I asked Karlsson to put me in touch with Calderón. Maybe they realised the investigation was closing in on them?'

Del Rio was writing in his notebook. 'That's an interesting idea, Ana. Thanks.'

'So can I go now?'

Del Rio looked up, surprised. 'We're not done yet. I said before you're not a suspect for the killings,' he glanced at Rodriguez, 'even if it might have sounded that way. There's another matter we want to discuss.'

'Fine.' Galíndez sat back in her chair. 'So what is it?'

He picked up an envelope from the table and took out a colour photograph. 'I'm about to show you a photograph retrieved from

Inés Fuentes's iPhone. Sargento Mendez, as Dr Galíndez's union representative, will you describe the photograph for the recording?'

'Certainly not,' Mendez said, angrily. 'That's your job. I know what it shows and I object to you asking me to do it. I'd like that protest placed on record, *Comandante*.'

'So noted.' Del Rio scribbled on his pad.

'What photo?' Galíndez looked at Mendez then Del Rio. Neither seemed to want to meet her eye. She leaned across the table and snatched the photograph. As she stared at it, she pressed her knuckles to her mouth. She was shaking.

The two men waited in silence.

Mendez looked down at her papers. 'For fuck's sake, one of you two do it.'

Rodriguez reached over and picked up the photo, embarrassed. 'The photo shows Ana María Galíndez, aged twenty-six, a resident of Madrid. The picture was taken at the house of Capitán Luis Fuentes in the guest bedroom. The location has been confirmed by witnesses.'

Galíndez twisted a lock of hair tight, as if that might make the image go away.

Rodriguez continued. 'The subject of the photograph is naked. She's kneeling on a small divan in front of a window, one arm outstretched towards a pile of what appear to be white towels. Her body is slightly twisted at the waist, exposing her—'

'That's enough,' Mendez cut in. 'You already said she's naked.'

'The point is,' Del Rio said, 'the photograph seems to be a glamour-type shot, with Dr Galíndez kneeling on the divan and displaying her... herself.'

'Don't...' Galíndez whispered.

'I agree. Let's stop there.' Mendez was raising her voice now.

Galíndez sank back in her seat, suddenly unbearably hot.

Del Rio took the photo from Rodriguez and slid it back into the envelope. 'I'm sorry, but we had to make clear the basis of the charge.'

'I want to place on record a request for this photograph to be marked with a unique identifier to prevent anyone making unauthorised copies,' Mendez said. 'Because if this appears on the net or in any other public domain or is used to harass Dr Galíndez in any way, the union will immediately instigate legal proceedings against the *guardia* and both the Internal Affairs officers present. Are we clear?'

'We are,' Del Rio muttered.

'I came out of the shower.' Galíndez's voice was faint. 'There was no towel in the bathroom so I went to look for one. I saw a pile of towels on the window sill. I knelt on the divan and leaned over to get one. When I got up, Inés was at the door, watching me.' She wiped something from the corner of her eye. 'She must have taken this as I reached for the towel.'

'That's your story?' Del Rio interrupted. 'I'd say the photo looks like you posed naked while an eleven-year-old girl took your picture.'

Galíndez shook her head nervously. 'That's not what happened. Inés was just inside the door, staring. When I saw her, I wrapped a towel round me and told her to knock next time. I didn't see her phone.' She stopped. The explanation sounded lame, even to her.

'You don't have to say anything, Ana.' Mendez put a hand on her arm. It was the first time she'd given her any comfort during the hearing and Galíndez gave her a faint smile of thanks. Mendez took her hand away.

'That's it for today,' Del Rio said, getting to his feet. 'We're not going to charge you yet, Dr Galíndez. But be aware we're thinking in terms of a count of indecent behaviour with a minor. We won't arrest you, but if you do anything stupid between now and the court hearing, we'll haul you in and you'll stay locked up until the trial. No one wants to make this any more difficult than it has to be.'

Galíndez blinked. Her world was falling to pieces.

Del Rio reached over to the tape recorder and spoke briefly, terminating the interview before turning the machine off. He picked up a paper and read from it. '"Ana said I could take the photo but I shouldn't show it to anyone, but *Mamá* saw it and she told *Papá*."' Del Rio gave Galíndez an icy look. 'That's part of the witness statement. You might like to bear it in mind when you think about how you conduct your defence. Obviously, a court will look unfavourably on a not guilty plea, if it means the minor has to appear in court.'

'That's outrageous,' Mendez said. 'You can't tell a colleague whether she can plead guilty or not.'

A colleague, Galíndez thought, *not my colleague*.

'All off the record, *Sargento*,' Del Rio said. 'I'm just making Ana María aware of the seriousness of the charges.'

'Oh God,' a voice said. Galíndez realised it was hers.

'Anything else you want to say?' Del Rio asked.

'She has no comment to make right now.' Mendez took Galíndez by the arm and steered her to the door. She paused. 'I take it that's all?'

'Not quite,' Del Rio said. 'I'll need your ID card, please, Dr Galíndez.'

Reluctantly, Galíndez took the laminated ID from around her neck and handed it over. She saw the small photo on the card, remembering the day it was taken. She bit her lip.

'You'll get this back if you're cleared,' Del Rio said. 'Have you got a weapon?'

She shook her head.

'Then that's all for now, Dr Galíndez. Thanks, *Sargento*.' Del Rio opened the door and Mendez led Galíndez out into the corridor. The door closed behind them.

'I'm finished, aren't I?' Galíndez muttered.

Mendez gave her a strange look. 'What in God's name were you thinking of?'

'You don't seriously think I let Inés take that photo?'

Mendez didn't answer.

'Christ, you don't believe me either, do you?' Galíndez said. 'Inés took the photo while I was getting a towel. I swear to God.'

'You always had a wild streak, Ana. Remember when you used to come to the dojo?'

'That was different. I was only sixteen. Inés came in without me knowing and took a picture. End of story.'

'So why didn't you tell her parents that she'd burst in on you like that?'

'I didn't want to make a fuss about it. Besides, I didn't know she'd taken a photo.'

'Sure you didn't have a rush of blood to the head? She hero-worshipped you and you got overexcited?'

'Don't be stupid. All we did that evening was practise a few moves on the lawn.'

'So there was physical contact?' Mendez groaned. 'I don't want to hear any more. You and me go back a long way but I can't handle this. I'll ask the union to assign someone else to your case. I'm sorry. You take the lift. I'll use the stairs.'

Galíndez twisted a piece of hair as she watched Mendez go down the stairs.

'Dr Galíndez?' Two uniformed officers came down the corridor. 'We've got instructions to escort you from the building.'

Galíndez nodded. All she wanted was to get outside.

'Do you need anything from your office?' These guys weren't so bad, she thought as they towered over her in the lift. It wasn't their fault.

'I've got some sports kit in my locker... No, it doesn't matter.' Clearing out her locker would be such a final act she wasn't sure she could handle it right now.

They went with her to the exit. 'Anything else we can do? Get you a cab or something?'

Get me out of all this. 'No, thanks. I'll be fine.'

Outside, she saw a normal day. People crowding the pavement, patrol cars pulling up, flashes of green and white as others drove away. Her mind whirled with things she should have said or done. Things that might have kept her from running full tilt into the shit.

She almost turned back to look at the dark bulk of the HQ building one last time, to try and accept she wouldn't be coming back. But that meant acknowledging her worst fear had finally come true. The fear that had dogged her since she'd joined the *guardia* to follow in *Papá*'s footsteps. *I'm a failure. Christ, people* said it enough: *Miguel was* guardia *through and through, shame about his daughter.* They could add a postscript now: *We knew she was no good.*

She kept walking, a question hammering in her head: why had Inés lied? Her fists clenched, her nails digging into her palms There was no use asking. No one would believe anything she said because their minds were made up the moment they saw that photograph. Christ, even Mendez thought she was lying.

As she walked, she wondered about calling someone. She took her phone from her pocket and scrolled through her contacts, looking at the names one by one. Slowly, she put the phone back in her pocket.

She was on her own now.

CHAPTER 29

The door to the *pensión* was open. There was no reply when Guzmán called Señora Olibari's name and he went in. Moving quietly through the hall, he passed the big dining room where he had eaten so well a few days earlier. A chair had been moved away from the table, he noticed. One chair. He drew the Browning and went in search of Señora Olibari.

At the back of the house, he found the old lady lying face down beneath the open wall safe, still clutching a German Luger. Guzmán whistled in admiration. So the old girl was one of Gutiérrez's agents. Out of practice though, since the fake Viana had anticipated her intentions and put a bullet in the back of her neck once she'd unlocked the safe. Even so, she'd managed to cut the phone cable before he got to her. Guzmán had quite liked the old battleaxe. She spoke her mind and was a formidable cook. Viana would suffer for this.

The safe was empty. That meant Viana had the file. Without it, Guzmán didn't have a clue what Gutierrez wanted him to do. He put a hand on Señora Olibari's arm. She was still warm. It was possible Viana might still be nearby. He thought for a moment, trying to imagine Viana's next move. Without doubt, he would need to inform his bosses of the contents of the file. To do that, he would have to use the phone or the radio at the *guardia cuartel*.

Guzmán left the *pensión* and hurried down the track. The door of the *cuartel* was open and even before he stepped inside, he could see the pool of blood spreading across the floor. Keeping the Browning raised, he went into the laundry room. There were two bodies lying close together, surrounded by a slick of congealing blood. Viana was lying on his back, a woodsman's axe buried in his chest. It was an impressive wound, and Guzmán casually wondered if he'd suffered. He hoped so.

The other body was a surprise: it was the big wood-chopper Jesús Barandiaran, face down with two bullet wounds in his back. Close range too, Guzmán noted, seeing the scorch marks on his shirt. Viana's gun lay nearby, suggesting he'd made an attempt to defend himself. Even so, it was hard to see how he could have shot Jesús in the back before being killed. Someone else had fired those shots.

Guzmán left the corpses and began to search the barracks. In the radio room, he found the lance corporal behind a desk. He too had been killed by an axe blow.

On the table near the smashed radio, he saw the red cardboard folder and, by it, the phone with its wire severed. So Viana had read the file? That hardly mattered: with the radio and phone out of action, it was unlikely he could have passed on the information to anyone else before he was killed. Guzmán picked up the file. Three people had died on account of this document. It made sense to read it.

He pulled up a chair and opened the file at the first page, seeing entries dating back to the end of the Second World War. He skimmed the pages, reading of official fears that resistance groups along the lines of the French Maquis might spring up. Several pages listed suspects to be detained and questioned. Some were shot as a precautionary measure, others were placed under close surveillance and some were imprisoned. They still would be, Guzmán noted, given the length of the sentences.

The surveillance continued for years. Countless searches and interrogations led by General Mellado, the Military Governor. Mellado's brief was simple: strike fear into the populace and terrify them into submission. He had followed his orders to the letter.

Impatiently, Guzmán skipped forward to the entries for the last couple of years. Reports of Red guerrillas being smuggled into Spain by a French gang, the Çubiry. He took a deep, angry breath.

If Gutiérrez had given him this material when he'd arrived, he might have had the job done in a day or two. He needed to have words with the *general de brigada*.

He read on, impressed by the extent of the surveillance operation. The later sections of the report dealt with a cell of young would-be guerrillas who met regularly in a schoolhouse in a tiny *pueblo* called Ihintza. Meetings organised by one Fernando Etxarte who had attempted to buy arms from undercover agents. A handwritten note in the margin: *Immediate Action*. Signed by General de Brigada Gutiérrez. Alongside that, dated a few weeks ago: *Allocated to Comandante Guzmán for action.*

And here was a much more recent scrawled note from Gutierrez: *The Resistance have an anonymous quartermaster, according to Guzmán.* Next to it, an entry noting Guzmán had terminated the cell. A list of the names of the dead students, and Etxarte, of course. An addendum that as well as the quartermaster, two other members had not attended that night. Fortunately, after further enquiries, the two had been identified by an informant. Guzmán clenched his fists. This was something else Gutierrez had kept from him.

A heading at the top of the next page: *Detain as part of Saturday night's operation.* There followed a long list of suspects to be arrested across the region. He stared at the list, puzzled. *What fucking operation?* He read the details quickly, his surprise growing as he saw the instructions for mass arrests, detentions without trial, and a few cases considered so dangerous they were to be summarily executed.

Guzmán frowned. Gutiérrez was full of fucking surprises. He was about to do precisely what he'd said he didn't want to happen: send in troops to arrest and torture suspected members of the resistance. Christ, Franco himself had forbidden those things so nothing would compromise the *Yanquis* making the payment for the trade deal. If Mellado learned of this he'd try to muscle in, hoping to grab the glory. That would be a disaster for all concerned. Guzmán wiped his hand across his face, suddenly tired. What a fucking day. Surprise after surprise.

And here was another surprise, one he could never have anticipated. The arrest of the two who'd avoided Guzmán's massacre at the schoolhouse had been postponed, the notes said, until the informant confirmed their identity. That confirmation had now been received. They were Begoña and Nieves Arestigui, aged thirty-five and eighteen respectively, residents of Lauburu Farm near Oroitz. They were to be arrested, along with the other subversives during the operation scheduled for today.

Guzmán stared at the typewritten notes, struggling to think how such mistakes could have been made in a report of this importance. Because it had to be a mistake. He read the details again, slowly, numbed by the slow, cold realisation there was no mistake.

He wiped sweat from his forehead, feeling the throbbing pain in his arm as he cursed Begoña and Nieves for dabbling in things they knew nothing of. Clearly, they had no fucking idea what the consequences would be. Worse, this operation was not something he could interfere with. Things were beyond his control now. He was helpless.

A memory of cold air, his feet hammering down the stone steps into the darkness. Raising his lighter, seeing Arantxa on the rubble-strewn floor of the cellar, her mutilated body sagging against the ropes that still bound her to the chair, her dark, dead eyes staring at him.

He had been helpless then as well.

Guzmán looked at his watch. It was five forty-five. Even if he phoned, Nieves and Begoña wouldn't have time to get away. Exasperated, he pounded the table with his fist. Phone them? They didn't have a phone. *He* didn't have a phone. This wasn't Madrid. No one could help them now. Certainly he couldn't. Trying to interfere was the most stupid thing he could do. It was treason, collaboration with enemies of the state and more. It was inconceivable for someone in his position to do such a thing. If Begoña and Nieves were guilty, they deserved to be punished. Every action had its consequences.

He thought about those consequences, his eyes narrowing as he imagined them at the drunken mercy of General Mellado and his thugs. The usual cycle of torture: the humiliation of being forced to strip and then the rape and abuse before the torture began in earnest. Electric shocks, beatings, immersion in freezing water, the sequence quite possibly culminating on Mellado's garrotte. That was the way these things were done. He could do nothing now. Trying to help them would not only be stupid, it would be the end of his career. Maybe the end of him.

But it could be done, though he would need to drive fast if he was to get them over the border before the authorities closed down the region. He'd done stupid things before and survived. Once in France, they would be safe. He could probably lie his way out of it after that. And another thought nagged him now. Magdalena had said she would be at Lauburu around seven. That meant she would arrive to make her collection just as the might of the security forces closed in on the farm. Who knew what Mellado's psychotic *legionarios* might do to a woman on her own?

He had a sudden recollection of a witch's eyes looking up at him in the cellar at Villarreal. Nieves' eyes. His mind made up, Guzmán went to the door.

Seventeen years ago, he couldn't save the mother. Perhaps that had been her destiny. But he could save the daughter. Perhaps that was his.

OROITZ 1954, CARRERA DE LAUBURU

Heading towards Lauburu Farm, Magdalena Torres slowed as she saw a line of cars ahead by the verge. As she passed, she glanced at the men standing by the vehicles. Heavy-set faces with dull expressions, broad shoulders crammed into suits that looked out of place in the countryside. And, as she passed, she caught a glimpse of the white hair and ragged clothing of another century and her heart sank. They had arrested Mikel Aingeru.

Something weighed in her stomach. Turning a bend, she pulled over by a tangled clump of gorse and reversed the car off the road, into the bushes. She sat motionless, resting her hands on the wheel. How typical of the secret police to pick on an old man like Mikel. The only crime he ever committed was to teach the forbidden language of his people. His clandestine teaching had awakened a generation of children to their heritage. And he had taught Magdalena so much more.

She climbed from the roadster and retrieved the Colt from under the spare wheel in the boot. Mikel once told her there was a time to help and a time to be helped. It was time for her to help him now.

Keeping low, she worked her way through the scrub until she was close enough to hear the men talking.

'What do you want?' someone asked. It was not Mikel's voice. But it was Mikel who answered and Magdalena listened, her eyes widening with horror. She listened to it all and then, as the men's talk turned to other things, she slid away, silent and careful, making her way back to the spot where she had left the Pegaso.

A hundred metres from the car, she stopped and lowered herself into the grass, her heart pounding as she watched the burly man in a dark suit examining the vehicle. Staying low, she moved stealthily towards the trees and crawled through them, not daring to stand until she reached the far side of the wood. Then she started to run.

OROITZ 1954, CARRERA DE LAUBURU

Guzmán drove fast, ignoring the squeal of tyres as he took the bends of the steep mountain road without slowing. His head rang with a single question. What the fuck were Begoña and Nieves thinking of? They should have been tending their farm, not involving themselves in something that carried the death penalty.

He struggled to put his anger aside. The women needed his help, that was all that mattered. He would drive them to France and drop them somewhere on the border away from the customs posts. There were Basques across the frontier, they would still be among their own people. He turned onto the road leading to

Lauburu Farm and accelerated, hearing the Hispano Suiza's powerful engine rise to the challenge.

Up ahead, he saw workmen standing by a line of cars parked at the side of the road. *Fucking roadworks.* He floored the accelerator and the Hispano Suiza hurtled forward, the wheel vibrating in his hands.

Guzmán didn't see what hit him. He heard only the sudden devastating noise of the impact as the car flipped over, skidding across the road in a shower of sparks, the metal screeching as the vehicle righted itself and careered into the verge on the far side of the road. A sudden sharp pain in his ribs as he slammed into the steering wheel. Unsteadily, he climbed from the wrecked vehicle, clutching his side. Around him, dark shapes emerged from the trees. He was surrounded by soldiers. A hundred metres away, a black sedan emerged from a narrow track in the woods and purred down the road, gliding to a halt alongside him. He watched as the rear window slid down.

'You're a fucking terrible driver.' Mellado laughed. 'Good job my lads only clipped you. Didn't you see them waving for you to stop?'

Guzmán saw now what had hit him: a military vehicle, the front bumper reinforced with a protruding steel frame. A roadblock.

'What the fuck's going on?' He reached into a pocket for his handkerchief to mop blood from the cut over his eyebrow.

Slowly, Mellado got out of the car. 'You're in a hurry, Leo, where are you off to?'

Normally, Guzmán was attuned to self-preservation. This was no normal situation. He had to think carefully.

'I asked where you're going.' Mellado's voice was sharper now.

'To make arrests at the farmhouse,' Guzmán said, thinking quickly. 'I need to question the two women there.'

'Really?' Mellado's face showed no interest. Certainly no sign of belief.

'El Lobo's been hiding out near here,' Guzmán said, getting into his stride. 'I want to arrest the women at Lauburu, they've been involved in the robberies.'

'I know about them. I'd have known sooner, if you'd bothered to tell me.'

Guzmán winced as a shard of pain shot through his ribs. 'I didn't get a chance.'

'Good job I don't rely on you for my information.' Mellado waved to the driver of a dark SEAT sedan parked up the road, its engine idling. The car rolled towards them.

'All these Basques know each other, Guzmán,' Mellado said as the sedan pulled up. 'Many are only too pleased to pass on all they know. That's how we recruit so many agents here.' He gestured to someone in the car. A man got out, brushing down his velvet frock coat, smoothing his hands over the mane of silver hair tied back in a ponytail.

'*Comandante.*' Baron Çubiry bared his teeth, though the gesture was far from a smile. He turned to Mellado. 'I've provided you with both information and a spectacular amount of money, General. I believe it's time to honour your side of the bargain?' He turned to Guzmán. 'Blood is thicker than water, I think you said, *Comandante*?' His mouth set in a thin smile. 'You spilled my son's blood, now I'd like to return the compliment.'

'Give him the pistol,' Mellado said. A man in a dark homburg and overcoat stepped forward, taking a pistol from his coat pocket. It took a moment for Guzmán to recognise Faisán. The young man smirked as he cocked the pistol and handed it to the Baron.

'All yours, Monsieur Çubiry,' Mellado said, taking a step back. 'You wanted the *Comandante* and you've paid very well, so make the most of it.' He smiled at Guzmán. 'See? I can get information from other sources beside you. Carry on, Baron.'

Guzmán locked eyes with Çubiry as he took a step towards him. *Fuck him. Fuck them all.* He no longer cared. Perhaps Begoña and Nieves might still get away without his help. But he knew that was not true. By the time they realised what was happening, it would be far too late.

'A last word?' Baron Çubiry smiled. 'Some last futile curse, perhaps?'

'Your son died squealing like a pig,' Guzmán said through clenched teeth. 'He shamed himself, he shamed you and he shamed the bullet I put in his cowardly head.' He spat onto the ground. 'At least it put an end to your family line.'

'Not at all.' Çubiry grinned. 'You forget my daughter. She's more man than my son ever was. Who do you think organised the robbery of your bank shipment?'

Baron Çubiry raised the pistol, aiming into Guzmán's face. Guzmán stared back, waiting. Faisán moved back, watching over the Baron's shoulder as Çubiry pulled the trigger.

A thin, metallic click as the hammer fell on an empty chamber. Surprised, Çubiry turned to Mellado, about to ask what was going on. No words came as he stopped, staring as Mellado lifted the lid of the boot and stepped back to let him see the contents.

'*Mon Dieu*.' Çubiry's eyes were wide with horror. 'My child…'

Faisán shot him in the back. As Çubiry sprawled on the ground, Faisán shot him twice more, the body jerking at the impact of each bullet. Faisán put away the pistol and went over to the General's Cadillac.

'You should see your face, Leo,' Mellado cackled. 'It's a picture.'

Dazed, Guzmán looked at the crumpled body in front of him.

'As if I'd let a bandit shoot you. You might be a bad bastard but you're our bad bastard. Çubiry's a Frenchman – you think I'd trust him?'

Guzmán ran a hand over his face. 'Who the fuck's that?' He pointed to the woman's body crammed into the boot of the sedan, her mottled face staring out at him, the great black tongue lolling from her lips, her pale naked body covered in bruises.

Mellado laughed. 'Jeanette Çubiry. Perhaps you knew her as Jeanette Duclos, that was her married name. Yet another favour I've done you.' He slammed the lid of the boot. 'Although, to tell the truth, killing the Baron was a favour to someone else. I just let you share it.'

'Who?' Guzmán glanced along the road to the farm. Time was running out.

463

'One of my informants, Leo. A proper informant, better than anyone Gutiérrez ever recruited, I bet. Or you, for that matter. And someone who wanted Çubiry dead very badly.' He gestured at the body lying in the road. 'That French bastard thought he could use the money he stole from your bank truck to bribe me into letting him kill you.'

'You got the five million back?'

'I did. But my informant gave me something worth much more: the names of resistance groups all over the region.' His eye glittered. 'I've declared martial law, Leo. We're picking up suspects right now, traitors every last one.'

Guzmán thought quickly. 'Let me arrest those women. This is personal.'

'No need, Leo. I've got people to do that.' Mellado gave a signal and an open-topped khaki truck pulled away from the line of military vehicles waiting by the verge. It drove past slowly, giving Guzmán time to see the sullen faces of Mellado's bodyguards staring at him over the tailboard. He felt something twist in his stomach.

'I want to do it,' he said. 'They thought I was stupid. Let me deal with them.'

Mellado shrugged. 'You'll have to walk then. I can't spare another vehicle and I've got the harvest ball later. There's still a hundred things to do.' He walked back to the Cadillac and Faisán opened the rear door for him. As the car's powerful engine throbbed into life, Mellado leaned out of the window. 'Did you think about my job offer, Leo?'

'It sounded good.' The words were like soot on his tongue.

'Good lad. You go and help the boys clear up at the farm if that's what you want. They're keen to get it over with so they can get back for the ball. It's just along that fork in the road back there, if you fancy dropping in. I reckon we'll be up all night, don't you, Faisán?'

Faisán smirked. 'I certainly hope so, *mi General*.'

'We'll discuss the job later, then, Leo,' Mellado said. 'Iron out the details.'

Guzmán leaned against the car, exhausted. Through the half-open window, he smelled the air inside the vehicle: a sour odour, fetid and rank. Mellado said something to the driver and Guzmán stepped back as the car moved off, followed by the line of vehicles carrying the general's entourage. Within a couple of minutes Guzmán was alone, with only his wrecked car and the corpse of Baron Çubiry for company. He looked up the road, seeing the olive-green truck in the distance lumbering towards the farm, carrying Mellado's battle-hardened mercenaries, all keen to get their work over so they could attend General Mellado's annual night of depravity.

He started to run.

OROITZ 1954, LAUBURU FARM

Begoña Arestigui stood in the doorway of the farmhouse watching the sun set. Behind her in Grandfather Arestigui's study, Nieves was lighting the big oil lamp. Begoña took a seat at the table by the window and put on her reading glasses before she went back to her needlework. 'I should have told you about your mother,' she said softly. 'She was such a wild one, she couldn't bear country life, that's why she went to the city. We heard she'd joined the anarchists but nothing more until the war began. She sent me one letter and the next I knew was when a drover arrived with you, wrapped in a blanket. All he said was that someone had paid him to bring you here. Much later, I found out she'd been killed. I should have told you, I'm sorry.'

'It's Comandante Guzmán I'm angry with,' Nieves said. 'He was there, and yet he never said anything to me.'

'But he didn't kill your mother,' Begoña said. 'You said yourself it was León.' She got to her feet. 'There's something I should have showed you years ago.'

She went across to the old portraits and family photographs on the wall and reached for a large framed painting of the beach at

465

Zarauz. She turned it, revealing a somewhat blurred sepia photograph of a tall, well-built young soldier with brilliantined hair, his arm around a young dark-haired woman, dressed in militia uniform. A note at the bottom of the photo, in Begoña's careful handwriting. *Arantxa, Bilbao, 10 Mayo 1936.* 'I don't know who the soldier is, the detail isn't very good.'

Nieves shook her head slowly. 'It could be me in that picture.'

'I know. I see you sometimes and I think she's come back.' Begoña nodded.

Nieves turned up the lamp, filling the room with a soft glow as she leaned over Begoña's shoulder to look at her needlework. 'What's that you're working on?'

'Just a little picture of the farmhouse. Grandmother Arestigui did one in 1864. I thought I'd hang this one next to it.' She looked up, adjusting her reading glasses. 'Maybe you could do one in ten years? Keep the tradition going?'

Begoña frowned as she heard footsteps outside. '*Dios mio*, I wonder who that could be?' Someone pounded on the door and she hurried to open it.

Magdalena Torres tumbled into the room her face flushed, her shoulders heaving as she tried to catch her breath. '*Buenas tardes*,' she panted.

Begoña and Nieves stared at her. This was not the Magdalena Torres who appeared in the society pages of the local paper, her hair styled like Graciela Kelley. Her hair was tousled, speckled with bits of bark and leaves, her expensive boots caked in mud.

'I'm dreadfully sorry to bother you,' Magdalena said, putting a hand to her chest as she tried to steady her breathing. Begoña noticed something else. Magdalena was frightened.

'*Kaixo*, Señorita Torres,' Begoña said. 'Did you find the figurines by the gate?'

Magdalena took a deep breath. When she spoke, her voice trembled with emotion. 'In the mountains, the snows are burning.'

For a moment, time stopped. 'Santa María. So it's you?' Begoña said, her eyes wide.

'It is indeed,' Magdalena said, almost apologetic. 'And I've got bad news.'

Begoña took off her apron and carefully placed it on the table. Then she took off her reading glasses and put them on the apron before turning back to Magdalena. '*Ongi etorri*,' she said. *Welcome*. She opened her arms and they embraced.

'*A sus órdenes*, señorita,' Nieves said. 'We never expected to meet the quartermaster.'

'That was the idea,' Magdalena said. 'To preserve secrecy. But things have changed.'

'What's happened?' Begoña asked, unsettled by the tone of her voice.

'Mikel Aingeru betrayed us. He gave the cell away to the fascists and now they're coming for you.'

Begoña gasped. 'Why would Mikel do such a thing?'

'He's finally taking revenge on Baron Çubiry. They're going to kill the Baron in return for betraying us.'

'What do we do now?' Nieves asked, pale-faced.

'I don't suppose you have any weapons?' Magdalena held up her small Colt. 'I've only got this little thing.'

Nieves went to the grandfather clock and opened it. Carefully, she lifted out a canvas bundle. 'It's a British Webley,' she said, unrolling the bundle to reveal the pistol inside.

Begoña knelt by the fireplace, rolled back the rug and lifted one of the floorboards. She took out another canvas-wrapped package. 'We've a couple of Mausers as well.'

'*Eskerrik asko*.' Magdalena took the pistol from her. 'So what shall we do?'

'You're our leader now,' Begoña said. 'We'll do what you say.'

'I haven't had much practice at this, I'm afraid,' Magdalena said. 'Hardly any, in fact.' She thought for a moment. 'We stand a better chance outside,' she said finally. 'It's dark and they don't know the countryside like we do.' She gave Begoña an embarrassed smile. 'I mean like you do, señoritas.'

Nieves replaced the carpet over the loose floorboard. When she got up, she was holding a Mauser. 'You're right,' she said. 'We can hide near the sacred pool. In the dark we'll have the advantage.'

Begoña drew back the curtain. 'There are headlights coming up the road.'

'We'd better hurry,' Magdalena's voice was tense.

As they went to the door, Magdalena saw the photograph of the tall soldier and a woman she thought might have been Nieves but for the date on the picture. She stopped, surprised.

'Who are they?' Magdalena asked, realising she already knew the man.

'My mother. I don't know who she's with,' Nieves said. '*Mamá* died for the Cause.'

Magdalena squeezed her arm. 'You must be very proud of her, señorita.'

Leaving the lanterns lit, they went outside, moving through the lavender towards the track. Nieves was the last to leave and she paused to lock the door, leaving the key on the window ledge.

As they reached the track, Magdalena stopped and turned. Someone was running up the track towards them.

Nieves signalled to the others to go into the trees as a man appeared in the ring of soft light from the house. Harsh, deep-set eyes, stubbled cheeks, leather straps glinting across his dark uniform. He slowed, staring at the pistol in Nieves' hand. A fatal hesitation.

The blast echoed among the darkened trees. A sudden uproar in the distance; men shouting, the sound of running feet. Nieves hurried after the others into the shadows.

OROITZ 1954, LAUBURU FARM

It was a mild evening and Guzmán's shirt was soon drenched in sweat. He gulped air, forcing himself to keep running as familiar landmarks began to appear from the evening shadows. A half-kilometre more and then the road would rise to the farm, corn to one side, green vegetables to the other. And then the lavender garden where Begoña had served him lunch and sensed the coming rain.

He had just reached the slope leading to the farm when the shooting began. Muffled small-arms fire, occasional white stammers of light in the darkness. His breathing was so loud now it was hard to tell how many weapons were involved.

The firing lasted several minutes, ending as suddenly as it had begun. And then a few desultory shots, followed by silence.

Guzmán lurched forward, panting so hard it seemed the ground was shaking. In fact, he realised, the ground *was* shaking. The truck came down the hill without slowing, forcing him to leap aside as it rattled past, crammed with hard-faced men who looked at him with hostile stares as they drove off down the road.

The farmhouse was in sight now and he stumbled forward, breathless. There had been no sign of bodies on the truck. Perhaps Begoña and Nieves had outwitted the troops, using their knowledge of the land to avoid capture. He imagined them hiding among the ferns, or behind the rocks near the sacred pool, letting their pursuers stumble around in the dark until they tired and broke off the search.

There was no sign of Magdalena's car on the track leading to the farm and that raised his hopes further. She must have made her collection and tired of waiting for him.

As he reached the farm, he slowed, choked by the acrid smoke from the burning farmhouse. The lavender garden was trampled underfoot. The table where he'd drunk their home-made cider was overturned and broken. Inside, the house was wrecked. Drawers had been emptied on the floor, crockery and glasses smashed, even Grandfather Arestigui's maps had been slashed or torn down. The big telescope was strewn over the carpet, smashed to pieces. Someone had started a fire in one room and the flames were now taking hold on the old wooden furniture. There was no time to deal with that and he went back outside.

Across the track, by the edge of the woods, he found the body of a man, one of Mellado's bodyguards, shot in the eye. So, Nieves and Begoña were armed? He felt a curious pride at the thought. He left the track and followed the path to the grove, stumbling over stones and roots as he approached the pool where a few days before he'd spied on Begoña and Nieves bathing. Through the pine-scented darkness, he heard the endless cadence of the waterfall and slowed, picturing the women struggling through these trees, pursued by Mellado's crack troops. His eyes stung and he wiped them with his sleeve. The smoke was getting to him.

Near the pool, he saw another uniformed body lying in the soft grass. Meeting resistance must have come as a surprise to Mellado's troops. Once they'd come under fire, they would have taken cover instinctively. And maybe, while the troops had peered into the darkness seeking a target, the women had slipped away. They knew this countryside better than these African-trained soldiers. Right now, they were probably holed up somewhere. He clung to that thought as he searched the wood.

A few minutes later, he found Nieves.

She was sitting propped against a tree, looking in the direction of the pool. The dark hole in the side of her forehead was scarcely visible in the darkness. Her eyes were blank and empty, as the eyes of the dead always were, though her mouth was set in a stern rictus of anger. She was angry, Guzmán guessed, because this was her first and last battle and she knew it was lost before it began. He hawked and spat as he searched the glade, his eyes growing accustomed to the darkness. A few metres away, he saw a crumpled shape in the long grass.

Begoña lay face down. She had been shot a number of times and her face was no longer recognisable. She had not gone down without a fight: he saw the body of another *legionario* nearby. Guzmán admired her for that.

Something rustled in the bushes and he spun round, aiming into the dark.

'Help.' The voice was faint, the clipped tones unmistakable despite the heavy inflection of pain, bringing the terrible realisation that his final hope was dashed. He took out his lighter and used the flame to find her.

Magdalena was lying on her back among the ferns. Guzmán knelt by her side, clumsily trying to make her comfortable. She winced. 'Don't, Leo, please. It hurts too much.'

He lifted the lighter, illuminating her pale face, seeing the holes in her sweater, the black glint of blood. 'You'll be fine,' he lied. 'I'll get help in a minute.'

'Can't help me, Leo.' Her voice was distant.

Even now, he still felt the need to tell her he'd been right. 'I found an underground room at your hunting lodge,' he said. 'Jiménez organised the resistance from there.'

Magdalena laughed. The movement made her cough and he saw blood on her lips. 'Don't be stupid, Leo. That was my room.' A spasm of pain convulsed her. 'Esteban helped me set it up after the war, when all things Basque were forbidden. Down there, away from my murdering father, everything was Basque, including me.' She moaned in pain as she pressed a hand to her breast. Blood welled through her fingers.

He remembered the photographs, the papers, the cartoons and drawings, the childlike captions. Her prize-winning poem. 'It was you.' A statement, not a question.

'Mikel Aingeru betrayed us,' she whispered. 'He's a traitor.'

'I'll get you to a doctor.' His voice was hoarse, his words meaningless. When there was no reply, he raised the lighter again. Her blue eyes still looked at him, though she saw nothing in this world now. He closed them slowly.

The world was changed, as if he saw it through someone else's tears. He returned to the farm and found a spade in an outhouse. He would bury them in a corner of the glade where the fragrance of pines softened the air. They would become one with their land. In time all things were forgotten, but not here. Here, time was written in stone.

The soil was moist and heavy and the moon was high by the time he finished digging. Since she was the youngest, he laid Nieves between Begoña and Magdalena. They would look after her. For a few moments, he held her face in his hands, seeing another face in another time. A sudden rush of questions burned through his mind; none would ever be answered.

Out of respect, he took Begoña's scarf and laid it over her shattered face. Finally, he said goodbye to Magdalena. She was a Basque warrior, he whispered. She deserved to be laid to rest with a great sword or the splintered armour of her vanquished enemies on her breast. Since he had neither, he drew the Browning and closed her fingers around it. It could serve her in the next world as it had served him. In return, he took her small Colt as a keepsake.

The gun was tiny in his hand as he knelt by the grave, thinking of all the things he should have said to her but had not. Those words were worthless now and so he said nothing. He filled the grave with clods of rich damp soil until the odour of loam and pines overpowered the cloying smell of blood. When he was finished, he washed in the sacred pool and returned to sit by the grave, staring into a cloudless sky washed by moonlight.

In the darkness, a twig cracked. Guzmán tensed as he heard footsteps, careful and measured, growing closer. He moved towards the sound, slow and silent. Someone was standing by the pool. A familiar sour odour, fetid and rank. The smell of sheep.

The old man was talking to the water, the Basque words echoing softly from the cliffs overlooking the pool. When he had finished, he took a stone from the ground and threw it into the pool. A gesture of reconciliation, perhaps. Guzmán stepped out from the shadows, sensing Mikel Aingeru's surprise as the old man turned, peering at him in the dark.

'You betrayed everything.' Guzmán's voice was flat. 'And everyone.'

'A cause like ours demands sacrifice.' Mikel shrugged. 'They're Basque heroes now. For each that died, there'll be ten for the next group I recruit.'

'I should kill you,' Guzmán said. Behind him, he heard the voices of the dead.

'They trusted my decisions, *Comandante*. And it was my decision to let them die.'

'That was before they knew you were a traitor.' The voices were louder now. 'You used them to get revenge for yourself, not for your cause.' He tried to control his anger. 'You even shot your own son in the back.'

A bitter laugh. 'Jesús was no loss to anyone. My true sons died long ago when Abarron Çubiry slaughtered my family. Letting Jesús live was a joke he played on me.' He sighed. 'How else could an old man take his revenge? I gave everything for the Cause. I was a king, Magdalena and the others were my pawns. I lost far more than any of them.'

'Not everything.' Guzmán raised Magdalena's pistol and fired. The shot hit Mikel in the chest and pitched him backwards into the pool. Expanding rings of dark water lapped against the banks, the widening ripples bright with moonlight. Gradually, the water grew calm again.

Guzmán returned to where his friends waited among the trees. There was no more to be done and he sat in darkness, listening to their voices echo around the glade. At dawn, he left them. They would lie beneath the dark silhouette of the mountain for ever, long after Franco was dust and long after Guzmán's timely or untimely demise. Time was written in stone.

He walked, oblivious to the vast landscape, seeing nothing but the road ahead, hearing the sound of his own breathing as if for the first time.

The sun rose. After several kilometres he saw a field ahead, decked in ribbons and bunting. At one end of the field was a bandstand, now a chaos of overturned chairs and scattered plates. Huge marquees had been erected, hung with flags and banners. In the distance, behind high walls, was Mellado's country house. The gate was open and he saw groups of women wending their way towards a row of vehicles. Some were dressed as ancient Greek slaves, one wore a bullfighter's glittering suit of lights. Further away, near the marquees, he saw several bodies in the grass.

It had been a feast of excess, judging from the debris around him. A line of griddles, heaped with burned meat. Piles of bottles

473

ankle deep, broken crockery. Crates of vintage wine piled by the gate. Nearby, several young women in various states of undress were assisted into a truck and driven away.

Mellado was standing by his black limousine near the gate. The general was in his shirtsleeves, his gold braided uniform jacket thrown to the ground. He was holding a champagne bottle, taking inaccurate swigs that soaked his clothes and boots with foam. Faisán sat with his back against the vehicle, fast asleep, his chin resting on his chest. When he heard Guzmán's footsteps, he opened his eyes, looking up at him without interest.

'Fucking hell, you're late, Guzmán.' Mellado coughed a stream of champagne over his boots. 'It's been a hell of a night. The lads were celebrating after mopping up the resistance, as you can imagine.' He waved at the piles of untouched food. 'And they say people are starving in Spain?' Faisán joined in the general's laughter.

Guzmán looked at them, expressionless. He saw a grave beneath the pines. An old man floating in a pool. A naked girl strapped in a garrotte.

Mellado was in good spirits. 'I bet Gutierrez is tearing his hair out, wondering how he managed to fuck everything up.'

'I expect he would,' Guzmán agreed. 'If he had any hair.'

Mellado roared with laughter. 'He arrived in San Sebastián last night,' he said, taking another careless mouthful of champagne. 'By now he's probably on his way back to Madrid to hand in his resignation. That means you're out of a job.'

Guzmán nodded, listening less to Mellado and more to the rising chorus in his head.

Mellado took out a cigar, bit the end from it and spat it away. Faisán hurried to give him a light and the general exhaled a cloud of fragrant smoke. 'So, did you think about the job?'

Guzmán had thought about it. It was an interesting offer, there was work to be done here. The resistance was not finished. Without doubt, there were other cells, growing slowly, patient and painstaking in their preparations. They would strike in their own time, and when they did, this region would burn. It would need men like Guzmán to stop it. Mellado would be difficult to work with, not least because he was insane. But he was easily manipulated. They could rule this land like robber kings. Guzmán would have power again, all the power he ever wanted.

'For fuck's sake make up your mind.' Mellado blew a cloud of smoke into the air. 'I'm not going to beg. Double your present salary and I'll throw in an apartment.' He looked over to where two men were carrying the limp body of a woman from one of the tents. He turned away, disinterested. 'A sea-view apartment.'

Behind them, the last of the vehicles were driving away back to San Sebastián. The grass was yellowing on the hillside. Patches of reluctant snow on the mountains, gleaming in the bright sun. Winter not far off. There were worse things than working here. Being poor, for one.

Guzmán shrugged. 'I'll take it.'

Mellado's bloated face cracked into a smile. 'Excellent. Let's have breakfast and a few drinks to celebrate. What do you think?'

'I think it sounds good,' Guzmán said.

Faisán climbed behind the wheel and started the engine.

'By the way...' Mellado paused, resting one foot in the car. 'I was right about that girl you asked about, María Vidal.'

Guzmán stopped. 'What about her?' His voice was heavy, pensive.

'She was a member of the resistance.' Mellado heaved himself into the back seat and fumbled with the catch on the cocktail cabinet. 'Do you want a Bloody Mary? They're like food. Tell you what, I'll make us all one.' He splashed vodka into the glasses and added tomato juice, stirring in the Tabasco and Worcester sauce with a glass stick.

Guzmán rested his hand on the car roof, listening to the brittle clink of glass as Mellado stirred the cocktail. 'How do you know she was in the resistance?'

'We arrested one of her friends,' Mellado said. 'She confessed. Turns out little María Vidal killed one of my men after that charity ball.'

Guzmán frowned. 'Who said so?'

The repetitive tinkle of glass on glass.

'María told us everything before she went in the garrotte, didn't she, Faisán?'

'She did.' Faisán sniggered. 'Though it took a while.'

Guzmán looked into the car, watching the glass stick circling in the tomato juice, chinking against the glass again and again, getting faster. 'She didn't kill the legionnaire.'

Mellado looked up. 'Of course she did. She confessed.'

'People admit to anything under torture.' Guzmán's voice was lower now.

Mellado stirred the cocktail. 'You can only go on what people tell you, Guzmán.'

Guzmán looked down at the blood-red mix in the cocktail shaker. Sunlight glinted on the thick crystal glasses. He saw the handle of the Walther at the side of the cabinet. 'You think a young girl could slash a trained legionary's throat with a trench knife?'

The tinkling of glass slowed to a harsh brittle pulse. Then it stopped. 'How do you know how he was killed, Leo? Those details were hushed up. No one knew that except the killer.' Mellado put the cocktail shaker down. 'More pepper. That's what we need.' Slowly, he reached into the cabinet.

A single shot, deafening in the confined space. Mellado slumped forward against the front seat, a chaos of broken glass and tomato juice.

Faisán screamed, scrabbling desperately at the door handle.

Guzmán leaned forward and pushed the muzzle of the Colt against the back of his head.

'Don't kill me,' Faisán shrieked. 'I'll give you money.'

'No, you won't,' Guzmán said. When Faisán screamed again, he pulled the trigger.

His ears ringing, Guzmán climbed from the car. A bottle of Napoleon brandy rolled from under the front seat against his foot. He opened it and doused the bodies and the inside of the car, pausing to take a swig before he emptied the rest over Mellado. He took out his lighter and held the flame to the rear seat. It ignited at once and blue fire danced over Mellado's uniform. Within moments, the vehicle was filled with flames.

Guzmán walked away, ignoring the pain in his ribs and the chafing wound in his arm. His head still pounded with the triumphant voices in his head. Behind him, the car burned fiercely. It was over now. He was over.

He had been walking for an hour when a car appeared along the road, heading towards him. Guzmán saw two men inside. The man in the back seat was bald while the driver was pasty-faced, with thick round glasses. The car stopped and Guzmán peered into the interior as the rear window slid down.

'We've been looking for you,' Gutierrez said. 'The corporal thought you might be at Lauburu Farm.' Behind the wheel, Corporal Ochoa nodded. He didn't look at Guzmán.

'No need to tell me,' Guzmán growled. 'I'm finished.'

'Finished?' Gutierrez stared at him. 'That's rather modest, *Comandante*, since you've done everything I asked. Mellado was expressly forbidden by Franco to take action while the US Ambassador was nearby and he did it anyway. That's his career finished, just as I hoped.'

'You couldn't be sure he'd do that,' Guzmán muttered.

'I knew exactly what he'd do, the moment he read the file I sent you.'

Guzmán frowned. 'How did he know what was in it, did Viana tell him?'

'Whoever Capitán Viana really was, he wasn't working for Mellado,' Gutierrez said. 'There are other people in the game now and, unfortunately, they're not on our side.'

'So who gave Mellado the information?'

'Señora Olibari had been a double agent since the war. I knew she'd let Mellado know what was in the file as soon as it arrived. She had the only telephone in the village, you know.'

Exhausted, Guzmán rested his hand on the car roof. For a

moment, he saw a powder-blue silk dress across a crowded dining room, crimson lipstick on the rim of a glass.

'Snap out of it,' Gutierrez said. 'You destroyed a resistance cell, killed its leaders and got rid of El Lobo. Not to mention removing Baron Çubiry and his repulsive offspring. We've even retrieved the missing five million pesetas from Mellado's mansion.'

Guzmán stared over the car roof at the foothills. Above the brow of the hill, a column of smoke rose into the clear sky, darkening as the petrol tank caught fire. 'You set all this up.'

Gutiérrez laughed. 'Oh no, you planned it. That's what I told Franco this morning, so it must be true.' He noticed the column of smoke in the distance. 'What's burning over there?'

Guzmán shrugged. 'General Mellado and his assistant.'

'A traffic accident? How very convenient. That saves the bother of arresting him.'

Guzmán shook his head, trying to clear it. 'So you've won.' Behind him a flurry of black smoke and sickly flame shot into the sky as Mellado's car exploded.

'You mean *we've* won,' said Gutiérrez, 'and since the *Yanquis* have paid the money for the trade deal now, I can't imagine how things could get any better.' He pushed open the door. 'Do you want a lift back to Madrid, or would you rather stay here with the goats?'

Guzmán climbed into the car. As he slammed the door, Ochoa accelerated, heading to the coast to pick up the highway.

'It's beautiful here, wouldn't you say?' Gutiérrez said, looking out at the hills.

Guzmán shook his head. 'They're all traitors here. You can't trust any of them.'

He slumped against the window, staring at the mountain tops, their peaks glittering as if the snows were burning. And he heard the voices of the dead, fading in the distance.

CHAPTER 30

MADRID 2010, CALLE DE LOS CUCHILLEROS

I t seemed she'd been walking for ever. Moving through crowds, along busy roads, down tree-lined avenues in leafy parks, seeing none of them. She walked slowly, like a drunk. Her head ached and strange strands of light floated across her vision. That worried her. Every time it had happened before, it had ended with her blacking out.

A sharp pain shimmered through her temples, another symptom. *Got to get home, don't want to collapse in the street.* Leaning against a wall, she pushed her hair away from her eyes, hoping no one was watching, thinking she was some sad junkie desperate for a fix.

She set off again, following narrow streets with walls covered in garish patchworks of election posters, huge pictures of politicians and terse, ambiguous slogans. The buildings around her seemed familiar and she saw the equestrian statue of Felipe Tres, felt the cobbles beneath her feet. Somehow, she had found the Plaza Mayor. She was almost home.

She went down the stone stairs at the corner of the plaza into the Calle de los Cuchilleros. A hundred metres away, she saw the window of her flat and the small bar below. Opaque grey shapes blurred her vision and she blinked, trying to clear them away. A vicious barb of pain lanced through her head.

'*Holá*, señorita.'

She peered uncertainly at the man sitting on the steps of the Meson del Champiñon.

'What, you don't you recognise me? It's me, Alberto. I must be losing my looks.'

'*Lo siento*. I'm not feeling well,' Galíndez said, fumbling with her key.

'Did you see the election debate on TV? It's going to be close, I reckon. Maybe the next lot will be better for business. I certainly hope so.'

'Maybe.' She nodded, forcing herself to be polite as she struggled to turn the key.

He wasn't done. 'What do you think about the shooting? Terrible, isn't it?'

She looked at him, blank faced. 'What shooting?'

'Rosario Calderón, the minister of the interior, was shot dead this afternoon.' He looked surprised. 'Didn't you hear the news?'

Lights flashed in front of her eyes. 'I must go, I'm ill.'

'Sorry to hear it, señorita,' Alberto said. 'Come and have some mushrooms when you feel better. Have a go at the karaoke. With that husky voice you might win first prize.'

Inside the lobby, she leaned against the wall, trying to catch her breath. *Just let me get up the stairs. Don't want to pass out here.* A large package was waiting on top of her mailbox. A heavy printed label: **AMAZON.es**. She took the package and went upstairs.

By the time she had unfastened the triple locks her head was pulsing with darts of pain. She pushed the door to, deciding the locks could wait. Too much trouble.

Leaving the package on the table, she walked unsteadily to the bedroom and tumbled face down onto the bed. She kicked off her shoes and lay still, feeling the dull pounding in her head recede a little. She wondered about calling Isabel. She was still thinking about it as she fell asleep.

It was dark when she woke. Her mouth was dry and her feet ached from the long hours of walking, though at least the headache was gone. The clock on the table said eleven. She leaned over to her bedside table and turned on the radio.

'... occurred around four o'clock when Calderón returned home. She was shot on the steps of her house by three masked men and was pronounced

dead when the emergency services arrived. Police
sources suspect the slaying is almost certainly linked
to her husband's recent murder when...'

Galíndez turned off the radio and went into the living room.
Opening the window, she breathed in the cool night air. Below, a
chorus of voices, laughter, the chinking of glasses, the smell of
frying mushrooms and garlic. People living their lives.

She went into the kitchen and got a bottle of *agua con gas* from
the fridge. The fizzy water was sharp and cold, taking away some
of the strange taste in her mouth.

The Amazon package lay on the table. Finally, she would be
able to view the reel of film from Ochoa's apartment. Tearing the
cardboard wrapper open, she took out the 8mm projector. Her
phone vibrated on the table. She picked it up and looked at the
screen. UNKNOWN CALLER. A short text message:

You Killed Her

Galíndez put the phone down slowly. Rosario had told her she
would get them both killed when they met in the Retiro. And now
Rosario was dead, along with her husband and his business partner
Jesper Karlsson. She realised she'd been correct when she'd
suggested to the two investigators from Asuntos Externos that the
killing of the men was some kind of warning. Rosario's was too.
They were a warning to Galíndez.

There was only one person she could trust when things got
tough and that was Uncle Ramiro. The best thing was to tell him
everything, all the dirt on Rosario, the stolen children and GL
Sanidad as well as the adoption certificate currently hidden under
her carpet. Come clean about it all, before someone decided she'd
had enough warnings.

The clock said eleven thirty. Ramiro always worked into the
early hours so there was plenty of time to get cleaned up and check
Ochoa's film before she made the call.

She went into the bathroom and turned on the shower, letting the hot water pound her aching shoulders as the small bathroom filled with steam. Leaving the fan running, she padded into the bedroom, grabbed a Barcelona shirt from the wardrobe and pulled it on, impatient to see what was on Ochoa's reel of film.

The projector was easy to set up. An instruction sheet with a large diagram in seven languages helped her get the spool of film fixed in place. She arranged a chair alongside the table and focused the projector beam on the wall. *Probably vintage pornography.* She turned out the overhead light and slumped into the chair, reaching for the button to start the film. *A night in, watching a movie all on my own. Been there.*

The light of the projector cut through the semi-darkness, filling a section of the wall with a blurred monochrome rectangle. Strange shapes floated across the wall, the result of dirt or dust on the film. And then the image changed as the person holding the camera adjusted the lens, bringing the picture into focus.

A view from a car. The cameraman in the front passenger seat, pointing the camera through the window: streaks of dirt on the glass. The car slowed, passing a line of grey and ochre houses. A bakery, then a grocery by the look of it, shelves outside laden with fruit and vegetables, dried hams and pimientos hanging in the window.

The car came to a halt and the camera moved slightly, showing more of the windscreen. Some fifty metres away were several new-looking houses, the sort they built in the seventies and pulled down in the nineties. The camera focused on the entrance of one of the houses, capturing it in all its grey detail. Galíndez felt a growing sense of unease. Her mouth was dry and her breathing grew faster as she recognised the door that now filled the flickering picture. As the door opened, a figure appeared in the doorway and her body turned to ice. Despite the fluctuating quality of the film, she knew exactly when this film had been taken, and who was about to come through the door. And as the figure came into view, she mouthed a single word. '*Papá.*'

Her father, just as he was in photographs. Tall and muscular, his square jaw covered in dark stubble. Deep-set eyes fixed in a stern frown, his *guardia* uniform immaculate, the gun belt gleaming. *Papá*. Her father as she had never known him or, at least, never remembered him: alive. Her skin was painfully cold and she squirmed in the chair, hugging herself, chilled by the sense of encroaching darkness. Knowing this would get worse.

Papá walked out of the door and down the path. He stopped and turned back to the open door, waiting for someone. And now that someone stepped out from the dark hallway, skipping through the front door into view. A little girl, big dark eyes blinking in the light of a spring morning. Eight-year-old Ana María Galíndez, wearing the uniform of the *Colegio del Niño Jesús*, an oversized satchel swinging from her shoulder as she turned in the direction of the camera, unaware of its presence, cocking her head to one side as her father spoke to her, her face wreathed in a smile.

Galíndez clenched her teeth, trying to stop them chattering, shaking as she watched these flickering images of her obliterated childhood. She blinked, feeling warm tears spill down her cheek. And then a barb of pain lanced through her head, the pain convulsing her, distorting her vision. Her hands tightened on the chair arms.

Little Ana María skipped to the kerb. The camera panned back, revealing a line of parked cars between her and the camera, shielding the unknown observer from view. *Papá* bent low for a goodbye kiss then pointed to the house. The little girl nodded, walking obediently to the door. A sudden recollection: *Mamá used to walk me to school.*

Ana María standing by the door, waving. The camera panned back slowly, showing Miguel Galíndez as he crossed the road, car keys in his hand, behind him the blurred shape of the little girl, out of focus. The camera zoomed out as *Papá* opened the car door, throwing his shiny leather tricorne onto the passenger seat before turning to wave goodbye to his daughter. He looked towards the camera, the image shifting as the camera moved to one side to avoid him seeing it, the driver's arm raised towards the windscreen, the hand open in brief greeting. *Papá* waved back in casual acknowledgement. And then the camera zoomed in again as Teniente Miguel Galíndez climbed into his car on that spring day in 1992. Just as he did every day, though today was special. It was the last day of his life.

Tears came down her nose as Galíndez watched the film through a storm of strange lights and needles of pain. Something was very wrong. This was far worse than any of her previous episodes. A thin string of drool hung from her lips. And still she watched.

Papá closed the car door and the camera panned to the little girl, focusing on her face, her hand waving with the indefatigable persistence of a child, determined to continue until her father drove around the corner and out of sight. The rectangle of light from the projector filled with the child's face as *Papá* started the engine and pulled away from the kerb, capturing her expression of disbelief as the explosion lifted the car into the air, flinging it along the road in a disintegrating fireball, recording the girl's transition from happiness through startled incomprehension to sudden, horrified understanding. The tears. The silent scream. The camera remained fixed on her face as she sank to her knees, looking up as her mother ran from the house, depicted by the camera as a skirt and legs, dark shoes, stumbling past the child in an attempt to save her husband from the inferno now cremating him.

And then the camera moved in slowly, amplifying the child's face, moving inexorably to her eyes, enlarging them into huge, impossibly dark shapes that filled the picture until, with a sudden dry flutter, the spool of film ran out.

Galíndez slid from the chair and lay on the floor, shivering, unable to move. Her mind was on fire and her body trembled with strange spasms. She tried to pull herself forward, feeling the rough carpet against her elbows. A faint sound outside on the stairs. *Help me.* But the words were in her head not her mouth. She looked up, realising the door was ajar. Perhaps she could attract attention, get help. She reached for the door and saw her hand fall limply to the carpet. It was the last thing she saw before she lost consciousness. By the time someone knocked, Galíndez was beyond hearing it.

The door opened. Two men in black ski masks. A fat man holding a pistol, the other short and skinny, carrying a Taser. Both stared at the woman sprawled face down on the floor, the Barcelona shirt rucked up around her legs.

'What the fuck?' An East European accent. 'Is she dead?'

The short man knelt by Galíndez's side and felt for a pulse. 'She's alive. Maybe she's high or drunk. Whatever. She's coming with us.'

It took less than a minute to secure her. The fat man opened a small haversack, waiting as his companion pulled Galíndez's hands behind her back, securing her wrists with plastic flexi cuffs. Her hands now immobilised, he crossed her ankles and bound them with duct tape. Finally, they turned her on her side as the thin man unrolled a black plastic body bag. His companion cut a piece of duct tape and taped it across her eyes. A moment later, he placed a second piece of tape firmly over her mouth. Together, they manhandled her into the black plastic shroud, leaving only her face still showing.

She was easy to carry. One took her shoulders, the other her feet. They went down the stairs with hardly a sound except for the rustling of the black plastic as they negotiated the bend in the stairs. The man in front stumbled.

'Careful,' the other one said, 'they won't pay if she's damaged.'

They hurried out across the deserted road to a van parked by the far kerb. Two more men waited by the rear doors, watching as Galíndez was carried to the back of the vehicle. One of the men was tall, his biceps covered in obscene tattoos, the piercings in his face twinkling in the half-light. Standing next to him was an old man, tall and dapper in a suit and tie.

As the East Europeans pushed Galíndez into the van, a cat sidled across the road from the Mushroom Bar and brushed up against the old man's legs. The cat screeched as the old man lashed out, kicking it halfway across the road.

'Fucking hell,' the big man said. 'That's a lousy thing to do.'

'Just do your job, Sancho,' the old man grunted. 'Or I'll kick you.'

'We get paid now?' the larger of the two East Europeans asked.

'You do.' Sancho nodded. 'She was no trouble then? That's a first.'

'Fast asleep. I think she's pissed.'

Sancho unzipped the black plastic bag and pinched Galíndez's cheek. There was no response. 'Is that a Barcelona shirt she's wearing?' he asked, amused.

A nod. 'Says Messi on the back.'

The old man came closer for a better look. Sancho noticed his odour again: a blend of Cuban cigars and brandy. A dry crackling in his throat that might have been a laugh.

'She's been wanting to meet me for some time.' He chuckled. 'It's her lucky day.'

'You're not kidding. It's going to be a real surprise when she wakes up and finds you standing over her.' Sancho pulled the zip on the body bag higher, leaving only her nose exposed.

'She thinks she's tough,' the old man muttered. 'A few hours with me and she'll eat shit if I tell her to.'

Sancho took a drag on his cigarette. 'Just like the good old days, eh?' He looked round at the others. 'Anyone want a look at her tits before we set off?' The two East Europeans nodded vigorously as he reached for the zip of the body bag.

'No,' the old man said. 'It's always better to undress them just before they're tortured. It adds to the stress.' He glowered at Sancho. 'I'm used to dealing with professionals.'

'Oh, you're the expert all right.' Sancho flicked his cigarette into the gutter. 'Let's get going then, Señor Guzmán.'

The two men got into the cab, and the East Europeans scrambled into the back alongside Galíndez. Sancho started the engine and the van moved off down the cobbled road, heading for Calle de la Colegiata. From the small bar below Galíndez's flat, laughter and loud voices echoed in the night air. A sudden blast of synthesised drumbeats.

The karaoke was beginning.